Gallping into Marriage

SONJA GUNTER

To anyone who loves horses. May you find this story inspirational to help save them. And to all the horse sanctuaries out there, your job is never-ending, but know that you are appreciated, and non-horse owners are with you.

Dear Rosalind,

If you're reading this letter, it's because I've passed away. I've assigned Sam as your new trustee. I'm sorry. It was the only way. I had to make sure you'd end up happy and not alone later in life.

Remember I love you and this is done out of love. You're a very wealthy young lady. Every young and old cowboy is gonna want to marry you. So, I've laid down some stipulations you will need to follow in order to use your trust fund.

On your thirtieth birthday, you'll be in full charge of all the money. Until such time, a monthly allowance will be deposited into your bank account in the amount of thirty-thousand dollars. If you marry before turning thirty, the trust fund will also be turned over to you, so long as your husband is not involved in the rodeo in any form. If your new husband has anything to do with the rodeo, the trust fund will be disbursed in the amount of ten thousand dollars yearly until you reach your thirtieth birthday.

You're probably very upset. That's to be expected, but don't do anything you'll regret later. You're headstrong like your father was at your age. I want you to live, to have children, and to be able to grow old with them. I don't want your children having to grow up with only one parent or none at all the way you did.

Love, Grandpa Rodney

CHAPTER ONE

Rosalind Dunne led Dawn, her four-year-old golden Quarterhorse mare, to the heavy metal gates. Many fellow competitors commented on how beautiful the horse was. Dawn's light champagne coloring with a touch of cream on her forehead down to her nose and her hind legs just above her hooves were two of the reasons she'd chosen her on sight. Plus, her mane and tail matched, but were a deep metallic gold coloring, reminding her of the early morning sunlight.

She nodded, acknowledging their compliments. The hum and excitement from the crowd inside the Las Vegas Sagebrush Ranch Arena for the Annual Barrel Race, brought on a smile and a feeling of being home.

"Watch out for turn three," Sam said as he took hold of the bridle.

"I've heard. Other riders have complained to the officials about some rowdy dudes in the grandstands." His years of being on the circuit with her multi-titled grandfather gave him the expertise she needed to compete.

"Be careful and remember to count."

"Yes, I will." Rosalind gave him a smile. Sam's broad shoulders and stocky build were that of a man who'd ridden hard in the day. Even though he was her guardian because of the trust her grandfather created, Sam took his responsibilities too seriously and worried too much. As far as she knew they'd been fierce rivals until they became too old to compete and became business friends.

"I'm headed to have a talk with the officials."

Sam patted Dawn's hindquarters and Rosalind observed him taking deep, labored breaths before he walked away.

Was he sick? He hadn't said anything.

She forced herself to concentrate on her run in the clover leaf pattern. With the first barrel to her right, she'd circle it and go across to the second barrel, and then on to the last barrel straight ahead of her. But her mood veered to disgust as she glanced at the crowd. Her gaze narrowed when she spotted the group of boisterous spectators obnoxiously heckling each barrel rider at turn three, the one straight ahead of her.

All men. It figured.

One, two, four, eight, nine in the bunch. They were whistling, hollering, and waving with what she guessed were newly acquired bandanas and cowboy hats.

Rosalind angrily kicked at the dirt as she waited for her number to be called. Definitely not real cowboys. Only-Wannabes.

Why today? She couldn't afford to lose.

Horses and people were counting on her. If she won today's forty-thousand-dollar purse, she'd be able to give the money to the real-estate agent, Mr. Kennedy.

She'd missed his call this morning due to poor cell service. He'd left a message, informing her Mr. Hillsboro wasn't willing to wait any longer for her to make good on her guarantee to buy the land. The down payment had to be paid with the signed purchase agreement and a closing date set before the end of the year, or the land would be put on the market.

Six months ago, she was ecstatic when Dwight Hillsboro, the owner of the adjacent ranch to hers, called and gave her the first chance to purchase his seven-hundred acres. They hadn't discussed a timeframe, but apparently now he wanted to sell fast.

"Good luck, Rosalind."

She blinked and saw David Billy, the number one bronco-rider, standing next to her. She tried not to stare at him. He was one cowboy that could do damage to a heart with his dark brown eyes, thick eyelashes, and lazy smile.

"Thanks. You ridin' last today?"

"No, I drew fifth. Not worried though. Careful around your last turn."

"I will. Sam went to talk to the officials."

"Okay, make the dirt fly." David winked and strutted away.

He was so damn handsome. Blue jeans hugged his ass and thighs. It was too bad he was already taken. His wife, Suzy, was definitely one lucky cowgirl to have that fit body in her bed every night. Rosalind could even see herself relinquishing the land to be married to the likes of him.

Time wasn't on her side nor was it her friend. Instead, a must-win situation had cropped up. The land couldn't slip through her fingers, not when she was so close to purchasing it. Everything would've been completed last month if Sam hadn't reminded her about her grandpa's will and his old-school marriage stipulation.

The parcel of land she wanted...no, *needed*, wasn't going to sit idle for her to turn thirty. At twenty-five, she couldn't wait five more years to be given permission to use her money when-ever she wanted or needed it. She'd been through hell the last two years since her grandpa had passed away. His unexpected death due to a heart attack had left her numb and lost. He'd been her only family after her parents had died. Running the ranch had been left to her too. Bills, payroll, and upkeep had been her life, racing whenever she could.

Then a plan had formed in her head. If she could get a hold of the bulk of her inheritance, she'd have the freedom to do what she wanted to do, which was to follow her mother's dream of saving horses.

Once everything fell into place, she'd be able to get the ball rolling for a sanctuary on behalf of ageing and abused horses. There were several animals on her wait list. It all came down to the land. It was everything.

Damn it.

The horses needed her. She wanted that land.

Dawn snorted. It was a sure sign, her anger was showing, and Rosalind sensed it. "Easy, girl. Sorry, I'm just mad."

She tried to calm her raising temper and let up on the reins. She had to get her hands on her trust fund by the end of the year. How could Grandpa have been so cruel?

Sam came up to her. "They ain't gonna do anything. You'll have to ride with them in the stands." He appeared winded and then coughed.

"You, okay?"

"Don't you go worrying about me. Could be the onset of a cold."

"Sam, Mr. Kennedy called to—"

"Stop. I don't want to hear it. Mr. Kennedy can wait. Concentrate on winning."

He was right. She had to focus on the run. She put the land, the realtor, and her irritation on the rear burner, clearing her mind.

Mounting up and squeezing Lizzie, as she liked to call the saddle horn, she settled into the leather. Suddenly, the drone of the crowd grew louder. If she took a wild guess, it would be another rider must've taken turn three.

Those men had to be drunker than a peach orchard sow or crazier than a parrot eatin' stick candy.

Without missing a stride, Rosalind prodded Dawn closer to the posts to have a clearer view. The arena had seating on three sides. It wasn't the norm, but in Las Vegas, it was all about the money and spectators. The next rider raced around the barrels. She recognized the woman's black hair. Alisa Highland. Instead of watching her rival and friend, as she should've, her gaze homed in on the men.

One of them wore a sign, 'About to Be Hitched.'

At least it was his choice. He wasn't being forced into marriage, like she was if she wanted to get her inheritance.

Boy, to be that lucky.

As she watched, Alisa approached the third barrel. All at once the party of men stood, waving and howling. Her horse spooked and slowed down.

Not good.

Alisa reacted and maneuvered her horse quickly. It was too late! The damage was done. She'd lost precious time.

Where were the officials? They should kick those men out. Someone or someone's horse could get hurt.

Stupid wannabes.

Her gloved fingers tightened on the reins. Dawn jerked her head in protest. Disgust replaced Rosalind's smile. She reached down, petted her mare's neck. On the edge of refusing to ride unless the officials did something, she sensed being watched. She scanned the crowd. Her search ended when she reached the group. One of the men stood. His bold, unbroken stare gave her butterflies in the pit of her belly.

Omigod.

He's so hot he could melt ice cubes on a cold day in Minnesota.

He didn't compare to the tough, good-looking bull, bareback, and bronco riders she was around all the time. This man was different.

Blond hair.

I need to breathe, damn it.

His sun-kissed locks, however, stuck out like a casino in a church district. Her smile turned to a chuckle when she noticed the way his midnight black Stetson was angled on his head. Didn't the man know wearing his hat that way meant he was single and looking for company?

Her lips curled upward, and she returned his stare. Tipping her hat to him, she looked away first, not liking the unsettling feeling he gave her.

"You ready, Rosalind?" Sam patted her leg.

"Yeah, as ready as I'll ever be."

"Focus on the run. And only the run." Sam tightened the cinch, ensuring the saddle wouldn't slip during her run, before stepping away.

She nodded and ran through her routine checklist mode. First, she brushed at her fringed western shirt to make sure it was tucked into her jeans. Absentmindedly, she touched each of the white-coated snaps, ensuring all were fastened properly. Next, she tugged her hat string tight for good measure and turned her head to feel the weight of her braid on her back.

Everything was set.

It was one of the things her grandpa had drilled into her. She couldn't spare any deductions for improper dress. The National Barrel Horse Association judges were strict when it came to points concerning the dress codes and could fine members up to twenty-five dollars per violation.

"Rosalind Dunne, rider number fifteen, to the gate."

With her legs, she nudged Dawn forward to the starting

line and turned her attention to the signal. The flag was her center point, second to the words. She waited and waited.

"Ready," the voice paused. "Go!"

The flag dropped.

Dawn didn't need any urging. She tore off like the proverbial bat out of hell. It was why Rosalind never had to use spurs or kick her horse at the start of the run.

Fifteen, sixteen, and turn, Rosalind mindlessly counted off in her head to assure herself she was in time with each long stride Dawn took. They rounded barrel one and then barrel two with no problems. As they neared the third barrel, the dreaded turn, she heard the shouts, whistles, and the catcalls. She used all her experience to avoid a catastrophe during the turn.

Out of the corner of her eye, Rosalind didn't miss seeing the blond-haired man stand and wave. For a split second, her attention was taken away from Dawn as the man lurched, ready to fall face first into the arena. She braced herself for disaster, except at the last second, another spectator saved the falling man.

Even with the distraction, she completed the hairpin turn with the stirrups nearly touching the ground. She steadied herself for the last leg of the run by loosening up on the reins and giving Dawn her head. They blasted toward home at a dead run.

With unbelievable speed, Dawn ran.

Her adrenalin was high. She loved the feel of the air on her face and the power of Dawn beneath her.

"Fifteen-point-nine seconds for Rosalind Dunne." The announcer shouted into the intercom.

Hot damn. Record time. I did it.

She'd secured a coveted spot at the BFA World Championship Barrel Futurity, in December. She let loose a cry of happiness. Her heart was pounding so fast she could hardly breathe.

She wouldn't have to enter any local events with limited purses and could concentrate on the ranch and opening the horse sanctuary.

Somehow, Rosalind managed to keep her composure, smile and raise her arms in victory. She rode Dawn to the center of the arena and waved to the crowd. The young mare danced in time to cheers and applause.

During Dawn's cool-down, in an adjacent corral, a crowd of well-wishers gathered. Most were other riders, and some were spectators. This was the part she didn't like, but she put on a smile.

"I'm so happy for you."

"She's a mighty fast filly."

"Good run, missy."

"Maybe next time you'll give me a chance."

Rosalind turned, recognizing the voice from the last comment, and dismounted. Alisa Highland was walking her horse and had come up to her. "Not this year. I'm going all the way."

"I'll be there to take it from you," Alisa stated.

Before she could reply, others came up to her. Between the handshakes and conversation, she curiously glanced toward the stands. She couldn't stop her eyebrows from raising in astonishment. The same man who'd almost fallen into the arena had followed her and was standing in the stands staring at her. He seemed to be weaving a little, but his strong gaze never faltered.

Who was this stranger?

She didn't recognize him or anyone in his group. Was he and his gang here for entertainment? Or was he a city boy in town for the weekend?

To her dismay, more rodeo participants jostled closer, blocking her view of him as they shrieked out more praises and trapped her. By the time she broke free, it was time for her to receive her trophy and take a victory lap. When she rode Dawn back to the main arena and galloped around the ring, she noticed the blond, blue-eyed man and his friends were gone.

Damn, back to square one.

He might've been her ticket to financial freedom.

What happens in Vegas stays in Vegas, right?

Her plan to marry while she was here seemed less likely now, with no candidate. She frowned. A roll of nausea hit her stomach at the thought of all of her inheritance sitting in the bank, with her unable to get at it.

All she had to do was get married.

She'd have full control of her money then.

The evening was still young. Plenty of time to find a greenhorn to marry her for money and agree to divorce her for a huge bonus. Her plan ought to work. It was simple enough. The marriage would be a business agreement, no night of bliss, and no husband to go home to.

Traditional marriages only caused heartaches.

CHAPTER TWO

"Your Granddaddy Rodney would've been so proud of you, Rosalind." Sam stashed the last bag into the truck.

"Thanks, I miss him."

"Don't be getting all sad. He's here with you. You did good today..." Sam was interrupted by a coughing attack and pulled out a bandanna, wiping his mouth. "Sorry, must've swallowed wrong. We should be on the road by six a.m. We'll swing back here at five. I know you checked in on Dawn. We pay extra to have a stall on site. The guys will keep her company. You shouldn't worry, Max and Walt always take good care of her for you. They should have Dawn and the trailer ready when we get back. I want to make Rawlins by nightfall."

"Yeah, yeah, up with the crack of sunlight and on to Wyoming. They did have Dawn secure. You know she is my number one priority." She caught his grin before he opened the driver's door. Removing his hat, he smoothed down his short hair. She hesitated, about to tell him she wanted to go out on her own, but she didn't and walked around to the passenger side.

Minutes were ticking away, and she didn't have a man willing to be her husband.

Through the years she'd learned to be tough and stand on her own in a male-dominated universe. No one pushed her around and got away with it, which included Sam or her deceased Grandpa Rodney.

Once she was seated inside the truck she took a deep breath, it was now or never. "Alisa invited me to Gilley's Saloon to celebrate with the others. Everyone is going."

Sam shook his head, and she noticed his gray locks seemed to be getting thinner. "It's not a good idea for you to go out."

Always a man a few words when he wanted to be and now seemed to be that time. The light from inside the truck made him look worn and tired. Her big plans seemed small now and she was about to change her mind and skip husband-hunting.

She appreciated why Grandpa had set down rules. Not very many young women inherited more than fifteen million dollars. She'd been prepared to hold out until her thirtieth birthday, until, almost a year ago, a television commercial featuring stories of young, old, and abused horses caught her attention and touched her heart.

Anxious to help the poor animals, she had contacted the agency. Linda, the caretaker-owner of the sanctuary, explained donations were always helpful, but the use of land was more important. In that instant, Rosalind decided to open her own sanctuary.

Night and day for a week, she sat planning during her free time on how to do it. However, the numbers wouldn't work out. Her monthly allowance of thirty-thousand dollars wasn't enough, not with running the ranch and all of those expenses. She needed to secure about five hundred thousand dollars of her inheritance to see it through.

When she called the lawyers to try to persuade them to go

against her grandfather's will, they had refused. Their nonchalant attitude sparked her anger. They couldn't have cared less about the abused horses or her dreams of a sanctuary. They simply reminded her she'd have to wait six years, get married, or obtain her trustee's approval to release the funds.

Sam refused to talk about letting her have the money early, repeating often he was simply abiding by her grandpa's wishes. They argued to no avail. He wouldn't give his blessing. Her only choice at that point had been to bite the bullet and get married to a green rider or a damn Yankee.

The roar of the truck engine brought her back to the present.

"Did you forget Tom Clark is in town, too? I'm sorry, I'm only looking out for you." Sam checked the rearview mirror before signaling a left turn.

At his reminder, Rosalind's revulsion surfaced. Her head snapped up and she peered at him. "I heard he was."

Just because a cowboy is a looker doesn't insure, he's as polite as a preacher talkin' to the devil.

She'd learned the hard way that Tom, her ex-boyfriend, had a tainted temper which showed like yellow snow in the winter. He was meaner than the bulls he rode. Tom wasn't about to ruin her plans. If he showed up, she'd deal with him.

Shrugging her shoulders with determination, she shifted to face Sam. "Why don't you come along and see for yourself? I'll be fine."

"I'm tired, missy, and you're not going alone."

"I'm twenty-five years old. I can handle myself. Why did you have me take those self-defense classes?"

"You know why."

"I want to celebrate my win with my friends. Please." She clasped her hands together on her lap.

"Rosalind, I said no."

"Please?" She pursed her lips, pretending to pout, knowing she really didn't need his approval. But they had a long ride the next day together. It was better to stay on his good side.

The lines on Sam's face softened. Her pouting worked and she exhaled the breath she'd been holding.

"What the heck, you're right. We should celebrate. We'll go for a spell."

"Yahooee. All right!" Rosalind pounded her boots into the floorboard.

"If everything is fine and I *mean* okay, I'll leave you to have fun. If Tom shows his face, we're leaving."

"No worries. He won't show. No one likes him. Once you see all my friends there, you'll know I'll be fine. And you won't have to stay. Maybe we can take both trucks."

"I guess. You do deserve time for yourself. We'll change and then swing over to the arena for the other truck. I'm too old to celebrate all night." Sam pulled into the hotel parking lot.

Rosalind smiled, ticking off problem number one, which was not knowing any men outside the rodeo. Visiting the bar would give her access to local city folks and tourists.

Problem number two was trickier. How to smooth-talk a man to fall in love with her quickly. Would twenty-five thousand dollars be enough to entice someone?

Who'd make a good husband?

All the men she'd ever associated with were bull and bronco riders, cowboys, or steer wrestlers. Barrel racing was all she'd ever had time for.

Hell, and damnation.

Did she want the man to fall in love with her?

No, love wasn't in her plans as she hunted for a husband. She giggled, not wanting any man in her life for a while.

Sam glanced over his shoulder, his eyebrows raised as they climbed the stairs to their rooms.

"What? I'm excited to celebrate. I did win a big event."

"Yes, you did. Meet me in a half hour."

"A night on the town in Sin City."

This time Sam chuckled. Whistling, he went into his room. She went to her room, swiped the keycard at the lock, entered and went to the bed. Sitting, she took a moment to consider what she was about to do, ticking away at her problems.

Number three was the hardest to solve. Once she picked the man, how did she get him to agree to go to a wedding chapel?

Getting married wasn't as easy as she thought it would be.

Undressing, she hurried into the shower. If she could persuade a wild stallion to let her ride him, she should be able to talk some man into marrying her. And the last one, number four, the divorce.

Easy to deal with by offering a bonus for his trouble.

The parking lot of the Las Vegas Gilley's was packed, which wasn't a surprise with the rodeo in town. Having been to the one in Texas, this one looked identical to it. She'd heard this was the place everyone went to celebrate or drown his or her sorrows. They had returned to the arena and picked up the other truck, before heading to the bar. Driving separately was a step in the right direction for her plan to succeed.

When Sam pushed open the door to Gilley's they were immediately greeted with loud music. Rosalind took a handful of steps inside and the crowd cheered her name. Smiling, she hollered her thanks to several people and spotted David Billy who pointed to an empty barstool.

"I see David. I'll sit with him. He'll make a good bodyguard."

"Okay, I'll find a table."

Sam gave her a half smile and wandered into the crowd. She weaved through the mass of people to the bar.

"Hey, thanks for the seat." She popped up beside David.

What a cutie. Her pulse did a happy dance as she tried not to look into his yummy chocolate brown eyes. She could look at him twenty-four-seven knowing it was safe too since he was a happily married man.

"Can I buy the champ a drink?"

"I could use a Miller. I missed your ride today. I heard you stuck like a tick to a lamb's tail."

The bartender put a bottle of cold beer in front of her. She took a sip, letting the liquid burn its way down to her nervous stomach.

"I did. I felt like I was knockin' a hole in my chest with my chin." He turned and flattened her with one of his heart-breaking smiles.

"I bet. You finished with a personal best time too, I heard."

"Yeah, and I'm feeling it. I saw your ride. You kept me standing the whole time. I knew you'd be breaking the record." David tapped his beer with hers in a toast and together they chugged.

"It felt good. I wanted it pretty bad." Rosalind turned in her chair to view the crowded room. "I see everyone who's anyone is here tonight. Nice place."

"It's a place to bend an elbow with friends. Alisa's holding court as usual. Your first time?"

"What gave it away?"

"You're acting like a long-tailed cat in a room full of rockers. Bet you a new pair of boots you won't go thirsty tonight."

She eyed him suspiciously, not sure who would be buying her drinks. Or why they'd bother. "Oh, really?"

David nodded and leaned against the bar to face the throng

of people. She followed his stare to a group of men sitting at a table close to the dance floor.

Holy cow. It's meant to be. The good-looking blond guy. "Isn't that the group of troublesome greenhorns from the Sagebrush Ranch Arena?"

"Yup. Security escorted them out after your run. It's a bachelor party. The one wearing the ludicrous sign is getting married, as if you couldn't tell."

"Looks like his bride will be getting the short end of the stick tomorrow night."

They laughed and Rosalind raised her beer to her lips. Mr. Blond stared and winked. Uncomfortable with the attention, she turned away. Yet she couldn't help thinking, just maybe good fortune was on her side for once.

Her plan might be on the verge of working. She placed her hand on David's arm, moved closer, and whispered, "Dance with me, so Sam will see everything is fine. He's worried Tom Clark will roll in. Sam won't leave until he's sure I'll be safe."

David drained his beer and draped his arm around her in a protective manner.

"You're safe with me and the other boys. Sam shouldn't have worried. Besides, everyone knows Tom Clark is a bad egg. I'd like to see him banned from the circuit."

"You and Sam think alike."

Rosalind set her half-empty bottle down and took a deep breath, sensing her life was about to change.

David winked. "Come on, let's celebrate our wins."

They stopped at the table where Sam was sitting before hitting the dance floor.

"Don't worry about our special girl here, Sam. Me and the boys will take good care of her."

"I'll be holding you and the other boys to those smart sprinkles. I'm gonna hightail these old bones out of here and drop off the truck at the arena. Max or Walt can take me to the hotel. You behave, young lady."

"I will. No drinking and driving."

Sam stood, gave her a pat on the back, and presented David with his death stare. They watched him hustle to the door. David grinned and drew her into the group of other twosomes currently line dancing.

As he'd predicted, she never lacked a dance partner or a full bottle of beer. She kept her promise of not over-drinking and set each bottle down after a small gulp.

The dancing helped her to relax. After three songs in a row, she gracefully declined another, pleading she needed to sit. Rosalind found an empty chair, and someone handed her a cold beer. More praise came her way from cowboys she didn't know. With David and his group surrounding her, none of the regular patrons could even ask her to dance.

Should she approach Mr. Blue Eyes? Or someone else? But who then?

She scanned the saloon for another candidate who didn't look like a cowboy but found the pickings slim. As she brooded over the room, to her surprise the blond guy sat in the chair next to her.

Rosalind feasted her eyes on the prettiest pair of baby blues she'd ever seen. Seeing them up close had her appraising him further. He gave her a boyish smile and her heart jumped a beat. His lips were firm and had a sensual curl to them, showing perfectly even white teeth. She found herself drawn to his very evident masculinity even with his wanna be cowboy hat, denim jeans and white button-down shirt.

"I saw youuuu earlier. You rode a horse...a horse fast. My name is Alllannn. What's yours?"

Trying not to laugh at his slurred speech, she casually set

her untouched beer down. "I did ride my horse fast. First time at a rodeo?"

"Yesssss. See the neat hat...neat hat I bought? We don't have rodeeooooos at home."

Bingo. He's my man.

He dragged his chair closer to hers, and their knees bumped. She about leaped off her chair at his touch. Her pulse quickened. Men in general didn't have this effect on her. Taking a quick glance at his hands, she noted he wasn't wearing a ring.

Think.

Start talking.

"Where's home? Are you from around here?"

"No, I'm here for my best...best friend's wedding. He's getting hittchedd. I'm from the Big Apple...the Big Apple. You know, New York. Hey, I think you'rrre pretty."

She couldn't hold in her laughter any longer and let it loose.

He found her pretty? A woman who never wore a dress or any makeup and had stubs for fingernails. Was he too drunk to know what he was doing?

"Rosalind, is this man bothering you? Do you want me to ask him to leave?"

David's question ended with him glaring at Allan. It was a comfort to know he would take the guy outside in a heartbeat to show him where rattlers lived if she nodded.

"No, it's fine. He's harmless," Rosalind said.

"She's a pretty cowgirl, don't you think soooo?" Allan gave David a toothy smile.

While Rosalind laughed behind her hand, David poked his finger into Allan's chest. But he kept his gaze on her. "If he begins to act like a mule, you let out a holler."

And then David walked away but peered over his shoulder once more at them before rejoining his buddies at the bar.

Playing with her almost full bottle of beer, she decided to see if he would fill the criteria for a husband. "Allan, are you married?"

"Meeee? Are you kidding? Hell nooo."

His reply ended with a hiccup. She produced a smile without laughing. One thumb up. One more question to pass the test. "What do you do for a living?"

"I'm... I am a stockstockbroker."

Allan gathered her hand into his. She didn't pull away even though she wanted to. The heat of his palm was like being prodded with an electric stick.

It was now or never. He was inebriated yet didn't seem totally smashed. She might have a chance with this candidate.

"Allan, how would you like to make a fast twenty-five thousand and another twenty-five thousand as a bonus?"

His blue eyes widened as he tried to focus on her and a lock of his blond hair came loose from beneath his hat, falling onto his forehead. She knew she had his interest. A good sign his drunken mind still worked.

He leaned in and a whiff of alcohol mixed with his after-shave—smelled like *Polo*—hit her. Unexpectedly her insides jangled with excitement, reminding her she was a woman.

"Twenty-five thou—thousand dollars? Investment? Lot—a lot of moneeeey. What would—what would I have to doooo? Which stocks do you want to buy?"

"I don't want to buy stocks. I want you to marry me. Tonight. And in a month's time, divorce me for the bonus."

He nearly fell from his chair as he rocked backward and laughed.

"Me, marry? No, it's...no. My friend's wedding."

He was drunker than she first assumed. Scanning the bar for a new prospect, she exhaled in frustration. Maybe this wasn't meant to work after all. She wouldn't be able to save the horses and open the sanctuary.

She ignored Allan's rambling but froze when he put his arm around her and drew her close.

"Do you want...want to have sex? You have a sexy...sexy body. Weeee could go to my room."

Rosalind choked back a cough at his forwardness. His state of intoxication might work to her advantage. If he couldn't remember getting married, he might be motivated for a quick divorce. And she might not have to pay the extra twenty-five-thousand-dollar bonus, as she'd promised.

"Where's your hotel, Allan?"

"At the Hil...Hiltonnn, number five-forty-one. I have a great room."

Rosalind stood with determination and helped Allan gain his feet. Once her arms were around his waist and he leaned on her shoulder, she led him to the exit. Checking behind her once, she made sure no one pursued them.

David and his buddies were facing the other way. Allan's friends were all at their table, not even aware he'd left them.

Allan stumbled several times, but she managed to maneuver him around tables and chairs to the door. With her booted foot, she kicked it open, allowing the fresh night air to greet them as they stepped outside. She took one last confirming look behind her.

The coast was clear.

She was at the point of no return and walked further away from Gilley's. The parking lot was less crowded, and her blue Chevy Silverado stood alone. She escorted Allan to the passenger side and shoved him in with his hat half-cocked.

Next stop, the Las Vegas Marriage Bureau.

CHAPTER THREE

Las Vegas, known as Sin City and the Wedding Capital of the World, worked in her favor. The tourism webpage indicated anyone could apply for a marriage license any time of the day or night and get it in a matter of twenty minutes or less.

No questions asked.

No blood tests.

Googling the Marriage Bureau Office of Las Vegas on her phone, more than a hundred wedding chapels came up, but only one branch that was open twenty-four-seven. Rosalind drove to the location, parked the truck, and had to help Allan out of the passenger side, setting his hat on the seat. When they entered there were three couples waiting, each pair kissing and hugging.

She tried to act normal, except she didn't know how. Taking a set of chairs, the furthest away from everyone else, she propped up Allan. Thankfully, the other couples were so into themselves they didn't notice her and Allan, not showing how much they loved each other. She checked her phone every minute for any messages from Sam and had to push at Allan when he'd nod off and slump over on her shoulder. Tapping her boots on the rungs of the chair wasn't making the time go faster. Soon two more happy-go-lucky couples came in and their number was called.

Holding unto Allan, they made their way over to a bald-headed clerk and she heard the man mumble, "Drunken marriages never last."

Rosalind forced her lips upward into a cheerful smile. "Hello, we'd like...we want to obtain a marriage license."

The man peered above his thick framed glasses. "Are you sure about this, young lady?"

"Yes sir, we love each other." Rosalind hid her nervousness by snuggling closer to Allan but had to keep pushing at his roving hands.

A second clerk, a woman, joined the first one.

"Behave." Rosalind hissed into Allan's ear.

"I want toooo kissss youuu."

"Shhh, later."

Watching the clerks, she wondered if they would refuse to give them a license due to Allan's garbled speech.

Her fears were for nothing. The male clerk gave her some forms to sign. She filled them out the best she could and handed them back. The clerk scanned the papers and pointed to some empty spots.

"You missed the address section, social security number, and Allan's full name."

"Oh, sorry."

Think fast. What would have his name and address on it?

Something in his wallet could. Men always carried one. She patted both his butt cheeks and located a lump in the left pocket of his jeans.

Bingo, wallet.

As she shoved her hand into the pocket, she couldn't help

but notice how her soon-to-be husband had without a doubt a cowboy's ass.

Tight and firm.

The black leather wallet hadn't provided any type of shield from the warmth of his body heat. A sudden urge to cradle his billfold to her chest triumphed and on its own, her arm rose. Rosalind stopped it in mid-stride when the clerk cleared his throat. The offending black object dropped from her hand as if she'd been caught stealing.

And with some luck, it landed open on the counter.

Exhaling, she chewed her lip in apprehension, and carefully removed his driver's license with only her fingertips.

"My husband-to-be's name is Allan Richard Smith. His address is eighty Riverside Boulevard, Unit two-six-one-zero, New York City, one-zero-zero-six-nine."

The clerk nodded. She spotted, adjacent to the driver's license, his medical insurance card which included his social security number.

Holy Beejesus. Sweet, everything in one shot, halleluiah.

She rattled off the numbers and replaced the wallet, careful not to touch his butt.

Less than five minutes later, the clerk handed them their official original marriage license and a single copy.

"Congratulations and good luck." The male clerk pushed his glasses further onto his nose. She ignored the clerks as they stumbled away like tumbleweed on a windy day in Texas. As soon as the doors closed behind them, Rosalind let loose the laugh she'd been holding.

I know what I'm doing.

A bright neon sign caught her attention as it flashed eleven o'clock. She had to make it back to her hotel by one.

Looking around, she spotted 'The Little White Chapel,' thankfully within walking distance of the courthouse.

"Allan, we need to walk across the street."

"Walk? I want to sleep."

"Not yet. Stay with me, Allan." She gently tapped his face twice to get his blood flowing.

"Hey, stttoopp..."

"Shhh, here we go, walk."

He did what she demanded, and they reached the chapel's entrance. She propped Allan against the wall, held him with one arm and yanked open the heavy white doors. She heaved him inside while he groped her at every chance.

An older woman with black hair, wearing a form-fitted dress, hurried to them. "Welcome to The Little White Chapel on your very special day."

"Hi, thanks." Rosalind took in the interior walls and floor. Everything was white. It was overloading her mind, but in an odd sort of way. It made the room appear very traditional, even respectful, elegant, and clean. Right out of a movie.

A large built man with gray hair, a short beard, and glasses joined the woman. "My, my, welcome. If you're looking to tie the knot you've come to the right place."

"Do you have a selection of packages?"

"I'm Fanny, by the way. Sit and we can discuss how to create a special day for you."

"Yeah right, some special day, forced into marrying a man I don't know," Rosalind thought and had to push Allan in the direction of the couch. He stumbled a few times, but she caught him and sat him down. She took the spot next to him, while the woman sat in a chair across from them, holding a large book.

"I have three packages." Fanny opened the book and turned it. "The first one is 'The Sin.' It's only the ceremony." She then turned the page. "Second is 'The Roulette,' it's the most popular. You get the ceremony performed in our famous Casino Chapel, matching silver bands, a red rose for love, and a wedding photo." She flipped the page and pointed to the next page. "The third, 'The Royal Flush,' gives you matching gold bands, a deluxe rose bouquet, a set of twelve coffee cups and four key chains with your wedding photo on them. You can share them with family and friends."

Rosalind pondered the three options, wondering if Fanny ever varied from her well-rehearsed speech. "What about the marriage certificate?"

"Our gift to you, we laminate one."

"I'll...we'll take *The Roulette* package."

Allan suddenly burst out in a baritone voice, singing lyrics to an old school song about getting married in a chapel.

Fanny smiled and closed the book. "I see someone is excited. We're ready when you are, so you can go right in."

"Sweetie, time to get married." Rosalind hauled up Allan off the couch and directed him toward the chapel room.

Once inside, she saw him blink several times and then he asked. "Where is everyone?"

His remark made the two witnesses' heads turn. The older man with glasses was now wearing a white minister's smock and stared at Allan with a questionable look. It wasn't hard to perceive their unspoken questions. A wave of apprehension washed through her as she pictured being grilled over how many drinks, she'd let her 'boyfriend' suck down.

"Please excuse us. We hit a huge jackpot on the way and stopped to celebrate. I guess one of us drank a little too much champagne." She kissed Allan for appearances.

"Oh, how wonderful. What a way to start off your marriage." Fanny beamed at them and tugged down her fitted dress.

Rosalind returned the smile, relieved they'd accepted her explanation.

The altar seemed to click and ring bells. She realized it

was actually a slot machine. Other slots and computerized blackjack tables played by themselves. It looked and sounded like a casino. She moved Allan in front of the ringing slot-altar.

"Whyy are we ooa an...another rehe...ooarsal?"

"Shhh, honey."

"Where'ssss Johhn?"

To quiet Allan, she clasped him to her and kissed his lips. The kiss worked. He stayed quiet. Although he wobbled a little, at least he was paying attention to the minister.

"Let's begin. We're gathered here today to unite this man and woman in matrimony. Do you Allan Richard Smith, take Rosalind Susan Dunne, to be your wife in sickness and health, for richer or poorer, till death do you part?"

No sugar frosting or words of advice, merely a sampling of the time-honored words. She held her breath.

"I do."

Rosalind blinked. He'd said the words in such a clear voice, she thought for a millisecond he meant them. His blue eyes were focused for the moment.

The minister turned to her. "Do you Rosalind Susan Dunne, take Allan Richard Smith, to be your husband in sickness and health, for richer or poorer, till death do you part?"

All she had to do was say the words and she'd be one step closer to securing her inheritance. A speck of doubt inched its way to the surface.

"Yes, I do." Rosalind rushed the words before the ramifications could make sense to her.

"You may now kiss the bride," the minister stated.

It was done. She was married.

She turned, then stopped short like a fifth ace in a poker game when Allan heaved her into his arms and planted his mouth on hers in a gentle yet persuasive kiss. It was nothing like the kiss she'd given him. Her knees went weak, and a weird fever seared its way down past her abdomen.

As a tide of desire swept through her, she felt herself transported, her emotions unfamiliar. Their tongues met. Rosalind wrapped her arms around his neck and ran her fingers through his hair as the kiss went on and on.

Her self-made defenses weakened. The sound of someone clearing their throat forced reality forward. The crux of the game she was playing hit her hard. She jerked away from Allan, and they stared at each other.

"Sorry," Rosalind whispered.

Man, could he kiss. She wouldn't mind being called a Wingless Angel to spend a night with him. Maybe she should, seeing as he was now her husband.

"Here is your paperwork. Congratulations, you're one lucky lady," Fanny said, nodding in Allan's direction.

Slowly and sadly, Rosalind moved to her handsome husband's side and gripped his hand.

As if the man could want someone like her, who spent days on end mucking out stalls and smelling of horses instead of some expensive perfume. He was simply a stepping-stone to her inheritance, business only.

"Honey, we have an audience, let's go to our room."

"Mmmmm, you taste good," Allan whispered.

He tried to pull her into his embrace despite the fact she held him at arms' length, unsure if she could handle another round of kisses from him. "We're done here. Time to go to the hotel."

Rosalind tugged Allan from the bizarre Casino Chapel to the front doors, waving to the man with glasses and Fanny.

They weaved and stumbled their way across the street. The neon clock displayed eleven-thirty.

Shit. Sam would have her hide if she was late.

"Move, Allan. We need to get to your hotel." Rosalind threw his hat into the backseat and had to push and shove him into the truck as if he was an ornery bull. Once she buckled him in and closed the door, she climbed behind the wheel and checked her iPhone. Eleven-forty-five.

"Yessss, my rrrroom to have sex."

She turned to answer him, just as her new hubby's head lobbed to the side and hit the window with a loud thud.

He'd passed out, thank God.

Her simple plan had worked. Get married. Get money. Get a divorce. The blue, signature Hilton Hotel sign loomed in front of her. Now, the hard part. How would she get him to his room?

She drove to the side of the building and found a spot to park, away from all the other vehicles. Cutting the engine, she gripped the steering wheel, took a number of deep breaths, and shut her eyes.

She could handle this. If she could drown in her own sweat while working, she should be able to half carry a man, if need be.

On the count of three, she opened the door and stepped down. Before closing the door, she reached underneath the driver's seat and withdrew a large brown envelope. She folded it and then tucked it into the inside of her shirt along with the copy of the marriage certificate. The heels of her boots clicked as she dashed to the passenger side door and yanked it open. Allan's face almost ate the tar, saved only by the seatbelt.

"Shit." She reached across him, unsnapped it, and he fell toward her. She clutched him by the shoulders and shook him. "Mr. Smith. Allan, wake up."

His eyelids fluttered, then opened, and he smiled in an erotic way.

Crap, his smile was sexier than David's.

Her heart raced faster than a bucking wild horse. Rosalind tried to look away from his impish smile but failed.

"Hey honeyyy, are youuuu cooome...are youuu cominggg to my roommm?"

"Um..."

All at once, Allan straightened and slid out of the truck. She stood ready to catch him, but instead she was wrenched into his arms, and he kissed her. Her own eagerness to kiss him took her by surprise and she wondered at the spiral of lust coursing through her.

Allan's arms locked her tight against his body. His telltale desire pressed into her. Her protective fence fell again. Recklessly, she allowed her dormant desire to take over. Somewhere in the depth of her consciousness she knew she should step away, but she couldn't. His hands held her hips closer, until there wasn't a bit of spare space between them. All her rational impulses vanished as she clung to him.

She'd ended up with a drunken rooster with octopus' hands. Lordy, lordy, Tom's kisses never had her feeling like this.

And the kiss continued.

Their tongues battled like a bunch of rattlesnakes, neither winning. Through the fog, Rosalind heard a clock chime.

Midnight.

Time for the fairytale to end. But she was no Cinderella.

Once again, this time regretfully, she pushed herself from Allan's arms and seized his hands.

"Yes, we'll go to your room. Now come on."

"My rooooom? Naked?"

Allan untangled himself and dove at her. He missed and stumbled. She reached to catch him and found herself in his arms.

She exhaled. "I don't have time for this."

With some twisting and turning, she wiggled out of his

embrace, put her arm around his waist, and urged him to walk. He staggered next to her as she half-carried him. Encouraged by the fact no one was around, she hurried them to the lobby. To her horror it was bursting with activity. Rosalind steadied Allan and moved toward the elevators.

"Your room key, please."

They stopped and she stared at the security guard.

Damn. Shit. And a pile of cow manure. She had to think fast. "Honey, the man needs to see our key. Which pocket is it in?"

"In myyy wallet, not mmmyyyy pocket."

For heaven's sake. Not the wallet again. It displayed a life of its own. Without thinking she dug her hand into his rear pocket for it but couldn't stop her thoughts of how nice his ass was. It was too nice.

Unable to resist, she pinched the firm piece of flesh.

"Hey, thattt wasn't nice."

"Shh," she muttered, and flashed the keycard at the guard. "Here it is."

"Thank you, have a nice night."

"Whyyyy did you pinnnch my ass?"

"Shhh, someone will hear you."

Rosalind plastered her mouth against his to shut him up, but Allan abandoned her lips to raise her hand and kiss the inside of her palm, then her fingers. Stunned, she couldn't move or think. Desire flushed through her body, crying for release.

The elevator doors opened. The sexual spell he'd evoked dissipated. She escaped his grasp and wrapped her arm around his waist to support him.

She guided him into the waiting elevator and turned. No one seemed to be aware of them or recognized Allan. Luck seemed to be on her side.

As soon as the doors closed, Allan's hands traveled from her neck to the front of her, capturing one of her breasts. He whispered in her ear and her body quivered at the warmth of his breath as it touched her skin. Yet she felt compelled to fight his embrace.

In the foreplay battle, one of his hands abandoned her breast to encircle her waist. He won and clasped her tightly to him. She felt his fingers unbutton her shirt. Sudden shivers cascaded down her spine as his warm palms moved over her bra.

The doors opened. Rosalind jumped back fast, as if someone doused her with cold water and repositioned the envelope inside her shirt.

His embrace was dangerous. Her skin tingled, branded by his touch. "Behave. We're almost to your room, get those legs moving."

"You have a lus...lussciouus body. What's your name?"

Laughing, she took one of his hands into hers and led him down the hall.

Luscious? That was one word no one had said to her before. Allan must be three sheets to the wind.

"What's your room number? We can't get into bed naked unless we find your room."

"Fivvvve-forrrty-oneeee."

They had to backtrack a few doors. She slid the card into the key slot. Bingo, a green light blinked, and she pushed the door.

"Thisss is itttt. Weeee get nakkked nooowww?"

"Yes, it is."

Naked, oh yeah. She would love to see him in his birthday suit.

No, this was a business arranged marriage. He was off limits, and he was drunk.

Allan pushed past her into his suite. Shaking her head, she took a quick glance down the hallway. Not seeing anyone, she kicked the door shut and turned to find Allan walking half-naked toward a pair of French doors. His discarded shoes, shirt, and belt lay on the floor. They seemed to cry out, 'Follow me for a reward!'

"Mister, what are you doing?"

"Getttting naked. Timmme oo have sexxxx."

"Oh, right."

He was definitely eye candy, but she reminded herself she wasn't here to have sex with him. Having seen a good many bare-chested men while working and living on a ranch, she was surprised how Allan's shirt had hidden far too well his muscular shoulders, chest, and a six-pack abdomen.

With her mouth open, she watched him take off his socks and jeans, revealing burgundy satin boxers. Rosalind licked her lips. He disappeared into what she assumed was the bedroom. She followed, stopped a tad inside the room, and flipped the light switch. He stood next to the bed clad only in those sexy shorts.

Oh, sweet Jesus. She sure would like to sample what he was offering.

Again, she had to rid her mind of such thoughts and focus on the main reason she was in his room—*bedroom*. She reached inside her shirt, took out the marriage certificate along with the thick envelope, and held it toward him.

"Umm, thanks for doing this for me. Here's the money. I'll call you in two months or when I have the divorce papers in my hands."

"Divvoorce. Not married yet."

"Yes, you are. We are..."

A loud belch cut her off. Allan raised his hand to his mouth. "Parrrdonnnn."

His word hung in the air, then he fell like a ragdoll and landed halfway on the bed with a leg hanging over the side, completely passed out.

Chuckling, Rosalind set the envelope filled with cash and the document on the table. She went to him, straightened his leg onto the bed. In shock, she stepped backward as his willy played peek-a-boo from the boxers' flap.

Oh boy. God had made him every woman's dream partner.

Although no one else was in the room, she glanced around anxiously before giving his body the onceover from his toes to his head.

An uncontrollable sexual desire took hold of her even though it shouldn't have. He was better looking than anything she'd seen on a Saturday night at the bar in Fort Ripley.

For the first time all night, she really studied Allan's face. He was gorgeous. In his peaceful, inebriated state, his square jawline and high cheekbones gave him a quality most men took for granted. His nose sported a bump toward the arch, and she wondered how he'd broken it. In a boyhood fight? Or in a contact sport like football?

She blew out a quick, short breath. With her fingertips she brushed aside several strands of golden hair that cloaked his eyes.

If he hadn't come to the rodeo, would their paths have crossed? Did he have a girlfriend or a fiancée?

What had she done?

For a split second, regret nagged at her, clouded by her fiery attraction to him. About to place her hand on his calf, she stopped. The man, her husband was passed out. It would be wrong to let the sexy hairs on his legs and thighs tickle her hand.

Leaning over him, she pulled the blanket onto his body, but

he moved, and the edge of the silky boxers revealed his dormant manhood that was now long and stiff.

Rosalind shifted her eyes to his face to see if he had woken up.

But she saw no movement. His eyes remained closed and his breathing even.

This time, she yanked the blanket and was tucking it in around him, when he pushed it off again. She grabbed the blanket for a second time, but her hand fell onto his chest. Afraid to move, she stayed motionless, with her fingers spread out over his six-pack. Her hand rose and fell with each breath he took. His light brown coarse hairs curled around her fingers.

She sat on the edge of the bed and stared at Allan.

Who was he? God had to forgive her for what she'd done, right?

Confident he wouldn't wake up, she slowly lifted her hand off his chest and stood. Stepping over to the table, she paused and noticed Allan's discarded jeans. She bent down and picked them up, but his wallet fell out. Hesitating because she knew it had a life of its own, she bit the bullet. However, this time when her fingers touched the leather, it was cold and heavy, not warmed from his body heat as before.

About to set it on the table with the papers, a business card on the floor caught her attention. She retrieved it.

Smith and Associates Brokerage Firm, Inc., Allan Smith, President.

In panic mode, Rosalind dropped the jeans and the card and hurried to the door. With her hand on the knob, she stopped short and forced herself to breathe in, and then exhale.

Pivoting, she proceeded back to the bedroom.

Shit. He was going to be meaner than a wet cat, when he

woke up and found he was married to someone he didn't know.

She scooped up his wallet and laid it on the table. This time, she slid the business card into her jeans pocket and neatly hung his jeans over a chair.

Taking one last quick look at the man who was her husband, her gaze lingered on his handsome face. Regret dominated the moment, knowing she'd never see him again.

Allan was probably a very nice man and hadn't deserved being a pawn in her plan. She grabbed a pen and wrote him a note.

Rosalind laid it, along with the money and a copy of the marriage certificate, on the table for him to see. With a clenched jaw, she hurried out of the hotel room.

What's done, is done.

CHAPTER FOUR

Ringing tore through the silence of Allan Smith's darkened hotel room. He flung his hand toward the sound, the first attempt unsuccessful, hitting the lamp and then the wall.

"Fuck!"

Finally, he grabbed the phone on the nightstand. That stopped the annoying noise, and he held the receiver to his ear.

"Hello," he groaned and slowly opened his eyes.

"Hello? Allan, where are you?"

A loud agitated voice interrupted the quiet. "In my room."

"You're ten minutes late."

"Late?" He fought through the fog of an instant headache and swallowed to moisten his dry lips and throat.

"Come on, stop kidding around. What the hell happened to you last night? You left the bar without telling us."

Allan tried to comprehend the words sadistically thrown at him as pain riveted through his forehead. The red numbers on the clock indicated it was eleven-fifty.

He was Mr. Time Management. He was never late. But he couldn't remember what he was late for.

Fragmented pieces of the night emerged. Bachelor party. A

damn stupid rodeo. Being kicked out for being rowdy. A limo ride to a country western bar. Drinking tequila shots and buckets of beer.

His lips thinned, and his nostrils flared with a mounting rage. He hated tequila. It was the most senseless thing he'd done in a very long time.

"Sorry, man. I forgot to ask for a wake-up call. I need to take a quick shower. Give me ten minutes."

"I need help down here now. Damn it, Allan. John is ready to bolt, he's so nervous."

"Right, John's wedding." At last, through the haze he remembered he was in Las Vegas for his best friend's wedding. The rehearsal thing had been last night. They'd gone out celebrating.

"This is not the time for you to be indisposed. I'm doing your job here. For God's sake, you're the best man, not me."

"I'm the best man? Shit. I *am* the best man."

Laughter erupted from the phone, triggering Allan's head to pound even more. The ceremony was today.

Why hadn't he stayed in his room like he'd planned?

Damn it.

The Amazon insider trader paperwork and reports from his lawyer were still in his briefcase, untouched.

The annoying voice on the phone continued to talk in excited tones. Allan managed to sit vertically and swing his bare legs over the side of the bed.

"How did...how did I get undressed?" He held the phone to his ear with one hand and rubbed his face with the other.

"I don't know. John is asking for you."

Trying to ease the tension along his forehead proved fruitless. Instead of relief from the pounding, something hard and foreign on his hand initiated more pain.

Snapping his hand away from his face, Allan stared at a

simple thin band encircling his ring finger. Straightening, he gawked at it, as waves of shock wracked throughout his body.

Left hand.

Ring finger.

Wedding ring?

Disconnectedly, the meaning slipped into his mind. Tension filled his entire body, and he held his breath. Turning, he looked over his shoulder, expecting to see a woman or worse, Katherine, his current girlfriend lying in his bed.

The other side of the bed was vacant, the bedspread untouched, and there was no evidence of another person having been in bed with him. His gut quivered as a sick feeling mounted.

It can't be.

There's no way in hell, he'd marry anyone. Ever.

"...are you sure you're still not impaired from drinking? Allan! Are you there?"

"Yes, yes. Did you guys play a prank on me last night?" He paced around the room as far as the short phone cord would allow.

This bore all the components of one of John's signature schemes. When they'd been in foster care together, pranks offered them a meager form of salvation to avoid the hurt and mistrust they had to deal with after moving from one home to another.

As he waited for details of his friends' sick practical joke to come out, an odd feeling in the pit of his stomach wouldn't cease. A pair of delicious lips kissing him surfaced in his fogged memories of the night.

"What are you talking about? You left with the cowgirl from the rodeo. Hurry up and get your ass down here."

"All right, ten minutes."

He peered at the ring as he replaced the receiver into its

cradle, ending the call and inspected the room a second time. The bedroom door stood open. His white Charvet French dress shirt lay on the floor. That wasn't right. He stepped toward the shirt and stopped. On the table was an envelope and papers.

Allan smiled. Okay, so this was all a hoax.

John better be prepared, he knew paybacks were hell.

Time stopped as he picked up the envelope and tore it open.

Cash. Hundred-dollar bills.

He counted it, separating the hundreds in piles of tens. When he hit two thousand, the rest of the money fell unheeded onto the table, most of it landing on the floor.

"No way. No way in fuckin' hell."

He stared at the paper.

Marriage Certificate.

"Holy shit!"

The curse vibrated off the walls. He pulled out the closest chair, sank down, and stared at the paper. His hands trembled. John would never consider marriage a joke.

After ageing out of their last foster homes at the age of eighteen, they'd formed a pact to never get married, knowing firsthand the trouble it caused. They worked the system to acquire money for college, food, and housing. John graduated with a degree in political science, while he'd obtained a degree in finance and a minor in law. Then last year, John came to his office, shocking him by declaring he'd found a woman he wanted to marry.

Allan's jaw tensed in frustration as his signature taunted him on the marriage certificate.

Fifteen years, their pact had lasted. It should have been forever. Beyond common sense, he closed his eyes trying to visualize what could have transpired in the past twenty-four hours.

He remembered the guys passing around shots of something in the limo as they headed to the rodeo. After climbing the metal grandstand steps, his knee ached, so he'd taken a Vicodin.

No, he'd taken two.

The first one he'd taken had been before they left the hotel.

Crap.

As hard as he tried to remember anything from beyond watching the rodeo, he couldn't.

Nothing. Not a goddamn thing. Not a single moment.

His eyes flashed open.

Fool. Vicodin and alcohol. No wonder he had a headache and couldn't remember.

Damn his friends. He could see them now, all laughing their asses off. The certificate might very well be a fake. Anyone could've printed one from the internet.

Or was it blackmail? Who would've done this? What if someone had successfully extorted him after all these years?

This can't be real.

He'd play along until someone admitted what they'd done. Yet doubt crept in as he stared at the money, the certificate, the note, and the final receptor, the warmth of the metal on his finger. A cold, harsh truth settled in.

I'm married.

A new level of questions rushed through him.

Who was his bride? Was she pretty? Had she been a good kisser? Had they sexually pleased each other?

Allan closed his eyes again, trying to see an image of the woman who was now his wife. It failed. Nothing came forward. He tilted his head. This seemed to work, as an odd sort of room with bells ringing and an older man and woman flashed for a moment. It faded and he opened his eyes.

Had he married an old lady?

Concerned, he absentmindedly combed his fingers through his hair and cursed when the ring caught, pulling strands out.

"Shit."

Cautiously, he reached for the other paper. The loathsome note seemed more damning in his hand than propped on the table. He lifted one corner hesitantly, and then all the way, revealing a handwritten scribble.

Allan,

Thank you for helping me. I left you a copy of the marriage certificate and the specified amount of money for your time. I'll contact you in two months to conclude our agreement. Rosalind

This confirmed what he'd guessed, and the authenticity frightened the hell out of him. Allan's gut gurgled and acid caught in his throat.

Shit. Shit. Shit.

Who the hell is Rosalind?

Perhaps one of the strippers the other groomsmen hired for the night?

The name didn't evoke a face and he wondered when the nightmare would end. His long line of foster parents taught him not to trust. Trepidation became the driving force that made him successful in his business transactions. Someone would pay dearly for this stunt. If, heaven forbid, this was real, he couldn't allow it being leaked to the news.

The illuminated numbers on the clock showed he had a few minutes left. He'd have to deal with this Rosalind person after John's wedding. Opening his briefcase, Allan grabbed the money and the offensive marriage certificate, tossing them inside. As he did, his prescription bottle rolled with a flash of its red warning label.

'Do not take with alcohol.'

By the time Allan arrived downstairs in the lobby, showered and dressed in his navy tuxedo, a crowd was gathered around the groom, who was hyperventilating. He laughed in spite of his own annoying situation.

He calmly walked to his best friend and yanked away the brown paper bag he held to his face, which compelled John to fling his arms around to reclaim it.

"John. Look at me."

Panic emanated from the groom's eyes, the same look he'd seen the first time he and John met, years ago in the middle of the night at the foster home. He'd heard the caseworker say John's parents were drug addicts and they'd been living out of a car when the police found them.

As he did all those years ago, he clasped John's hands and placed them on his knees. The raspy breathing didn't stop. Allan took hold of John's head and tilted it higher, so they were face to face. He gazed into John's brown eyes.

"John McNeil, you're about to marry the woman you love. Do you want her to see you like this?"

John blinked. "I'm not..."

The dazed look began to fade, replaced by confusion. Allan's concern for his best friend diminished too. "Do you still want to get married, or do I need to take you to the hospital?"

"No, no. I'm fine." John had replied in between gulps of air and heaving shoulders.

"Show me. Act like a *man* who is about to marry the most gorgeous woman I know."

"You're right. It's a new beginning. I love her. She loves me. I want this. I can do this, Allan."

"Yes, you can. Now, on your feet, John." He glanced over the crowd, looking for someone to help, but the other groomsmen stood around like statues.

As John's panic began to subside, Allan had to wonder if he

was the only sane person here, even with a splitting headache. "John, concentrate. What time do we need to be at the church?"

His question broke the groomsmen's zombie-like state. Several immediately consulted cell phone calendars and notepads for last-minute checks. Seeing them all with phones out, he checked to make sure he had his. He located it in his breast pocket. Then, as if on cue, the limo arrived on the scene to take them to the church.

The ceremony began without any more drama. He was positioned to the right of John and found himself recalling fragments of the previous night. He and a woman had stood before an altar much like the one in front of them at the moment.

He was concentrating so hard on the image in his mind, he missed his prompt to hand the wedding rings to John. Someone nudged him in the side, and he instantly snapped to, reaching into his pocket for the rings and setting them on the Bible the pastor held.

Too late, his mistake was visible for all to see. Instead of two rings, three lay on the Bible. The pastor gasped. So did the bride and groom. Seeing his error, Allan snatched up the shiny silver ring that stood out like a sore thumb next to the gold circlets.

Shit.

Unwilling to draw attention to himself until he knew exactly what was going on, he'd taken the damn ring off and shoved it in his pocket earlier. The slip was now a blur as the rest of the ceremony went on without any further incidents.

Allan focused on his best friend who appeared happy. When John leaned in to kiss his bride, a woman's face flashed before him, along with a lush body he'd held in his arms. He remembered a pair of waiting lips and the never-ending kiss they'd shared. An unexpected sexual ache spread to every nerve in his body, and he shifted his stance, frowning at his reaction. The vision was gone before the woman's face became clear.

Loud musical chords from the organ played, signaling the end of the ceremony. Allan shook his head to clear his mind and followed the happy newlyweds down the aisle.

Frustration set in as he struggled to enjoy the reception. Not only did he not know who his wife was, but how was he going to break the news to Katherine? He wasn't too worried since they'd tired of each other anyway long before she left for an all-expense paid trip to Europe.

He grimaced. Paid for by him.

Several guests and bridesmaids tried to entice him out onto the dance floor, but he declined. He couldn't get into all the merriment. He'd done his duty for his best friend. All he wanted to do now was escape to his room.

With a pounding headache and his knee throbbing, Allan reached inside his tuxedo coat for a Vicodin and stopped. He couldn't chance a repeat of the previous night. He scanned the room. It was time to cut loose from the celebration, so he'd have time to figure out why he married a woman he didn't know. None of the groomsmen offered a single word about his so-called marriage. It was as if it never happened. He was almost convinced it was a joke, but the image of the money and the damn certificate wouldn't leave.

It was real. It had happened.

Time was ticking away, and he'd stayed long enough. Allan maneuvered toward the doors. Unfortunately, one of the bridesmaids, whose name he couldn't remember, slipped her arm through his, delaying his exit.

"Help us get the bride and groom to leave for the wedding suite."

"Sure, I'll get John. You ladies take care of the bride." This worked in his favor. He'd be able to make his escape then too.

Upon completion of their errand, along with all sorts of sexual jokes about the wedding night directed at the happy couple, the same bridesmaid who'd asked for help put her mouth to his ear.

"I'd love to have you join me in my room."

The other bridesmaids laughed and giggled, offering the same.

"Sorry, ladies. I need my beauty sleep. Thanks for the invitations."

Ignoring the pleas and the pawing hands, Allan escaped. He wanted no part of them, which surprised him. He'd never turned down an invitation for sex with a gorgeous woman.

What had gotten into him?

Allan looked at his ring, then continued on alone to his room.

CHAPTER FIVE

"I had no choice. I did what I thought I should do." Rosalind had kept her marriage and the wedding in Las Vegas a secret from Sam until they'd arrived home in Minnesota, hoping if she waited, he and the lawyers wouldn't be able to do anything.

"It was wrong."

His three words hung in the air. She didn't have a reply.

They'd finished lunch when he'd brought up her marriage for the thousandth time. She nibbled her lower lip and placed both hands on her hips as confusion and indignation set in.

Mr. Smith wasn't going to be happy about the divorce being delayed. Then again, she hadn't heard from him. With no other options in her playbook, she'd wait this one out.

"I got married to get the seven-hundred acres for the horses. I can't allow any more of them to die. A handful are scheduled to be put down soon. If the damn lawyers hadn't requested confirmation my marriage was legitimate, I'd have my money."

"It's part of their job."

"No, no, no. They can't keep refusing to release the money until I provide more verification. What more do they need?

They have the signed marriage certificate from the state of Nevada. It's not fair. This is throwing me off schedule."

"You should've thought about this before—"

"You knew the land was important to me," Rosalind cut in. "And you could have helped, not thrown up roadblocks."

"It doesn't make what you did right."

He bobbed his head, pursed his lips, and strolled from the kitchen.

The silence wasn't her friend. Sam's chiding tone infuriated her. She threw the dirty lunch plate into the sink. The clop and clunk sound of the dish breaking irritated her further.

"Great, now I have to clean up that mess too."

No one was in the kitchen to hear her complaint. The lawyers stepping in and denying her the money seemed to be a heaven-sent message to Sam. He hadn't overreacted when she'd let the cat out of the bag about her sudden marriage to a man she didn't know. He'd been very quiet and almost pleased. He didn't have to be the bad guy anymore. No, he appeared relieved to let the lawyers take control of the situation.

It brought up the question, why were the lawyers requesting more proof? Had Sam instructed them to?

To her surprise the afternoon months ago when she had revealed the fact, she'd gotten married, Sam hadn't lectured her or anything about her deceitful marriage. He only warned her not everything stayed the same, change was a good thing, and not all men were as easy to control as her horses. When she'd tried to question him, he had raised his hand, signaling the conversation was finished.

Frustrated at his M.O. these last weeks, they barely spoke. He seemed to be avoiding her or would leave the room when she entered and go upstairs to his room. She often found his dinners half eaten.

With the deadline of the second month fast approaching, it

was time to have an all-out shouting match with him whether he liked it or not. He was a guest in her home. She had invited him to take Grandpa Rodney's bedroom, just to have another person in the house.

The stairs creaked as she climbed up to the second floor. Rosalind slowed her steps as Sam's bedroom door loomed in front of her. Her confidence faded.

The sudden ringing of the land-line phone saved her. She abruptly turned away and raced down the stairs.

"Hello."

"Is Mrs. Smith available?"

"Who... I'm sorry, this is she."

"Hello, my name is Mr. Haugen, from Johnsen and Haugen Law Office. I'm calling to let you know your inheritance will be in your control in seventy-two hours."

"It's about... I mean, will all of it be transferred to my bank account?" Rosalind fisted her free hand uneasily, wondering what changed their minds. All she needed was the five-hundred thousand right now to complete the purchase of the adjacent land to her ranch.

"It can be, or would you like a portion of the cash and the remaining amount invested?"

"Can I have one million?" The amount sounded strange to her own ears. Listening to herself say it aloud caused her to smile.

"Yes, I'll have it arranged to be transferred in forty-eight hours. Did you want to establish an annuity for the remaining fourteen million?"

A small gasp of delight escaped her. "Oh, I'm not sure. Can I call you tomorrow?"

"Yes, we can have you signed any agreement via the phone at that time, Mrs. Smith. Is there anything else I can help you with today?"

"No. Thank you, Mr. Haugen, for calling." She hung up the phone with shaking hands and hid her excitement, knowing Sam would be able to hear if she screamed. She withdrew the now worn business card from her rear pocket.

Two p.m. in Minnesota, an hour ahead in the Big Apple. All her worries would soon be settled.

Allan, her so-called husband, would be removed from her life for good with no harm done. The quicker they pushed through the divorce, the better. Simply saying the word *husband* left a sour taste in her mouth. Without delay, she punched in the number from the card.

"Good afternoon. Thank you for calling Smith and Associates Brokerage Firm. How may I direct your call?"

"Hello, Mr. Smith please."

"I'm sorry, he's on the phone. May I take a message?"

"No... I will...it's very important I speak to him today. This is his wife." Holding her breath, she waited. The meager self-confidence she'd gathered withered away. "Hello, are you still there? Did you hear me? I am his wife. I need to have a word with Mr. Smith."

"Sorry. Hold please."

The woman's tone had become curt and unpleasant. She heard a click and then music.

Now what? What if he couldn't talk, and another day went by without contact?

It was already late afternoon, and she didn't know if she'd be able to make it into town to FedEx the divorce papers. All she wanted to do was be courteous by letting him know the papers would be arriving.

After holding for a short time, she was ready to redial when the annoying music stopped, and the unemotional voice came on the line. "Thanks for holding. May I have your first name?"

"My first name? It's Rosalind..." Before she could say

anything more, she heard another click and the pointless music.

Well, if that doesn't make a bull ornery. Allan needed to hire a more courteous secretary. As her temper climbed, unexpectedly the irritating music cut off.

"Who the fuck are you? Who are you working for?"

The familiar male voice cooled her fire, but another kind of burn flared in a different area as her pulse skyrocketed. She'd been unprepared to hear the huskiness of his voice even though it was laced with fury.

Her knees weakened and her stomach flipped. "I'm not... you're being rude."

"Listen, you money-hungry, conniving bitch. I want a divorce."

She gripped the phone tighter, in spite of her sweaty palms. An unexpected image of him lying in silky boxers, with that sexy, hairy chest and his handsome face, caused her body temperature to rise.

"Excuse me. You don't have to shout or call me names. That's why I'm calling." Rosalind forced the sexy visualization to dissipate. "I wanted to thank you again, Allan. For helping me and to let you know I'll be sending the divorce papers today."

"You didn't answer me. Whom do you work for? How much are they paying you to do this? I could have the Feds at your doorstep in no time for blackmail."

The sternness in Allan's voice told her this wouldn't be a walk down the yellow brick road. Blackmail? She was paying him. He wasn't making sense. "I don't work for anyone."

"Why haven't you contacted me before this?"

"You agreed to help me. I've been trying to tell you I have the divorce papers. I'm going to get them out to you this afternoon, so you'll have them in the morning via next day air."

"Come on, this is a joke, right? You're doing this for John."

"Who's John?" She realized Allan didn't remember anything about them getting married or the reason why. If he demanded an annulment because they hadn't slept together, she'd be screwed. Would Mr. Haugen and Mr. Johnsen demand she return the money?

Damn. That wasn't going to happen.

"Never mind. You have divorce papers for me, already?"

"Yes, as soon as you sign them, I can submit them to the court here in Minnesota. When the divorce is finalized, you'll receive the second part of your payment."

"Money? How much?"

Rosalind took a deep breath. "Mr. Smith, it seems you've forgotten our agreement."

"I don't even know who you are. *And* I surely wouldn't have agreed to marry you, or anyone for that matter."

"Oh, yes you did, and we are married. You agreed to help me for twenty-five thousand dollars up front, which I left on the desk in your hotel room. And then upon completion...um, our divorce, I'm paying you another twenty-five thousand dollars. Is this ringing any bells? You were a smidgen drunk, but it *is* your signature on the marriage license and the certificate. You agreed."

"I see my name, goddamn it! I have the proof right here in front of me. This doesn't answer my question of why. And you said no one *paid* you. Why would I have married you for fifty thousand dollars?"

"Are you sure you aren't drunk right now, Mr. Smith? Who would pay me? I paid *you* to marry me. You have the initial payment of twenty-five thousand dollars."

"I'm confused. Why would I want, need, or take your money?"

She heard the candor in his voice and her temper rose. "I

don't know. Only you would know that. If you think I'll give you more than fifty thousand, you've got another think coming, mister. The agreed amount was twenty-five thousand dollars when we divorced. Not a penny more."

"Fifty thousand dollars total. That's all?"

"Listen here, Mr. Smith. Being president of a big company doesn't mean you can push me around. I don't know who you think you are. You're not getting a dime more than the agreed upon amount." Rosalind stood and paced around the kitchen to calm down, thankful for the long telephone cord.

Holy Mother of pastures if this didn't make pigs shit. Was he trying to collect more money from her?

Damn. What a mess.

About to fly off the handle with insults, instead, she heard laughter on the other end of the phone.

"I don't give a damn about the money. Keep it. And for your information, I wasn't drunk. I developed a reaction to some medication I took. It didn't mix well with the handful of drinks I enjoyed. Why on earth am I explaining myself to you?"

"Not sure. It's not my problem. The divorce papers will be overnighted to you, and you'll have them tomorrow. Please sign and returned them to me, so I can file them here in Minnesota with my lawyer."

"Let me get this straight. You're saying no one paid you to blackmail me?"

Undecided if she should be angry or laugh, Rosalind held her temper in check for the moment. "Yes, I've been trying to tell you you're wrong. You're not listening. I never mentioned anything about blackmail. You did."

She heard more laughter followed by what sounded like choking. Great. All she needed was for the man to die before signing the papers. "Mr. Smith. Mr. Smith, are you all right?"

"Rosalind? Is that your name?"

His tone was much calmer and controlled. On the other hand, it now held a hint of amusement. "Yes, that's my name."

"There are certain things you should know about the person you married. The firm I own and am the president of, is one of the top Fortune Five Hundred companies in the United States. I am, and have been, one of the most sought-after bachelors in the world. Somehow, you have done what others haven't been able to do. You got the best of me. I'll be more than happy to sign the papers when they arrive. And forget about the money. I don't need it. I don't want it. I want the divorce. I can't be married."

"I'm sorry, Allan, I had no clue who you were...are. As I said before, I want this divorce as badly as you do. The documents will be FedExed before five today. Thank you very much, Mr. Smith."

"The sooner the better for both of us. By the way, Rosalind, why did you need to get married, or should I rephrase, why did we get married?"

How was she supposed to reply? By saying she was being selfish and childish. Why would some billionaire care that she needed money to save horses? What did she have to lose at this point, being honest would be the best answer.

"My grandfather was kind of old-fashioned. In order for me to receive the bulk of my inheritance before my thirtieth birthday, I had to get married. Like you, I didn't want to be anyone's wife or have a husband. I found you at the bar in Las Vegas. I'm sorry your drunkenness gave me... I'm not like...the—our marriage was meant to be very short." She held her breath and waited for his response.

She'd given him part of the truth. The silence was broken by more of his husky laughter. His deep booming laugh brought a smile to her lips and something intense raced through her system.

"Rosalind, I can't say it's been a pleasure. I contemplated hiring a private detective to find you. Get those papers to me ASAP."

"I will. Thanks."

"Goodbye."

She hung up and did another happy dance around the kitchen. Now, she'd be able to concentrate on Dawn's workouts and training for the championship, instead of how to get her inheritance.

CHAPTER SIX

"Fifty thousand dollars," Allan grumbled in disbelief as he placed the phone in its cradle. *That's pennies in my world.*

Why would he have agreed to accept money to get married? He didn't need any.

Removing the impertinent ring from his inside breast pocket, he turned it over in his fingers. He'd carried the damn thing around every day since Las Vegas. He opened his desk drawer, took out the copy of the marriage certificate he'd kept hidden, and stared at the words with contempt.

Marriage.

The word and the idea of it left a bad taste in his mouth. His parents' marriage had been turbulent for as long as he could remember back. Even now when he thought about his parents, he felt an uncontrollable fury. They'd had to move almost yearly to a new home, until they were forced to leave that one, due to not paying rent. His dad drank heavily, which caused him to lose whatever job he had at the time.

While his mother tried to give him a home, she never took her medication for depression and things got out of hand until she would take it again for a while. Allan did have to give her some credit for trying, but with no support from his dad, it was no wonder life was hell.

The day his life changed, he'd been coming home from high school, when he saw several police cars parked in front of the house they were renting. He walked up the sidewalk and they told him his parents had died in a crash. He'd learned later that his dad was drunk and the cause of the crash. That had begun four years of being in the foster care system, since he didn't have any grandparents, aunts, or uncles.

Rosalind's phone call had thrown him a curve, by bringing up unwanted old emotions. He'd been prepared for some sort of blackmail plot. He even had his lawyers along with special agents on call if he heard from his so-called wife. Now that she'd surfaced and she wasn't blackmailing him, he was in uncharted territory and didn't know what to do.

He'd been so positive someone was tryIng to extort money from him. Now there was no need for the police. His lawyer should be able to handle a very quiet divorce. But in general, he was on his own to fix this mess. Yet a smidgen of skepticism lingered. Perhaps, this whole thing had been a set–up.

Of course, it was his own damn fault.

He knew better than to drink when he took his medicine. John and the gang would have to own up to their part in this insane marriage.

Allan swiveled and leaned back in his chair to take in the New York City skyline, with the One World Trade Center that had replaced the destroyed Twin Towers.

"Excuse me, Mr. Smith. You need to see this."

Allan whirled around and stared at Paul Harrington, his Vice President waiting in the doorway. His thin frame and tallness gave him a certain kind of lankiness, but the man had a very mathematical mind. They'd worked together for a number of years, even though Paul was older by about ten years.

Allan waved for him to come into the office. "What's the concern? Did someone find out about a couple of our investors being involved in the Amazon insider trader lawsuits?"

His VP hurried toward the desk, holding out a newspaper. He seemed agitated. "No, I haven't seen any movement yet. I'm not sure how to tell you. This morning's paper has a picture of you on the front page."

Paul's face was tight with emotion and Allan saw that his knuckles were white from his grip on the paper. Standing, he walked around his desk and grabbed the paper from his hands.

In black and white, was a picture of himself with a woman he didn't know locked in an embrace. "What the hell! This can't be happening!"

"Do you know this woman? It's all over the Internet too."

Allan ignored Paul's question and statement. It was a very unflattering photo of him. He appeared plastered and was groping a woman in a cowboy hat. The caption read:

Allan Smith, one of the world's most sought-after bachelors, is no longer on the market. He married Rodeo Queen Rosalind Dunne the same weekend he attended a friend's wedding in 'Sin City,' also known as Las Vegas—

The paper fell from his fingers, floating to the floor.

Damn. His perfect world was about to bust in all the wrong places.

He never thought the media would find out about his marriage. If Paul said the picture was on the Internet, did they have more? The tabloids would soon get a hold of them too and feature his disgrace for all the world to see.

How was Katherine going to react?

Shit.

Who in the hell leaked the story? Where had the damn pictures come from?

Then he recalled a message he'd received days ago about someone wanting to talk about Las Vegas. He'd been too busy trying to figure out his damn marriage to think about it. Running his hand over his mouth and chin, Allan forced himself to gain control of his raging emotions.

"When did the story hit?"

"This morning. There are about a dozen or so pictures and a long article on the Internet. I found a few videos on TikTok. Should I order a cease and desist?"

"What about YouTube or X or Twitter whatever people call it now?"

"Yes, and yes. You are all over everything."

Allan paced around his office as numerous scenarios played out in his head. "Any inquiries yet from clients or the media?"

"Seven to be exact. I've been able to throw them off for the moment. I'm sorry, I should have been prepared."

"How could you have been? You didn't know. It's all my fault. I thought this marriage thing would disappear, go away." Allan inhaled deeply and exhaled hard as he stopped pacing. "I should've told you when I returned from Vegas that somehow, I got married. Damn it. We'll have to work fast. Get Ms. Becker—no, I mean Mrs. Parker—back from her honeymoon. Tell her I'll send her and her new hubby anywhere they want to go after she takes care of this problem."

"Is it true?"

Allan drifted over to the window and regarded his beloved New York skyline. It gave him a calming feeling every time he gazed at it. He loved the Big Apple with its myriad lights. It was all he'd ever known. He braced his hands on the windowsill.

If he could work through the Kraft Heinz Corporation

losses, along with the Securities and Exchange Commission probe, and the stock market falling hundreds of points during the COVID shut down, the pictures of his tactless wedding shouldn't be problematic to handle. His shoulders were wide enough to carry the burden.

"Yes. It turns out I was the wrong person, at the wrong place, at the wrong time. As you know, timing is everything," Allan said without turning.

He'd been so careful to conceal his tracks so the paparazzi wouldn't ruin John's wedding day, which had been a success. But somehow things got out of control during the bachelor's party outing. Whoever leaked the pictures was going to be in deep shit when he found them. Once he did, that person or persons responsible, he'd make sure they burned in hell.

"Sir, I'll contact Tiffany myself. The least number of people talking about this the better. If you don't mind me asking, how did this happen? Are you being blackmailed?"

"No, I'm not being blackmailed by the woman who is my wife. I can't explain everything at this moment. If the papers... shit. If anyone calls for a statement, tell them we have none at this time. I'll wait for Tiffany to arrange a press conference. Once you have her itinerary, bring it to my office. I'll fill you both in at that time."

"Of course, give me fifteen minutes."

"Thanks, Paul."

With the clicking sound of the door closing, Allan rubbed the tense cords on the back of his neck and groaned. The news photo surprisingly brought into place some missing pieces.

His unknown wife was the beautiful cowgirl from the rodeo. He remembered how she'd ridden her horse like it had been a part of her. A sharp image in flashback mode placed them sitting in the country western bar. Next, came a white room, music, and a man in front of a slot machine. Lastly, the kiss.

The woman he'd been dreaming about since returning From Las Vegas was his wife.

Rosalind.

Every damn night he dreamed of them kissing. He'd awaken wanting, aching for her. It frightened him. He'd never felt such an explosive attraction to a woman before. Not even Katherine had been able to keep his interest, as this mysterious woman was able to.

Was this the thing John tried to explain to him last year? The reason their fifteen-year-old pact meant nothing?

The lure to be close to the woman, who he now knew to be Rosalind, his wife, was weirdly intoxicating, yet he couldn't remember them having sex. It had been years since he'd taken pleasure in sex without the safety net of the relationship contract, that he'd dubbed the 'Social Climbers Agreement.'

Thankful for the privacy of his office, Allan buried his face in his hands, trying to erase his tiredness. The past was haunting him in his business dealings and now, his personal life.

As he lifted his head, the picture of his wife in the front page of the newspaper laying on the floor caught his attention. The old saying, *A Picture is Worth a Thousand Words*, came to mind.

What was her real story? What would have mandated a woman to become so desperate that she'd marry a stranger? She'd indicated something about a trust and a stipulation. Who did that nowadays?

He knew appearances could be deceiving. His phony foster parents said they cared for him each time he was greeted into their homes, but they just wanted the money the state would send. Girlfriends professed their love for him, although usually it was feigned in order to continue reaping the benefits of the relationship. Executives inflated their company's financial resources to later find the firms insolvent due to stupidity.

He had a right to be apathetic and uncaring. It was what most people expected, and he obliged them.

How many hours did he have to act as if he didn't care what people thought of him? Twenty-four, thirty-six, forty-eight? Or would it be days?

Allan pondered the unsaid question of why he wasn't immediately going after the woman, his wife, who'd created this media mess. Could it be because she bested him when no one else ever had?

CHAPTER SEVEN

"Mr. Smith, my husband said you owe him big time for cutting short his honeymoon."

Allan raised his head and set the damning newspaper aside. His angel had arrived although he hadn't given her a choice. Tiffany, his faithful secretary, walked closer to his desk sporting a sunburn and about a million braids in her dark hair. Her petite body made her appear delicate, but he knew her to Be a little spitfire. And right now, she was all business despite her casual outfit—slacks, a sleeveless top and sunglasses perched on top of her head.

"From the looks of it, you didn't need any more sun."

"For your info, sunbathing wasn't the reason I was on vacation." She flicked her beaded hair over her shoulder. "Remember?"

"I'm sorry, Tiffany. Thank you for coming." Allan stood. He slid out a chair for her. "Paul is going to be joining us, too. I'll send you and your hubby anywhere you want to go after this problem is taken care of for me. I'll even extend it to a month."

"A month? Who's going away for a month's vacation?"

"Good evening, Paul. Me." Tiffany waved her hand and smiled.

Allan regarded the two best people on earth, here to help him out of his predicament. It had taken Tiffany less than eight hours to return to New York City from the Bahamas. How Paul had done it he didn't know.

"Oh, I see." Paul shut the door and took a seat at the conference table. Tiffany settled back into her chair with her iPad. He joined them and placed the newspaper in front of her.

"Launch your tale from the beginning. What happened and when? Don't leave out anything. Paul and I need to know the entire scope of the situation in detail."

"I don't know. I don't remember." He closed his eyes, as if that would bring it forward. "I awoke the morning of John's wedding with a killer headache, discovered the ring on my finger, and found a note with an envelope full of cash."

"And *that didn't* cause you any concern?"

Allan heard the disappointment in Tiffany's tone and refused to look at her or Paul. She was right. He couldn't answer her simple questions. It did concern him. That's what frightened him the most. The unknown.

"No...yes, damn it. I thought it was a joke. You know, like the groomsmen pranking me after a night out for the bachelor party. We went to a rodeo. My knee was killing me, so I took a Vicodin. Maybe it was two. Then we went to a bar. The other groomsmen were all acting like sex-craved idiots. That's it. The next day was the wedding, and no one said anything to me. They didn't even comment on why I wasn't wearing a wedding ring. Even after John's wedding when I came home and ignored the problem."

He pushed his chair away from the table and stood. Pacing around the office, he waited for the two of them to say something-anything.

Tiffany stopped typing on her iPad. "Show me the marriage certificate."

He went to his desk, pulled out the document from its hiding spot and handed it to her.

"I can call the police," Paul suggested.

"No." Tiffany shook her head and placed the document next to the paper on the table in front of her. "This marriage certificate is real. Mr. Smith will have to file for a divorce. Unless you never—" She cleared her throat before she began again. "Excuse me for the bluntness, but if you never consummated the marriage, a judge might allow an annulment."

The room went quiet.

Allan pressed his lips together and clasped his hands behind his back, then resumed his pacing.

He couldn't answer that question. He wasn't sure if he'd had sex with the woman claiming to be his wife that haunted his dreams.

What a fucking mess.

Paul broke the silence. "Tiffany's right. It might be the loophole you need. A judge could say in your drunken state, mixed with the painkillers you'd taken, you temporarily lost the ability to make rational decisions. Such as agreeing to get married."

"I don't recall having sex with the woman. Shit. I didn't even know what my so-called wife, Rosalind, looked like until you-Paul, showed me the paper yesterday morning." Allan folded his arms irritably across his chest. "This can't be happening. I'm at a loss here. I have no solution. What should I do?"

"You're married, Mr. Smith, whether you like it or not. It's a good thing Katherine went on her grand European vacation before your return from Las Vegas," Tiffany stated. "We need to think about the press and what you want them to know."

At the mention of Katherine, Allan clamped his jaw. He

realized she hadn't even called him once. Why he'd ever started a relationship with her wasn't clear to him.

"We shouldn't say anything. Let the tabloids run their course," Paul chimed in.

If he did nothing, would his life be the same? Allan frowned. "Rosalind, my wife called yesterday, telling me she was sending divorce papers and the other twenty-five thousand dollars. I told her to keep the money. They should be arriving in the morning. Maybe I should sign them and put an end to this madness quickly."

"Interesting. We still need to make a statement," Tiffany said. "Think of the company's clients."

"Fine. The company can't lose clients. I've worked hard advocating for them to believe in us after the Amazon disaster. I don't want to give the impression I act impulsively, when it was simply a case of an accidental mixture of alcohol and a pain medication." Allan shoved his hands into his pockets.

"We can acknowledge the marriage," Paul pointed out.

"Make it short. I thought someone was blackmailing me, but Rosalind paid me and was willing to send me more money. Nothing adds up. We'll release more details if the tabloids get wind of the divorce or pertinent information about the week-end." Allan took his seat at the table ready to work.

Still behind closed doors, his office became chaotic. Paul typed up a statement to send to the clients and Tiffany started on the PR news releases. When two a.m. came around, Allan announced it was time to call it a night. They all left together and said goodbye when they reached the parking garage.

Tired, angry, and hungry, he arrived at his condominium at The Rushmore. To his surprise, Katherine was waiting for him, dressed in a short black skintight dress and high heels when he entered his condo. Her freshly dyed blonde hair hung long and straight down to her waist. Her make-up was picture perfect.

"When did you return from Europe?"

"This morning. Did you miss me?"

Her sweet childlike tone made him sick to his stomach. Whatever he had seen in her, he didn't know.

Miss her? Heavens, no.

He avoided her question and went to the wet bar and poured himself a vodka on the rocks. Taking a sip, he faced her. "Did I forget about a dinner appointment or something?"

"No, Allan. Sweetie, are you getting a divorce?"

He gulped down the remaining vodka. It wasn't Katherine who invaded his dreams and left him wanting her so badly he'd had to take cold showers, but his wife. Which he hadn't comprehended until today. "That's the plan."

"Good."

Katherine sniffled. He watched her wipe at a tear she'd somehow produced, and saunter over to him. Her stilettos clicked on the tile floor. She placed her cold hands on his chest, unbuttoned his dress shirt, and leaned in for a kiss. He indulged her and met her lips briefly. She pressed her body tight against his, wrapping her arms around him.

"I'm willing to be your mistress for a million dollars a year. I don't mind sharing," she whispered into his ear.

Disgusted, Allan unwrapped Katherine's clinging arms from his body and held her at arm's length. "You've exhausted your time here. You need to leave."

Tightening his jaw and clamping his teeth together, he was afraid he'd say something he shouldn't. For her, now an ex-lover, to suggest a fee for sexual favors, wasn't nor would it ever be in his game plans.

He released his grip on her arms and ignored her as she tried to grasp him again. Letting his arms fall to his side, he moved away from her and headed to the bedroom. He took out his cell phone and pressed star-nine to summon the doorman.

"Start packing your stuff."

"Allan?"

"Don't say another word. You're on very thin ice right now." He threw two suitcases on the bed. "Now! Unless you want to leave with nothing. It's your choice."

Slowly she emptied drawers and the closet.

How dare she imagine he'd pay her one million dollars a year to be his mistress. If and when he chose to have one, it would be on his terms. Was she blind? He'd given her more than that in jewelry, designer clothes, shoes, and purses. Not to mention the trips. It was one thing to pay for his girlfriend's living expenses and other items, but to be expected to flatly pay for sex was unacceptable.

He'd never do that in his lifetime.

So long and good riddance, Katherine. One less problem to deal with in his messed-up life.

"Please Allan, let me stay." She stood by the stuffed suitcases, now dressed in pants and a blouse holding items of clothing that wouldn't fit into the bags.

He slammed them shut and forced the zipper to close them just as the doorman knocked announcing his arrival. Tugging them off the bed, he wheeled them to the front door, and she reluctantly followed.

"I'm sorry, please let me stay. You won't owe me a penny."

Her tone of voice had changed from a whine to on the edge of hysteria when he opened the door. "Kindly escort Ms. Williams from my home and remove her name from the approved guest list. She is never allowed in here again."

Allan blocked the rest of Katherine's pleas from his mind as the doorman led her to the elevator. Breathing deeply when the doors slid shut, a quietness came over him. She'd lasted six months, which was a record for him.

It was for the best.

Fuck. His perfect life was crashing around him.

He became conscious of the fact he and Katherine hadn't been intimate since before John's wedding. She'd refused to go to Vegas with him and instead flown to Italy. Then she called to inform him she'd extended her trip with stops in France and England.

He hadn't complained. He'd granted the lengthy tour with an underlining objective of it being a goodbye gift. Their relationship, with all of her constant demands and overspending, had become more burdensome and boring than fulfilling on his part.

Being single was what he liked.

Women. And more women.

Anytime he wanted one. A true bachelor for life.

No wife for him

He could never love one woman. Not when there was such a variety of ladies in the Western and Eastern Hemispheres yet to meet.

Sex was his second area of expertise. Hot and sweaty. Fast and hard. Or slow and wanting. It depended on his mood. The women he dated always returned for more.

His reputation as a lover was well known. Due to his wealth, notoriety, and dating habits, his lawyers mandated an agreement be signed in order to protect him and his money from unscrupulous women. Tiffany referred to it as the *Social Climber Document*. It was intended to prevent the women from disclosing any details about them or him, either during or after the relationship ended. This included interviews with the press or tabloids, writing memoirs, or discussing any aspects with the public.

There was to be no expectation of support or palimony payments. The woman had to assert she was entering into the relationship of her own free will and was not being coerced in any way, nor was she executing the document under duress.

It further provided in the event of any child or children being conceived during the dating period, a paternity test must be performed to prove he was indeed the father. The care and custody of the said child would be vested in him, and the mother would have limited to no contact with said child.

Should the woman fail to abide by these terms, severe consequences could be imposed. If the woman refused to sign the agreement, he simply walked away. Without this protection, he'd be dead in the water for any and all kinds of blackmail conspiracies and other legal complications.

In the past, several women tried to negate the document, to no avail. The agreement was binding in all courts of law, foreign or in the United States.

During the last several years, one-night stands were the easiest. He'd have them sign the agreement on the way to his condominium. For the lady of the month, he would sweeten the deal with an exclusive Black American Express card for the entire time they were together. Katherine had been a test to see if he could commit to one woman for a longer time-period, but they hadn't lasted.

During his college days, he'd lost his heart to Megan. She'd been from upper class society. They'd been happy, until her fiancé came to the campus. Heartbroken, he and John had come up with the pact, to never marry or fall in love ever.

After college, when he'd became a stockbroker and began to make lots of money for clients and for himself, women wanted to only date when they envisioned how much he was worth and wanted a piece of it. He obliged by lavishing them with jewelry, clothing, shoes, and vacations. In a way, he was paying for sex. However, he chose when and how to part with his hard-earned money.

The second reason he'd never wanted to marry was divorce. His parents' unsuccessful marriage was the number one reason. He'd seen how destructive marriage could be to men with money after becoming well-off. The laws never went easy on wealthy men like himself. He could lose half or more of his net worth to an ex-wife. Even with an ironclad prenuptial agreement.

Allan showered and lay down to sleep, however the bed reeked of Katherine's perfume. She must've taken a nap before he'd gotten home. His eyes remained open as thoughts and scenarios kept his mind working, not allowing him to rest. Finally, around five a.m., resigning himself to not getting any sleep, he dressed and returned to the office.

Nerves assailed him. All his planning and fail-safe precautions hadn't saved him.

The rodeo queen had snared him.

Instead of pressing the button for the twentieth floor where his office was, he stopped on the sixteenth floor to check on the European markets before they closed. Brokers ran around making last minute trades. In talking to a few of them, Allan discovered that news of his marriage had affected the market by about a four percent drop. Since their day was almost complete and the U.S. brokers would be arriving for the starting bell, he headed to his office.

Feeling more at ease with his decision to sign the divorce papers, he waited for them to arrive. As the morning progressed and the U.S. markets opened, all hell broke loose. He received word clients were calling to cancel their accounts and requests for withdrawing funds were flooding in. Then to add insult to injury, the stock market plummeted one hundred plus points, due to an interest rate hike.

His reputation was on the line, he had to stop the bleeding fast. Being only thirty-seven years old, he'd had to fight for the last seven years to gain the trust of his clients and prove he was going to be around for a long time. Many well-known stock-broker firms and financial institutes had labeled his firm a non-starter.

It didn't matter how much money he made for clients if they thought of him as a loose cannon. They'd look the other way at how many women he dated, but to marry a woman from a rodeo while in Las Vegas was over the top. Allan stalked around his office dwelling on the ramifications, before sinking into his desk chair, frustrated.

Could his marriage work like an investment? What if he could make her hold on to it until it hit rock bottom?

"Excuse me, Mr. Smith, I have the divorce papers. Do you want our lawyers to review them before you sign?"

Allan spun his chair around. Tiffany stood dressed in business attire but looked out of place with her braided hair and Paul appeared fresh in a navy suit ready to help fight his battle.

While he on the other hand still hadn't shaved or slept. "No."

"They should take a look at them. They might—"

He interrupted what he knew would be words of advice. "Tiffany, I've decided on a new course of action. I'm delaying the divorce. Maybe I'm sleep deprived, but my wife needs to be taught a lesson. No one messes with me and wins. I aim to ruin Mrs. Smith's life as she has mine."

He never lost when it came to stocks. The only way for the value of something to rise was to nurture it slowly. On his terms. And his marriage was going to be one of those stocks.

Sex and relationships were his expertise. He was the king of investments. He grinned when he realized how his thoughts might prove to be viable.

"I have to advise you not to contact..."

Allan raised his hand. "I know it's a huge risk, Tiffany. What do I have to lose at this point? My clients are running. Katherine and I were finished before my marriage to Rosalind. The hell with it. I'm leaving today. I want to talk to my wife."

Tiffany's and Paul's surprised expressions caught him off guard. Allan clasped his hands behind his back and waited for them to speak.

Paul took a step closer to him. "Don't do this. I'll persuade our clients to change their minds. You're a grown man. Marrying someone won't affect how you do business or handle their accounts."

"Katherine left?" Tiffany tilted her head and the beads in her hair clicked at her movement. "It's a good thing she's been out of the country for months. Otherwise, your wife could sue you for infidelity. The Social Climber Agreement is only for relationships. You don't have anything in place if you ever did have a wife."

"I kicked Katherine out last night. She asked for a million dollars a year to be my mistress."

Paul cleared his throat and coughed. "You shouldn't treat women as the new penny stock waiting to hit the bull market. I know what you're thinking. You can't keep tossing them away for futures. They can burn you if the entities in question rebound."

Tiffany laughed, and then bowed her head when he gave her his death stare as she set the divorce paper packet on his desk.

Rebound? How? He held all the trump cards. All the women he'd allowed close to him were treated like goddesses until he found another one to drool over and conquer.

Maybe he did treat women like personal portfolios of stocks and dealt with them to his benefit until he lost interest. Allan shrugged. It didn't matter, he'd never truly love anyone.

He stood abruptly, causing the chair to hit the wall. "I'm

leaving. I'm going to meet Mrs. Smith in person. I'm not ready to sign the papers yet."

Allan scrutinized Paul and Tiffany as their mouths dropped open and walked out of his office with the unsigned divorce papers in his hands. He would be king again.

———

Gripping the steering wheel, Allan stretched and rolled his shoulders to ease the tension in them. He couldn't believe his private jet hadn't been able to land closer to the town of Randall. Who would've thought the place where his lovely bride lived wouldn't have an airport? The lack of anything resembling a runway forced him to land at Minneapolis-St. Paul.

Where does she live, Timbuktu?

He'd hoped to have been there by now. Instead, he found himself in a cheap, rented car driving north to some unforsaken town, not even a city. Thank heaven the damn white stuff wasn't coming down.

He hated snow. If it had been snowing, he would've been ticked off. Living in New York City for his entire life, all thirty-seven years, had turned his enjoyment of winter to dislike. He'd experienced enough of the white crap to outlast anyone's appreciation of it for a lifetime. It wasn't the snow that bothered him, but the bitter cold that went right through to the bone, the number one reason he headed south to Florida for long weekends.

With the car heater turned to max, the rental's GPS system flashed one-hour drive time. His next priority was to find the nearest Starbucks for a desperately needed vanilla latte. The GPS indicated one was close. Allan spied the green-white sign and grinned. John called him a coffee sucker. So, what if he

75

spent twelve to twenty-four dollars a day on his drinks? He drank a lot of coffee.

The first sip hit his taste buds with irresistible satisfaction. In the rental, he concentrated on his next destination, Randall and then his revenge.

His cell phone rang, interrupting the local radio channel chatting about the weather, via the car's Bluetooth.

"Hello, Tiffany."

"Have you arrived? How did she handle the papers not being signed?"

"Still *en* route. She lives in no man's land. Any leads?"

"I'm making progress on how the newspapers mysteriously learned of the wedding and broke the story to the damn globe. My hubby is pulling strings at the *Times* to confirm who leaked the pictures. There must be a money trail."

A muscle quivered in Allan's jaw. He slowed the car as the speed limit dropped to thirty.

"Thank him for me. It's fucking freezing here. Schedule a week at my house in Naples, Florida to thaw out, in a few weeks."

"Not before I finish my honeymoon," Tiffany laughed.

"You're right. I'll call you later once I've talked to my wife. I'll return Tuesday."

"Take my advice, sign the papers. You don't want to provoke her. Remember the saying about a woman scorned. Walk away while she doesn't want anything from you."

Allan sneered. He'd been the wrong person at the wrong place. A quick and short marriage wouldn't have been a problem to a plain Joe, except he wasn't a plain Joe. She had no idea who she'd royally screwed with.

"I wouldn't be here, if anyone had been able to make the actual marriage cease to exist. The damage's been done. I can't reverse time. I have to live with the consequences. Got to go. Talk to you later."

He pushed disconnect and was about to call back to apologize for his impertinence. She couldn't have made the marriage non-existent because it was a binding contract. He knew that. He'd make it up to her somehow.

The GPS announced forty miles to reach his destination.

Rosalind Smith, aka Dunne, was about to be taught a lesson. Not to meddle with Allan Smith.

Time to even the score. How could he make her life miserable?

"Turn left in one mile," the GPS announced.

All his life, he'd been one step ahead of the other guy until this chick trounced him at his own game of using people. The more he thought about it, the more furious he became. A woman had gotten the best of him.

Would she turn the tables once she discovered his net worth?

Fuck. He didn't want to be married.

How would she react when he arrived at her doorstep with the unsigned divorce papers? If she refused to have sex, he'd stay for a while in this frozen tundra and force her to live together as man and wife.

Childish? Yes, but he didn't care at this point in time.

Retribution was a bitch.

"Your destination is ahead on the left in two miles."

It was a sound plan. He excelled at making people regret crossing him. He could provide Rosalind with a resume full of statements from past girlfriends, clients, and employees. In New York and around the financial industries, he proudly wore the '*Terminator Ass*' title. Just like in the movies, he always came back with full vengeance to get what he wanted.

Allan mindlessly tapped his finger which sported the shiny ring on the steering wheel as he drove closer to hell.

CHAPTER EIGHT

Rosalind halted the brush on Dawn's neck in mid-stroke. The hum of an engine from outside the barn caught her attention. She strained to hear voices. Her arm finished its downward motion when the sound of a door slamming made her pause. Her eyebrows drew together. She wasn't expecting anyone other than the FedEx truck, which had a loud engine.

She waited another moment. No one came into the barn, so she continued to move the brush over Dawn's girth and down her side in easy strokes. Sam's voice, and another she didn't recognize, drifted into the barn. In the middle of an upward brush stroke, the great barn door opened. Rosalind straightened and turned.

"Sorry, girl." She patted Dawn, opened the stall door, and stepped into the middle of the barn.

Who had Sam allowed into her private domain?

The sun obscured her vision, and she used her hand as a shield. A tall figure in a black coat, driving gloves, and sunglasses advanced toward her.

"Good morning, Rosalind honey. I brought the papers to you personally."

She almost tossed her cookies when the man spoke.

Allan Smith? Here?

Pulling off her work gloves, she swiped at her bangs. She ventured closer, out of the offending sun, to scrutinize the man whose voice could make her knees go weak. He looked better than a wild stallion, in his expensive overcoat in the middle of the dusty and putrid barn, standing out like a can of red paint in a white room.

"Mr. Smith, coming here wasn't necessary. FedEx would have worked." She widened her stance challengingly.

An uncomfortable silence lingered inside the barn as they stared at each other. She saw he held the brown envelope she'd mailed to him. Her false confidence faded. Rosalind shifted from one foot to the other, not sure what to do or say.

From the corner of her eye, she spotted movement. Sam leaned against the wall with his arms folded, wearing a knowing smirk.

Well, he'd warned her not to mess with Mother Nature.

She switched her gaze from Sam to Allan Smith as he closed the space between them. He held out the envelope with a smile etched on his handsome face. Suspicious something wasn't right, she took it, tore open the seal, and scanned the papers.

Nothing was signed.

"What the hell?"

"Rosalind, love of my life, I'm home. I've decided being married has its advantages. Most women called me a *Don Juan* before I met you. I've come to claim my husbandly rights. It will be a joy to have a woman around twenty-four-seven to tell what to do. Night and day. Day and night."

"No way, City Boy. You said you'd sign them!" She held the papers out to him.

"I changed my mind. If you want those papers signed, you'll

do what I want. Or there's this thing called an annulment. If we never had our night of bliss, you'll have to return your inheritance, won't you?"

"When pigs fly!" Rosalind threw down her gloves and stomped her booted foot.

Dirt, hay, and other barn floor detritus flew onto his shiny black shoes.

"Maybe I should say, checkmate instead."

She shook the papers in his face. "Checkmate? This isn't a game, you piece of scum. I need the money, damn it!"

The man was crazy. The horses needed her. People were counting on her.

"You left me no choice. Clearly you don't—"

"*Asshole.* Sign the papers. I don't want to be married!"

"You should have thought about that before you signed the marriage certificate. I'm all yours. You have me now. You know, for better and worse, in sickness and health," Allan stated.

She noted his thin-lipped smile was without humor. A dangerous gleam had formed in his eyes. Tossing her braid over her shoulder in defiance, she boldly met his glare. She was in a pickle that was for sure. "Go to hell, Mr. City Boy."

"Calm down, Rosalind. You're upsetting Dawn and the other horses." Sam moved to stand between her and Allan as the other barn door opened and a few ranch hands came inside. "You need to keep this private. Go to the house. There's no need to let others hear. We can discuss what you're gonna do, young lady."

Dawn's nickering and kicking the wall prompted Rosalind to rein in her fury. She tucked the papers under her arm and stomped to the stall. "Hey, girl. You're fine." She rubbed the horse's nose as she withdrew a sugar lump from her pocket.

Once Dawn was settled, she collected her gloves from the middle of the barn's floor, whacked them against her leg, and strode past the man who was attempting to ruin her life. When she shoved the barn door, it swung fast and hard, hitting the side of the building with a deafening smack.

———

Allan glanced at the older man. With a shrug, he gestured, and they both followed Rosalind. The barn door missed hitting him in the face on the backswing only because the old man's arm stopped it. Allan had one last glimpse of her retreating figure before the house door slammed shut, too.

His mouth curved in a smile, and he rubbed his gloved hands together, not for warmth but in enjoyment. When Rosalind's chin had lifted, he'd seen her eyes tighten in hatred, her expression priceless.

So worth the long-ass drive.

"Is the Rodeo Queen always this rude?" Allan noticed he left white puffs in the air as he spoke.

"To men trying to take away her freedom."

No friend or ally there. The old man's reply had been laced in sarcasm.

He didn't care. Being on his own during his teenage years had forced him to be strong. He followed the shoveled narrow path in the snow to the house and walked inside.

Examining the rustic interior, he noted most of the furniture was mismatched. Definitely not Fifth Avenue quality. Not sure which way to turn, Allan waited. The older man pushed past him and led the way down a narrow hallway.

It opened into a large kitchen decorated in ugly reds, yellows, and of all things, roosters. A lingering smell of coffee greeted him. Allan stared at his wife, leaning against the counter with a mug in her hands. She'd shed her Nanook coat and wore a plaid flannel shirt, jeans, and a western belt.

The newspaper picture hadn't been very clear. Now that he saw Rosalind in person, he vaguely remembered her face. However, it was her body that triggered memories of them in an embrace.

She had long legs. A dream come true when it came time for sex. She wasn't wearing any makeup and yet was drop-dead gorgeous. He studied her pretty face, which featured a square chin, with high cheekbones. Her lips were full and when she opened her mouth, he'd seen perfect white teeth. But the feature that captured his attention were her green eyes. He'd never seen eyes that color before.

"Mr. Smith, I'm Sam, Rosalind's trustee. Would you care for a cup of coffee?"

The old man's question broke the standoff.

"I could use one. It's rather chilly in here."

Rosalind pushed off the counter and made herself as tall as possible. He watched with interest as she parted her legs, set her mug down and placed her hands on her hips.

"You don't want to be married. I don't want to either. We have something in common. Why did you come all this way to hand deliver unsigned papers?"

Allan accepted a cup of coffee from Sam and pulled out a chair. Ignoring her question, he took a sip. And almost spewed the hot liquid from his mouth. "You call this coffee? Are you trying to poison me? This is the most awful tasting shi—stuff I've ever tasted."

"Well, City Boy, you might call that *stuff* those fancy coffee shops serve coffee. This is the real *stuff*. Sign the papers and you can get a cappuccino on your way home."

Allan wiped his mouth. She was tougher than he'd anticipated.

Damn it.

He couldn't give in this soon and sell the stock. He had to

teach her a lesson. "Do you read the newspapers or tabloid papers?"

"No, I don't have time to read trash. What does that have to do with why you won't sign the divorce papers?"

"Once upon a time a Rodeo Queen married a Stock Market Prince. Somehow the press got wind of our storybook marriage. They plastered our precious wedding photo all over the New York City papers and other no-nonsense gossip magazines, not to mention the Internet. I didn't find out the 'good news' until after we concluded our conversation the other day."

He put on a half-smile, reached for the cup of coffee, and took another sip. This time his taste buds might have been prepared, but he wasn't, as the bitter taste hit him once again. Swallowing, Allan grimaced and observed Sam propped against the doorframe, laughing.

"If everyone is done laughing and bellowing, I'll finish. I've been bombarded with requests for exclusive interviews. My company is losing clients right and left. Nasty divorce issues may hinder my ability to work for them. All in a single day's time. So, you see, it would be in my best interest for us to stay married."

Why did he say that? One night of hot sex was all he wanted.

"Stay married? No way. I want the divorce now. You can't stay in this house with me!"

He decided to play along, enjoying her anger. "You know, it will be to your advantage to have our honeymoon, since we never had a wedding night."

"I *will* not have sex with you."

"You have no desire to sleep with one of the world's most eligible males? You're hurting my feelings. Is there something wrong with me?"

He stood, shrugged off his overcoat and held his arms out,

making sure she could feast her eyes on everything he had to offer a woman.

"Mr. Smith, you surely don't have anything I would want. To me, you look like a prissy City Boy, who wouldn't know the difference between a mare and a stallion. Sign the damn papers, and I'll give you an extra twenty thousand dollars for your trouble."

Who did she think she was?

No woman had ever turned him down for a night of sex. "I told you, I'm not signing any papers unless they are annulment papers."

"Annulment?"

"You wanted a husband. You now have one."

"This isn't what we agreed to. You said on the phone you'd sign them."

"Sometimes life's a damn surprise, Mrs. Smith."

Rosalind uttered a string of unladylike words for the second time in a matter of minutes.

He let them roll off his back and lifted his chin. "Now will you please show me to the master bedroom? I need to prepare for our long-overdue wedding night. Our marriage has yet to be consummated. Or I'll order it to be annulled. I would've remembered making love to an ice queen." Rosalind's tight-lipped, stunned expression gave him the added fuel to continue. "I see you comprehend *my* terms."

She looked like an animal who was cornered. Her green eyes narrowed, and her lips were a tight line. She peered over at Sam, who smiled, unfolded his arms, and ambled out of the kitchen without a word.

Allan settled his coat over his arm and waited.

Checkmate.

CHAPTER NINE

Too rattled to talk, Rosalind stole a glance at Allan. His hungry coyote eyes traveled the length of her body. A lurch of excitement coursed through her, weakening her knees.

He couldn't stay.

Her body was reacting to him in ways she didn't want it too. If he did stay, would she be able to keep her hands to herself?

He had to leave. She had paid him for his time and the use of his last name.

Had he discovered how much her ranch, and its adjacent land, was worth? Did he want part of that twenty million dollars because he was her husband?

Fed up with his cat and mouse game, she wanted answers. "If you intend to stay, you can sleep in the barn."

Allan's low deep laugh quickened her pulse, and she watched him step toward her. Breathing deep to calm herself proved to be the wrong thing, because she inhaled his musky cologne.

Saved by the landline phone, she ran from the kitchen.

"Hello. Yes, Mr. Kennedy—no, I'd like to have a mortgage on the land. The cash will come in handy to nudge the ball rolling for other projects. Yes, I have an appointment with the Farmer's Bank and Trust today. I've been pre-approved for the purchase price."

The floor creaked next to her, and that wonderful, heady smell invaded her space again. She turned. Allan stood inches from her. A tingling spread to places it shouldn't and she stared at him, forgetting time, the phone to her ear, or the fact she wasn't supposed to want him close.

She blinked, ending her insane thoughts. "Sorry, I'm still here. I'll bring the paperwork with me. Thanks for calling. See you tomorrow. Goodbye."

Rosalind hung up the phone. With narrowed eyes she tilted her head and slapped her hands on her hips. It was her "don't mess with me" look. It should've turned him into a frozen icicle, however, it didn't work. He smiled and showed his perfect white teeth.

Urrrrg, Mr. GQ had to leave.

"Mr. Smith, we have unfinished business, but I don't have time to argue with you right now. You can spend *one* night here. This way to the guest room."

"I knew you'd see it my way."

She ignored his smart-ass comment. "You know where the kitchen is. If you need anything, you can get it yourself. My home isn't a resort."

"I can tell. I hope you have clean sheets."

"If you find my home offensive, there's a motel in town." A hint of humiliation and shame surfaced at his insinuations about her home and her temper began to climb.

"I'll survive without the comforts. How can we have a night of hot sex if we're not in the same room?"

"One night. Then you'll leave in the morning. Do you understand?"

"That depends on you. I'm ready to do it now."

She stopped and spun to face him, letting out a gasp. "Over my dead body."

"Let me warn you, we will be sharing the same bed. If it's not tonight, I guess I'll be here for more than *a* night."

Who did he think he was? God's gift to women? No way.

Rosalind turned away from her very attractive husband. Her heart raced. Since Las Vegas, she hadn't been able to forget the salacious memories of his kisses. She knew firsthand what lay beneath his suit and his boxers. His body had muscles in all the right places. A hairy chest, long muscular calves, and she couldn't forget her glimpse of his manhood falling out of his boxers.

She'd lain awake for hours craving his mouth on hers the past few weeks. With him a step behind her, all she'd have to do was stop and his body would press against hers.

No.

She couldn't give into him, no matter what her body was telling her. When she did stop at the guest room door, her wish of their bodies touching almost became reality.

"Is this *our* room? The honeymoon suite?"

He stood inches from her. She smelled coffee on his breath. About to reach for the door handle, she touched his hand which was already on the knob.

"This is the guest room. Yes, the sheets are clean. Don't get too comfortable because you won't be staying long. I would suggest changing into some jeans. I wouldn't want to be responsible for you ruining your suit."

What was wrong with her? She wanted him out of her life and here she was wanting to succumb to his damn charm. Rosalind attempted to step to the side, to put open space between them, but couldn't. Allan's other arm trapped her. He leaned in. She turned her head away.

"Thank you, honey. Are you sure you want me this far away from you on our first night together?"

Allan's whisper close to her ear left her motionless. She tightened her jaw and waited for him to move away. "There will be no first night together. Ever. Period."

"I'll leave the door open in case you want me to show you why I'm called a '*Don Juan*.'"

"Don't you get it? I don't care. Our wedding is a business deal. The extras weren't included. All I need is for you to sign the papers and be on your way."

Rosalind remained still, with her hands fisted behind her. She closed her eyes and silently counted to ten. His body brushed hers as he stepped into the bedroom. She moved forward and found herself facing him when she opened her eyes again.

"Baby, the only way to close our so-called business deal is for you to give me *our* wedding night."

"I have an appointment, so you'll be on your own until I get back. Now if you will please move out of my way."

"I'll be waiting. Oh, and don't forget the condoms. You'll note I used the plural form of the word."

She pushed against his shoulder, slipped past him, and dashed down the hall. "No way!"

CHAPTER TEN

"You can run, Rodeo Queen, but you can't hide from me." Allan followed Rosalind into the hall, intrigued by the sway of her hips in her tight jeans.

"Um, I did for six plus weeks."

Disliking the satisfaction he heard in her voice, he shook his head when she disappeared from sight. A burning hunger to get Rosalind into his bed intensified. The undeniable ache left him unsatisfied. The door slamming brought him rudely back to the problem at hand as his ardor cooled.

The change of emotions he'd seen on Rosalind's face, annoyance, stress and then something else when he accidentally brushed against her was puzzling. His immediate reaction to her had been unexpected, as a vague memory of their bodies pressed against each other ebbed and flowed in his head, teasing him.

Man. If an Ice Queen could make him as hard as a stick, he did need to get laid.

Taking his cell phone from his pocket, he called his office. "Mrs. Parker, I've reached my destination."

"Good afternoon, Mr. Smith, it's so nice of you to call. You already owe me big time."

"Yes, I know. I need you to find out what Miss Dunne, I mean Mrs. Smith, is looking to buy. And get me her financial statements."

"Do you want a full credit history?"

"No—on second thought, yes. I want to know everything about my bride."

"I have some leads in regard to the leak of the photograph and information."

"Good. One other thing, there's an older man staying in the house. Find out who he is. I only know his first name which is Sam," Allan said.

"Will this get me a two-month vacation? My husband is very agitated about having his honeymoon cut short."

"Tiffany, I'll give you a two month all-expense paid belated honeymoon. Call me with any info the minute you get it."

He heard her colorful laughter and then the click as she disconnected. He didn't know what he'd do without her. She'd become more than his assistant in the past years. She was the person he trusted the most. When he needed something taken care of, whether it be some woman he wanted to date, or a woman he wanted out of his life, he knew without a doubt she'd take care of it. No questions asked.

Problem gone.

Quickly and efficiently.

Their relationship hadn't always been professional. She'd been Paul's secretary before she became his, and he considered her fair game in his book. On their first date, they'd kissed, and it lacked the passion of a lover, more like kissing a sister. With mutual agreement they ended their dating, realizing the chemistry wasn't meant to be. Their relationship took on a different tone at that point. He became the brother she never had and she the sister he'd wished for all those lonely nights when he was younger.

A surge of wind rattled the windows and reminded him his luggage was still in the car. With his coat on once more, he headed out the front door.

The bone chilling air slapped at him as he walked to his rental car.

As he reentered the house and stepped on the wood floor, his feet slipped out from under him. The weight of the suitcases threw him off balance and his shoulder hit the wall. He fell backward and landed on the hardwood floor with a thunderous boom followed by a clunk as one of the bags fell inches from his head.

He slowly moved each part of his body. Inching higher on his elbows, he observed a trail of melted snow from the front door to the guest bedroom. Attempting to stand, he heard heavy footfalls from above. Next the bark of a voice broke through the quiet.

"What in God's name is going on down there?"

Deliberating his plight from a half-sitting position, Allan met Sam's gaze, who'd just come down the stairs.

Did the man ever stop smiling? Why didn't he leave him alone? He was in enough misery as it was.

Looking away first, he tried standing, but almost lost his balance again. "Er, damn."

Refusing to look at the older man, he stood and collected his suitcases. As he walked away, he heard the man's loud, jovial laughter. "Apparently you find another man's misfortune funny."

Sam approached him, still tittering, and then spoke. "When it suits me. I haven't had this much fun in years."

"Fun? This isn't fun in my domain."

"Don't get me wrong, boy. But be assured, I'll watch from

the sidelines as long as I believe she doesn't need me. She got herself into this mess." Sam paused to cough. "She is gonna have to get out by herself. I'm warning you, if you hurt Rosalind in any way, no amount of money will get you out of trouble with me."

Allan's brows shot up as his anger escalated. "I am not one to—"

"Do I make myself clear, boy?"

Sam's tone was demanding. They stared at each other as if they were about to duel.

"Yes. But your Little Ice Princess will have to work hard for me to sign the papers. I don't want or need her money. I want compensation for ruining my life." He lifted his suitcases, noting a smile still plastered on Sam's face. Turning sharply, Allan headed toward the dungeon bedroom, leaving Sam standing in the middle of the room.

Inside his self-made prison, Allan sat on the edge of the bed. He rubbed the lump on the back of his head and lifted his leg to the bed to ease his throbbing knee. Reaching for his briefcase to get a pain pill, he hesitated.

No, he couldn't take one. He wanted to be sharp and fully awake when Miss Attitude returned.

His hasty decision to go see his wife now became apparent. He'd entered a hostile place. He could be home in his luxurious apartment or on his way to his beachfront villa in Florida.

The ringtone he'd assigned to his office broke into his reverie and he pulled the phone from his pocket. "Hello."

"Mr. Smith, I have some news for you."

"Go ahead, Tiffany."

He wandered to the window, hoping for an enhanced signal. He noticed for the first time a fenced corral, a handful of long buildings, including the barn he'd gone into when he'd arrive surrounded by empty land.

"Mrs. Smith has a bid on the adjacent property. It's about seven-hundred acres. The sellers have been waiting for the down payment, before moving ahead with the transaction. Her bank account shows a rather large transfer recently."

Allan limped around the room massaging his knee. "Was I blackmailed? Remember those earlier emails requesting money that I thought were spam? Maybe they weren't. Could the money that was transferred into her account have been a payoff?"

Shit.

If his Little Ice Queen was involved in a plot against him, heads were going to roll.

"No, the money received came from an investment company. I did some research and found an old newspaper article. Mrs. Smith didn't lie when she said she needed to get married to acquire her inheritance."

"Have my bankers make the sellers an offer they can't refuse for the land. Tiffany, I want the land in my name by tomorrow. Also, see if you find a piece of property in town to establish an office there." He heard the harshness in his own tone and told himself to calm down.

"Are you having second thoughts? Your plane is still waiting in Minneapolis." Tiffany laughed.

"Very funny. This adds spice to my plans. Tell the pilots to call it a day and book them into a hotel. Give them a card for food and other things. Next, make sure the bankers use the Portfolio Management Firm as the buyers. I don't want Miss Dunne—Mrs. Smith to know it's me who's outwitting her."

"Are you sure you want to do this, Allan? All the reports I've received indicate your wife is a nobody. Sign the papers and come home. She didn't know who you were."

He knew the moment she used his first name that Tiffany was trying to appeal to his better nature. It was her way of being the concerned sister. He wasn't sure why he wanted to stay on course or why he felt compelled to remain here longer.

Could it be because he didn't recall the night, he'd gotten married? Other than a pair of lips belonging to a body that left him wanting more.

Shit.

A vivid image of them in an embrace, kissing her, her body pressed against him, came to mind. Her lips had parted, and he'd taken control of the kiss, knowing she was his for the taking.

There had to have been a night of sex. He always finished what he initiated.

Rosalind had a body to make a man salivate, and her green eyes, how they intrigued him. A man could get lost in them, and he did.

Allan felt a tightening in his pants and the desire to have sex with her became urgent.

"Are you still there? Did I lose you? Allan?"

"Sorry, Tiff. Yes, I'm here. I need to do this. Send me a text, the cell service sucks. I want to know immediately when everything is completed."

Silence.

"Tiffany, did you hear me? Tiffany?"

Allan stared at his phone.

No bars. Damn. He'd lost the signal.

He wasn't ready to throw in the towel on the game and would leave on his terms, not a minute before. It was essential to solve why he had such a burning ache to see the Ice Queen again.

CHAPTER ELEVEN

A mixture of gravel and snow hurled from behind the spinning tires as Rosalind drove away. Her gloved hands tightly gripped the steering wheel as the truck swerved toward a snowbank. Madder than a charging bull, the truck was her victim. She yanked the wheel to the right and then to the left. Straightening out, she counted to ten for the hundredth time since leaving the house.

Why hadn't City Boy signed the papers? What could he possibly want from her? He had everything. It wasn't her fault the newspapers printed something on their marriage.

She didn't have time for all this nonsense. Today had started out like any other. She and Dawn worked hard during their practice runs and had been rewarded with a best new time. Every second and one-hundredth of a second counted. They had to be in top form for the Barrel Futurities World Championship scheduled the week before Christmas. She needed to improve their time to win and prove she was a skilled trainer.

The day had gotten even better. During Dawn's cool-down walk on the ranch, Rosalind spotted and marked an evergreen to cut for her Christmas tree. Memories of her father planting the baby trees brought tears to her eyes. He'd said it was to make sure they'd have a tree for years and years to come.

The hunt for a perfect Christmas tree had been a family tradition and one of the happiest times she remembered. When they found the finest one, Mom would head home, leaving them to cut it down. A wonderful smell of hot chocolate and freshly baked cookies greeted them when they returned with their prize.

After her parents' unexpected deaths in a car wreck when she was ten, she'd made sure to take care of the trees. She and Grandpa Rodney followed her dad's example by planting a new tree the next spring to replace the one they'd cut. Sam's reminder that it wasn't wise to take things from the land without giving something back in return for its bounty rang true. He always said, "If you were good to the land, the land would be good to you."

The single traffic light in town turned red. She let up on the gas to hit the brake and skidded to the intersection. Rosalind slapped the steering wheel, wishing it was Mr. Allan Smith.

A blaring car horn broke through her moment of daydreaming. Rosalind blinked. The light had changed, and she waved to the car behind her. Crossing through the intersection, she made a left turn into the Farmer's Bank and Trust parking lot. Finding a plowed space big enough for the truck, she parked and hurried inside the bank.

The receptionist greeted her. "Good morning, Mrs. Smith. I'll let Mr. Fergussen know you are here."

"Thank you."

Rosalind frowned. The woman hadn't called her by her first name as usual. And why was she calling her, 'Mrs. Smith'?

"You may go in now."

She entered Mr. Fergussen's office. He stood fidgeting with a newspaper he held.

"Morning, Mr. Fergussen."

"Good morning, Mrs. Smith. I'm glad you were able to come in. The snow we received last night was unexpected."

"Mr. Fergussen, what's going on? Why are you calling me Mrs. Smith?"

"We here at Farmer's Bank and Trust, pride ourselves in knowing everything we can about our customers. We recently learned of your marriage. Congratulations. Your grandpa would've been very proud."

"Thank you." When he continued to fold and unfold the newspaper in his hands, she shifted impatiently. "Can you get to the point?"

"Yes, sorry. Based on your marital status, we're able to grant you a generous line of credit based on your husband's financial position. Good news, you won't need to have a mortgage on the new property you wish to purchase. We can deposit the funds into your checking account in a matter of minutes. How does a line of credit for one million sound to you?"

Dumbfounded for a moment and riveted by Mr. Fergussen's remarks, she managed to repeat, "One million dollars?"

"Yes, isn't that enough? Would you prefer two million?"

What in heaven's name was going on? The bank could give her two million dollars, just because she was now married?

"There's been a mistake, Mr. Fergussen. Yes, I did get married. I'm filing for a..." Rosalind paused and thought hard, then smiled prettily at the bank manager. City Boy was in for another round, she was about to even the score. Mr. New Yorker would regret not signing the papers and stepping into her domain. "A million will do for now. Thank you."

"Great. Sign here."

She signed "Rosalind Smith" by the X.

"I understand you already have clients for your business venture," Mr. Fergussen said.

"I do. Thank you. Can I get a letter to show the realtor?"

"Yes, yes of course. I'll be right back."

Unable to sit, she stood and noted some commotion at the bank entrance. People with cameras were in the lobby and three security guards were holding them back and directing customers out the doors.

Curious, Rosalind stepped outside Mr. Fergussen's office just as a few cameramen pushed a guard away.

"There she is!"

Someone in the crowd screeched, and the entire mob rushed toward her. A reporter jammed a microphone in her face. "Can we have a word with you, Mrs. Smith?"

"Mrs. Smith, how did you and Mr. Smith meet?"

"How did you snag the world's most wanted bachelor?"

Another newshound interrupted. "Did you marry Mr. Smith for his money?"

Frightened, Rosalind stumbled backward until a desk stopped her. She watched wide-eyed and open-mouthed as the crowd of people pressed forward and flashes popped.

Out of nowhere, Mr. Fergussen and another guard emerged from the crowd. They pushed and shoved their way through. The two men reached her and slammed the office door shut.

"I'm sorry, Rosalind—er, Mrs. Smith. I don't know where all these people came from. The police are on their way. Sit. You'll be safe in here."

Rosalind continued to stand, unable to move or form words. She could feel her mouth hanging open. But she accepted Mr. Fergussen's hand on her arm and let him guide her to a leather chair.

As the crowd's chants grew louder outside the office, she raised her hands to her ears to block the noise.

This wasn't happening. What was going on? Who were those people? What did they want from her?

"May I get you some water? You're looking pale."

She didn't know what to say to him and nodded. With nausea threatening her stomach, she accepted a bottle of water. The glass window kept out some of the rumble as it became less intense. The sound of police sirens mixed with the loud voices had Rosalind holding onto the water as if her life depended on it. She opened her mouth to speak, but Mr. Fergussen spoke over the shrieking noise.

"Please stay in my office until I come back for you. I'm sorry this happened in my bank." He rested his hand on her shoulder and then stepped to the guard, whispering something to him. Together they exited. Thankfully, two uniformed men outside of the office blocked her from any prying eyes.

The guards moved aside, revealing the police had arrived. People crammed into the bank lobby and a ton more were outside. Camera flashes went off amid excited shouting.

"Mrs. Smith, you need to stay in my office," Mr. Fergussen said as he returned.

"What's going on? Why is everyone here?"

"They're here to see you."

"Me? What for?"

The two guards glanced at each other, then smiled but remained silent.

"It seems your husband is someone of importance. Since word of your marriage became public, the townspeople are keenly interested in a multi-billionaire." Mr. Fergussen sat on the corner of his desk.

"For real? I thought they knew about my inheritance, my millions. I don't have billions."

"You do. What is your husband's is now yours."

Shit.

The damn town's gone loco. They'd known her since birth. She was one of them. This was ridiculous.

A knock sounded on the closed door. Rosalind, Mr. Fergussen, and the guards turned. A police officer opened the door a crack.

"We'd like to move Mrs. Smith's vehicle to the employees' entrance. We'll be able to control the mob and protect her better using the side door."

Rosalind stared at the guards and officer. Control the mob? Protect? "Everyone's gone crazy," she muttered.

"Mrs. Smith, can we have your keys?" The officer extended his hand.

Confused, she didn't respond right away.

"Rosalind, they need your keys," Mr. Fergussen urged.

"Oh, sorry. Still getting used to the name. It's a blue Silverado."

She handed the keys to one of the guards and he left with the police officer. The remaining security guard moved to the door.

"Mr. Fergussen, I'm sorry." She raked a hand through her hair, beyond irritated.

"Don't worry. We'll be better prepared next time."

"Oh, right. Next time," Rosalind echoed.

They sat in silence. Not knowing what to say, she played with her phone as the noise gradually lessened. A few minutes later, the door opened, and the two men returned.

"If you're ready, Mrs. Smith, we'll escort you out."

Rosalind nodded. The men flanked her as they exited Mr. Fergussen's office and escorted her through the bank.

Safely in her truck, she swore as she clutched the steering wheel for the second time in an hour. Honking the horn, she inched away amidst a crowd of people. In the rearview mirror, she saw the blue and white patrol car following her.

So much for keeping a low profile. Focused on the road, she fumed with anger.

How dare he do this to her?

How was she supposed to go into town for groceries?

He'd ruined everything.

The lone gravel road with the sign *Dunne Ranch* came into view, and she signaled for the turn. The patrol car blasted their siren for a second, then went on their way.

Rational reasoning seeped in as she neared her house. She wouldn't be able to intimidate, pressure, or blackmail Mr. New Yorker into anything he didn't want to do.

Oh my God, she'd just taken a million dollars from him. Crap. She was back to square one. How was she going to persuade him to sign the papers?

Then it dawned on her.

Sex.

She'd play his game. He'd been talking about getting her into bed.

She'd have sex with Mr. New York City.

Though Rosalind hadn't been with anyone since she and Tom had sacked their relationship, she couldn't deny she'd enjoyed Allan's kisses in Las Vegas. He'd made her feel things she'd never felt before.

Could she, do it? Could she trust a man again?

Pieces of a new plan formed. She'd agree to a single night of sex. Or, as Allan informed her, they'd have *his* wedding night. The catch would be only if he'd sign the divorce papers first.

Happy with her decision, she parked the truck, and proceeded to the house with her head held high. Her new plan would work, wouldn't it?

CHAPTER TWELVE

The ding of the phone woke Allan. Dazed from sleep, he grabbed his phone and saw his office number.

Tiffany.

"Hello."

"Mr. Smith, the property is now owned by your firm. The owners, an elderly couple, hadn't wanted to make a deal at first. Something about promises and knowing Ms. Dunne—sorry, Mrs. Smith, all her life."

"I'm assuming it will take about a month for all the paperwork to be completed."

"Yes, there was a mortgage to pay off. I kept raising the price. They finally caved at well above the asking price. I'm sure we overpaid," Tiffany said.

"Any amount of money will be worth it. Obtaining my revenge is priceless. Anything on the old man?"

Allan combed his fingers through his hair. Yawning, he realized he must've dozed off. He glanced at his Rolex.

Two hours?

Shit. He hadn't time for a goddamn nap.

"No, not yet. Still working on it. Will you be calling in, or should I call you?"

"Anything you find can wait till tomorrow. I'll check in at nine o'clock. Don't forget to find me an office in town. I'm using my hotspot for service. The internet connection sucks."

"Yes, Mr. Smith."

"Thanks, Tiffany."

"Have a nice night."

"Yeah, right." The phone went dead, and Allan opened his suitcase just as a fist pounded on the door. "Who's there?"

"Who do you think? The maid."

He recognized Rosalind's voice, but it had taken on a pissed off tone. "Give me a minute."

Allan unfastened the first two buttons of his dress shirt and quickly tugged out his shirttails, creating the look he knew made women swoon. When he wanted a woman, he got her. Before leaving he'd have sex with Rosalind if it was the last thing he did.

Opening the door, he placed a hand on the frame. Caught off guard for a moment, Allan stared into an unusual shade of green eyes. He hesitated, unable to speak.

No wonder he'd been dreaming of a woman with eyes the color of emeralds.

Neither said a single word. Knowing he'd mastered the art of turning females into hungry women, Allan's mouth curved in a smile. He saw her eyes darken, now they were a deeper green, tinged with desire. Rosalind slowly licked her lips.

She was his for the taking.

He leaned in toward her, removed his hand from the door, and placed it on her waist. Her breath warmed his cheek, half an inch away. Soon he'd be able to feel her. Taste her.

"Rosalind," Allan breathed softly against her lips.

The pending kiss never happened. Rosalind stepped away abruptly at the sound of heavy footfalls on the stairs, only to be stopped by the opposite wall. What had occurred earlier at the bank faded as she stared at Allan, unable to remember the reason she'd knocked on the door in the first place. She could smell his spicy, musky cologne and it triggered images of their night in Vegas.

She wanted to kiss him, to be able to run her hands over his broad chest and feel the warmth of his exposed skin against the palm of her hand.

"Rosalind, is that you? You're home early. How did your appointment go with Mr. Fergussen?" Sam's voice bellowed from the second floor.

Her eyes stayed focused on Allan's face. She needed to breathe.

"Fine. I mean fine and terrible. Because of..." As her words tumbled out, she remembered the crowd at the bank, the police, and she pointed an accusing finger at Allan. "It's all *your* fault. I'm not able to show my face in town without a police escort."

She poked Allan in the chest. Giving him a shove, she turned and stalked away. She met Sam before he had reached the last step, her temper at its boiling point.

She'd almost kissed Allan and knew if she had, she would've followed him into his bed if he had asked. If she had, he would've been gone by nightfall.

She didn't want to look at the most hunky, clean-cut man she'd ever seen outside of the rodeo circuit. She felt Allan's presence behind her as she followed Sam into the family room.

The tension in the room grew as thick as fog on an early autumn morning. Allan, still half dressed, leaned against the nearest wall. His penetrating glare was hot enough to light a campfire and she refused to look at him. The two men waited for her to speak. Sam slowly crossed over to his favorite recliner.

So unfair. Two against one.

Rosalind paced around the family room not ready to say anything with her hands on her hips. Her emotions spiked from nervousness to defiance.

"Missy, tell me what's the matter."

She stopped her pacing and related what happened at the bank, purposely withholding the fact she'd taken a million dollars of Allan's money. "He's ruined my life, Sam. I want the divorce. He won't sign the papers." She fired her verbal jab in Allan's direction. He pushed away from the wall and stood with his hands in his pockets. The pose emphasized his groin. She couldn't look away from the bulge in the front of his pants.

"*I* ruined *your* life? Excuse me, Miss Rodeo Queen, but it's the other way around. I never wanted to get married. If and when I did, I wouldn't have picked a complete stranger. I was an unwilling partner, and I'll tell your trustee or trustees we never consummated our sham of a marriage. You'll have to surrender all your money."

He sauntered closer to her as he spoke. His explosion of words hurt. Blinded by her wrath, Rosalind met his advance. "I paid you. I sent you the divorce papers. Nevertheless, here you are, delivering them *unsigned*. Sign them. You can be on your way in a few minutes. I'm never letting you touch me."

Now face to face, with only inches separating them, both fumed at each other.

Finally, Sam stepped in. "No 'OK Corral' arguments in the house. Mr. Smith, Rosalind deserves your anger. In spite of her actions, she is right."

In unison, they turned to stare at him, and Rosalind took a few steps away from Allan.

"I'm the trustee."

Allan's eyebrows had lifted when Sam had revealed he was her trustee. She couldn't help her lips curving into a smile.

She'd won. Sam was on her side.

"Then you need to do something. She shouldn't have been allowed her inheritance. If you don't put a stop to this madness, I'll call my lawyers and sue."

"I'll tell you what I'm gonna do, Mr. Smith. You'll have one year from your wedding date to convince our wild filly, Rosalind here, to have a wedding night. If the year passes and you're unable to consummate the marriage, I'll have it nullified."

Sam sat in the recliner, like a king taking his throne.

Rosalind gaped at him. "No."

"Yes."

Allan's stern one word reply echoed in the room. He had removed his hands from his pockets and now stood with them crossed over his chest.

"If you're unable to spend one night with your husband in a year's time, Rosalind, you'll have to return the inheritance plus interest." Sam folded his arms over his chest.

"No way. This is unfair, Sam. You of all people know why I did what I did. How I planned to use the money. I have clients waiting. You can't expect me to wait another four years."

Her pleading had no effect on Sam. He sat stone faced. She ignored Allan as she paced the room again.

"This is for your own good. You cheated, young lady. What you did was wrong. Did you think I'd stand by and allow you to take advantage of our friendship?"

Damn. Damn. Damn. She couldn't return the money. "Sam,

you can't be serious. Why would I allow *him* to have sex with me? I don't even know him."

"You knew him enough to marry him."

"That's unfair. Besides, he has a city boy attitude." Rosalind stopped her pacing to glare at her husband.

"Thank you, Sam. You won't have to worry," Allan said. "I'm able to tame the best of the best. It's the letting go that women have a problem with on my end. Nevertheless, be assured I will walk out of here with no regrets after I've completed your terms. It should only take a week or two, and I'll be gone."

Rosalind fumed while Allan strutted toward her. She braced herself for another round of his verbal assault as they faced each other. Instead of words, he reached out and gently touched her cheek.

The sound of her hand hitting his face snapped like a fire-cracker.

"Don't ever touch me again." She whirled out of his reach, grabbed her parka, and slammed the front door.

———

"Does she ever shut doors quietly?"

"Yeah, when it suits her." Sam chuckled and then coughed.

Allan rubbed his cheek. "She has a mean right. Is her left as quick?"

He opened and closed his mouth to test for damage, then pushed aside the thick curtain to watch Rosalind's retreating figure. Her hips swayed enticingly even through the thick coat she wore.

Maybe she'd ride him tonight.

He turned from the window and the disturbing picture she made, unsure why his emotions were so affected.

"What type of proof will you be requiring?" he asked, trying for a businesslike demeanor.

"I don't think I'll be needin' any."

Sam's voice had held a laughing tone. Why wouldn't he need proof? There was only one reason he could think of and he frowned. "Are you saying she's a virgin?"

"No, no boy. She's had several boyfriends. There was one boy who'd meant more than the others did. They were young and in love when he asked her grandfather, Rodney was his name, for her hand in marriage. Rodney by the way was my best friend, we went back years, no decades. Anyway, he placed the stipulations on her inheritance. The boy was eager to marry Rosalind, before her grandfather could file the papers. He pressured Rosalind for a quick marriage..." Sam trailed off at the sound of the barn door slamming.

They both looked toward the window. Allan glanced back at Sam who shrugged, then continued, "Rosalind wouldn't do what the boyfriend wanted and tried to end the relationship. The boy got mean."

"Mean? How mean?"

"Enough to scare her away from men."

"I'll go about this slowly. It'll take longer than I'd expected, but I'll get the job done." Allan frowned. This would be harder than he thought. Shyness and timidity weren't in the women he dated.

"I'm gonna go check on her. I'd advise you not to follow." Sam pushed out of his chair, coughed a few times, and followed Rosalind out of the house and headed to the barn.

Allan raked a hand through his hair. For the first time in his life, he was questioning his sexual expertise. He might lose this battle. Women who'd been abused by men required support, sensitivity, and an emotional commitment. All things he'd never put into a relationship.

He hadn't expected this. He'd only wanted to teach Rosalind a lesson. Why was it so important to have sex with her? Why did he want to?

No answers came.

He could still cancel the land deal. How would she react when she found out she lost it? And why did he care?

Suddenly chilled, Allan headed to his room. Her story touched him. And consequently, threw him a curveball. He was usually so good at appraising women. How could he have misjudged her? How could an unpretentious cowgirl have gotten the better of him more than once?

What kind of sick bastard gets physical with women in a malicious way? It's no wonder she was jumpy.

He unpacked his bags, took off his suit, and changed into a pair of jeans, all the while planning his next strategy. She wasn't turned on by his charm, so there would be no quick surrender. As timid as a virgin, yet she could hold her own in a fight. Allan tested his sore jaw again.

He'd become her friend. Definitely, friends with benefits as the saying went.

New, improved plans formed as he stuffed boxers into an empty drawer in the dresser. And he'd start tonight!

CHAPTER THIRTEEN

The creak of the barn door alerted Rosalind. She wasn't alone anymore. She continued to hug Dawn in hopes the person would leave. Only one person would dare follow her.

"Rosalind?"

Ice encased her heart and hardened at the sound of Sam's voice. He'd betrayed her. His footsteps grew louder when he approached Dawn's stall. Reaching inside her pocket for a lump of sugar, she found a leftover piece and held it out to the mare.

"Rosalind, I know you're in here."

Dawn nickered and raised her head in defiance.

"Shhh, it's okay, girl," Rosalind murmured. She moved to Dawn's opposite flank as her irritation at him and Allan cooled. Sam was usually on her side, but for some reason he'd chosen a stranger over her. It was clear she'd disappointed him.

Everything she'd done was to save the horses. Clients were counting on her to help them. She'd made promises. She couldn't let them down too.

"You have to stop running." Sam leaned against the door.

"I can if I want." Rosalind tipped her hat low to shield her face and wiped at her tears.

"You need to go inside and talk to your husband."

"I'm not saying one word to him. I hope he's packing his bags."

"He isn't." Sam paused and cleared his throat. "Your husband will be staying for at least one year unless you agree to return your inheritance."

She stayed hidden in the stall using Dawn as a shield, not ready to face Sam. She was cornered and as useless as a four-card flush in a poker game.

"Mr. Lover Boy better be packing, and I don't mean a gun," she hissed, not able to ignore her swirling emotions and loss of control over the situation. "I'll give Mr. Kennedy a call after dinner, to tell him I won't be able to purchase Dwight's land. Will that make you happy?"

The sound of the bolt sliding back annoyed her. She eyeballed Sam over Dawn's hindquarter. He stepped into the stall and gripped the wood as he coughed several times.

Her anger faded, replaced by concern. "Should I take you to the doctor?"

He continued to cough and placed a hand on his chest. Rosalind ducked under Dawn's neck and went to him.

"No, I'm fine. It's only the cold air in these old lungs," he said and wiped at his mouth with a handkerchief.

"I'll look for some cough medicine. If Allan spends the night, I'm sleeping in the barn."

Sam chuckled and coughed again. "I wouldn't be so quick to put your tail between your legs, like you've done something wrong. Your grandpa raised a smart granddaughter. I'm not hearing or seeing that person right now."

"I don't have my tail between my legs." She raised her head

high. She'd kick Mr. New Yorker's ass over the water trough for causing all this trouble.

"Come on now. Don't show me your temper."

"I know what I did was wrong. I'm admitting defeat." Rosalind exhaled, before adding, "There's nothing wrong with that. I've nothing to be ashamed of, unless you're saying because I'm conceding, I'm weak."

"No, what I'm saying, girl, there isn't a reason for you to concede this soon."

"You think I should have sex with a stranger?" She spoke through gritted teeth, trying to hide her exasperation from Sam. The thought of Allan's hands on her breasts again excited her so much it scared her. Tom, who'd she'd thought had been the sexiest bareback bull rider on the circuit, never left her as hungry for his touch as Allan had.

"You chose Allan for a reason..." He raised both hands to stop her from interrupting. "Even if they were the wrong ones. Someone must be looking out for you. Mr. Smith could've sued your ass, but he didn't. He offered you a compromise. I don't agree with him. He made a good point, however."

"A compromise? You call having a one-night stand a compromise? Have you lost your mind?"

"Now, calm down, he's your husband after all. Who knows, you might find him to your liken'. Your grandfather's wish was for you to find someone to love. I want you to experience real love, too. I never did, being a rancher and on the rodeo circuit, wasn't the kind of life I'd expect any woman to agree to. Just like your grandfather, he never found anyone after your grandmother had died long before you were born. We became two bachelors. Well, I did and your grandfather a widower."

She met Sam's eyes. "You're the only one left who I love. Loving someone means you can get hurt. I loved my parents and they died. I loved Grandpa Rodney and he's gone too. You're gonna live forever."

"Rosalind, Allan isn't like Tom. I know a gentleman when I see one, city boy or cowboy. He might not want a commitment, but all men are womanizers to a point. They love women, then either leave or stay. They don't get their reputation for nothing. Believe it or not, I've left behind my fair share of women. Never wanted to be tied down either." He laid his hand on her arm.

As Rosalind considered Sam's admission, a new plan was formed. "I'll agree to your terms. After the deed is done, I can send Mr. Prick home with his taste of sugar. I can't let the horses suffer any longer than I'm capable of allowing."

She smiled and angled her hat back further on her head. It wasn't as if she didn't have to have sex with Allan, it was the marriage thing. She'd been thinking a lot about Allan's kisses since Las Vegas. It didn't mean she'd give in to him easily. Two could play the sexual game. She could make his life a living hell of unsatisfied lust.

"Good, it's settled. Let's go inside." Sam wheezed and hacked, covering his mouth.

"Are you sure you don't want to see the doctor?"

"Yeah, I still have cough medicine from the last time. I'll take it after dinner."

"All right, but if it's not any better in a day, Sam I'll make the appointment for you."

"Don't worry about me. You have a husband to think about."

She sure did and he would be regretting it. Together they walked from Dawn's stall. He checked on a few of the other horses and she did the same. It was too soon for the ranch hands to be doing it for the nightly checks. They worked in silence.

When they left Sam shut and bolted the heavy outer door

and held out his hand. "To reiterate our deal. Mr. Smith has one year to convince you to consummate the marriage. If it doesn't happen, you'll deed the land to me to pay off the amount of money you illegally obtained. I'll hold on to the land until you reach your thirtieth birthday. At that time, I'll deed it back to you."

"Deal."

She shook his hand with an ear-to-ear smile. She was going to enjoy teasing Mr. Smith, the good-looking, heart-stopping kisser with a gorgeous body. And the best part, putting him to work as a ranch hand. She'd be the winner both ways and he'd be the loser.

CHAPTER FOURTEEN

A pungent, spicy aroma drifted into Allan's room, engulfing him in the mouthwatering smell. He stretched, realizing he'd fallen asleep again waiting for Rosalind and Sam to return after their desertion. A loud grumbling noise emitted from his stomach. He checked his watch, startled to see it was past five-thirty.

No wonder, he was famished.

Checking his phone revealed no bars. He moved toward the window and got one bar, plus three missed calls and voice-mails. Sliding the bar across the screen, the *No Service* reappeared. He held the phone higher. Still nothing.

Frustrated, he slipped his phone into his pocket and opened the bedroom door. His nose led him to the kitchen where he paused at the display of unbound spontaneity from Rosalind. She stood at the stove and was singing.

Shit. She's beautiful. And had a nice ass.

He blinked and adjusted his jeans. The country western song complemented the tone of her voice. As the chorus started, Rosalind turned and stopped in mid-word.

Their eyes met.

Allan swallowed. His appetite changed from food to an undeniable desire to pull her close. An apron decorated with roosters was tied around her small waist. Her long, rich brown hair framed her face, pushed behind her ears. Her cheeks were flushed from the heat of the stove.

Had he walked into a *Hallmark* movie? How could this woman get him all heated up whenever he looked at her?

He cleared his throat. "Do you have enough for company?"

———

Rosalind clicked off the radio and hastily smoothed her hair. "Oh yeah, I was about to come get you." She took in his changed appearance. "I see you packed jeans."

"These are *Balmain*. I wear them on casual days at the office."

An easy smile played at the corners of her mouth. "Oh, designer jeans, not Wranglers."

"Wrangler jeans? Do they still make them?"

"You're not a *Gap* kind of guy, I take it."

His shocked look expressed it all. She couldn't keep the grin from widening. He still sported his white oxford shirt with only the top button open and tucked into his jeans.

"The smell is wonderful." He inhaled animatedly and placed his hand over his stomach. "What are you cooking?"

"It's chili night." A beeping sound interrupted any further conversation. With an oven mitt, Rosalind removed a tray of cornbread from the oven.

"Let me help."

Allan quickly moved two potholders that were on the countertop closer together. She placed the hot tray on them. His body brushed hers, sending sparks of excitement through her.

Rosalind deliberately moved to the sink. He followed and to stop him, she opened the silverware drawer.

"I'm sorry for slapping you. It was wrong of me."

"You have a powerful swing."

"Well, I *am* a cowgirl." She inhaled, held her breath for a moment, and then exhaled. "Maybe we should start over. If I want to keep my inheritance to buy the land, I have to be nice to you. But you'll have to give me time and space. I'm not...not the kind of woman... I mean... I don't sleep around."

Lost in the depth of the blueness of his eyes, Rosalind leaned in, like a moth drawn to a flame, willing his lips to smother hers. He shoved the drawer shut, laid his hand on her waist, drawing her to him, and her eyes closed in anticipation.

"Is dinner ready? I'm hungry enough to eat my shirt."

At Sam's abrupt intrusion, Rosalind stepped away from Allan, opening the cabinet door to use as a shield.

"Yup, setting the table."

———

Allan put as much space as possible between himself and Rosalind while she positioned herself next to the refrigerator. Sexual tension filled the air as Sam took a seat at the table.

Fuck.

The old man had the worse timing ever. It'd been twice now he'd ruined his advances toward Rosalind.

"Good evening, Mr. Smith. I see you've found your way to the kitchen. Rosalind is a damn good cook." Sam patted his protruding belly. "Her chili has won first place the last five years at the county fair."

"I can hardly wait to sample it." Allan glanced at Rosalind, who gave him the cold shoulder as she efficiently moved around the kitchen.

"I'm not a betting man, but I'll place a wager you'll have to be getting new clothes before ya leave. You'll be adding on pounds for sure," Sam chuckled. "Come sit next to me."

Allan joined Sam in a quiet laugh and took the empty chair. Rosalind placed the pot of chili on the table along with the cornbread. She chose the seat across from him.

Sam carried on a lively conversation throughout dinner. Allan listened with mixed interest as Sam reminisced about a young Rosalind, her trials of barrel racing, and days spent at the rodeos. He caught her staring at him. She looked away first. The more he learned about his wife, the more he felt like a total cad and wished he hadn't instructed Tiffany to buy the land Rosalind wanted so ardently.

He should've unconditionally signed the goddamn divorce papers. Simply mailed them to her. How could he back out gracefully?

He tapped his fingers on the table in exasperation. When he hadn't known anything about her, he'd simply wanted to bed the Rodeo Queen and leave. She would've been a night of sex in the dark. A one-night stand, but now it wouldn't be right.

How had his plan fallen apart in the last few hours? For Christ's sake, he felt like a heel. Tiffany was right again.

"Excuse me, I'm gonna take my coffee to my room. The two of you need time alone." Sam's chortling caused him to hack and wheeze on his way out.

"Goodnight, sir."

"Night." Rosalind stood and took her plate over to the sink.

Allan followed her lead and helped clear the table. "I'll help with the dishes. I'm not a very good cook. But I do know my way around a kitchen."

"I can handle it on my own." She kept her eyes averted from his.

"No, I insist, as repayment for dinner. It was the best chili I've ever tasted."

"There is no dishwasher."

"By hand it is, then." He turned on the water, filled the sink, and rolled up his sleeves.

While they worked together neither said anything, but the friction thickened. Running water and the clatter of dishes were the only sounds. All of a sudden Rosalind wiped her hands on a towel, put her hands on her hips, and faced him.

"Listen, I'm sorry I got you into this mess. Will you be able to take time off from work? 'Cause I've changed my mind. I won't be honoring our wedding night festivities."

"I own the company," Allan pointed out. "I have as much time as I need. Do you have Wi-Fi? The 5G on my phone is slow."

"Yeah, I'll give you the code."

He drained the sink and dried his hands, then walked to the cleaned table and took a seat. "Rosalind, sit down. We have to discuss the mess we're in. Our only solution is to have sex. We are adults. We should be able to enjoy our encounter."

"Don't you get it? I will *not* have sex with you. Sleep with you. Or have you touch me."

Allan took no heed to her outburst. "Sam's trumped us both. You're in a no-win scenario. If we don't, you'll have a houseguest until our anniversary. And if I ask for an annulment, you're screwed either way." Unable to hide his amusement, he rocked the chair on two legs.

"Funny guy. I suggest you keep your day job."

She poured two cups of coffee and set one in front of him. He sobered for a moment. None of his past girlfriends, including Katherine, would've brought him coffee, but it was Rosalind's way of life to be thoughtful. Something he'd never been accustomed to. The foster homes had been a 'you're on your own' way of life.

"I talked myself into sleeping with you, but I can't. We're strangers. I told Sam I'd return the money, plus the line of credit the bank offered to me. You won't have to stay around for our anniversary." Rosalind sank into her chair, twisting the towel she held on her lap.

Contemplating her request, Allan weighed the options and outcomes. The pie chart in his mind was heavy on one side. She'd offered him a simple solution.

Get out quick when the going is good, as he did with some stock. "Nice offer…"

He stopped as he caught the slight upward turn of her lips. Damn. She was playing him at his own game.

"It's settled then, right? You can leave in the morning."

He drummed his fingers on the table. He'd almost handed everything to her on a silver platter.

No way, honey, he would be sticking around. No one got away with making Allan Smith look like a fool twice even if that person was a woman with a tempting mouth. Yet he couldn't resist.

"I like people who are straightforward. I also like my women to be willing when I make love to them. You see, I'm a breast and thigh man." The chair screeched as he moved to face her. Testing her, he placed his hand on her thigh. The heat of her body encouraged him to slide his hand around to the inside of her leg. "I love to feel that smooth skin beneath my fingers."

"Take your hands off me, you sleazy snake."

Rosalind's demand sobered him. And in a blink of an eye, she'd reached across the table, grabbed the butter knife, and pressed it against his exposed throat. Allan stretched his neck to move away from the threatening cold metal.

She moved it closer. He felt the dull blade press into his exposed skin.

———

Through gritted teeth, Rosalind repeated, "Take your hand off me. Now. Do it or you'll regret ever touching me."

"I've never used butter in foreplay before."

She pushed the knife against his skin. He removed his hand. She studied his facial expression, forcing herself not to react with anything he could identify as desire.

"I'm not into bondage, but if you insist..." Allan began.

To her shock, he gripped her wrist and pushed away the knife. He stood, seized her other hand. The knife fell to the table. She craned her neck to stare at him.

"This could've been easy. One night. Take it or leave it. I won't force you. You'll come willingly, which is one wager I'll easily make. I'm ready for the long haul. Even if I have to live in this two-by-four you call a house. I have the time. Do you, Ice Queen?"

She heard his voice change from sternness to desire. Her arms now behind her back, she was nestled against his body. Before she knew it his face was inches from hers.

Oh, my.

He was going to kiss her.

Her arms imprisoned, Rosalind couldn't do anything. She thought of turning away but didn't. Her lips met his surprisingly soft kiss. She willed herself not to react. He applied more pressure. Her insides flopped like a bunch of tumbleweed, twisting, and turning.

Any thoughts of what was right or wrong faded. She relaxed and enjoyed his kiss. Rosalind closed her eyes to block out the desire she could see in his face.

Allan knew the signs of a woman letting down her defenses. He took advantage and slipped his tongue into her mouth. Their tongues now battled a different kind of fight. Releasing one of her arms, he slid his hand into her hair, pulling her closer.

The kiss went on and on.

A sudden jarring noise from upstairs broke them apart. He freed her other arm and tenderly placed his hand on her cheek. He brushed his thumb across her swollen lips. "Spend the night with me. I know you want to. I'll be gentle."

"Please move away from me."

With much regret, Allan did.

"I can't do what you want. I'm not that type of girl."

"Okay, we'll take it slow. Tomorrow is another day." He sank back into the chair and linked his hands together behind his head.

"I have an early appointment tomorrow." She sat down too and folded her hands on her lap. "Everything's gotten way out of hand. I don't know what to think anymore. My plan sounded so simple. I never imagined it wouldn't work. I never thought anyone would get hurt."

He saw tears forming in her eyes. Not expecting tears from her, but for some reason seeing them in her eyes struck a chord of protectiveness in him. He stroked her arm. "You've made my astuteness problematical. Done damage to my firm. Nevertheless, both will survive at a cost. What we need to do is conclude our dealings so we can get on with our lives. I'm ready to go to Florida so I can thaw out. This godforsaken state is too damn cold."

She laughed. "Thanks for your practicality. I can't make you wait for the annulment. I don't think I could handle you around twenty-four-seven for any length of time, City Boy. The sooner you leave, the better."

"Sounds like a plan."

What she said made sense. They'd both win. He'd be able to manage the press she couldn't.

"We can talk to Sam tomorrow. Maybe he'll agree to the annulment early," Rosalind said.

Allan stood and held out his hand to her. Shaking her head, she stood, pushing her hair from her face, shoving her hand in her back pocket.

They stared at each other.

Mentally he tried to figure out why she had a hold on him. His gut feeling told him this was bad business from the beginning, but he'd almost given her everything. Unheard of in his book, a woman saying no.

The quicker he left, the better.

"Good enough, we'll talk to him in the morning." She turned and walked out of the kitchen.

In slow motion he followed, telling himself not to stare at the movement of her hips.

Neither said a word. She headed to the stairs, and he went down the hall to his room, lost in his own private realm of inner turmoil.

CHAPTER FIFTEEN

Voices and the smell of recently brewed coffee lured Rosalind toward the kitchen as she entered the house. Unzipping her parka, she hung it on the coat rack. Her nine o'clock meeting with Mr. Kennedy and his explosive announcement echoed in her mind. She found an old napkin in her coat pocket and wiped her eyes.

"Don't show defeat. Be strong," she said to herself.

From the kitchen doorway, she saw Sam and Allan at the table. They looked like best friends, talking and enjoying coffee. About to turn away, she spotted her file of abused horses between them. Suppressed fury surfaced. "I've been calling the landline and your cell phone, Sam."

Both men peered over their shoulders and stared at her.

"It hasn't rung, and I don't have my cell phone on since I'm at home," Sam said.

She took the cordless phone from the counter. Dead silence. Shaking her head, Rosalind placed the handset in its cradle and watched until the red-light indicator came on.

"How many times have I told you to replace the phone in its holder? It has to charge."

"Sorry. Were you calling to tell me when we can dig the foundation of the barns?"

"No, and we won't," Rosalind said.

"What? Why not? You have the money to get the project in motion."

"I have nowhere to build them. Someone bought the land out from under me yesterday."

Sam pushed his chair away from the table to look at her. "Who would do such a thing to you? The whole town knows you wanted the land."

"Right. Mr. Kennedy said a management company paid five times the asking price." Rosalind paced the short length of the room. "Can you believe that? Not double or triple, but five times the listing amount. That would be almost four million dollars. Damn Mr. Hillsboro. He promised to sell it to me for seven-hundred-fifty thousand dollars. Who in their right mind would pay such an exorbitant price for that land?"

All at once Allan began coughing and choking. She glared at him.

"Sorry, I'm still not used to the bitterness of the coffee. How terrible to lose everything at the last minute. I stay on top of my acquisitions right up to the moment I sign the papers."

"Are your bags packed, Mister New Yorker? I want you out of my home. I'm ready to give back my inheritance." She halted her pacing and stopped next to him.

"There must be something you can do," Sam urged. "You had a contract first. I was showing Allan some of the abused horses we were gonna be boarding."

She shook her head. "There's nothing I can do. How do I explain to Linda and the others, I can't take or even help the horses? They need me. And now they'll be killed!"

Tears filled her eyes. A lump rose in her throat. Taking a deep breath, she poured herself a cup of coffee and leaned against the counter, her pose giving a false impression of calmness at best as she sipped. The hot liquid flushed a warm trail down her throat. Both men still regarded her. She refused to look at Allan, although the shine of the knife lying next to the butter dish held her attention. She raised her eyes to meet his.

Why had she grabbed it last night? Self-defense?

A sudden blaze of desire swept over her as she stared at him.

That's why.

Mr. Fancy Pants with his handsome face, square jaw, and crooked nose. Not to mention his flashing blue eyes.

"Perhaps the company that purchased the land would be willing to lease it to you until they need it. Maybe they aren't planning to develop it anytime soon."

Allan's voice made her knees weak. She hadn't really listened to his words. All she saw was his lips moving and wanting them to kiss her.

"Sounds like a grand idea. Rosalind, you—"

"Sam, stop. Don't listen to Mr. Rich Boy. Like I can call some firm and say, 'you know that land you stole from me, can I borrow it?'"

"I wouldn't use those words," Allan stated.

Rosalind turned away from them both and topped off her cup of coffee. Then she joined them at the table. She frowned as she touched the file.

Sam slid his chair back to the table and faced her. "Do you want me to call Attorney Haugen and ask if he can help? It ain't right. Your contract should've been enough."

"Whatever, I don't think they'll be able to do anything. Mr. Kennedy wouldn't give me any information on the new owners. This is totally insane." She smacked the tabletop with her hand. Coffee cups shook and their brown liquid spilled and aimed her eyes at Allan. "First, you appear with the unsigned divorce papers and ruin my day. You demand to have sex with me. The police had to escort me home yesterday from the bank. And now this. I can't take any more."

"You should make an effort to get in touch with the new owners," Allan repeated.

"You believe everything is simple. Well, at least I don't have to worry about the divorce since I too can file for an annulment. The money isn't any good to me now. The land is gone. Mr. Smith, you won't ever be getting any wedding night. Pack your bags and leave. This is a family matter, and you're not family."

She purposely glanced at the butter knife to get her point across to him, stood, and stormed from the kitchen.

———

A loud bang shook the house. Allan flicked a glance at Sam. "Does she always walk...run away from her problems?"

"I'm afraid she's a tad spoiled. Her grandfather hardly ever told her no, and unfortunately, I've followed in his footsteps. I'm gonna lie down. I'm tired and I have a headache."

"If you don't mind, I'll make a few calls. See what I can do to help."

"You do that, boy."

Etched into the old man's face was pain and weariness. Allan could see it for himself as Sam nodded and slowly shuffled from the room.

Man, oh man alive. This sucked.

It was the first time in all his business dealings that he saw firsthand what happened when a short sell occurred. Shit. He didn't like it at all.

He took out his iPhone and tapped his office number.

"Hello, Mr. Smith."

"Tiffany, can we cancel the purchase of the land?"

"No, the money was wired, and I'm sure it cleared already. The paperwork should be arriving. Why? What's the problem?"

"You were right. I should've signed the divorce papers and dealt with the ramifications from my office. My plans have changed. Write a land lease proposal. Rosalind wanted her inheritance to buy the land to board sick and abused horses."

"Mr. Smith, will you repeat the first sentence? I want to hear it again."

Allan took a sip of his coffee. His lips tightened and he shook his head. He needed a real cup of coffee. He didn't have time for Tiffany's sassiness.

"Yes, you were right. I've said it twice, and I won't say it again. Fabricate some sort of letter saying the company will consider a land lease option. She can't know I own it. Did you find me an office?"

He heard Tiffany's laughter and frowned. She cleared her throat. "No, I haven't. The letter and lease can be ready this afternoon."

"Okay, call when you've got that office. Goodbye."

He clicked off his phone and picked up the butter knife. He stroked it absentmindedly. His wife had spunk and guts. A slow smile came to his lips. They both owned the land. They were still married, hallelujah. Since he bought the land yesterday, it meant she owned it too. She never signed his prenuptial agreement.

'Bad guy, good guy' came into play. There was a chance he'd lose half of everything if she figured out, he was worth billions.

Holy crap.

All his hard work over the years to secure his holdings, were at risk.

He lifted his hands and wiped his forehead. No sweat.

Being noncommittal had its advantages in his playbook. However, when money was involved, he worried. Even the highs and lows of the stock market could cause him grief.

Why was he not more bothered by the fact he could lose half of everything he'd worked so hard to achieve?

Allan slid his chair away from the table. Time to find his bride and talk to her.

Somehow, a hometown cowgirl—Rodeo Queen was turning his life and heart upside down.

———

Rosalind swore as she hurried to the barn. She slipped her phone from her jeans pocket and pressed Linda's number.

"Hello."

"Linda, this is Rosalind."

"Oh hi, I've been waiting for your call. Do we have a move date?"

"No... I'm sorry... I've run into some problems."

"Problems?"

"Someone bought the land before I could get my inheritance in place to purchase it. This isn't how I envisioned things."

Rosalind yanked the metal bar and opened the barn door. The earthy smells calmed her raging emotions.

"We were counting on you. If you can't help, I won't be able to provide for the horses. Decisions will have to be made. I had high hopes for your help."

Rosalind heard Linda's disappointment in her voice, she fisted her hand. Waves of sadness coursed through her. She kicked at the floor and inwardly swore again. "Okay, what decisions do you have to make?"

"Some of the horses' medical needs outweigh the money

available. The money I do have needs to be spent on the ones I can save. Samson's medicine—"

"Don't do anything yet, Linda. I'll send you some money. It should get you through until the end of the year. I have the BFA World Championship in December. If I win, I'll send more."

"Thank you. You're an angel. Samson's medicine is expensive. The veterinarian was here yesterday. His diagnosis wasn't good. Samson's left leg is deteriorating from his days on the Barrel Racing circuit. He needs extra care."

Crap. She couldn't let Samson die.

His previous owner had passed away, and the family hadn't cared what records he'd held or who would care for him. Thank goodness Linda's organization stepped in when they heard he was scheduled for a slaughterhouse in Canada.

"Hang in there. I'll pull together something soon, even if I have to build a new barn on my land. Keep me informed if you need anything," Rosalind said.

"Okay, I will. Bless you for taking care of us."

They disconnected.

Damn that City Boy. Why hadn't he signed the divorce papers? Everything revolved around having sex with Mr. Wonderful. Sex. Money.

A tiny smile tweaked her lips as a new plan edged itself forward. If she had sex with Allan, she could keep her money and use it to build a new barn. It would mean putting off the training facility she'd planned to add to her existing barns and property.

Her mind was like a damn yoyo.

Sex.

No sex.

Sex.

No sex.

She could treat herself to a night in Mr. Wonderful's arms. It would be exciting and no doubt pleasurable.

Dawn's loud neigh drew her attention to her job.

"Yup, I'm late. We'll work harder today."

Dawn shook her head and snorted as if in approval.

She began grooming Dawn for their runs, but her mind went over possibilities to fix the problem of not being able to afford extra hands around the ranch if she sent money to Linda. It irked her to no end, that she had millions waiting for her, but couldn't use it. Her mind went back to the sex. She should just do it, get it out of the way and Allan would be forced to depart back to New York.

He'd come for a one-night stand. Made it very clear, except now she didn't know if she wanted him to leave, even if they did have sex.

CHAPTER SIXTEEN

Fresh snow crunched beneath the borrowed boots Allan wore. He gripped the lapels of his coat and snuggled into its depths as a gust of cold wind blew. The sun had long since vanished, leaving a grayness in its wake and layers of clouds.

Jesus Christ, it's freezing.

Had he lost his mind? New York was never this frigid.

Movement to the left of the barn caught his attention. A cowboy sat on top of a fence with what appeared to be a stopwatch, focused on a rider poised at one end of the corral on a light brown horse. A handful of other men stood along the fence.

Rosalind?

It had to be, but she wasn't wearing her red coat. She had on a jean jacket. Wasn't she freezing?

Before Allan reached the corral, the cowboy with the stopwatch hollered, "Ready. Set. Go!"

She urged a golden-brown horse with her legs, and they took off at high speed toward a tall barrel to her right. Her hair flew out behind her like a scarf blowing in the wind. When she reached the barrel, they rounded it, and she pressed the horse on to a second barrel at the opposite side.

"Five, seven, nine..." Stopwatch Guy shouted.

The horse and Rosalind circled the second barrel, faster than the other two sprints. She pressed on to a third barrel and skillfully guided the horse around it. Allan's eyes widened as her boot almost touched the ground.

Holy shit. She was the Rodeo Queen.

Some of the fog, which had haunted him since Vegas, lifted from his brain. The image of a woman sitting regal-like on a horse pushed through. He remembered how intrigued he'd been with the way her hips moved as one with the animal. From this perspective, it was like the new panorama 4K television, but in 3D.

"Fourteen-point-thirty-two seconds!" The stopwatch cowboy screamed and jumped from the wooden fence in excitement. The others came to stand near the cowboy cheering too.

Not sure what all the excitement was about, Allan moved closer. "Is that good?"

Stopwatch cowboy turned, grinning. "Oh yeah, it's better than good. Hey, are you the man she married to save the horses?"

"Yes." His one-word answer was all he was going to say and then was about to plead the fifth.

"It was awfully good of you. Very noble thing, you know, to help her. Nice to meet you. I'm Joe."

Before Allan could reply, Joe sauntered toward Rosalind, who still sat astride the horse. Allan stood alone a short distance from the fence, feeling sick. His perfect life lost a layer or two. Her plan had been an unselfish act, while his actions were purely egotistical.

She looked more like a queen today than before with her

cheeks flushed and eyes sparkling despite the dullness of the sky.

Would she have that same look after he made love to her?

God, he wanted her now, more than ever.

"Are you sure?" Allan heard her ask Joe as soon as he reached her. He nodded and held out the stopwatch. The handful of men lingering around the fence went into the corral to check the time.

"Holy conniption. I did fourteen-point-thirty-two seconds in the cold and with all this gear on. I'm for sure gonna take first place next month if I stay at this pace."

"Don't be celebrating yet," Joe warned. "That's bad luck, you know. Dawn shouldn't be out in the cold too long. Get her inside for a rub down. You don't want her sick."

"Yeah, but first I want to do a quick cool down. Can you and the others check the placement of the barrels? Number two is off."

"As if you need to ask. Walt checked them before you came out, but I'll personally see to it."

Allan strolled closer, wanting to be part of the enthusiasm, not a bystander. Seeing his bride carefree and having fun had a contagious effect. Soon the other three men and Joe moved away, chatting about her accomplishment.

These cowboys were wrapped around her finger. Was she sexually involved with any of them? It would be a total pisser if she was.

Her gaze drifted over to him as he walked toward her. "Did you come to tell me you're leaving?"

Her don't-mess-with-me attitude had returned. Allan disregarded it as he stepped to the horse.

"No, we need to talk."

"You can't possibly have anything to say that I'd want to

hear. Nonetheless, if you think you do, we can talk in the barn after I'm done with Dawn's cool-down."

Not allowing him to reply, she abruptly steered the horse away. He returned to the fence and kept his eyes on his wife as she walked the horse around the corral. Allan frowned and his jaw tightened. He didn't have a plan yet. Hell, what could he say to her about the land?

"You were right," Joe yelled, "six inches off."

"I knew it. Dawn was off a step when we rounded it. Make sure it gets fixed." Rosalind continued to ride around the course.

"I'll have it corrected for tomorrow's run."

"You mean Friday. Tomorrow is Thanksgiving."

"No, I mean tomorrow. You need to do the run every day." Joe moved to intercept Rosalind.

She came to a halt. "Fine."

Allan observed the exchange and saw Rosalind stick out her tongue at Joe, who waved it off. He had to chuckle. Everyone was so interesting here. Not like at his offices where stress left his employees short-tempered and moody. This was a real working ranch. Family. Not just co-workers. No one complained; they all did what needed to be done without being told or reminded. He'd have to tell Paul to schedule a team building retreat.

The sounds of the horse's hooves hitting dirt had Allan focusing on Rosalind. She rode the horse around the yard four more times, dismounted, walked another two times, and disappeared into the barn from a side entrance.

By the time he entered the warmth of the building, he saw she'd removed the saddle which now rested on a half-wall. She gripped a long, wide brush with a band holding it in place over her hand, pulling it over the horse's coat.

Her hand and brush moved as one unit, back and forth in

sync to some unheard music. Her other hand trailed close behind and caressed the sleek animal. The rhythmic motion was strangely mesmerizing. His eyebrows drew together as flitting memories of them at the wedding chapel lurked at the edges of his mind. They slipped away, leaving him in the dark once more.

Nothing made sense. Seeing her, being close to her, felt confusing and maddening.

Allan stepped closer to her. No, he was drawn to her, but his voice sounded harsh to his ears, but it wasn't from anger. He wanted her, in a way he'd never desired any other woman. His Ice Queen was destined to melt in his arms. "You have a gentle touch."

———

"Dawn has never complained. She waits for this after our rides."

Rosalind paused for a heartbeat as Allan moved into Dawn's stall. He stood too close for comfort. His musky, spicy scent was a pleasant alternative to the barn's usual odors. Outlandish, but somehow it felt right.

She remembered wanting to glide her hands over his almost naked body in the hotel room. Oh lordy-lordy, she had wanted to touch his six-pack and his broad shoulders and chest.

What had triggered that memory all of a sudden?

"Rosalind…" He murmured her name, and she turned.

When had he moved so close to her?

Before she could react, Allan engulfed her within his arms, kissed her mouth and sifted his hand through her loose hair. Her lips pressed firm against his. As in Vegas, his mouth created a fervent pleasure, weakening her resolve. The brush dropped from her hand, and she wrapped her arms around him.

Take that, City Boy.

Lost in sensuality, she wondered who was really in charge. She moaned when his cool, ungloved hands found their way inside her jean jacket. Her skin tingled as his fingers explored every inch of her back. The pressure of his need pressed against her. To her dismay, his mouth left her lips.

"Let me make love to you."

"Allan..."

He kissed her lightly, cutting off her response, then his eyes met hers as their lips parted.

"I remember who you are. You were at the rodeo, in Vegas. I saw you ride your horse. I wanted to meet you, but regrettably we were asked to leave before I was able to make your acquaintance."

"You were drunk. You can't remember me."

Rosalind put inches between them but rested her hand on his chest. It rose and fell in a steady pace. She couldn't let him touch her again. She wanted to cave in to her own need of wanting him.

"I wasn't drunk. You were waiting for your turn to enter the arena and sat on your horse as if you owned the heavens."

"So, what..." she paused, swallowed. "You almost fell into the arena. I could've lost."

Allan shook his head, reached down, and took hold of her championship silver belt buckle, drawing her toward him. She gasped and held her breath.

"John fell into me. If I'd been drunk, we would've landed in the arena. I wasn't drunk. I'd had a reaction to some medicine I'd taken."

"No, you were drunk. You slurred your words."

He slipped two fingers behind the buckle and pulled her

closer to him. She gulped as her hands drifted across his broad chest.

"Yes, I probably did slur my words. I don't recall much after we left the rodeo. I thought I'd be safe taking a Vicodin for the pain in my knee. However, instead of returning to the hotel the limo took us to the bar for more shots. Booze and Vicodin isn't a good mix. That's when you found me."

She lowered her eyes, not wanting him to see her desire, as his fingers proficiently undid her buckle. She moistened her swollen lips, willing him to kiss her again. His breath touched her mouth.

She couldn't take any more of this foreplay.

Rosalind stepped to the side, out of his embrace, snatched the fallen brush, and hung it on the hook. Then she shoved Allan from Dawn's stall.

"Rosalind, please..."

"Don't speak."

Metal scraping against metal had Dawn nickering as Rosalind latched the bolt. "Shh. Sorry girl, I don't have time for more."

The lost warmth of his arms left her feeling empty. She wanted them around her even more. He was a step behind her and all she'd have to do was stop and turn.

Suddenly he gripped her arm and for a second time, drew her into a hug. "I want you."

Body to body.

Face to face.

She was forced to decide. "Do you get everything you want? I'm not interested in becoming a notch on your bedpost. Or whatever you use to keep track of your...women."

"Yes. *No.* At first, I wanted you for revenge, but since I've been here, spent time with you, all I want is to make love to you. Not sex. Making love."

"If I have sex with you, it will mean we're married. And I don't want to be." She couldn't fall under his spell. Again, she put space between them and checked the time.

Twelve-eleven.

The ranch hands would be heading into the bunkhouse for lunch at this hour after finishing up with the morning chores and other horses.

Maybe a quickie would get him out of her system.

"I'm not trying to trick you because of our damn marriage. You do something to me, Rosalind. For reasons I can't perceive, I enjoy the way your temper explodes. The way you walk. The way your hair smells like a fresh breeze."

"No, I don't want to hear this."

Allan took a handful of her hair and lifted it to his nose. "Mmmm, nice."

"Let me go, City Boy." Did he hear her heart beating? Could he know she was on the verge of accepting his proposal?

"See, there's your temper. It makes me want you more."

Rosalind opened her mouth to give him a piece of her mind, but he drew her against his body. Kissed her parted lips. She sighed as he gently sucked her bottom lip. As if on command, their tongues met.

As one they stumbled awkwardly backward, the intensity of the kiss remained persuasive until the rough barn wall stopped their movement. Her loss of breath momentarily brought consciousness to their actions. He wrenched her jacket off her shoulders, holding her arms captive by the sleeves. His fiery trail of kisses from her mouth to her neck had her heaving in anticipation.

"Your soft skin smells like a spring morning," he murmured between kisses.

Rosalind moaned as he nipped and nibbled the area below

her ear. She pressed her body into his, wanting more of his kisses.

He loosened his hold and his fingers skimmed over her shirt to her breasts. Her jacket fell to the floor, freeing her arms.

"Allan, stop. I can't. You don't love me. I don't love you."

Her tone sounded more like a moan than a demand. She forced her arms to stay at her sides as he kissed the area left open by her shirt.

Save her, Lord. He had charmed her.

Love?

Who needed it to enjoy what he was offering?

"You ride your horse in a very sensual way. I want you to ride me. We are married. No annulment would be necessary if you did."

She closed her eyes, fighting her inner self. The popping of her shirt snaps unnerved her. Cool air touched her skin as he tore open her shirt. She inhaled sharply as his fingers eased inside her bra and teased her nipples. She opened her eyes and gazed at him. He stared at her.

"Fine. It's here and now. No complaining like a mule about the cold or straw poking you. Sex. That's what it'll be. Just sex with no strings attached. Two adults satisfying their needs."

Rosalind pushed him from her and stomped to an empty stall. Spotting fresh straw on the floor, she grabbed three saddle blankets from a bench and threw them on top.

———

"This will be a first," Allan mused as he watched her preparing a bed for them.

He'd made love to women at four-star hotels, luxury yachts, but never in a barn. Not how he'd envisioned their first time together. She collected her coat and added it to the blankets.

Next, she removed her shirt and rolled it into a makeshift sort of pillow. He swallowed hard as he eyed her sexy derriere, and a tattoo that swirled along her beltline playing peek-a-boo every time she moved.

Lord have mercy on him. He was being tested.

Shit.

His hunger climbed by degrees that he hadn't known before. Allan stepped closer, mashed his groin against her butt, and gripped her hips. Her natural response of straightening up slowly and thrusting backward had him releasing a suppressed groan.

Surprised by her unconstrained, steamy desire, he wasted no time, and slid his hands to her breasts. He kissed the exposed back of her neck.

The feel of her hands sliding up his thighs and grasping his butt cheeks sent his craving surging out of control. She drew him closer. His hard manhood pushed against her. Rosalind's head fell back onto his shoulder, allowing him full access to her sensitive neck.

He found the front hook of her bra and quickly freed her swollen breasts. The minute he touched them he knew they were a hundred percent real, not man-made enhancements. The soft, natural, and yielding skin was more than a handful.

"Your breasts are beautiful. Why do you hide them?"

Not waiting for a reply, or expecting one, he whirled her, so she faced him. Lowering his head, he kissed one breast and paused for a second before taking the other.

Another tattoo. God wasn't listening.

She was killing him.

A single rose in full bloom with a stem that curved beneath her left breast became visible without her shirt and bra. The artwork was delicate, not overpowering like some of those old school tattoos. Gorgeous. He placed a gentle kiss on the red petals and tenderly traced the green stem with his thumb.

———

She whimpered and held onto Allan's shoulders for support as wave after wave of decadent craving let loose. **As if he** understood her want-her need, he stopped his intoxicating love licks on her breasts. The reprieve was short lived as he moved lower, leaving tantalizingly brief kisses in a path to her naval.

"An innie. I love it."

Smiling, Rosalind inhaled when he kissed her there. He stopped and tore loose her belt, opening her jeans. His mouth and tongue nipped at her panties, playing havoc with her fading self-control. His fingertips traced the jagged split heart tattoo on her upper thigh.

"Allan." Her knees gave way.

He caught her and tenderly laid her on the makeshift bed. "There are no words to tell you how beautiful you are, Rosalind. Three tattoos. Each one more intriguing than observing your ride."

"You find my works of art sexy?"

"I do."

"Do you have any?"

"Me? No." He laughed as he removed his coat, tugged his shirt from his pants, and undid the buttons. "Why a broken heart? Don't you believe in love?"

"It's personal." She was unwilling to break the sexual moment they were sharing by sadness. Time to change tones and get back to what they were about to do. "You're awfully slow at undressing, City Boy. Do you need my help? If you don't hurry, you'll be left hanging."

"Are we in a hurry? Don't you like what you're seeing?"

Allan kicked off the borrowed muck boots, unzipped his jeans, drawing one leg out at a time, discarding them with a flick of his hand.

"Plaid boxers. Nice, but the red ones were better."

"You're the one who's in need of undressing. You still have clothes on."

She had time to end this madness but couldn't as she let her eyes rake over his fabulous body. She smiled. Greenhorn on the inside he might be, but on the outside he bore the muscles of a bred stallion. He knelt and tugged her jeans along with her undies. Her boots stopped his progress.

"You have to take the boots off first."

"Right."

Rosalind chuckled as he tugged on one boot heel and almost went flying when it came loose. The second boot he gripped with more precaution. She helped and it slid off. Eagerness heightened her hunger for what was about to come.

"You ready to do the deed, Big Boy?"

"As if you have to ask. The proof is very evident."

And ready he was. In a sweeping motion he shed his boxers, now naked for all the earth to see, unaware of the cold, the horses, or the smells.

Allan knelt before her. Slowly his hands moved in a caressing motion up her calves to her thighs. His touch played homage to her broken heart tattoo until she threw her head back, enthralled at the unexpected and satisfying sensation.

Through half closed eyes, she saw him lower his head, and groaned when his tongue replaced his fingers.

To her delight his mouth and tongue worked as one and in no time, she exploded in an earth-shattering run of orgasms. She lay unmoving, drained by her uninhibited response.

What had he done to her? Tom had never made her feel like this.

Allan curled next to her on the makeshift bed, cuddling her close. "Have you come down from cloud nine yet?"

"Uh-huh," she murmured.

He stroked her hair and spine. Rosalind shifted out of his arms. Pushing herself up, the wintry air cooled her burning body.

Green eyes met blue.

"You ready for your ride, mister?"

His eyes darkened with desire. She saw her answer and straddled his bare hips. His hardness throbbed against her inner thighs. Half-sitting, she slowly guided it into her, savoring the sensation of the stiffness filling her.

With him nestled inside her warmth, she moved back and forth, bracing herself on his chest. Allan's eyes closed, his face revealing pure bliss and she grinned knowing she had him where she wanted him.

To heighten his pleasure, she pulled up slow, slid down slower. His groans of satisfaction encouraged her to do it several more times, only to be stopped by his hands on her hips. They held her in place, poised and ready at his tip.

"Rosalind, I'm ready to bust."

"Well, City Boy, you don't know how to ride a horse. Let me show you."

Bucking like a wild thing, she took off. Up and down. In her sweet torment, she heard his grunt and felt his pulsing release. Like hers, his came fast, and hard, spilling his seed into her. She collapsed over him, drained, and astoundingly fulfilled for the first time in her life.

CHAPTER SEVENTEEN

Wrapped in euphoria from their lovemaking, with only her hair encasing them, cold air ruined their moment. Rosalind shivered in spite of Allan's hands wandering over her back. The decadence of their self-indulgence faded.

She lay naked on top of a man she barely knew, in the middle of winter. And she wasn't one of those women who'd sleep with anything on two feet. A tremor of panic and apprehension coursed through her as deep shadows formed inside the barn.

Shit, what was wrong with her? Someone could walk in at any time.

"We need to make like the wind. Max will be arriving to feed the horses." She pulled away from him.

Allan's arms tightened. "Can I have another ride?"

Embarrassed, she bit his shoulder. He yipped and she used his surprised reaction to spring to her feet. Locating her undies and jeans, she snatched them up. He swatted her butt in retaliation before she escaped his reach.

"Ouch. You've had dessert."

"I'd enjoy a second helping. The first one was tasty, except not quite filling."

A huskiness in his voice compelled her to peer at him. He lay on his side, patting the spot next to him, visibly ready for a second round.

She smiled at Allan's very well-endowed manhood. It was definitely a ten. "Sorry I can't accommodate you. I've ridden enough for one day." Laughter edged on her lips. She tugged her jeans on and found her bra on top of his coat.

"Is it ever enough?" In one swift motion, Allan was on his feet and grabbed her from behind in time to cup her breasts before she closed her bra. Leaning into him, she confined his hands so he couldn't entice her into another ride as he whispered, "I can keep going all night."

"Breaking in a wild mare is hard work. We need to hurry. I told you Max should be here any minute. Aren't you hungry? I need to start dinner. Sam will be looking for me, too."

"Does this mean I don't have to pack my bags? I would like to stay a while. I could help you out . . . with stuff." Allan removed his hands and gathered his boxers and jeans.

"It's Thanksgiving tomorrow, and I was taught never to turn a hungry soul away from a bountiful table. I'm sorry for getting angry earlier. I have an awful temper. It makes me do things I regret later."

"I accept your apology. I tend to annoy people too. It's sad you won't be able to help those horses. Let me talk to the company for you. I'm good at negotiations."

As if on cue, the big barn door opened to admit Max, the very second Rosalind stepped from the stall. Thankfully, he was carrying buckets and wasn't looking straight ahead. She nervously peeked behind her at Allan, who'd managed to slip on his coat and move into the shadows.

"Max, make sure the horses have extra straw. The temperature is dropping. It's gonna be a cold one tonight," Rosalind seized a feed bucket herself.

His hat sat low in the front and despite his winter jacket, an outsider would think twice about getting into his space because of his burly body. He halted a few feet from the tackroom, and she saw when he tilted his head, his eyes held surprise.

She wasn't usually in the barn this late. In that instant the sexual thrill from the ecstasy Allan had brought about vanished.

"You still in here, ma'am?" He took out the toothpick he had in his mouth and then added. "Is there something wrong with Dawn? Or one of the other horses?"

"Ummm—no, I—I took my time." She carried the bucket to Dawn as a distraction to give Allan more time to dress.

"Extra straw, right. That's a given when it hits below zero. The other ten horses will be in heaven tonight. We brought the cats into the bunkhouse due to the drop in temperature. I heard about you not gettin' the land. We could've added ten more stalls to the barn. The guys and I were talking. We'd work for free, if you decide to go at it alone."

"My goodness, I wouldn't expect anyone to work for no pay. I haven't had time to think about it yet, but I'll work on the numbers this weekend."

Rosalind shifted her eyes toward the stall. No sign of Allan.

"Sure, let us know. Will you and Sam be okay tomorrow without our help?"

She caught Max glancing off to the right and she pivoted in that direction. Her mouth formed a tight line. To her dismay, Allan was emerging with his shirttails untucked.

Damn.

———

"Mr. Smith—Allan, my soon to be ex-husband, has agreed to stay the weekend. He's volunteered to get his manicured nails dirty."

Allan hung back in the shadows. Rosalind's words stung. His blood pressure increased. He rubbed the back of his neck. Her dismissal of him invoked memories of his long string of foster care parents, who'd uncaringly introduce him as their ward, never as their son.

He forced the uncomfortable feeling to go away. With a clearer mind he shoved his hands into his pockets and clenched his jaw. Gone was her kind, sweet, and sensual tone from moments before.

Manicured nails, my ass.

As if he'd ever step foot in a salon for one of those things. What could've triggered her temper this time?

Allan moved forward, determined to give his bride a taste of his temper, but her words stopped him.

"You found the outhouse. You must not be used to the cold. Were you in a hurry?"

"What?" Unsure why she was asking him about an outhouse. He didn't even know those things were still a thing. He caught the sharp rise of her eyebrows as her eyes flicked over him.

He looked down and saw his untucked shirt.

Shit. What in God's name was this woman doing to him?

Being used to quickies and nooners, he'd never failed to make sure he was presentable afterward. Allan casually strolled to Rosalind's side.

"I heard a noise, and I thought it might've been a bear or some wild animal. I—um—as you see I made a hasty exit. Sorry for my undressed state. Usually, only women I date are able to see me like this."

"Okay, then. We don't have bears here on the ranch." Max grinned and shook his head, causing his long beard to sway.

Rosalind's cheeks turned a nice shade of pink as Max marched to a stack of hay bales.

Allan shoved his shirt into his jeans. "Can I help?"

"No, I got it."

Max lifted the bale of hay as if it was a pillow and brought it to the middle of the floor. Allan was glad he had declined his offer of help.

"Call me tomorrow if you need anything, Rosalind. Have a Happy Thanksgiving. Mr. Smith, nice to meet you."

"Same here..." Allan tried to reply, but Rosalind's elbow hit him in his side. He glanced at her. She motioned her head toward the door.

Time to leave.

He took her hint knowing he'd dug himself into a colossal of a hole and knew better than to say anything else.

———

Together they headed out the door Max just came through. Rosalind's irritation rose in spite of the chilly air. The temperature had dropped, and heavy snow blinded their route.

The realization of her actions by giving him what he wanted weighed heavy on her soul.

Horse crap, he'd won.

He could go home, and she was still without the land she needed. Ignoring him, she set the pace and hurried to the house. She entered first and when Allan followed, the wind caught the door and slammed it shut.

"Wow. Burrr, it's cold here."

"It's Minnesota." The two words said it all. They took off

their coats and boots. He rubbed his arms. Rosalind rolled her eyes and headed to the kitchen with him a step behind.

"I'd love to stay for a home-cooked Thanksgiving dinner."

"Oh, sure, great. One more person."

"It doesn't mean I have to, I would have to kill the turkey, does it?"

She switched on the oven and leered at Allan. Her rage disappeared as fast as it had appeared. "Yeah, you will. Have you ever killed one before?"

"I've never killed anything before. I might have accidentally, you know...a squirrel once or twice. I don't even own a gun."

"Don't worry, no shooting involved. How handy are you with a hatchet?" She enjoyed his priceless expression. He was such a city boy to the bones. She tried not to laugh but couldn't help herself.

"I'll save you the aggravation. You won't have to hurt, shoot, stab, or hatchet anything. Sam hunted, butchered, plucked, and washed the turkey yesterday."

"Pluck? You mean pull feathers out of a...turkey?"

"Yes, it can't be cooked with its feathers."

"Right," Allan echoed.

"Have you ever cooked a turkey?"

"No, I have Tiffany, my assistant, call the corner butcher for a fresh turkey. They deliver it and I hire a chef for the day."

"Oh my God, are you for real?"

"Do you want me to hire one to come out here?"

Delightful shivers pulsed through her with each step he took. She leaned against the counter with her hands behind her. Her breath stuck in her throat at his nearness. When he reached for her, she closed her eyes, ready for his lusty kiss. Ashamed, she wanted him too. Instead of the pressure of his lips, his hand touched her hair. She exhaled and opened her eyes to find a piece of straw in her face.

"Oh, thank you."

He laid it on the counter and grinned, still within arms' reach.

"If you don't mind, I'll wash up before we eat."

"Sure. Go ahead. Dinner will be ready in about forty-five minutes."

As soon as he'd gone, Rosalind sat at the table and hung her head. Several pieces of straw fell onto the table as a cruel reminder of what she'd done.

This was all wrong.

She was supposed to hate him, not invite him to stay. She wanted a divorce. She didn't want to be tied down to anyone. What was she doing falling for the man she married?

More questions arose, adding to her confusion. Should she give in to her own sexual needs? He'd asked for seconds.

Pig shit.

Now that she'd tasted the honey he could provide, she wasn't ready to abandon the sweetness of the pot yet.

His touch ignited a fire in her unlike any of the cowboys she knew. An ache between her legs reminded her what he could do to her.

Friends or enemies?

Better to be friends, she decided. New rules. Allan's suggestion to call the new owners of the land could work to her advantage.

She stood, crossed to the refrigerator, and took out pork chops to fry for dinner. As the pan became hot, the meat sizzled, and then the sound of the sputtering water heater generated thoughts of Allan's naked body in the shower.

———

Allan's phone rang when he reached the bedroom.

"Hello."

"Mr. Smith, where have you been? I've been trying to call you for the last hour."

"Sorry, Tiffany. The signal is bad here."

"I have some information on Sam. His name is Samuel Hughs. No relation to your wife's family."

"A friend?"

"Could be. He used to participate in rodeos. Hasn't competed in years. I found out he's been visiting a cancer clinic in St. Cloud," Tiffany said.

"How did...never mind. Cancer. How bad?"

"I couldn't get much info. I did however find out your wife is worth millions. Not as much as you, but close."

"Millions?"

"Yes, sir. One part is the trust from her grandfather. If you calculate in the horses and the value of the ranch—."

"How come I've never met her?"

"Excuse me, she's a cowgirl from Minnesota."

Tiffany was right. Rosalind wasn't the normal spa-polished woman that caught his attention. She could be, should be, living in a mansion, not here in the middle of nowhere. Instead, she was using all her finances to rescue horses. A real purpose. Not spending it on tangible items or extravagant things like the women he knew.

The pictures Sam had shown him left him feeling nauseated. The horses were severely abused, and the shelters couldn't afford to care for them any longer. There were some very sick people in the world who needed to be punished for being cruel to animals. The true mystery of why Rosalind wanted her inheritance so bad finally came to light.

Man, he'd acted selfishly. He was such a heel.

He'd ruined her dreams to save them. All because he'd been pissed off. How could he reveal to her he owned the land?

No, they both owned the land since they were husband and wife. Not only in name, but in the meaning now too.

"Mr. Smith, are you there?"

"I'm here. Did you find anything else?"

"No. Paul wants to know when you will be returning. He said to call him."

"I'm staying the weekend. Tell the pilots to go home. Have them come back on Monday and let Paul know I'll touch base with him then also. Thanks, and have a great turkey day."

"Will do. I've been checking on a cruise in April, and a stay at a castle in Ireland."

"Anything you want. Absolutely. But don't confirm any dates until I return." Allan smiled when he heard her laughter. Leave it to Tiffany to find the most extravagant vacation as retribution payment.

When they disconnected, he wondered what happened to his original plan. He'd succeeded in his main goal to have sex with Rosalind and gained property to add to his portfolio. All in only two days. He should be ecstatic, on his way home, and interviewing for a new live-in girlfriend.

However, an image of Rosalind on top of him wouldn't leave his mind.

He cast off his shirt and a blade of straw fell on the floor. Allan saw his socks were covered with them too. As he shed his remaining clothes, more fell. It was worse than sand.

Tucking a towel around his waist, Allan left his room, and crossed the hall to the bathroom. He turned on the water and waited until steam filled the air before dropping the towel. He stepped into the shower, closed his eyes, and let the hot spray hit him as thoughts of Rosalind returned.

He hadn't expected her to be so skillful in a bed of straw, no less. She knew how to please a man. She'd been so uninhibited. Women he'd dated would never have stripped naked in the middle of a barn, or for that matter in the cold. They'd been high maintenance, but not Rosalind. She wouldn't be.

He lathered the soap and washed his hair. More straw fell to the drain. The swirling of it reminded him of the tattoo on her lower back. When she'd thrown down the blanket and he'd seen it, he lost his senses. The design was exceptional, angel wings surrounding a symbol. He'd have to ask her what that one meant. He could vividly recall the other two.

The stem of a rose began under her left breast and ran upward, curving along the inside swell and up the valley between. The flower in full bloom exploded on a section of her breast.

Magnificent.

No one would be able to see it unless she was topless. It was hidden very well. Without provocation he hardened with desire.

And the last one, a heart cut in half.

Personal?

Was it for an ex-lover?

The mystery behind the meaning had him experiencing jealousy. Something he vowed never to feel since leaving the foster care system. When other kids were chosen or adopted, he'd felt hurt, sadness and the green with envy bug hit him. But after he'd turned sixteen, he knew no one would want him and he'd be on his own.

He stepped from the shower, foregoing a much-needed shave as a wonderful smell filled the room. His stomach rumbled and interrupted his fantasies.

"Sam. Allan. Dinner is ready."

He opened the door. "Be there in a minute."

Walking to his room, he toweled dry his hair. He heard Rosalind call to Sam again. He didn't hear a reply, except the stairs creaked, then the sound of footsteps above his head. He tilted his head and reached for his pants.

Suddenly an ear-piercing scream vibrated throughout the rooms. Allan raced from the bedroom, taking the stairs two and three at a time. Another scream pierced through the house. He rounded the corner and charged through an open door. Rosalind sat on the bed next to Sam, holding him.

Allan rushed to her side as she stood, her eyes glazed. He checked Sam's wrist. "He has a pulse."

"But his eyes won't open."

"Rosalind, call nine-one-one."

She didn't move, just stood at the end of the bed.

"Nine-one-one. Call nine-one-one!"

She snapped out of her trance-like state, patted her pockets, and darted from the bedroom. He heard a muffled conversation as he sank to the mattress next to Sam.

"Come on, old man, open your eyes."

Allan sensed Rosalind in the doorway and turned. Tears streamed down her cheeks.

"Don't let him die. I can't lose him, too!"

"How long will it take for the ambulance?"

"About thirty to forty minutes." She choked on a sob. Her hands gripped the doorframe.

"Would it be faster to drive ourselves?"

"I'm not sure. It's snowing pretty hard. What's wrong with him? He was fine earlier."

"Maybe a stroke. I don't know." Allan knew better than to reveal what Tiffany had found out about Sam visiting a cancer clinic. He pulled the blanket up to Sam's chin.

Did Rosalind know Sam had cancer? Should he say something?

"A stroke?" Her face lost color. She used the doorframe to steady herself. "My grandfather died of a heart attack."

"I'm not sure," Allan answered in the most calming tone he could muster. He wondered if he'd have two patients. "He's still breathing which is a good sign. Why don't you go downstairs and wait for the ambulance. I'll stay here with Sam."

"All right. I need to turn off the stove and oven. I'll get everything ready so we can leave when they arrive."

He saw the anguish on her face before she disappeared down the hall. Allan took out his phone and slid his finger over the screen. Thank God, he had four bars.

Time to call in some favors.

CHAPTER EIGHTEEN

A pulsating, whirly noise compelled Rosalind to rush to the front window. She stared out in awe at the scene. A Flight-for-Life helicopter landed in her driveway and three paramedics jumped out and ran toward the house.

Go for blazes. What the hell?

She sensed Allan behind her. "How did they know to come? It looks like something from a movie. Where's the ambulance?"

"It's not coming. You said it would take more than a half hour for the ambulance to arrive, so I called the Flight for Life."

"Thank you so much. Is Sam, okay?" She brushed at the tears on her cheeks as they walked to the front door.

"I'm no doctor, but he's still breathing." Allan flung open the door, allowing the three paramedics inside.

"Where's the patient?" One of them asked, holding a case.

"Upstairs. The first room to your right."

The three men dashed up the stairs after Allan had given them directions. Rosalind followed them. Sam lay on the bed unresponsive while the men worked on him. An IV was inserted into his arm.

"Miss, is he allergic to anything?"

"No—I'm not sure. Is he going to die?"

"We have him stabilized for transport."

Rosalind leaned against the wall sobbing. Allan's arm slid around her, drawing her against him.

"Is there anything we can do?"

Allan's words brought her to a point of realization she hadn't been paying attention to Sam's needs for a while. How could she have missed that he was this sick? She raised her hand to cover her moan.

"It'll be okay," Allan murmured in her ear, tightening his arms.

She turned and laid her head on his chest. Closing her eyes to hide the scene in front of her didn't work. She still envisioned it.

"We're ready to take him down," an EMT stated.

"I'll get my coat. I'm coming too." She pushed out of Allan's arms.

"We won't be able to fly with them, Rosalind. Sam will get there quicker."

Moments later the EMTs wheeled Sam from the house, across the snow-covered yard, and loaded him into the helicopter. It took off in a rush of air, followed by a machine created blizzard.

Max, Walt, and Joe joined Allan in the yard while she ran to her truck.

"Rosalind no! I'll drive," Allan yelled.

"We have to leave now. You can't tell me what to do."

She slid into the drivers' seat, but an arm reached over her and grabbed the keys out of her hand. "What the hell? Give them back to me!"

"Rosalind, calm down. He's in good hands. He wouldn't want you to do anything rash. Do you have your purse? You don't even have your coat on. Let's go back inside and prepare to leave the right way."

The tears froze on her face as he led her back to the house. She wandered from room to room, unable to concentrate. As she waited impatiently at the door, she saw a Sheriff's car come into view.

"They'll be our escort to the hospital." Allan zipped up his coat. "Are you ready?"

"Does a chicken lay eggs? Yes, I shut off the stove. I have my purse and I have on my coat."

"That's the Rosalind I've come to know. I'll drive."

"Oh no, not in your rental. My truck will do better in the snow."

"All right, but you're still not driving."

"Fine." She handed him the keys.

They hurried out of the house. Bright blue and red lights flashed through the dark night. Rosalind's fear knotted inside her as they flickered. The truck lurched and she braced herself when Allan pressed the pedal to the floor to haul ass, keeping pace with the police car.

Why had her whole life been such tear squeezers? Just when she thought things were going good, something bad had to happen.

"He'll be fine."

She didn't want to answer him and lowered her head from the distracting lights.

"Rosalind, be strong. I'm here for you."

Allan's calm voice soothed her. He reached over and took her hand. She felt his strength. This act of kindness was all it took for her to focus on him with tearful eyes.

"The night my parents died, I was riding in my grandfather's truck, and we followed an ambulance. The lights remind me of that night." She wiped at her tears with one hand, and left her other hand in his, thankful for the support. Allan's fingers tightened on hers.

"My father's name was Marty. I loved him so much. He was the best dad ever. He always had time for me and was funny. As a family, we went on many exciting adventures, both at home and at the rodeos. He'd been the top bronco rider at the time. Everyone came to see him ride and to try to beat his best time. He still holds a handful of records. Susan, my mother, was my dad's and the circuits' rodeo queen and barrel rider...like me. She taught me how to ride and treat the horses. It's sad. I was too young to perceive what it was all for."

"I'm not an expert, but you're very good."

Allan merged onto the highway.

"Thanks. Granddaddy completed my training. He'd taught my mother too. The day of the accident we'd all been returning from a competition. I'd fallen asleep in the backseat of the truck, but my mom's screams woke me. I heard tires squealing, horns honking, and glass breaking."

"You don't have to talk about it, Rosalind. I lost my parents too when I was fourteen. And several of my friends lost their parents and grandparents on 9/11 in the towers."

"I want to talk about it." She blew out a breath. "To this day, I remember my dad calling my name. I'd never heard him yell like that before in my life. I told him I was fine, but something was blocking my way from sitting up. He told me to lie very still, and said the situation was like hair in the butter."

"Hair in the butter?"

She broke into a reminiscing smile for just a moment. "It's a saying my dad loved to use whenever he couldn't figure out something. He called my mom's name repeatedly. She didn't answer. There was only silence. My dad swore. You see, he never used those kinds of words in front of me before. My dad told me to be a big girl, and someone should be coming very soon to help." Rosalind choked back tears and wiped at her eyes. "I didn't want to be a big girl. Damn it, I was only eight years old."

"I'm so sorry. There's nothing I can say. My parents also died in a car crash, but I wasn't with them. The police came to the house. I remember it clearly too."

"How awful. I didn't know. I'm sorry. I know personally that words don't help. Are you sure you want to hear the rest?"

"I do."

Rosalind eyed the flashing lights and took a deep breath.

"My dad continued to talk to me until we heard voices. My Grandpa Rodney was the first person to reach the truck and us. I cried out how scared I was, but no one answered. It was like they'd forgotten about me. I was alone, but I heard my grandfather's, my dad's and several other voices all talking at once. I couldn't see anything. I couldn't move. I don't know how long I waited before someone told me to unbuckle my seatbelt. After I did, the voice told me to crawl toward the front of the truck.

"A tree limb had come through the windshield all the way to the backseat of the truck. If I hadn't fallen asleep lying down, I would have died too."

"Oh my God, Rosalind."

She swallowed the lump in her throat and wiped her eyes. "They helped me crawl through the opened windshield. I tried to," she paused and took a breath, "to see my mom, but I couldn't. It was too dark. My dad kept telling me to look at him as the men hauled me out. He'd protected me even though he sat there knowing he was dying himself."

She stopped, unable to share the rest of the horrific scenes and memories.

"I'm so sorry. No child should have to go through what you

did. It's one thing to lose your parents when you're older but losing them when you're young is harder."

She heard the strength and the sincerity in his words.

Maybe he wasn't such a City Boy after all.

"It was the last time I talked to my dad. The ambulances arrived. It was too late for my mother, she'd died on impact when the truck hit the trees. They tried to save my dad, but he died at the hospital of internal bleeding."

"Did you see him again?"

"No. He spoke his last words to me as the men helped me through the broken windshield. He told me to never forget that they loved me very much."

"Do you know the reason the truck went off the road?"

"Yes, my father hit an elk. He swerved to save the trailer of horses we'd been pulling. The road was wet, and he lost control of the truck. He hit several trees when he went off the road. No horses were lost that night, although two precious lives were taken." Rosalind shivered in spite of the hot blowing air from the vents. "My grandfather was always there for me until he died almost five years ago. And then I had Sam. He was, is my grandfather's best friend. I don't know their entire story. All I remember is he has been at the ranch for many years. I can't lose him too. He's all I have left of what I can call family."

Neither said a word when she finished. The silence deepened. The past faded away. Rosalind regarded the man driving her truck.

Allan did things she never thought a man like him would consider doing. He'd taken control, stayed with Sam, called in the Flight for Life, and talked to the paramedics in a commanding tone. While they worked on Sam in the bedroom, he'd called Max and told him to take care of the horses. And he'd simply driven her to the hospital.

He's done everything without complaining. Who was he?

These things weren't what a wealthy tenderfoot from New York was supposed to do. He wasn't anything she'd expected him to be.

At times, his tenderness and gentleness, especially during their wild lovemaking, surprised her. She'd caught a glimpse of something in his expression which showed her he wasn't like any other man. She knew he'd held his tongue several times when she'd made him livid.

The truck jerked. She blinked. The past disappeared as the flashing lights stopped. They'd arrived at the hospital.

She didn't want to go inside to hear what the doctors or nurses had to say. What if Sam was dead?

But, that question, she knew to be false. Her heart was telling her Sam was alive.

"The helicopter is here. Ready to go in?"

She nodded. "I'm worried about Sam. He's never been sick before. I don't know what I'll do if I lose him."

It was hard for her to let Allan see how weak she'd become. No one had ever seen her cry at the ranch, but here he was, about to see it for the millionth time in a couple of days.

When they entered the ER, Allan took charge again and she allowed it. He offered her a bottle of water which she held onto almost like a shield. She kept an eye out for the white coats and jumped, dropping the water, when two doctors entered to greet them.

"How is he—Sam? Is he alive?" Her voice sounded strained to her ears. She cleared her throat.

"Yes, and he's resting. Mr. Hughs' body has shut down. His cancer has progressed faster than we thought it would."

"Cancer?" She stared at the doctor. "No, that can't be true. He's tired, that's all. He said he had a stomachache and had a flu bug."

Sam had cancer.

When had that happened? He'd never told her.

The doctor slid his hands into the huge white pockets of his smock. "Ms. Dunne, he has Stage Four lung cancer. At this point all we can do is make him as comfortable as possible. He is a DNR, do-not-resuscitate patient."

"No. No, you're lying." She squeezed her eyes shut and shook her head.

"Rosalind..."

"They're lying." She opened her eyes and scanned the doctors' faces. The truth was on them. Unable to process their looks of pity, she stormed from the room and left Allan alone to contend with them.

Sam was dying. He might not make it through the night. He couldn't cash out and leave her alone. Why hadn't he told her about his cancer?

She needed him in her life.

Question after question raced through her mind as she bolted from the hospital. She embraced the cold air, feeling it ice her skin and her temper. She didn't have a plan.

Rosalind needed to escape. The doctors hadn't even tried to use baloney words. Their non-emotional voices rippled through her mind and her body making her weak. She flung her arms in the air.

"Why, God? Haven't you taken enough from me?"

Didn't death mean anything to doctors? They simply told her without any sugar coating, or beating around the bush that Sam was going to be making the big jump to greener grass.

Fresh tears froze on Rosalind's cheeks as they tried to fall in the bitter cold. She detected someone behind her and knew it was Allan. The moment his arms encircled her, she broke down and lost control of all her bridled emotions, sobbing.

They clung together in the cold night, gathering warmth for their hearts, souls, and bodies.

"You're shivering. We should go inside. The doctor said you'd be able to see Sam when they move him to his room. He's awake."

She twisted, laid her head on his chest. Kept her face hidden until her wracking sobs subsided. "Allan, I can't. I want to, but I can't be strong for him. He'll see right through me."

"I don't think he's expecting you to be. I do know he would want you to talk to him. The doctor said he's been asking for you."

Rosalind hesitated for a moment, then pushed away from the security and comfort of Allan's embrace and studied his face. His words hurled through her mind. She had to be strong for Sam.

"You're right. I'm ready."

She followed him inside. The white corridors were quiet as they approached the intensive care unit. The glass doors made for easy viewing. She spotted Sam instantly.

He wore a breathing mask and a variety of flashing, beeping machines were hooked up to him. She didn't have a clue what they meant. It didn't matter as long as they kept Sam alive. As she neared the door, Allan released her hand.

"Don't make me go in by myself. Please." Rosalind grabbed his hand and looked at him, her eyes brimming with tears.

"All right, I'll be here for you as long as you need me. I won't leave your side."

Opening the door, still holding on to his other hand, Rosalind's fears subsided. Together, they advanced toward the bed and stopped. She paused, her booted feet planted, and her chin held high for an air of confidence.

"Sam?"

As if he'd been waiting for her voice, his eyes opened, and he smiled. "Honey, I'm sorry for all the trouble. I was looking forward to pork chop night."

In one fluid motion, laughing and crying at the same time, she laid her head on Sam's chest.

"Don't die. Don't let the grass call you over."

"Sweetie, you'll be fine. You are a survivor. I knew it the day I helped you through the broken windshield."

She gaped and lifted her head to stare at him. The voice from years ago, that had encouraged her to be strong, had been his.

"It was you, not Daddy?"

"Yup, I promised him and your grandpa I'd take care of you. I can't any longer. You have a husband now. It's his job."

He wasn't lying. His face told her. "Oh my God." Her voice quivered.

"Hush now. No tears."

Rosalind laid her head against his chest again, and Sam touched her hair with shaky fingers. He stroked it as he'd done all those years ago when she'd been a frightened little girl.

"Why didn't you tell me? Oh, Sam, you can't die."

CHAPTER NINETEEN

Allan met Sam's stare over Rosalind's body and nodded. The silent message was clear. He'd stay by her side and help her through the next days, weeks, and months.

If it had been any other woman, he would have walked away. Or better yet, run back to New York. Why was he acting like a damned knight in shining armor?

Rosalind lifted her head and looked back at him. Her now misty green eyes from sobbing her heart out caught his attention. He panicked as a shocking realization became evident to him. That he, Mr. Non-Commitment, had fallen in love with his wife as a man was meant to love a woman since the beginning of time.

With his heart racing, the truth struck him. Allan gulped for air as the room began to close in on him. The self-discovery he loved Rosalind seemed too much for him to acknowledge. With the object of his distress a foot from him, he backed away from the bed.

New York was safer. He knew what people expected from him, but here, he was dead in the water. An instant headache pounded at his right temple as he turned to leave.

"Allan, don't go."

Her cry stopped him. Rosalind was everything he'd avoided all these years. Her face didn't show love, only fear and grief. She wasn't asking him to stay because she loved him.

He couldn't and wouldn't leave because he loved her.

"I'll be back. Would you like... I'll find us something to eat from the cafeteria. If it's still open."

He kept all the emotion he could from his voice and used his hasty retreat as his liberation. He heard her call his name as he slipped out of the room but didn't turn. His emotional accountability had rendered him dazed and reeling. He roamed the corridors and half-heartily followed the signs to the cafeteria.

How in the hell had this happened? What a wake-up call.

Love.

Was this how John felt when he looked at his bride? Or the women he so coldly left behind when they said they loved him?

An image of Tiffany's smiling face flashed before him. She'd be laughing her ass off and opening a bottle of Dom Perignon to celebrate his dethroning as the King of 'Uncommitted Relationship Syndrome.' No one needed to know he'd been hit by Cupid's arrow. Not even Rosalind.

He didn't ask to love anyone but was very happy loving many women. These feelings he was having couldn't be love. He was a confirmed bachelor.

The words 'I love you' hadn't left his lips since he was a young boy. He wasn't about to say them now.

Allan reached for a sandwich when the lyrics to the canned music playing hit him. A teeny-weeny thing called a love bug. And how ruling the roost with many chicks got hit by funny feelings.

"It's fresh, sir."

He blinked and stared at the staffer who pointed toward the sandwich. "Sorry, thanks. Can I get another one of these?"

"Sure thing."

To hide his embarrassment of scowling at a harmless sandwich, he grabbed two bottles of water.

He was losing it. How could music be talking to him?

Going through the process of paying for the food, he once again walked as if in some sort of bad daydream.

He didn't have time to deal with a marriage and a wife. That's why he had come here to end his unimaginable husband status. He needed to sign the divorce papers and fly this coop.

The image of Sam lying in bed, riddled with cancer, came to mind. Allan slowed his pace.

He couldn't leave now. He'd promised to stay and help Rosalind. But if he loved her, why not stay married?

He had found their quickie in the barn exciting, yet only an appetizer. He wanted the main course and all the extras. Allan straightened as an idea flashed before him like a bull market before closing.

He could fly her to New York whenever he wanted. Or he could fly to Minnesota.

He foresaw a new Gulfstream G600 in his future. She'd be well worth the expense. But would Rosalind ever come to New York to visit? Her ranch and horses meant more to her than loving a man. She'd made that very clear. What if she refused to stay married? He couldn't reveal his true feelings. She'd laugh at him and leave him lying in horse manure.

Oh hell, her trustee was dying and here he was contemplating how to keep her with him.

So wrong on so many counts.

The glass doors loomed ahead of him. Allan paused to gather his thoughts and mask his emotions.

She sat in the same chair, next to the bed, with Sam's hand in hers. Her jaw was tight, shoulders squared, all body signs he was very familiar with in the business crowd. He'd seen it in people who were ready to fight for what they wanted. She was definitely the strongest woman he'd ever met.

He stepped into the room. "Rosalind, let Sam sleep. We need to eat. You need to eat."

She peered at him with glazed eyes, not seeing him.

Allan shook his head and stepped nearer. He shifted the food and bottled water to one hand and took hold of hers with his other, ignoring the tingling sensation the moment their fingers touched.

"Come on, take a break. He'll be okay while we're gone." He pulled her, and she followed like a zombie. They moved down the corridor and he found another waiting area away from the intensive care unit. They ate in silence, both absorbed in their own private hell.

"I should go to Sam. I've been away too long."

"All right. Do you need me to do anything?"

"The doctors say he only has a week to three months to live. Sam's admitted he's ready to go."

He heard the quiver in her voice and saw her struggle to hold in her tears. "I'm sorry. It's never easy to lose someone you care about."

"How can he simply leave me?"

"Sometimes people know when it's their time. They're ready. He's not doing this on purpose. He got sick. Sam must feel you'll be okay on your own."

"He won't be here to see our dream come true. He's the one who showed me what we could do to help all those poor horses I'd seen on television. I can't do it on my own."

"I'm sure—"

"No. Just because we had sex doesn't give you any rights.

Don't try to make me feel better." She tore her gaze away from his. "Thanks for supper. I'm going back in."

"Rosalind."

"I don't need your sympathy. Or for you to feel sorry for me. You got what you came here for, so sign the papers and go home."

They stared at each other, neither backing down. Finally, he sighed, "If that's what you want."

"You know it is. It's all I ever wanted." She stood, with her hands on her hips in a defiant manner.

"I'll stay till Sam is able to go home."

"Whatever. Do what you want. It's of no concern to me."

Allan reached out to her, but she brushed off his hand and stomped away. He watched her go, unaccustomed to being the one dumped. Unfinished feelings simmered. The need to comfort and hold her stunned him. He wrestled with uncertainty for the first time in his adult life. Walking to the family waiting area, he tapped his phone as he contemplated calling John.

Instead, he chose to text him.

Call me when you can. Odds changed.

The message was cryptic. They'd always used code. No one controlled the odds, only fate did. A rush of adrenalin filled him when his phone beeped.

K after turkey dinner.

Allan typed. *It's a portfolio problem.*

The message flashed, sent. He stared at the phone and waited.

K 4 real.

Allan smiled, pocketing his phone, satisfied John caught on how important it was that they talk. Real stocks and bonds were a lot safer than his portfolio of relationships.

He walked to the nursing station. An older woman sat

typing on a keyboard. "Excuse me, is there a room with a bed-chair?"

She looked up at him, nodding. "Yes, in the family room, down the hall. Turn left and it's the second door on the right."

"Thank you," Allan sighed with a half-smile. "Please have someone get me if something happens to Mr. Hughs."

"Yes, sir."

Allan stared at Sam's room. The curtains hung open. Rosalind still sat next to the bed. He hesitated for moment before turning away in search of the family room. Stepping inside, he reclined in the first chair he spotted. As he closed his eyes, he thought of his life without love and how he could change it.

CHAPTER TWENTY

"What the hell!" Allan's eyes flashed open as a burst of light ended his dream of Rosalind.

An older woman wearing a volunteer badge stood in the doorway. "Sorry, I didn't realize anyone was in here. Would you like me to turn off the lights?"

He stared at her volunteer badge, vaguely noting her name was Alice. The night and early morning came back to him, and he stood to stretch and ease his sore and stiff muscles. He rubbed his hands over his face, the growth of whiskers scratching his palms.

"You can leave them on. What time is it?"

"Six o'clock. Are you okay? Do you want me to check on someone for you?"

"Yes, I'm fine. No, I'll get out of your way. The nurse said I could use this room. Thank you, though."

A wonderful aroma of coffee reached Allan. His sleep deprived mind and body instantly sharpened. With widened eyes, and his mouth watering, he turned his head, forgetting his disheveled state. The woman held a coveted cup of coffee.

"Coffee? Where can I get some?"

"Before you get to the cafeteria, there's a coffee bar."

"Thank you. Three hours of sleep—need coffee." He needed coffee. Real coffee.

Caffeine cravings would have to wait though, until he checked on Rosalind. He stepped out into the hallway.

The corridors were active with nurses, doctors, and patients. He pushed the door button for the ICU doors and found her still asleep in a chair at the foot of Sam's bed. Someone had covered her with a blanket, but it had fallen off her shoulders, exposing her lace bra. The rise and fall of her breasts teased him with a tantalizing peek-a-boo show of her rose tattoo. Desire rippled through him.

What's wrong with him?

A man was dying, and he couldn't control himself around his wife.

An unexpected answer came.

Because he loved her.

How and when it happened was unclear, except now his plans were changing. Allan left her and Sam and strode to the nurses' station.

"Excuse me, can I have an update on Mr. Hughs?"

The nurse eyed him. "Are you family?"

"No. Yes. I'm Rosalind's husband."

"His condition hasn't changed. We've increased his morphine levels for the pain."

"Thank you." Allan turned back to the doorway and looked in. Not seeing any movement, he headed to the cafeteria for a morning cup of coffee. To his delight he found a Starbucks station and ordered a French Vanilla Latte and regular dark roast.

His mouth watered as the smell engulfed him. The first swallow was pure heaven.

"Ahhhhh." He lifted the cup for a second precious sip when

his phone beeped. He dug his phone out of his pocket. A text message flashed.

Three-three-three.

With only one bar, Allan set his and Rosalind's drink in a cup tray. Before obtaining full bars, his phone beeped two more times as he stepped outside of the hospital.

"Tiff, what could be happening at the office on Thanksgiving Day? We're closed."

"Mr. Smith...Allan, we have a problem."

"Clearly, since you sent the emergency code. I'm standing out in the freezing cold. Now what?"

"A YouTube video has been posted. Plus, more pictures in the morning paper and on the internet. The heading reads, *'Who is the turkey on Turkey Day? Mr. Smith, or his wife Mrs. Smith?'* The words Mrs. Smith are crossed out and replaced with Miss Dunne."

"Slow down, Tiffany. You're not making any sense."

"Okay, listen. The front page of today's paper has a picture of your wife, Rosalind, leaving your hotel room in Las Vegas."

"Who dared to shove my private life into the public's view?"

"I spoke to the editor at the *New York Times*. He said it came from an unidentified source, who also claims he can prove your marriage was a huge scam. The papers want to know if your so-called marriage was a ploy to drum up business and take away pressure from the Amazon insider trading investigation."

"Fuck." Allan stood motionless on the sidewalk, his precious cup of coffee going cold in the tray, unable to believe what he was hearing.

Tiffany's voice broke through his state of shock. "Paul is with me. He says the article gives a website and has several other pictures of you and Rosalind."

"What kind of pictures?"

"Looks like the two of you in a bar. And another, of both of you leaving the courthouse."

"Could they have been photoshopped?"

"Paul's shaking his head, so no. The other video is of your entire ceremony at *The Wedding Chapel*."

How in the hell did that happen when he couldn't even remember it? "What else?"

"Images of you entering the hotel, leaning on your wife."

"Can't you get them extracted? What am I paying you guys for?"

"I'm trying. Whoever this is, they are steps ahead of me. I can't explain it. My contacts have no idea who it is or who they're working with to get the pictures out there," Tiffany said.

"Goddamn it. I want the website taken down. Now." Allan paced outside in the cold to keep warm.

"We're trying."

"Do whatever it takes."

Tiffany sucked in what sounded like a fortifying breath, before adding, "There's one more thing. A second YouTube video of you and Rosalind in a very hot and steamy kiss in the Hilton Hotel elevator along with a timeframe has been released. To rivet the audience, it shows the time she left. Seven minutes."

With one hand holding the coffee to-go tray and the other the phone, he couldn't run his typical frustrated hand through his hair, so instead he kicked a snow chunk into the street. All of New York and the entire globe was about to find out they'd never consummated the marriage before when the divorce papers went public.

Rosalind wouldn't survive this kind of a scandal. He set the tray on top of the garbage can and rubbed his chilled fingers on his chin, the stubble prickling his hand.

"Mr. Smith, are you still there? Did I lose you?"

"Jesus, Tiffany, take it down. Have Paul call the lawyers to file lawsuits against the newspaper and the hotel. And I want to know who betrayed me."

"Paul's been working at it and says the site should be down within the hour. I wanted you to know right away." She paused. "One last thing. The press knows you're in Minnesota with your bride, not to have a honeymoon, but to obtain a divorce."

"Shit. You guys need to find out who is leaking this information ASAP."

"We are working on it."

"Keep me posted." Allan ended the call.

An ambulance with flickering lights drove by and his temper cooled, replaced by annoyance. Everything seemed out of control, his structured life in chaos.

As he stared at the hospital portico, Rosalind's face flashed before him. Should he leave to take care of business or stay to protect her? Tiffany and Paul would do what was necessary to stop the damage at the office, but here, Rosalind might need his help. Would his *Ice Queen* come to love him if he remained?

He took a deep breath. Cold air filled his lungs. This rural town wouldn't be able to take on the reporters, the paparazzi, and journalists he knew would be arriving soon. Absentmindedly, Allan lifted the coffee to his mouth and sipped.

Shit.

Instead of hot liquid, ice cold coffee hit his tongue. He threw away both cups and retraced his steps to the cafeteria for fresh and hot coffee.

———

Rosalind awoke to the sound of a nurse bustling around Sam's bed, checking his vitals. She straightened in her chair, alert, but tired. "How's he doing?"

"He's hanging in there. His morphine level has been increased."

Rosalind frowned, her worse fears gnawing at her fragile control. "That can't be good. When will the doctors see him?"

The nurse fixed the blanket around Sam and wrote on his status board. "Dr. Haarstad will stop by sometime this morning to see him."

"Thank you. Where can I get a cup of..." Rosalind paused, glancing at the door. Allan was holding a to-go cup in each hand. She took one and brushed past him into the corridor.

"How did you know I needed coffee?"

"A guess," he replied. "Anything new? I saw you talking with the nurse. Is Sam awake?"

"No. They've upped his morphine. I haven't seen the doctors yet."

"They're making him as comfortable as possible." Rosalind averted her eyes while she sipped her coffee, trying to control her labored breathing at the sight of him. Her knees had gone weak. He looked too handsome in his rumpled clothes and her heart began to pound at his two-day beard growth. "They want him to stay the weekend."

Suddenly, she longed for an escape route from him and turned away slightly.

"That's good and bad."

His hand settled at her waist, and she was tempted to brush it off, but its warmth and strength was a comfort.

Why was he still here? She'd given him his way out.

Dipping his head slightly, his voice softened, and she almost missed his question. "The cafeteria is offering a Thanksgiving Day meal of turkey and all the extras. Would you like to go down later to eat?"

"That would be nice. It'll be kind of weird, this will be the first time in years I haven't cooked the turkey." She moved to stare out the window.

"Is there anything I can do for you? Should I call someone?"

"I'm Sam's only family that I know of. Come to think of it, he's never talked about a wife or kids. Thanks for the coffee, though. Keep it coming."

"I can do that." He moved a step away from her, drumming his fingers on the paper cup. "Rosalind, we need to talk."

"Later, after I have a conversation with the doctor."

She turned toward Sam's room and didn't wait for him to follow. She reached the bed first, pausing at the sight of Sam. He looked so peaceful with his eyes closed, the thought that he might be dead crossed her mind, so she touched his hand. Then she felt Allan next to her and again, he settled his palm on her waist.

A gruff, harsh voice had her look toward the door. An unsmiling middle-aged man in a white coat walked in.

"Are you Dr. Haarstad?"

"I am." He held out his hand and took hers.

"I'm Rosalind. Can you tell me what's going on?"

"Sorry, there's nothing we can do for him that we aren't already doing. He is in the last stages of his cancer."

She raised her hand to her face as Allan took the cup from her. "What about chemo?"

"No. Chemo isn't an option. All we can do is make him as comfortable as possible. Mr. Hughs has a DNR order."

A soft cry escaped her. "I know, but—"

"It's hard to accept. We have to honor his wishes. I've ordered him to stay here in the ICU," Dr. Haarstad stated.

Rosalind folded her arms in front of her. "No, there has to be something else. Another hospital that specializes in cancer."

"I'm sorry, there isn't. I'll send up counseling to discuss the events with you."

Allan moved next to Rosalind. "Dr. Haarstad, have all avenues been tapped?"

"Yes. It's never easy at this point. We have obtained all his records. As I said, we're doing everything for him to ease the pain. I'll check back in a couple of hours."

Rosalind sat with her head in her hands as the doctor left.

Allan joined her and wrapped his arm around her. "Let's go eat."

"I can't leave him. Look at him. This isn't right. I realized that I don't really know anything about him. Only that he has been with my family for a long time. I let him take my grandpa's old room. He never spoke of any family."

"You need to eat, come on." Allan stood and held out his hand.

Even as she eyed him, ready to refuse, her stomach growled.

"See, there's your answer."

She grinned and reluctantly followed him to the cafeteria. Neither tried to make conversation. Once seated, she picked at a cranberry muffin, all she could handle at the moment. Not able to finish it, she pushed it aside. "I'm done."

"Should we get another cup of coffee?"

"Sounds great." Rosalind stood. Uneasiness swept through her. She didn't want his empathy, but his presence was becoming a relief and a norm.

With their new dose of caffeine, they walked back to Sam's room. The machines beeped, but Sam slept on, undisturbed. The afternoon progressed slowly. She and Allan took turns going to the nurses' station for updates.

"I'm going to stretch my legs. Ready for another coffee and a Thanksgiving feast?"

For a businessman, he couldn't hide his candid expression from her very well. Yet he hadn't complained once, simply stayed by her side, ready to do anything for her.

"Only coffee, this one went cold some time ago. Make sure it's a dark roast, no sugar or cream."

"Gotcha. Why don't you take a break? I'll meet you in the waiting room."

"I guess. I do need to stretch my legs too." After Allan left, Rosalind stepped to Sam's side and took one of his large, callused hands, squeezing it before she shuffled from the room.

The other rooms were quiet, and the nurses smiled at her as she walked past. The waiting room was empty. The only sound came from the television. As she paced, she glanced at the screen and halted in mid-stride.

What the hell. She was on the news?

Rosalind stood transfixed. It was like watching her wedding day from a bystander's point of view or a movie. She observed herself give in to Allan's kisses. Her arms went around him. They came together as if she couldn't get enough of him.

Now everyone would see how her body had betrayed her. Allan could see she'd yielded to his charm. She'd made a fool of herself and for what reason? Her shame came full circle, as a video of their ride in the elevator played.

"Rosalind?"

She turned toward the sound of Allan's voice. He stood next to her. Without hesitation, she raised her arm and slapped him.

The tray he held wobbled. "Ouch, what the hell!"

Seething with anger and mortification, Rosalind spat, "Why am I—are we on television?"

She searched for the remote control.

"Listen to me." Allan set down the tray with the coffees. "I'm sorry. Tiffany called to warn me—us. I haven't..."

She found the remote and pushed the volume button, drowning Allan out.

"...Rodeo Queen, Ms. Rosalind Dunne, couldn't keep her secret. We have learned this unknown woman has taken Allan Smith off the market. They were married in Las Vegas three months ago. As you can see from this video..."

Allan snatched the remote control from her hand and turned off the television. "I told you we needed to talk, but all day you've put me off. I only found out myself, this morning. I'm sorry, honey."

"Honey?" Hands on hips, she glared at him. "How dare you. All I wanted was to buy the land to save horses. Now look what I got!"

"Rosalind, please let me explain."

Her nostrils flared with new fury, enough to kick a hog barefooted. He'd known since this morning and hadn't said anything to her. Seeing herself on television in his embrace dredged up feelings she didn't want to remember. How his hands felt on her breasts. How his lips sent shivers down her spine when they touched her neck.

A new set of conflicting emotions wiped away her frustration.

She wanted him to hold her and make love to her. She wanted the release he'd given her yesterday in the barn. What choice did she have but to hide these feelings from him, he didn't love her?

"I don't want to hear your excuses. The fact I have you, a husband I never wanted, and not the land I wanted, is worse than getting kicked by a mule." She poked him in the chest with her finger. "To add salt to my injured ego, people will now think I'm a con artist or worse, a slut."

She watched as his eyes narrowed and he clenched his jaw. Good, she'd hurt him. Let's see how he liked it.

"No, it's not how—"

"Why didn't you simply sign the papers? If you had, none of this would've happened. All of this is your fault. We consummated our sacred so-called marriage. That's what it is now. A real marriage. Monday morning, I want the divorce papers signed and you gone. Out of here. Out of my life. Do you hear me?" Her voice rose to a screech as she raised her hand to slap him again.

The sound of beeping, echoing down the hall, had them both spinning around in unison. Nurses came from all directions. Two sprinted, pushing a crash cart, into Sam's room.

She and Allan froze at the chaotic scene unfolding before them.

CHAPTER TWENTY-ONE

"It's so sad."

"Can't believe it."

"Is that her husband?"

"Poor girl."

Rosalind cringed at the whispers but sat stone still in the front row pew of the church, Allan at her side. She stared at each person's shoes as they filed past Sam's casket and avoided eye contact with everyone. Judging by the number of people who'd drifted by, it seemed the church would be filled to capacity.

Her brain churned with too many thoughts to sort out.

Allan squeezed her hand. She blinked and turned to look at him.

"Breathe," he whispered.

Nodding, Rosalind sucked in some air. Pushed it out. Her tension eased. His reassuring pressure on her shoulder was a comfort too. The church organist began to play 'Amazing Grace' and the pastor stood at the altar.

Had an hour gone by already? It was too soon.

Her stress returned. Rosalind glanced from the casket to

the pastor. His voice lulled her as he eulogized Sam. Dry-eyed, she half listened. Memories of all the good and bad times whooshed by in muddled scenes as if they were trying to tell her something.

"Rosalind, it's time to leave." Allan held out his hand to her.

She looked at him. Without any further encouragement, she rose, disregarded his gesture, and walked to the closed casket. She placed her hands on it and tried to feel Sam's presence one last time.

"Goodbye, friend. I'll miss you."

Then it hit her, really hit her.

Rosalind groaned and lost all composure. Strong arms gathered her close. Through the fog of grief, she knew it was Allan. She clung to him for support and this time accepted his help as he led her away to the car. She sat in a daze during the short ride to the cemetery.

"Would you like to wait for the hearse before sitting out in the cold?"

"The last time I was here was when my grandfather died," she whispered. "It was spring, and the flowers were blooming. Very different."

"It's never easy."

Allan took her hand. His warmth burned her cold fingers.

"I see the car coming. You wait here. I'll come and get you." He squeezed her hand and she nodded.

Through the windshield she watched him walk to the black car, joined by Max, Walt, and Joe, all hands from the ranch. The four men and the driver lifted the casket and carried it across the frozen ground to the freshly dug hole.

The passenger side door opened. "You don't have to go. You can stay here in the warmth."

"No. I'm ready, Allan."

She placed her hand into his and allowed him to lead her

along the shoveled path to an awning where her friends waited.

With her shoulders and back rigid, she sat in one of the chairs. When the time came to lower the casket, Rosalind jerked to her feet, numb to the bone, and made her way to the car.

Allan climbed in and laid a hand on her cheek. "You should have started the engine. You're freezing."

She blinked. "I don't care."

"Then it's a good thing this rental has heated seats."

His attempt at a bit of levity helped, and the corners of her mouth turned upward for a moment. But for the rest of the ride, she remained in her own bubble of misery.

Reaching the house, Rosalind recoiled at the sight of several vehicles parked in the yard.

"I don't want to see or talk to anyone."

"They're here for you."

She opened the car door and trudged to the house. Time crawled by slowly as families came and went. Rosalind smiled when she needed to and spoke when necessary. Mostly she found comfort in sitting in Sam's old recliner.

The house finally became quiet.

Allan squatted next to her chair. "Rosalind, the last of your guests have left. Would you like to lie down?"

"Yeah, I'm wiped out. My face hurts from trying not to cry."

Allan helped her to her feet and escorted her upstairs to her room.

"Do you wear a nightgown?"

"I have flannel pajamas beneath my pillow."

He hesitated, made a move to go get them, but stopped. "Do you... I'll leave so you can..."

"I just want to lie down." Rosalind yanked off her boots.

In her stockinged feet, she went to the bed, heaved back the comforter, crawled in, and closed her eyes. Allan tucked the blanket up to her chin, and then kissed her forehead.

"Stay with me."

"Sure."

Though his reply was slow and faded, she felt the bed sag. She moved to the middle, but he wrapped his arms around her, drawing her near. She rested her head on his chest and sighed.

———

Loud pounding woke Allan. He uncoiled from a sleeping Rosalind and quietly left the bedroom. Scurrying down the stairs, he tripped on the last step in his haste and stumbled to the front door.

Max stood on the porch. "Good evening, Mr. Smith. The guys and I want to know if there is anything we can do."

"Come inside out of the cold." Allan massaged his stubbed toes as he motioned Max inside.

"Thank you, sir."

Max took off his hat and ruffled his hair as he entered, holding it in front of him. Allan shut the door and absently brushed his hair from his eyes to clear the sleep from his mind. He gestured to a chair, but Max shook his head.

"Not sure you heard. We might get some unwanted media attention and visitors," Allan stated. "I talked to Sheriff Hoffman. He's been in contact with the police departments in Brainerd and St. Cloud. Until we call something in, there isn't anything they can do. Can you make sure they don't come as far as the house?"

"Already done. The gate we installed will keep any scamps out. We're taking shifts too." Max ran his finger around the brim of his hat. "I could use more hired help."

"Make it happen. And I have a request. Do you know anyone who can cook?"

"Yes, I do. Her name is Helen, Mrs. Knutson. She's recently widowed and needs employment, sir."

"You've saved the day. I can't cook and Rosalind hasn't been eating. Will you ask Mrs. Knutson to come by mid-morning while Rosalind is tending to the horses?"

"I will. Sir, thank you for taking care of Rosalind. I had my doubts about you..." Max shuffled from one foot to the other and lowered his head.

"You're welcome," Allan interjected and squeezed Max's shoulder. "We'll take one day at a time."

"Right," Max drawled and nodded. "Okay, see ya in the morning." He put on his hat and left.

Once the door closed, Allan pulled his phone from his pants pocket and pressed Tiffany's number.

"Hello, Mr. Smith."

"Tiffany, any updates?"

"Yes, I was about to call you. Paul is closer to obtaining this person's identity."

"Great. Make sure our names don't appear in any papers."

"Will do. I'll email you a brief update before I go home. Remember, I have a husband."

"Yes, of course. Take him out for a nice dinner on me. Thanks again." Allan ended the call and hoped he hadn't woken Rosalind. She'd fallen asleep almost immediately when he'd taken her into his arms. He'd been on the verge of doing the same when he'd heard the knock.

Quietly Allan returned to her room. He found her still asleep and settled next to her. She curled into the curve of his body. He studied her pale face and didn't miss the dark circles around her eyes.

What was he supposed to do? He didn't know how to take care of a woman, besides buying them things.

He closed his eyes and breathed in Rosalind's flowery scent with a smile.

I'll figure it out.

———

Allan awoke when he felt Rosalind inch away from his embrace. Faking sleep, he opened his eyes a sliver, enough to observe her. She tiptoed from the bedroom. He heard the toilet flush and water running. He opened his eyes as he stretched and waited.

The water stopped and he pretended to be asleep again. She returned to the room wrapped in a towel. Rosalind glanced in his direction and dropped the towel. He forced his body not to react to her nakedness.

She slipped on blue undies and then her jeans which fit like a second skin. The waistband of the jeans hid her red, blue, and yellow tattoo. He struggled to hold back his desire. In the barn he hadn't been able to see the alluring colors. His need to have her, escalated to an unbearable ache. He unleashed a loud snore and rolled to hide his very evident hardness.

Rosalind turned. Allan groaned this time when she flashed her breasts at him and showed him her rose tattoo in all its glory.

She quickly raised her hands over her chest. "You awake?"

"I am. Want to come back to bed?"

"In your dreams." She grabbed the rest of her clothes and scurried from the bedroom.

For Christ's sake what was wrong with him?

He wanted her so bad it hurt. He ached to be inside her and run his hands through her long, soft hair.

"Shit. I'm in deep here. Pretty soon she'll have me riding and shooting like a cowboy," he mumbled and sat up.

He reached inside his jeans and adjusted himself before following her downstairs. The front door shut as he took the last step. He wasn't done with her yet. They still had unfinished business. She could try to run, but not for long. He'd catch up with her!

CHAPTER TWENTY-TWO

The sound of a car outside the barn stole Rosalind's attention away from Dawn. She used her coat sleeve to wipe at the fresh tears and gave her beloved horse a hug. "Crap, I don't want company."

"Is everything okay?"

Max's question jolted her. She'd forgotten he was in the barn. He'd been her shadow every day since Sam's death.

"Yeah. I'm tired of people lingering around me like I'm something fragile."

"They care about you."

"If you say so. Whoever it is can wait." She resumed brushing Dawn, blinking away tears.

It had only been four days since Sam had been put into the ground leaving her alone. All alone, she corrected herself. She missed his grumpiness, his half-left smile, and most of all his friendship.

"I can finish the chores," Max yelled from the other side of the barn.

"No, I'm about done. Thanks though." Rosalind dropped

the brush into her bucket. She wiped her eyes with her sleeve again.

"You know, me and the guys are here for you."

Still not ready to face Max, she puttered around in Dawn's stall. The memories of the last few days were too fresh, and a new round of tears fell.

Her argument with Allan still hurt. In her opinion they had unfinished business to deal with. If they hadn't argued about the news report on the television, she would've been with Sam when he'd had his heart attack and could've said goodbye. By the time they'd reached his room, doctors and nurses were crammed inside. There'd been no way for her to get close to Sam. She'd been helpless as a cow stuck in the mud.

The doctors said he'd lost the will to live. They were wrong. Sam knew how to die standing up.

Damn cancer.

Knowing her safe haven time was up, she moved to the door. "I'm practicing today."

She locked the stall door as Dawn nickered and Max stepped out from the storeroom. Placing the bucket next to the bench, she met him in the middle of the barn ready to put up a fight if he said no.

"Okay, we'll have everything ready. Let me know the time." He sighed and patted her shoulder.

"Early afternoon." She moved subtly and his hand dropped. Max's concern hindered her steadfastness to show no emotion.

"Sounds good. Dawn's been restless the last couple of days. She needs exercise. The guys want to know when they can get goin' on the new barn."

"New barn?"

"Yeah, since you lost Mr. Hillsboro's ranch, we decided to help build one. So, you can bring those horses here."

"Oh, no..." she jammed her hands onto her hips. Her thoughts went from one possibility to another, not wanting to succumb to defeat. "I didn't know. It would mean... We'll talk later."

Everything was Allan's fault. He'd ruined her perfect plan.

She stomped to the entrance and used all of her pent-up frustration to slam her hands at the barn door, pushing it open. A rush of cold air took her breath away and erased the telltale evidence of her morning cry.

"Can't the weatherman ever get it right? Sunny and forty-five, my ass," Rosalind growled. She eyed the recognizable blue and silver car, then dashed to the house.

Expecting the aroma of Mrs. Knutson's famous cinnamon caramel rolls, instead mouthwatering smells of fried bacon and eggs greeted her. Hunger pangs, sounding like a diesel tractor, erupted from her belly.

Oh my God, real food. Not that crap Allan had been trying to pass off as edible.

Discarding her outerwear, Rosalind went straight to the kitchen. She smiled at the sight of Helen, gray-haired and plump, standing next to the stove.

"Mrs. Knutson, what are you doing?"

"What does it look like, sweetie? A teeny birdie told me you weren't eating. Why the formalities?"

"Not sure." Rosalind hemmed and hawed, then looked at the table adorned with fresh, hot food. Her eyes darted to Helen as she took a pan of golden-brown biscuits from the oven.

"Thank you for coming. Those are some good-looking dough gods. My mouth is watering." She reached for one, but her hand was slapped away.

"You have to wait," Helen scolded. "I kept them warm for you. Go wash before they get cold."

Rosalind grumbled in an unladylike fashion, grabbed one, and stuffed it in her mouth before Helen could stop her.

"I told you to go wash. No dirty hands in my kitchen." Helen swished the towel she was holding toward the door.

A second roll found its way into Rosalind's hand before turning and heading out into the hallway. Her taste buds were alive as she savored the butter, her eyes closed with enjoyment.

"I heard Mrs. Knutson tell you to wait."

Opening her eyes, she saw Allan leaning against the wall with his arms crossed. The whiteness of his teeth only added to his bemused smile.

"I don't know what you're talking about." She swallowed the incriminating evidence, shoving her hand behind her to hide the other biscuit she held. "Now if you will kindly move. I need to clean up for my first real breakfast in the last several days."

"By all means, Madame."

She ignored Allan's 'I caught you look' and retreated to the safety of the bathroom. She crammed the second biscuit into her mouth and brushed away crumbs from her fingers. The mirror showed more evidence on her chin. Smiling, she washed her hands then dabbed at her face with a wet towel. She should be mad at Allan for having Mrs. Knutson come by, even though it was a nice surprise.

No one had cared for her since her parents and Grandpa Rodney. Allan hadn't abandoned her like she'd expected he would've done. He'd taken charge of everything.

Without his help, she might've been lost, though she'd have figured out how to manage on her own. He was allowing her time to properly mourn.

Why? The man didn't make any sense.

One minute he didn't want to be married then the next, he was making love to her. Now he was taking care of her.

Confused, she hurried to the kitchen.

Helen stood by the stove. "Do I need to check your hands?"

"No, I'm not a little girl anymore. They're clean."

Rosalind held out her hands to Mrs. Knutson for inspection anyway and joined Allan at the table. She shoveled eggs and bacon onto a plate and began devouring the food. In no time, her plate was cleaned, and she filled it a second time.

"Whoa, slow down." Allan placed his hand on her fork.

"Honey, hasn't this young man been feeding you?"

Rosalind shrugged and yanked her fork free. "He doesn't cook. And I haven't felt like eating until today."

A few minutes later Helen cleared the dishes off the table and wiped it with a wet dishrag. "Rosalind, when will you put up your Christmas tree? Max already delivered mine. Why don't you go get one today?"

Christmas tree? Shit.

She'd forgotten all about cutting a tree. Sam respected the tradition and had gone with her since Grandpa Rodney's death. Now who would go along and find that special tree? "I haven't even thought about it."

"Can I help? I'll drive into town with you to get one."

Rosalind stared at Allan.

Was he from some other planet? He probably had an artificial Christmas tree and used a plug-in imitating the smell of pine trees.

"Why would I go into town? I have trees planted on my land. I also allow my friends to cut down their Christmas trees if they want." She paused, took a sip of coffee. "Would you like to come with me, City Boy? You'll have to ride a horse and swing an ax."

"Ride a horse? Cut a tree?" Allan slid his chair away from the table. "Isn't it easier to purchase one?"

"No." Rosalind glanced at Helen who was stifling a laugh.

"Why waste money when you can grow your own? That's how it's done here in the country. Cutting one is more fun than slapping money down and lashing it to the top of your car."

"Oh, I don't know. It's cold outside."

"Of course it is. It's November. Helen, thank you, it's a wonderful idea."

She watched as Allan's forehead creased and his lips formed a tight grin. "Sounds like an adventure. When do we leave?"

"Be ready in fifteen minutes." Rosalind saw his discomfort and chuckled. "The breakfast was a real treat, Helen."

"Oh sweetie, it was my pleasure. You know how much I love to cook. Besides, your hubby hired me. He's so very polite and well-mannered. Wherever did you find him? He's a keeper, for sure. I'll be here every day to cook and clean. It was so nice of him. The extra cash will come in handy."

Rosalind's mouth opened to protest, but she closed it. Helen said she needed the money. And if Allan was willing to pay, why not let someone else do some of the chores?

"Yes, it was nice of Allan. Why don't you move in? Then you won't have to worry about driving to and fro."

Rosalind rolled her eyes at him innocently. She liked this game they were playing.

"I don't know." Helen paused and eyed Allan. "It would be easier."

"If Rosalind wants you to stay, by all means do so. I agree, it will be better."

Helen joined them at the table, deep in thought. "I can stay during the week and go home on the weekends."

"Great idea. I'm sure you have things you'd like to do at home." Rosalind smiled at her husband before she directed her attention to Helen. "You can put your things in Sam's room."

"Oh no, honey. I can't do stairs."

Allan grinned. "There is a first-floor, guestroom. Why don't you take that?"

"My goodness, you two are angels. I didn't know what I was gonna do come the first of the year. My husband, Henry's pension benefits from being a mailman will come to an end soon, and his social security isn't enough. I'd planned on selling my home."

Rosalind grasped Helen's folded hands. "Why didn't you say something sooner?"

"I'm stubborn. I prayed something would work out for me." Helen muffled a sob. "I'll go home to pack a few things. When I return, I'll start dinner. I made some sandwiches for lunch."

"Sounds good. It'll be wonderful to have someone cook for me."

"She means cook for us, and yes, the breakfast was the best I've had in a long time. Nothing beats a home cooked meal," Allan added.

"It was my pleasure. I enjoyed cooking for someone again. See ya in a jiff." Helen stood.

Rosalind stood too and moved to the safety of the counter as Helen dried her hands on a towel and left.

At the sound of the front door closing, she looked at Allan. "You have about nine minutes left to get ready if you plan on going with me for a Christmas tree."

"I'll be ready." He rushed from the kitchen.

She bit her lower lip, unsure why her pulse was racing. He was giving up the first-floor bedroom and would be moving upstairs. Did he plan on staying in her bedroom? Or could it be because she'd suggested he go with her to look for a tree? She should be telling him to leave, not including him in family things or allowing him into her bed.

CHAPTER TWENTY-THREE

Allan walked out the front door with two minutes to spare. He'd borrowed a man's coat, hat, gloves, and scarf from a hook by the front door. Rushing to the barn, his breath made white puffs in the air. He opened the big door, wrinkling his nose at the mixture of farm smells. Then, he came to an abrupt stop. Max held the reins of a huge black horse with a patch of white on its forehead, while Rosalind sat astride a smaller, reddish and white horse.

"Where's the horse from the other day?" Allan recoiled a few steps backward, not sure he was ready for this escapade.

"Dawn is my barrel racing horse. I can't take the chance she'll get hurt. This here is Ms. Red, and she's my workhorse. Mount up, you'll be riding Midnight."

"It looks more like the devil in an animal form. Is Midnight a boy or girl?"

Max chuckled causing his beard to go up and down. He moved the beast closer to him and heard Rosalind's stifled laugh.

What had he said to cause them to laugh at him?

"Horses aren't boys or girls." She chuckled and bent low

over the neck of Ms. Red. "They're mares or geldings or stallions. Midnight is a mare. And Ms. Red is also a mare. You do know how to ride, don't you?"

"I have—no, I don't know how to ride. I've only been on a horse once and it was years ago in Cancun."

Allan sucked in a breath as he eyed Midnight.

Holy shit.

This horse was a black monster and a hundred feet tall.

Rosalind sidestepped her horse to him. Ms. Red snorted and stomped her hooves. Allan scrambled backward, afraid of the horse's actions.

"Don't worry, City Boy, Midnight will follow my lead. She's well trained. All you'll have to do is climb on and enjoy the ride."

Allan took note of how Rosalind's cheeks turned a light shade of red before she turned away. He'd caught the play on words too. Yes, he had enjoyed their ride right over to the left in the stall. And he'd like a repeat.

"Mr. Smith, place your left foot in the stirrup and swing your right leg over."

About to do what Max had instructed, he held some sort of rope in his hand that was keeping the horse in place. "Right. Shit, I'm not sure..."

With Max's help, Allan lifted himself up and sat astride the horse.

"Now hold onto the reins."

"Like this?"

"Yup, that's good. Hold them loosely but firmly in your left fist. Move your hand to the left to go that way, and to the right, to have her step in that direction."

Max demonstrated and the horse's head moved. Allan repeated the actions and Midnight reacted accordingly.

He worked in downtown New York City and walked, took

cabs, Ubers or drove himself. What the fuck was he doing on top of a horse?

"Take it easy. You're doing fine."

Rosalind had moved her horse next to his and touched his thigh with her hand. Even through the glove she wore, her touch ignited his lustful appetite for her.

"I put the rope and the folding bucksaw in the saddle bags and tied on the bow saw. You're good to go." Max released the bridle.

Rosalind made two short clicking sounds and the horses began to walk as they left the area near the barn. She took the lead and without any guidance on Allan's part, Midnight followed. They rode single file for at least fifteen minutes, but it seemed like an hour.

Having enough of this outdoors stuff, he tried to stop the horse. "The snow is deep. We should turn around. I'll buy you the biggest damn tree you've ever seen."

She turned sideways in the saddle. "You're okay. My horses are used to the snow. We'll be reaching the path soon."

A tamped down path appeared. She'd been right. It did make the ride easier. Snow crunched beneath the hooves of the horses, giving the quiet an uncanny, natural sound. Allan found himself relaxing as he scanned the scenery of trees and more trees. It was magnificent, so different from his normal view of tall buildings with endless glass windows.

Why wasn't he missing the noise of zillions of people or being inside all day? Must be all the damn fresh air.

"What do you think of my land?"

"You own all this?" Allan swung his arm wide in front of him, almost dropping the reins. Rosalind snickered and slowed her horse, so they were side by side.

"Yes, I do. I've received several offers to sell, but no way."

Allan glanced at her. Gone was her grief. She seemed carefree, transformed from her stiff and abrasive behavior. Her red nose matched her rosy cheeks.

"It's so vast. Tiffany, that's my secretary, talked about visiting a dude ranch in Wyoming for a team-building event. I imagined it would be like this . . . not with the snow of course. In New York we get plenty."

"You should see it in the summer. Everything is green." She pointed to the right. "See the line of trees past the field?"

"Yeah."

"That's the land I wanted to buy. It would've been a perfect fit, with plenty of space for the Heavens Kiss Sanctuary I'd planned on opening."

"If you own all this land, why did you need the extra acreage? You could've built the barns here." Allan scolded himself for making the purchase of it behind her back. He needed to have Tiffany do something, anything about it right away. He'd created a monster of a problem.

"Most of my land is in what is called the state's *Set Aside Program*, so I can't use it. My grandpa thought it would be best in the long run. I have several years yet before the restriction ends."

"Do you want me to call the new owners? I'm pretty sure I can convince them to let you use the land."

"No, I've decided to add on to my existing barn for now. I'm going to use some of my money for improvements on the barns I already have."

"I'm sorry the deal didn't work out for you."

"I'm over it."

Her reply was hard and forced, then she urged her horse ahead of him. They rode single file along the snowy trail and despite of his trepidations of controlling the horse, he found the animal easy to command and relaxed. For the first time since they left the barn, he studied the landscape. There were so many trees it was hard to see when they ended.

"We're here. I know which tree I want." Rosalind called out over her shoulder and stopped her horse. Midnight halted beside Ms. Red. "We need to dismount and walk the horses in from here."

Allan dismounted and walked to her as she was about to swing her right leg over the horse's rear end.

"Oh, I don't need help." She ignored his hand.

"It's the gentleman's way. You know, as in helping a lady."

Allan grinned and reached up, setting his gloved hands on her waist. When her boots touched the ground, she faced him. They stared at each other. If it weren't for their bulky winter coats, they'd be touching. Breasts to hairy chest, their mouths inches apart. Always the man who never passed on an opportunity, he leaned in and imprisoned her sensual lips.

Time stood still as their mouths became one. The kiss, even in the cold, sent an unfamiliar warmth surging through him. Unsure if the crisp air and nature played a part, he only knew the feeling felt right. He slid one gloved hand around her and up to the collar of her coat, to her neck, possessively pulling her closer.

Ms. Red snorted and moved abruptly, breaking the drugging kiss. "Sorry. I couldn't help myself. Your lips were so inviting. Must be all this fresh air."

"Right. Good thing I'm not packin' anything right now."

"Do you usually carry a gun?" Not sure if she was joking or not, he took a step backward.

"Of course. Don't tell me you've never shot one."

"Okay, I won't, but then I'd be lying."

"For heaven's sake. Grab Midnight's reins and follow me."

Her words matched the cold, but he knew how warm and

yielding her mouth could be. He moved around Ms. Red and collected Midnight's reins.

"I'd follow you anywhere."

"What did you say? You have to speak up. The wind is blowing against us, so the sound is carried away."

He cupped his hands around his mouth this time. "I mumbled to myself that this wasn't one of my wisest decisions."

Her laughter didn't disappoint him as they reached a copse of trees. They passed several evergreens before she halted in front of a mammoth pine tree.

"This is the one." She stopped and unbuckled the bow saw from the saddle.

"This oversized thing? It won't fit inside your house."

"Yes, it will," she chortled. "You saw and I'll hold the tree."

Allan retrieved a rectangle-shaped object with a jagged blade on one side. "What is this? Where is the ax?"

"We don't use an ax on this small of a tree." She brushed snow off limbs.

"As you're so fond of calling me, I'm a city boy. This might take me a while." He knew he'd be able to do it but took a look at the tree and sighed. One of his foster parents had signed him up for the Boy Scouts, which he never went to, but he'd read about Paul Bunyan.

Allan knelt, held a few branches back, and positioned the saw at the base of the tree. With a deep breath, he tugged and pushed.

"Ouch." He stopped as the branch he'd been holding hit him in the head.

"You have to crawl under the tree."

"I don't need your advice. I was a scout."

"Oh, a make-believe woodsman. Next, you'll be saying you're a lumberjack like Paul Bunyan."

Could she read his mind? Or was he that predictable?

Ignoring Rosalind's sassy remarks, Allan got on all fours, then to his stomach, squirmed beneath the branches, and repositioned the blade.

She could laugh all she wanted to. Paul Bunyan wouldn't fail him now.

Push. Pull. Push. Pull.

"Almost through. Four more pulls," Rosalind urged.

The tree loosened, fell to the snowy ground and the saw slid into the air.

Groaning, Allan stood, breathing hard.

Crap. His knee was throbbing, a sign it was beginning to swell. What he'd give for an hour in a hot tub.

While his breathing returned to normal, Allan watched Rosalind tie a rope to the trunk of the evergreen tree. She stomped in the snow to Midnight and attached the other end of the rope to the saddle.

"I'm impressed. I lost the bet."

"What?"

"Max said you'd be able to cut it down. I said you wouldn't, and I'd have to do it myself."

He came up behind her. She turned and looked at him with widened eyes.

"Rosalind..."

He didn't give her time to react as he leaned in, kissed her, then framed her face with his gloved hands and deepened their kiss. She wrapped her arms around him, and he softly nibbled her lips to play a cat and mouse game with her tongue.

They paused for air. His voice held a husky tone despite the cold when he rested his cheek next to hers. "I want to make love to you."

"I want you too."

"Are you sure? I don't want a butter knife at my throat again."

"Yes, I'm sure, but you should know I do keep something hidden under my pillow."

"Besides your pajamas? I guess I'll have to keep your hands occupied. Are you inviting me into your bed?"

"I have a king size bed. It would be more comfortable than the twin bed in Sam's room."

She flashed him a speculative smile and he was at a loss for words. She had invited him into her bed. "We'd better head back. I have to run Dawn through our daily exercise. Plus, you have to clean out your stuff from the guest bedroom Mrs. Knutson will be using before she comes to cook us dinner."

"So, no afternoon delight?"

"Let's ride, City Boy."

CHAPTER TWENTY-FOUR

"Shit. We have company."

Rosalind looked toward the house after hearing Allan. Six vehicles were parked in the driveway. She halted Ms. Red. Allan and Midnight moved up beside her.

"Who is it?"

Allan's breath whistled between his teeth as he exhaled. "The media are about to descend on us. Sheriff Hoffman said he'd only be able to keep them at bay for a couple of days."

She heard the tightness in his voice. "Is this because of the pictures on the Internet?"

"Yes. I've been trying to take care of it. I've clearly missed their determination to find me."

"We'll go through the back door of the barn. It should shield us."

Another interruption in her day. When would it end?

She took out her cell phone and called Max. "We're on the south ridge. We'll come through the west side door."

"I see you. Good idea. Sorry, Rosalind. Walt left the gate open for a delivery. I called Sheriff Hoffman. He arrived a few minutes ago."

"Good. Make sure the barn and horses are protected. No one, and I mean no one, gets inside."

"Yes, ma'am."

She shoved her phone into her pocket. "Max said Sheriff Hoffman is here too. Allan, I want those people off my property."

"Let me talk to the sheriff. The media shouldn't have trespassed onto the property." Allan smoothed his gloved hand over his thigh. "Once we make our way to the house, you'll have to be prepared not to say anything, to anyone, no matter what they ask or yell. Can you keep your temper under control?"

"I can't promise much at this point. Come on Ms. Red, let's ride." Rosalind used her legs to urge Ms. Red into a faster walk. She glanced over her shoulder a few times, making certain Allan was keeping pace with her. If they weren't in such a hurry, she'd have found the scene funny. He had a hard time dragging the tree behind Midnight, but he didn't quit.

They were almost at the barn entrance when it opened. A frowning Max held the door. He grabbed the reins from her hands as she dismounted.

"They've been asking all sorts of questions about you and Mr. Smith. We haven't said a word."

"Thanks. Take care of the horses and have someone bring the tree to the house later."

"Yes, ma'am." Max moved and held out his hand.

Allan dismounted, yielding Midnight's reins to him. Rosalind motioned for him to follow. They took a couple of steps, and his phone rang.

He pulled it out of his pocket. "Wait, let me answer this. It's Tiffany, my secretary."

Rosalind nodded and paused, studying him.

When did everything get complicated? Here she was,

working with him, and all she wanted was to have sex with him again. But she couldn't. They didn't belong together. And she didn't want a man in her life.

She was so confused.

She tried to sort through her thoughts as he talked softly into his phone. His rigid stance was familiar. Sam's coat was too big on him, hiding a view of his cute butt.

Holy cow. One minute she couldn't wait for him to leave, then the next she wanted him to stay.

She'd fallen for him. Damn it.

He wandered from one side of the barn to the other. She peeked out the door, but her gaze kept returning to Allan. When he let out a string of curses, Rosalind took a step toward him.

"Make it happen. Bye." Allan pocketed his phone. "I thought my people had everything in check. How could they—how could *I* let this happen? If the culprit or culprits are not found by the end of the week, my company will have a new vice-president."

He laced his hands behind his back and rocked on the heels of his borrowed boots. It was clear he was upset. She'd seen him act this way before.

"Allan, now what?"

"It's the Internet again. More pictures were posted on the fuckin' website this morning. I'm sorry my staff wasn't able to control the situation."

Rosalind observed him. His tone was stern, and he looked madder than a charging bull.

"I'm not sure why you're letting this affect you like it does. It happened. We got married." She strode to the door. "We didn't have sex. They're showing the truth. I've nothing to hide. Do you?"

"No, I don't..."

Not giving Allan time to respond further, Rosalind unfastened the door. Immediately they were surrounded by reporters with microphones and cameras when they walked out.

"Are you and Mr. Smith married?"

"Did you file for a divorce, Mrs. Smith?"

"Who was the mastermind behind this scam?"

She stood stone-faced. The pressure of Allan's hand on her back was oddly reassuring. The crowd of people moved closer.

"You're trespassing on private property. I have no comment. You all need to leave." Rosalind disregarded Allan's whispered words to stay calm and marched toward Sheriff Hoffman.

"Mr. Smith, why did you pick a cowgirl to marry? She doesn't compare to the beautiful women you've dated in the past."

Rosalind halted in mounting anger. Allan ran into her. She shook off his hand, but he took hold of her arm. As she twisted to free herself, he released her but stepped in front of her.

"Allan, move aside."

He ignored her. "People...people, please excuse us. My wife just said you're on private property. If you choose to stay, the sheriff will have to arrest all of you."

Sheriff Hoffman pushed forward. "Everyone move aside. The Smiths have asked you to leave."

The men and women slowly moved and formed a path, their questions ceasing for the moment. Allan grasped her hand and maneuvered her through the crowd of media personnel as they resumed shouting questions.

Inside the warmth of the house Rosalind's embarrassment bloomed beyond the point of no return. She fell against the wall as tears flooded her eyes. She bowed her head to hide them, but he pulled her into the safety of his arms.

"Sorry, the media can be cruel."

His soft words surprisingly calmed her. Yet she had to wonder why he'd stayed. True, she was a nobody. Yet whenever he kissed her, it was as if he cared.

"Why don't you sign the divorce papers and leave? You've won. We slept together. You've made my life miserable, and I don't need this now," she sobbed, even as she wanted to remain in the comfort of his embrace.

"Rosalind—"

A knock on the door interrupted.

"I don't want to talk to anyone, Allan."

"Go upstairs and lie down. I'll take care of everything."

Before she could protest, he took her face in his hands and kissed her. This time his kiss was gentle, different from the one in the woods.

"I'm holding you to the invitation in your kiss. Go on, we'll talk later." He turned her around, so she faced the stairs and pushed her toward them. She wiped at her tears. A second knock prompted her to move faster. Before heading upstairs, she took off her boots, not wanting to leave a wet trail of snow.

Allan had opened the front door. "Hello, Sheriff Hoffman."

"Mr. Smith, I'm sorry. They're leaving. I'll have someone stationed out by the road. I noticed the new gate. Do you know how they got it opened?"

Rosalind paused on the third step to listen to Sheriff Hoffman and Allan.

"It was opened for a special delivery. Will you be making sure they don't step foot on my wife's property?"

"Yes, sir. Everything's in place. A squad car is on its way to park at the entrance. You might want to install motion detectors if you don't have them already."

A small grin eased some of her saddened mood. He hadn't claimed her property as his. A sliver of her independence was still intact. Rosalind took the stairs two at a time, their voices disappearing. Instead of lying down like Allan suggested, she went straight to the bookshelf in her bedroom. Pulling out an old photo album, she flipped through the pages until she found the one she wanted.

She touched the photograph. "Dad. Mom. What am I doing? Everyone is gone and I've made a mess of my life."

The family picture had been taken a few days before her parents' deaths. Her mother's hand was on Rosalind's rear, helping her mount the racehorse Mom owned, while her dad held the reins.

Look at our smiles.

Was that why she hadn't pressured Allan into leaving? Could he make those feelings return?

She heard the front door shut, clutched the photo album, and drifted to the window. A line of vehicles headed toward the road. Sheriff Hoffman and his deputies were getting into their cars too.

Would Allan be coming to make love to her? If he did, should she let him?

Rosalind straightened and lowered the album, her thoughts as crazy as popcorn popping in a pan. Nothing was making sense to her.

The stairs creaked.

Hurriedly, she shoved the album onto the shelf. She looked to the bed and then the window seat, not sure what to do.

If she sat on the bed it might imply, she wanted him. If she sat on the window seat, would it discourage him from taking her to her bed?

"Why aren't you resting?" He stood in the doorway.

"I didn't... I see everyone's left. What did Sheriff Hoffman have to say?" Her tongue felt thick, and her voice sounded raspy to her own ears.

Allan leaned against the doorframe, arms folded. Who

needed cowboys in Wrangler jeans, when she had a City Boy in them. She moistened her lips.

"Yes, all the media have left. The sheriff has assured me an officer will be parked out by the entrance. He suggested putting in motion detectors."

"I have them in the barn, but not on the house or entrance. I never thought..." Her breath caught with each step he took toward her.

One. Two. Three.

She staggered backward and slumped into the window seat as he stood within arm's reach.

"Your social status has changed, whether you like it or not. I'll call around and have the best high tech one installed asap."

His next stride brought him inches from her. He laid a hand on her shoulder. She cleared her throat to corral her roaming sexual desires.

"It's okay. I'll get Max or one of the others to do it in the morning."

"Are you sure? I'd like to help."

She hesitated, not knowing how to act or what to do with a man in her bedroom. His fingers massaged her shoulder and the tension eased. "Have you—when will you be leaving? I've told you before, I need to practice for my upcoming competition. I'll need the money to—"

"I'm not leaving. I've decided to stay and help you through the championship. I doubt we've seen the last of the media. Besides, we've got a date for this afternoon." Allan knelt in front of her, slid his hands to her face, and tilted it until her eyes met his.

Then his mouth took hers, pressuring her lips apart. Before he could succeed, she nudged him away.

"Don't. This isn't a good idea. I shouldn't have encouraged you this morning. The reporters are right, you need to go back home—back to New York, to the life you're accustomed to."

She refused to look at him.

Before she made a fool of herself and Allan figured out, she'd fallen for him, he needed to go. He could have any woman. Why would he ever want her?

"I can't. I made a promise to Sam. He asked me to stay and see you complete your competition no matter what happened. My word is as good as gold. You're stuck with me until then."

"This is wrong. Neither of us wants to be tied down."

"I say we make the best of our...situation. My appetite for some afternoon delight needs to be satisfied. Let me pleasure you. Our first time was rushed."

Against her better judgment, Rosalind let Allan brush his lips on hers for a second time. In a slow seduction he nuzzled her lower lip and freed her shirt. His cold hands prickled her skin.

She gasped.

His fingers weren't calloused, but smooth. They roamed her shoulder blades and unhooked her bra. She fought against the agonizing, but welcoming desire.

Why not enjoy what he was offering? He's a damn good kisser.

Succumbing to the crazy moment, she wrapped her arms around his neck and drew him closer. Their tongues devoured each other's mouths.

Breaking contact with her lips, he looked at her. "Do I need to be afraid of any hidden knife? Or what is beneath your pillow?"

"It depends on if you please me or not."

He laughed richly, lifted her into his arms, and carried her the few steps to the bed. She took the lead and started to unbutton her shirt, but he stopped her.

"No. I want to undress you."

And he did. One button at a time until her shirt opened. His fingers stroked her bare skin and slid her shirt off her shoulders, immobilizing her arms.

Rosalind shivered as his lips touched her skin. His mouth left a fiery trail from her shoulder to her neck. As her own needs leapt swiftly, she tilted her head to allow him full access to the spot below her ear. His tongue, teeth, and lips sent explosive currents through her.

"Allan..."

"Do you want me to stop?"

"Ohhhh, mmmm..."

"I'll take it as a no."

His words were a whisper of a gush of warm air in her ear.

Lost in the sweet euphoria, she moaned again as he nibbled her earlobe. Allan traced her rose tattoo with his fingertips.

"Your breasts are beautiful. Women pay thousands of dollars to have them look like yours. This rose is so delicate and enticing."

She smiled. Only one other person had ever seen it. *Tom*. He hadn't liked it, said it was the mark of a slut. Allan, on the other hand, appreciated the rose's beauty. She slid to the center of the bed, allowing room for him.

Before he joined her, he discarded his shirt and borrowed boots. Once he was next to her, Rosalind's hands explored his chest, enjoying the texture of the coarse hairs.

Allan tugged her belt off, unzipped her jeans, and yanked them open.

"Blue lacy thong? Aren't such things incredibly scandalous for a cowgirl?"

"And what are you wearing, boxers? You being an uppity businessman and all."

He grinned, then placed a tender kiss on her bellybutton.

She shuddered in pleasure. He continued a path of kisses and nips, down to her panties.

"I'll need your help here. Your jeans are tight. Not that I'm complaining."

She laughed and wiggled out of her jeans. She heard his sharp intake of breath.

"What's wrong, City Boy? Cat got your tongue?"

He sat back on his heels. She watched the way his eyes appraised every inch of her, finding his leering sexy, and felt a warm gush between her thighs.

"Rosalind, I want you so bad it hurts. I promise to take it slow this time. I don't know why I thought you were an Ice Queen."

She positioned herself on her elbows and parted her legs. "Then what are you waiting for? I can see you're ready. Do all city boys take this long in satisfying their women?"

Her words came out as a purr. She unzipped his jeans, heaved them below his hips, and cupped his major hard-on with just enough pressure to obtain a moan from him.

The atmosphere had changed from fun and delight to a primal animal impulse. Allan yanked off her thongs. In the next moment he was standing and undressing faster than a jackrabbit on the run.

Naked, he crawled into her bed. She caught a wicked gleam in his eyes. In a slow deliberate move, he gently grabbed her wrists in one hand and held them above her head. His other hand glided over her bare skin to the place between her thighs. She ached with desire and need as she spread her legs wider to welcome him.

His hardness electrified her as her body accepted his entire length. His raw, untamed passion carried her to unexpected heights, and she raised her hips to meet his eager, fast thrusts.

"Kiss me."

Instead of her mouth, he kissed her breasts as he ground harder against her to reach her sweet g-spot. With her arms imprisoned she was helpless to control the passion. When she thought she couldn't take the enthralling sensation and was on the verge of losing it, he stopped thrusting and set her hands free.

"Rosalind, turn around." His command was a heavy, sex-laden drawl, and he slipped his hard manhood from her body.

She managed to position herself on her hands and knees, trembling. Gently and slowly, he pressed against her back, moving her legs to each side, then surged forward in a single thrust. He brushed aside her hair with one hand, and let his other hand trace her horseshoe tattoo.

"Oh my God. Don't stop, Allan."

He touched her nub, and her climax came fast.

Before she sank down on the bed, Allan thrusted again and again for his own release. They collapsed, holding each other.

"Hello? Hello, I'm back."

At the sound of Helen's greeting, their eyes flew open at the same time.

"Can we ever have time to ourselves?" Allan tightened his hold.

"I was thinking the same thing. I was hoping for a second round."

He kissed the tip of her nose. "My dear, I'm good for at least four times. Want me to show you?"

Not waiting for a reply, he stroked her nub and slid two fingers inside. She moved her hips, giving in to his mad, sensual teasing.

"Mr. Smith? Rosalind? Sweetie, are you in here?"

Fighting exasperation, Rosalind followed Allan as he scrambled off the bed and frantically looked for their clothes.

CHAPTER TWENTY-FIVE

"I'm coming," Rosalind yelled.

Allan looked at her and she stared at him. Without warning, she burst into laughter, making him grin. They scurried around, caught in a bout of afternoon delight.

"Why are we running around like two adolescents? We're grown adults. And married." Yet he held his finger to his lips, not wanting Helen to know he was with Rosalind.

Helen's reply drifted to them. "Okey—dokey, honey, I'll be in the kitchen."

Allan bent to retrieve his shirt and located Rosalind's bra. He threw it impishly across the room, his aim perfect, hitting her in the face.

Rosalind giggled harder and held out his torn plaid boxers. "Don't think you'll be able to put these on."

At the sight of the split piece of fabric, he laughed.

"Shh, Helen will hear you." Rosalind put her finger to her lips.

Her repeat of his earlier actions made him laugh more. She stood next to the dresser, buckling her belt, her hair a mess, her face flushed. Allan crouched to gather up his jeans and found Rosalind's lacy panties.

"Excuse me, did you forget something?"

Her head snapped up. Allan grinned and brandished her forgotten panties as if they were a prized possession.

"Well, I couldn't find them." Rosalind faced him with her hands in her back pockets. "Besides, I like free-buffing."

"Oh, very interesting. I thought only men liked commando-style."

"You *are* a City Boy," she taunted. "Get dressed."

Rosalind turned to leave the room. Allan caught sight of her frown, but at the last second her mouth lifted. "I saw that."

Her hurried footsteps were her answer.

Dear lord, his appetite for her was insatiable.

He viewed his unwearable boxers, puzzling over how they'd been ripped. Now what? His clothes were still downstairs.

Commando it was.

He zipped his jeans, wriggled his hips, and cupped his groin to adjust his private parts.

Not bad. It was weird, but sort of comfortable at the same time. He would need to do this more often.

Lips twisted in a smile, he headed to the kitchen where he found the two ladies talking and drinking coffee. Rosalind smirked at him, and he noticed a sparkle of desire flicker in her eyes before she looked away.

Did she want him again? With a sexual appetite comparable to his, they definitely shared a tangible bond. She simply hadn't realized it yet.

He nodded to Helen. "Hello, Mrs. Knutson."

"Good afternoon, Mr. Smith."

"Please, call me Allan."

"Thank you. I'm planning the meals for the week. Is there anything you'd like me to look for at the grocery store?"

"Yeah, Allan. Is there anything you might like?" Rosalind lowered her glance to his groin for a split second.

Two could play this word game.

"I like apples." He directed his glance toward Rosalind's chest and received the desired reaction. Her mouth opened, but she didn't say anything.

"Oh, apples. Good choice. I can make apple pie and apple-sauce." Helen mumbled the ingredients.

Allan busied himself by pouring a cup of coffee to hide his amusement.

Rosalind tapped a pen on the table. "Would you like me to help with dinner?"

"No, no, my girl. You do what you need to do. I'll deal with the laundry tomorrow." Helen continued writing on a piece of paper.

Allan turned and found Rosalind studying him.

Damn you, Rosalind.

If she didn't stop eying him with desire, he would carry her right back to the bedroom.

"Did you bring anything for me to carry into the guest bedroom for you?" He shifted his stance, liking the freedom of no binding of underwear. Rosalind lifted her eyes to meet his as he cleared his throat.

"I did. It's still in my car."

"Give me your keys and I'll bring your suitcases inside." This would allow him time to get his few belongings out of the bedroom without her knowing he and Rosalind had been sleeping in separate rooms.

Helen nodded. "Mr. Allan, that would be nice. Everything is in the trunk. Take your time, honey. Dinner won't be ready for a least an hour or more."

Allan set his half empty cup of coffee on the table and chanced a look at Rosalind, who gave him a mischievous leer.

Oh, God, it was time to get away from his wife.

———

Rosalind watched her husband leave, enjoying the private knowledge he wasn't wearing any underwear.

"Lordy, lordy is he hot," she muttered under her breath.

"No, I'm not hot. It's comfy in here. I've completed the grocery list unless you have something to add." Helen pushed a piece of paper over to her.

Oh, for heaven's sake, had she said that aloud about Allan being hot? She took the list, not really reading it. Allan had her so out of whack, not to mention she could smell his cologne on her.

"Okay, I'll get you some cash before you leave for the store."

Helen pushed her chair back and went humming to the stove. For a moment Rosalind sat, unsure what to do. She was the one who usually did the cooking, now someone was taking care of her. Allan. Her husband.

A pounding at the door snapped Rosalind out of her thoughts. "Now what?"

"Want me to go see who it is?" Helen wiped her hands on a towel.

"No, I'll go." She pushed out of her chair and headed to the front door. Pulling on the handle, it opened with a loud creak. Expecting a neighbor, the sight of Max holding the evergreen tree had her shoving the door wider.

It was the Christmas tree Allan had cut. Then an image of them in the woods alone and him kissing her, came to mind. "Oh Max, thanks. Put it in the living room next to the window. I'll get the tree stand."

"Yes, ma'am."

He progressed slowly into the hall. Seeing he had everything under control, Rosalind descended into the basement and removed the bin labeled 'Xmas' along with the green tree stand. When she reached the landing, Allan stood there.

"Let me help."

"It's okay, I've got it." She tightened her hold on the bin, unwilling to let him become a part of her traditions.

"Why are you so stubborn?"

Without warning, he snatched the red plastic container from her arms.

"Fine." She lifted her chin higher and rolled her eyes. "I'll go get the others."

Again, Allan was there waiting. This time she handed the container to him without a word. With the last one in her hands, she ignored him and carried it into the living room, leaving him in the doorway.

The fresh cut pine was perfectly placed in front of the picture window. All the bins were opened, ready for her to take out the decorations.

"Did Max leave?"

"He's in the kitchen with Helen. He commented about you not practicing today."

"Oh, right. Something else popped up this afternoon." The words slipped out before she realized how sexual they'd sounded. Rosalind caught Allan's smile.

Why did she keep thinking of sex when he was next to her? Or his naked body?

Crap.

"If you don't need me for anything at the moment, I need to go upstairs."

His unsaid words made her realize things were about to change in the house. "I'm okay."

"Yes, you are. Nice ass," he whispered and slapped her butt.

"Ohhhh." Rosalind lurched forward from the impact and spun around to glare at Allan. He didn't turn, only strutted down the hallway. She never thought it would be this hard to ignore him. Definitely a ladies' man, he had her bewitched.

Damn.

Lifting a box of ornaments, her tears fell sporadically when she hung a special ornament which reminded her of her parents, Grandpa Rodney, or Sam.

She could do this. No, she should put them away and start fresh with new ones.

"It's a gorgeous tree. What on earth are you putting on it? Those decorations don't look like Christmas ornaments."

So engrossed with selecting and hanging items, Allan's voice surprised her. She turned. He held and inspected a three-inch cactus with a Santa hat on one of the branches.

"A cactus. It's a Christmas cactus. I suppose you decorate with colored balls, wreaths, and angels."

"Not balls or angels. I hire a service. They bring in a ten-foot tree decorated in white lights and a variety of Christopher Radko ornaments."

Rosalind couldn't keep herself from chuckling. Allan's confused look made her laugh harder. "It figures. My family has always decorated our trees in Southwestern décor. We went against the normal traditional things."

An array of western boots, chili peppers, coyotes, and cactuses adorned the branches. Each one had a red Christmas hat, or strands of Christmas lights intertwined around them. Allan looked closer at several items on the tree and touched a few.

"What do you use as a tree topper? A bull?"

"No, a cowgirl angel."

She laughed. Instead of a smart-ass comeback, Allan sidestepped around the tree to stand next to her. Her smile disappeared, once again lost when she felt his masculine magnetism.

"Do you know what I do to women who find enjoyment at my expense?"

She hesitated and lifted her chin a notch higher to look at him. "What? Take them shopping?"

"No." Allan gently placed his hand on her cheek. "I teach them a lesson by..."

His fingers slid softly over her lips. She allowed them to part slightly and moistened them with her tongue.

Together in slow motion, they leaned toward each other.

His lips smothered hers.

Oh my gosh.

Rosalind didn't want him to stop. She was tingling all over. She wanted this feeling to last forever.

The kiss went on for eons, neither giving in to the other, allowing their hunger to take them to new heights. Allan's arms encircled her, one hand in the small of her back. She did the same, cupping his superb ass.

The clatter of dishes came from the kitchen, clearing Rosalind's thoughts. She moved out of his reach, knowing Mrs. Knutson might chance upon them in a lip-lock embrace. To make it harder for Allan to pull her into his arms, she went to the opposite side of the tree.

"If *that* was your form of punishment, I might have to continue my bantering." She selected a strand of chili pepper lights, smiled, and held them possessively in her hands while stroking them innocently. "Can you help me hang these properly? Sometimes they..."

To her astonishment she was in Allan's arms again.

"I warned you before about teasing." He buried his mouth on hers.

This kiss was demanding, making her knees tremble, and passion radiated from her soft core. Did they have time? Would Mrs. Knutson mind if they were late to dinner?

The forgotten chili pepper lights fell from her hands as she wrapped her arms around Allan's neck, drawing him closer. Another delicious shudder heated her body as his cool palm touched the warmth of her breast. His hardness pressed against her. Freeing one hand, she reached for him and unzipped his pants.

With no fabric hindering her search, she cupped his growing hardness.

CHAPTER TWENTY-SIX

"Yeeee...I'm—I'm sorry. Dinner is ready."

Rosalind thrust Allan away from her in time to see Helen's surprised expression before she spun and bolted away.

"You can hold my chili pepper anytime, all you had to do was ask." Allan zipped up his jeans and wiggled his groin in a sensual way, then followed Helen into the kitchen.

Rosalind leaned against the wall for support. He was going commando, same as she, which had her stomach tingling in a peculiar but exciting way. She lifted her hand to her thumping heart, then touched her swollen lips and realized she could smell him too. She'd have to wash her hands before dinner.

But the way she was feeling had her reminding herself, she wasn't a teenager anymore.

Sex with Tom had been enjoyable. However, when they finished the deed, they'd been done.

She pondered how different the two men were, understanding for the first-time sex verses love. Having very satisfying sex with Allan was like eating a pie with no crust. And here she was, wet from a simple kiss. And she couldn't get enough of him.

But he was leaving soon.

She stepped over the fallen lights, entering the kitchen in a dazed, exasperated state. The table was set for three, with Helen sitting in Sam's old spot. Rosalind's jaw clenched, but she forced the sadness to go away.

Going to the sink, she washed her hands and avoided any eye contact with Allan when she turned. "You outdid yourself, Helen. Everything looks so tasty. And smells wonderful."

"Thank you, dearie. It's my pleasure. I found some chicken in the freezer this morning and had taken it out to thaw. I simply breaded and baked it. The mashed potatoes were easy to make. Tomorrow's breakfast might be inadequate, since there isn't much left to work with."

"I know. I'm sorry. Time got away from me this past week." Rosalind kept her eyes downward not wanting to look at Helen, afraid she'd mention what she'd interrupted by the tree.

Almost finished with her meal, Rosalind chewed her third biscuit when she felt Allan's foot run up and down her leg. She jerked in surprise then tried to stifle her reaction as she peered at Allan across from her.

He snickered and winked.

How was he doing it? She still felt on fire from their kisses. Was she special to him, or only his new plaything?

Helen waved her hand and smiled. "No worries. I know what I need now. I'll go to town after breakfast for groceries."

"Would you like me to drive you?"

Rosalind rolled her eyes at Allan's chivalrous ladies' man performance. Good thing she was immune to his charm. Or was she?

"No. I'll go alone. You'll slow me down," Helen said and chuckled.

"Excuse me, anyone want more coffee?" Not waiting for their replies, Rosalind tugged her chair away from Allan's foot.

"Yes, please, dearie. That's so thoughtful."

"I'll take more too, and can you bring the sugar?"

Allan's tone had a sensual thickness to it, that she recognized. Sugar? Not in front of Helen, what was he thinking? She retook her seat after pouring the coffee, managing not to make contact above or beneath the table with Allan.

A sudden pressure between her legs unnerved her. Allan's shoeless foot had staged its own invasion, pressing into her center. She reached below the table and pinched his toes, hard.

"Ouch," he muttered.

"What's wrong, Allan?"

Rosalind sat with her arms on the table, innocent as could be. "Yes, is there a problem?"

"I bit my tongue. I hope it doesn't swell." He stuck it out for them to inspect.

She rolled her eyes. "It does look swollen. Maybe we can finish in silence."

For his reply, she felt his foot begin to make its way up her leg again, but she kicked it away and glared at him.

"When Max delivered the tree, he told me you haven't practiced for the competition yet. What are you thinking, little missy?"

"I'm not sure if I should compete. I've decided not to go." Her announcement hung in the air.

———

Allan stared open-mouthed at her. "Not going? Why not? Isn't this what you've trained for your entire life?"

She had to go. If she didn't, she'd never know if she would've won.

He remembered what it was like not wanting to go to meet

his next foster care parents. Would they be nice or mean? Did he have to change schools again?

Then there was when he wouldn't place an order to buy stock because he'd questioned his instincts.

"Yes, but it doesn't—"

"You're going. It's what your parents would've wanted. It was important to Sam, too. There are no buts. I can't let you concede so easily," he stated.

"I only did it to get my inheritance. I don't need the purse any longer. The land is gone. I don't want to race anymore. My heart's not into it." Rosalind hung her head and folded her hands in front of her.

He'd accomplished what he'd originally set out to do.

She was defeated. He'd won.

The satisfaction he'd normally experience with success never came. Instead, regret surged through him.

Somehow, he had to correct what he'd done. "I forgot to tell you, the new owners called me."

"You talked to them and didn't tell me right away?"

"I didn't get an opportunity. We—were—I was helping you trim the tree."

"Oh, right."

"They've agreed to lease us the land." He paused as her eyes sparkled, her blush very evident before she lowered her head. "Of course, they've asked for a fee."

"How much? Did they say? When can we start building?"

"Slow down. They're supposed to email the forms. I haven't seen anything yet. Once I receive the information, we can look at them together."

Gone was Rosalind's crestfallen frown. It was replaced with a look of total exhilaration.

This had to work, damn it. He'd make it work.

When she stood and paced around the kitchen, Allan willed away his desire to carry her upstairs.

"This is wonderful." Helen placed her hand on her heart. "Those poor horses will finally have a good home. The whole town has been buzzing about it since they heard you were gonna open a sanctuary."

"I have to talk to Max. He'll need to prepare Dawn for me to ride in the morning. And the course should be fresh. Guess I better take the first-place purse of a hundred thousand dollars after all."

The next thing he knew she was gone. Allan looked at Helen. "I guess it means you and I are on KP duty."

"Oh no, I'll take care of everything."

"If you insist." He gave her a wink and a smile that would melt any woman's heart.

Helen shooed him out.

Allan glanced into the living room, but there was no sign of Rosalind. He noticed her coat was missing from the front hallway rack. She hadn't slammed the door this time when she'd left.

Good. He had time to set things in motion.

He took the stairs two and three at a time. When he reached his new room, he called Tiffany.

"Hello, Mr. Smith."

"Tiffany, I need a land lease contract for the land I purchased. Make it out to Rosalind...no, to both of us. On second thought, have it addressed to Mr. and Mrs. Allan Smith. I'll fill in the figures."

"But...you already own the land."

He stepped to the window and scrutinized the barn. "Yes, I do. But Rosalind doesn't."

"Right," Tiffany replied.

"Any further info on who's been posting the pictures?"

"Paul has narrowed it down."

Allan watched Max, along with two other men, set up plastic barrels in the fenced area. "I want cold hard facts by tomorrow. And send the contract ASAP."

"Yes, Mr. Smith."

They hung up. Allan took a moment to catch up on emails and scanned the numerous lines. Then he saw one from his lawyers and opened it. His face hardened as he gripped his cell phone.

He didn't have time for this bullshit.

Clicking off his phone, he grabbed a clean pair of boxers and a towel, then headed to the bathroom for a shower.

How could he get Rosalind to admit she loved him?

He'd have to turn on the charm full throttle. She wasn't going to know what hit her.

CHAPTER TWENTY-SEVEN

"Hello?" Rosalind hollered when she returned to the house. No one responded. "Hey!"

Still no answer. The only sound she heard was running water. She proceeded toward the kitchen and found it dark. She went to Helen's bedroom. The door was closed and there was no light peering out from under it.

She was safe until morning. She wouldn't have to explain herself to anyone and headed upstairs. Allan's door was open. Unable to resist, Rosalind peeked inside. It wasn't very different from how Sam had kept the room. He'd changed out the bed quilt to a thicker comforter. She grinned. It was the one she'd used on cold nights. His suitcase lay open, empty. His laptop sat on the nightstand with his iPhone. Overall, a very neat person.

The sound of pipes rattled loudly as the water was shut off, a sure sign Allan's shower was finished. Quickly, she stepped into the hallway and eyed the bathroom door.

Would he come to her room? Should she go to his? Maybe he'd want to finish what he started earlier, next to the Christmas tree. Would she want him to?

Before she could choose an answer, the bathroom door flew open. Rosalind couldn't move. She was rooted to the floor like a tree in the ground. Her jaw dropped.

Allan stood in the doorway, one hand on the knob, and the other on the light switch. His hair was wet, a towel thrown over one shoulder, its end pointed toward his plaid boxers.

"Oh my," she groaned and zoomed past him with her head down, until she reached the safety of her bedroom. Before she closed the door, Rosalind took a second look at Allan's bare masculine chest and the six-pack she knew was real. When her eyes flicked to his clean-shaven face, he sported a grin.

She staggered backward and slammed the door, then leaned against it, debating if she should reopen it and invite him in. Her body cried 'yes.' She tightened her grip on the handle, ready to push down.

Crap. She needed to take a cold shower and go to bed, alone.

About to move away from the barrier, she heard his footsteps. They stopped outside her door. She held her breath.

Would he knock? Or disregard formality and come in?

The floor creaked and she heard his door shut. Rosalind breathed again. She grabbed her robe and towel, opened her door, and scampered into the bathroom.

She turned the dial to cold and stepped into the shower, closing her eyes to think of how he stood nearly naked in this very spot a few moments ago. Warm gushes of desire coursed through her body in spite of the cool water easing her overly heated skin.

Fantasies of him became suffocating. The water that ran down her breasts suddenly became Allan's hands. The droplets slid down her skin, forming into his fingers, following in streams to her stomach and lower. Lifting her head, she let it roll backward until the spray of water hit her face to shake away her imaginary Allan.

Rosalind's eyes flew open as a rush of air drifted into the shower. Allan, naked as a jaybird, held the shower curtain open, devouring her with his gaze.

"I thought you already took a shower," she stuttered.

"I did, but you were taking too long. So, here I am. I came to join you."

"I didn't invite you." Even as she spoke with fake calmness, Rosalind had caught the huskiness in his voice and could see the evidence of his desire.

"Can't you picture it? Our bodies entwined with water splashing on us."

"Maybe where you come from, City Boy, sharing a shower is a common thing. But here, we take ours alone."

Unable to believe she was having a conversation with a naked man in her bathroom, she fought the urge to cover her breasts with her hands.

Lordy, lordy, what was going to happen next?

She grabbed for the curtain, but his hand stopped her. He held onto it and reached into the stream of water with his other hand.

"A cold shower?"

"Yes, I like to take one before bed."

He stepped over the tub wall and turned the knob to hot. "I need to show you how this is done."

The curtain slipped from her grasp as her wet, cold body touched his, then molded to the contours of his, dry and warm. She did what she didn't want to do and wrapped her arms around his neck.

"Show me what you got, mister."

"Rosalind..." He claimed her lips in a savage, yet searching kiss, doing the impossible, making love standing with a curtain of water cascading on their skin.

It was so erotic; his kisses, his hands, the water, acting as one unit. She felt like an untamed filly. Her desire took on a new dimension.

"Allan, now."

He lifted her and entered her in one smooth thrust. She held onto him with her legs wrapped around his waist, as one climax after another took her to new plateaus. A hot tide of passion raged through them both.

Their needs were satisfied for the moment.

Allan broke the spell. "I believe we're done here."

She loosened the grip of her legs and stood on weak knees. He held her pressed against him and turned off the water. Rosalind kept her eyes closed as he carried her from the warmth of the bathroom. Her wet skin chilled. He laid her gently on her bed.

"You forgot the towels."

"Didn't think we needed them."

He joined her on the bed. She eased over next to him, their naked bodies touching. Allan pulled the feather-down quilt over their damp bodies. Without any coaxing, she snuggled closer to him, not wanting him to leave.

"Do you want me to go?"

"You're finished?" Rosalind sighed and ran her hand over his chest. "Is that all you got?"

"No, I thought you might be tired."

"As I see it, the night is young."

"In that case, I'll make love to you slowly and make you plead for me to take you, to satisfy your ache. And when I do, you'll beg me for more."

"Is that a dare?" She whispered into his ear.

His response was to take her hardened nipple into his

mouth. She moaned and her hands caressed his muscular shoulders.

"You're very beautiful, Rosalind."

She grinned. "Is this part of your so-called seduction?"

This time he left a trail of kisses to her abdomen, then to the tattoo on her hip.

"Let me mend your broken heart."

At that, Rosalind lost her private battle of resistance.

They made love several times during the night, each better than the previous. They found each other's secrets and learned new ones, together.

She didn't want the morning to arrive.

CHAPTER TWENTY-EIGHT

Rosalind didn't have to look at the time when she awoke. Her internal clock was right on target every morning.

Five-thirty.

She'd been rising before the sun since she'd been a young girl.

Stretching, she reached for Allan. The spot next to her was empty and cold.

What a wondrous night they'd had. His kisses enticed her to want more and more. His sweet touch had melted her desire into a liquid pool of longing.

She'd remember last night and early this morning love-making for the rest of her life, even after he was gone.

Rosalind hugged herself. A slow, satisfying smile spread across her lips, still swollen and tender. He'd been gentle yet sometimes demanding during their lovemaking, always making sure she'd been completely satisfied before giving in to his own pleasures.

Four times they'd made love. Not sex, but love.

She lifted the pillow he'd slept on to her face and sniffed.

His musky, woodsy scent engulfed her. Rosalind lazily sat, tossed the pillow aside, and glanced at the clock.

Five-fifty. Shit, Max would kill her. She'd promised to be on time.

She scrambled off the bed and dressed. In the hallway, she took a fleeting look at Allan's closed door.

"Mister, you and I have unfinished business," she muttered.

The aroma of brewing coffee caught her attention as she headed down the stairs.

"Good morning, Helen, thanks for the coffee. No time to talk. Max will have my hide if I'm late."

"Breakfast will be ready at seven-thirty."

Helen stirred a mixture in a bowl and didn't even turn to look at her. "Right. Bye."

Rosalind strolled to the barn, enjoying the morning, and sipping her coffee, when a wild thought crossed her mind. Would Max be able to tell she'd spent the night making love to the sexiest man she'd ever known?

———

Allan lay in his bed, missing the warmth of Rosalind's body pressed against his. He'd heard movement from her room and realized he'd left in the nick of time. Since she hadn't exactly invited him into her bed, he'd thought it best to leave before she awoke.

Should he have declared his love? No, it was too soon.

A beeping noise from his computer interrupted his thoughts. Throwing off the warm covers, Allan reluctantly left the bed. When his feet touched the cold floor, he swore. It reminded him he needed to buy some slippers. He didn't own a pair, but was tired of cold feet, and until she asked him to stay the night in her room, he'd be bed hopping.

He'd begun to sift through reports and data from Tiffany and Paul when Rosalind's voice drifted in from outside. Allan pushed back the chair and went to the window. It appeared she'd just finished a run and was about to take Dawn through the course again. The thrill of watching her ride was as exhilarating as the first time he'd seen her in Las Vegas.

He had to admit, he was glad he hadn't signed the divorce papers. If he had, he would never have met the woman who'd stolen his heart.

Without a second thought or a glance at his unopened emails, Allan dressed and rushed outside.

He leaned on the fence next to Max. Both of them kept their eyes glued to Rosalind as she rounded the second barrel. "How's she doing?"

"Her time is slow. Her posture is slouched. Dawn needs to be run more and Rosalind needs to arrive on time."

Allan looked sideways at Max, who had raised his eyebrows and was clenching his jaw as if he wanted to say more. What was with these Minnesotans being so straightforward?

Max's casual words hadn't slipped past him. He ignored the comment and stared at Rosalind. What happened between him, and his wife was no one's business but theirs.

Smiling, Allan calculated her every move. She approached the last barrel at an extraordinarily high speed.

Was she going too fast? It looked like she was to him.

She pulled the reins as she went into turn three. Suddenly, Dawn reared. From that point, time stopped and then moved in slow motion.

Rosalind falling to the ground with a thud.

Rosalind lying lifeless.

Dawn, high-stepping, and snorting.

"Rosalind!"

Allan and Max jumped the fence and ran to her motionless body.

No. No, she can't be dead. He loved her and hadn't told her.

He was the first to reach Rosalind's side. Allan stumbled to his knees. He yanked off his gloves and gently touched her cheek. "Rosalind."

She didn't move. Her eyelids fluttered.

"Rosalind! Are you hurt?"

Her eyes remained closed, but he saw the slight rise and fall of her chest.

Max strolled to them and caught Dawn's reins.

"Is the horse all right?" His question went unanswered. Had everyone lost their minds?

Rosalind was hurt, lying still on the ground, and no one seemed concerned but him. Allan fumbled to pull his phone from his pocket. "Don't move her. I'm calling nine-one-one."

He glanced down at Rosalind's face. Her lips were curved upward into a smile.

Damn her. She wasn't hurt. She wasn't dying.

He gritted his teeth and swung his head around to glare at Max, who'd erupted in a fit of laughter along with the other four men that had come out. Allan stood so quickly, Rosalind's head dropped to the ground.

"Ouch, what was that for?"

"You fell. Damn it, I thought you were dead or hurt."

Rosalind sat up, rubbing the back of her head, before getting to her feet. She brushed the dirt off her pants and took her hat from Max, sweeping it back and forth across her leg. Dirt and snow flew.

"Allan, don't go gettin' mad. It's a trick we play on all the greenhorns." She gave him a smile that could've melted all the snow in this arctic state. His anger faded but he still felt annoyed at being the recipient of the joke, as he slipped his phone into his pocket. His heart raced from the mere thought of losing Rosalind.

"That wasn't very nice. You know the old saying about crying wolf too many times, right? Next time, I won't come to your rescue."

Allan moseyed away, hid his smile from her, and strutted to the fence. He resumed his position by the post. Rosalind worked hard, but he caught her staring at him often. She ran the barrels three more times, then gestured for him to follow her into the barn.

She led Dawn to a stall. "Would you like to help? To see what this is all about?"

"I'm not sure how much help I'll be to you."

"The girth comes off first," Rosalind instructed as she unfastened the straps.

He observed how this allowed the saddle to be lifted off. Rosalind handed him the saddle and he almost dropped it. Allan shifted the weight in his arms. "How much does this monstrous thing weigh?"

"About fifty pounds. Why? Is it too much for you, City Boy?"

Allan ignored her feisty comment. "You do this every morning?"

"Do what? Ride or lift the saddle?"

"Train." He shifted the saddle to get a better hold of it in his arms.

"I run Dawn about three to five times through the course, when I have a show coming daily. I have trained other horses too, but I don't have any right now to train. My goal has been to take on the sanctuary."

"And here I thought you worked out at a gym to keep your body so toned."

She moved to the other side of the horse. He wrestled with the weight in his arms.

"I don't go to a club to exercise. The horses and the ranch are work enough."

"I see. No wonder cowboys are so fit." He carried the saddle to a short half wall and placed it on it like she'd instructed. Before he turned, Max handed him a sponge, soap, and bucket of water.

Allan regarded the thick, smelly sponge he held. "What in God's name am I supposed to do with this?"

"Today is the day to clean the saddle. You've been chosen to do it," Max said.

Wiping his brow with his arm, Allan sucked in a deep breath. Hard labor. She had a thing or two coming. It had been years since he'd stocked shelves at the local grocery store.

"I do? How much does this job pay?"

Laughing, Rosalind shook her head.

"What is that?" Allan pointed to a plaid blanket on the back of Dawn.

"This is a saddle cloth to protect the horse's body from the rub of leather. Stop wasting time, you need to take the soap, get it wet, and apply it to the sponge..."

"Okay, okay. I get the picture." He struggled with his task, getting more water on himself than the saddle.

"You're such a greenhorn. We have a saying about the unexpected and seeing a rattlesnake in your bed."

Allan dropped the sponge and glared at her, then Max. They in turn laughed at him. Disregarding their teasing, he noticed she was holding the horse's foreleg in her hands. She picked up what looked like a cross between a knife and a screwdriver, using it to dig dirt and other stuff from Dawn's hoof.

But what made him stare, motionless, was how Rosalind's

tucked-back hair revealed cheeks sporting a rosy tone. *Gorgeous.* Everything about her was real and natural. Even the barn, the horses, and the scents were a part of her.

"Do you go to one of those places to work out?" She turned to stare at him after finishing with the horses' hooves.

He was lost.

No woman had ever made him feel this much passion or the need to protect. Realizing she was waiting for his reply, Allan cleared his throat. "Yeah, my office has one available twenty-four-seven for all my employees. If I don't have a lunch appointment or the markets are calm, I go to the gym."

Unable to look away from her, Allan missed the bucket of water and the sponge fell to the ground. He bent to retrieve it and caught a glance at his watch. "We're late for breakfast, it's eight o'clock."

"I know. Helen said she'd have breakfast ready for us at seven-thirty."

"If she scolds us, it's your fault," Allan said.

Rosalind led Dawn into the stall, then locked it and before he could say or do anything, she was running from the barn toward the house. Leaving the sponge and bucket, he followed her. They raced, laughing, until they reached the door at the same time. Inside the house, they discarded their winter coats and boots in a hurried manner. As they made their way to the kitchen, he shoved her to be the first one at the table.

"You two are late. Wash your hands. No one eats in my kitchen with dirty hands."

"I'm sorry, it won't happen again." Allan kissed Helen's cheek.

"None of that, now." Helen brushed him aside. She placed a plate of pancakes on the table.

Rosalind took a seat and filled her plate. He joined her and did the same. When their plates were clean, Helen shooed them out of her domain.

"I can help," Rosalind protested.

"No, you scoot." Helen waved them off. "Remember I'll be going into town."

"Okay. I'll get you some money."

"Let me pay." Allan withdrew his wallet and plucked out a couple hundred-dollar bills.

"Oh my, my, it's too much." Helen refused to take the money.

He pressed the bills into her hand. "Keep the change for the next shopping trip."

"Thank you, Mister, um, Allan. I'll put this in my purse right now." Helen hurried from the kitchen.

Rosalind coughed.

"What?" He gave her a puzzled look.

"You have her wrapped around your finger."

"I warned you I have a way with women." He grinned when Rosalind rolled her eyes. "Let's go into the living room."

"Have you received the lease agreement?"

"Not sure. I haven't checked my emails since I left the house. I will now." Allan slipped his cell phone from his pocket.

"I'm—umm—I'll go take a shower..."

"I could join you." Allan stepped closer. "We could discuss it afterward if it comes. It'll be nice to be able to phone some contractors and inform the horse owners of the good news."

"Shh," she looked toward the hallway. "Helen might—"

He cut off her reply with a slow, caressing kiss. His lips left her mouth and nibbled her neck. "I want to make love to you, but you're right. We need to spend our time getting this project going."

"Yes, yes, I agree. I'll meet you in the living room in ten

minutes." Rosalind kissed his lips, and then took the stairs two at a time.

Allan grinned at the sexual rock of her pelvis with each step.

He clicked on his phone. Opened his emails. Two were marked 'urgent' from Tiffany. The first one was the land lease agreement. He pressed 'print doc' and opened the second one. His face darkened. He tapped the contact button, scrolled until John's name appeared, and touched 'call.'

———

Rosalind stood alone under the rain of water and waited for Allan to join her. Minutes passed and he didn't show. She sighed and finished. After she toweled off, she blow-dried her hair. Before heading to her room, she dabbed on perfume she'd found in the back of the vanity drawer.

In her room, she put on a clean pair of jeans, but struggled with which top she should wear. She didn't own anything sexy.

Everything in her closet was dull and boring. She couldn't compete with his rich girlfriends and their named brand clothes. She tapped her chin and settled on a tee shirt sporting a puppy on the front, and a blue zippered hoodie. Excited in spite of all the sadness of the last weeks, she hurried downstairs.

The living room and dining room were empty, but she heard Allan's voice coming from the kitchen. Her file lay on the dining room table. Opening it, she laid out the pictures of the abused horses, the sketches she'd done of the proposed barn, and a set of financials.

Engrossed in arranging everything, she smelled his after-shave before she heard him.

"This symbol matches your tattoo." He tapped on a sketch.

"It's the trademark I created years ago after witnessing first-hand the abuse of a horse. I had it tattooed on me as a reminder of all the lost horses."

"Wow. Maybe I'll have to get a matching one." Allan placed his hand next to hers. "Your plans are very good."

His closeness caused her to drop some of the papers to the floor. Her chest tightened.

"Thank you. I've put a lot of time and effort into this idea. Once *Heavens Kiss Sanctuary* is operational, the next stage is to open a training center for young girls or boys wanting to become barrel racers. The third stage is to teach kids and adults how to ride."

Rosalind sat and fidgeted with her fingers, feeling very nervous. Sharing her dream with him of all people was frightening.

He chuckled.

"What's so funny?"

"You...not funny, but amazing, it's a huge project. I can see you teaching kids."

She felt the pressure of a kiss on her forehead before he sat next to her.

"Thanks. It's a dream. One I've considered for a very long time. My mom had planned to open a training center. I couldn't do it on my parents' coattails. That's not how it's done in the rodeo circuit. I needed to make a name for myself, which I have. Now, it's time."

"Let's do it, make your dreams come true." He pointed to the papers. "The land leased id come in. All you have to do is sign it."

"Oh, my God. For real?"

"Yes, I left it upstairs. You can sign it later," he said.

They plotted, called contractors, emailed, and scanned proposals. Rosalind studied Allan. She enjoyed having someone to talk business with intelligently. He'd helped formulate her ideas into spreadsheets. He was smart and methodical. Sam had known some things, but he'd been old school. Her project was coming to life. Allan respected her expertise about the horses and the ranch and treated her as an equal.

This man was her husband, and he might leave soon. If he signed the divorce papers, he'd be free.

When pigs fly. She didn't want him to leave.

She'd fallen in love with him.

The admission came from a place outside of logic and reason. She cast him a sideways glance. He was on the phone and didn't pay any attention to her. His calls were mostly huge dollar amounts, numbers, and stock codes. She pictured him at his office, in a business suit, professional, handling problems.

She wanted to stay married to him.

Right now, he respected her. Would he believe her when she told him she respected him?

CHAPTER TWENTY-NINE

"Are you coming?" Rosalind yelled to Allan from the front door.

"I'll meet you in a few minutes. On a call with the office."

Scrunching her face, she mimicked his words. They'd fallen into a routine with their newfound truce. Neither spoke about the divorce, staying married, or leaving. She'd work Dawn on runs through the course in the mornings. He'd come outside most of the time. Together they'd take care of Dawn and the other horses until it was time for breakfast. It was weird, but exciting. They were acting like a couple.

Yet why did he continue to leave her bed each night, with only his lingering warmth in an empty spot?

"Okay, I get the picture. You don't want to do any hard labor today."

Allan peeked around the wall with his phone to his ear and held his finger to his lips. She gave him a smirk. He smiled and blew her a kiss. Her mouth opened, but he'd vanished from her sight.

She'd make him pay later.

"Come out when you can." Shrugging, after not hearing a

reply, she headed out into the cold, crisp air. Then hesitated for a moment as the hairs on the back of her neck stood.

The air smelled bad this mornin'.

She scanned the area. Nothing appeared unusual. She rubbed her thick jacket sleeves against her arms to brush away her ominous sensation that something terrible was about to happen and kicked at a chunk of snow.

Everything was going so good. But all good things never lasted long in her life.

Rosalind patted her gut, thinking she should skip Helen's delightful breakfast. She was sure she'd gained a least five pounds and would have to purchase new jeans for the competition.

She finished the exercise run and was in the middle of rubbing Dawn down when Allan decided to make an appearance. She noticed right away his mannerism was different, not his usual million-question self.

"I laid out the new budget for *Heavens Kiss Sanctuary*. So, do ya think we can get the buildings done by summer?"

"I believe it's conceivable," he replied.

She halted the brush in mid stroke, thinking he would say more, but he didn't. He past Dawn's stall with a hay bale. She realized he hadn't said much all morning or last night.

"Good. By the way, I need to confirm the plans for my trip to Oklahoma, for the competition. You're coming, aren't you?"

He didn't answer. She waited and waited. Rosalind stopped brushing Dawn and went to the stall door. She glanced around.

"Allan?"

He exited a stall two down from Dawn's with his head bent low.

This was it. The end. Her honeymoon was kaput.

"I have to leave in the morning." He hesitated and shuffled

from one foot to the other. "I'm sorry. I've delayed my return to New York long enough."

Leave? Now?

He couldn't leave. She wanted to stay married.

"Okay." She was able to choke out the one word but struggled to say more.

He raised his head. His eyes held a sternness she hadn't seen before. His mouth formed a thin line.

Had she lost him?

"I'm not sure if I'll be back for the competition."

"Oh, I see how the water flows." She paused for time to think and then in a firm and non-emotional tone, she added, "Make sure you sign the papers."

His movements were brisk and measured as he stepped over to Dawn's stall. "Papers?"

Unwilling to let him see how he'd hurt her, she held back the tears that threatened to fall as she stood by Dawn. "Yeah, remember the reason you're here. Divorce papers. You got what you came here for...sex."

She couldn't let him see how hurt she was.

The creak of the stall door told her he was coming inside. Rosalind stilled her arm, sensing he'd invaded her personal space. She fought the urge to face him and beg him to stay.

"I'm not leaving because I want the divorce. I have a meeting I can't postpone any longer. I need to be there in person."

"Oh, whatever..."

He turned her. His bare, now calloused hands touched her cheeks. His warm and inviting lips zealously took hers. Time stopped, like it did every time he kissed her.

"Rosalind, I..."

The crash of the door being shut silenced Allan. Rosalind stared at him, wishing he'd finish.

"I'm gonna make a *Do Not Disturb* sign for the two of you," Max hollered.

"Hello, Max." She rested her head on Allan's chest and felt his rumble of laughter. She breathed in deeply to savor his scent.

He didn't want the divorce either.

Hallelujah.

Rosalind stepped away from the comfort of his arms. "We will have... I have to leave Monday to meet up with the others for the competition. How long will you be gone?"

"I should be back Saturday."

"Ahhh ha, right, Saturday."

"I can't promise. If for some reason I can't be here, I'll join you in Oklahoma. I have a very important meeting I've put off several times." Allan gathered her back into his arms. "I don't want to leave, but I have to."

She looked into his eyes. At that moment she knew he'd stolen her heart and soul.

Heaven. Pure sweet heaven.

A City Boy-Greenhorn was the man she wanted to spend the rest of her life with.

She loved him. Should she tell him? Would he care?

To hell with her pride. Her unspoken words threatened to spill. A sense of indecision swept through Rosalind even as her body ached for his touch. "Allan, I..."

Her declaration was cut off by Allan's cell phone. They moved apart.

"Hello. Yes, I have..."

He talked to some unknown person as he walked to the main area of the barn. Rosalind followed and locked Dawn's stall. She tried not to listen but couldn't make heads or tails of the information.

He pocketed his phone and darted toward her. His mouth

was in a tight line and his jaw was clenched. Rosalind swallowed a sob rising in her throat as a chill settled on her.

"Sorry, my plans have changed. I need to leave now. That was my pilot. There's a winter storm brewing. He says we need to leave ASAP in order to ensure we make it out."

"I understand. Go get ready. I'll finish up here."

He gave her hand a squeeze before hurrying away. Pain crushed her tender heart.

What if he was walking away from her forever? She had to stop him. She had to tell him how she felt.

"Allan?"

Stopping, he pivoted around, and she walked to him. Without any hesitation, she flung herself into his waiting arms. Their mouths met hungrily. A moment later, he left her swollen lips, kissed the tip of her nose, then her eyes, and returned to her waiting mouth, sealing it with a gentle kiss.

"Rosalind, this isn't the place or time but," he paused and took a deep breath. "I love you. I don't want to divorce you. Ever."

His admission froze in her brain. It repeated itself over and over.

He loved her.

He didn't want a divorce.

He loved her.

Her heart jolted as if she'd drank a gallon of coffee. She'd heard the love in his voice and tasted it on his lips. She stared at him in a daze and found her voice. "I love you too, Allan. I was afraid to tell you..."

Her words were lost as he smothered her lips with his again. He pulled her hips to his. She felt his hardness. He buried his other hand in her hair as his tongue found hers.

Rosalind reached around and rested both hands on his sexy butt. She moved one hand to his belt buckle, ready to repeat their first lovemaking episode in the barn, when his phone rang for a second time.

The moment was lost. He moved away, but still held her imprisoned in his arms.

"I'm sorry, Rosalind. I'll make it up to you. I promise." He lifted the phone to his ear.

Still in awe he loved her, she rested her head on his chest, and concentrated on memorizing the sound of his pounding heart. When he finished the call, he kissed her forehead.

"We'll need to talk about this when I return. You're not going to back out of your admission of loving me, you're mine forever."

She smiled, then tears fell.

"Don't, honey. I'll be back before you know it. I promise to call you every night."

"This is crazy. I never thought we'd end up loving each other."

Allan smiled at her and slowly stepped away. "Me either. It doesn't change the fact I have to leave. I don't have much time. I wish to God I did. I want to make love to you right now."

She moved completely from his arms but clung onto his hand. "Get going, City Boy, before I hog-tie you so you can't."

"This is the only time I will leave you. Remember I love you."

She released his hand. He crossed to the door, turned, blew her a kiss, and left.

Rosalind stayed in the barn, not trusting herself in his presence. She didn't want to appear weak by begging him to stay or worse yet, asking to go with him. At the sound of a car engine, she walked to the closest window and peered at Allan getting into his rental car.

Then he climbed out. Her heart began to race. Was he coming back for her?

Instead of returning to the barn, he ran into the house. A few minutes later he came out with his briefcase and a brown paper bag. No suitcase.

He'd left his personal things behind. He would have to return. He'd told the truth.

The car backed up and he drove away from the house and her.

CHAPTER THIRTY

"Hello, Rosalind?"

"I'm here. You're breaking up. Can you hear me?"

"I can now. I promised to call you. I'm in New York on the way to my office. We missed the bad weather." Allan maneuvered his car through traffic *en* route to Fifth Street.

"I'm glad you made it out before the storm hit. It must have changed course because we don't have any winter storm warnings."

His phone beeped and he glanced at the screen on the dash. An incoming call from Tiffany. "I have another call, can you hold for a moment?"

"Sure, I'll drink some of your favorite coffee."

"I'm beginning to like that stuff you call coffee. Hold on."

He hit the button on the steering wheel, switching calls. "What's going on, Tiffany?"

"Paul and I, along with four FBI Special Agents, and your lawyer, will meet you in front of the office building. They have a subpoena."

"I figured. I'm ten minutes away."

"I'll let everyone know," Tiffany said.

Allan clicked the button. "Fuckin' A."

"What's wrong, Allan?"

He glanced at the screen and saw Rosalind was still on the line. "Nothing, just traffic. What did Helen make for dinner?"

"Meatloaf."

He heard a hint of mischief in Rosalind's voice and could picture her face with a smile which would've made her green eyes sparkle.

"I missed my favorite dinner?"

Her laughter lessened his tension.

"Yup. See what you get for leaving unexpectedly? Helen was making it for you. You snooze, you lose."

Allan wished he was back in Minnesota right now. He imagined Rosalind sitting in the family room, surrounded by papers, the fireplace aglow, and the Christmas tree lights shining bright.

"I'm not sure I'll be able to call you later or tomorrow."

"You sound—I don't know, nervous. Is everything good?"

"It's the damn New York traffic. Fifth Street is heavy as usual."

"Traffic. Right."

Rosalind's voice sounded flat. He knew he hadn't been very convincing. To ensure she didn't ask any more questions, he changed the subject for some normality. "Any new candidates for *Heavens Kiss Sanctuary*?"

"Holy cow, yes. I've gotten about thirty emails. There is no way I can take them all. Max and I are going over the applicants."

A red light gave him a few more minutes of freedom. "Why don't you build a third barn?"

"I don't have enough help to house twenty plus horses. Do you know how much the veterinarian fees would cost for all those horses? Not to mention the huge cost of feed and supplies."

"You'll figure out something. I wish I was there to help. Remember, I have money. On the other hand, you're right to go slow."

He smiled at her laughter and forgot for a moment the Feds were waiting to take him to jail if he refused to cooperate.

What if his lawyers were wrong and he wouldn't be back in time for her competition?

"Okay, Mr. New Yorker, like you'd be able to tell which horses we'd be able to help. Can you spot the difference between a mare or a gelding and a stallion yet?"

"Ouch, that was low." Allan paused and took a deep breath. His office building came into view. Flashing lights and cars parked on the street greeted him. "I'm pulling in the parking garage. The signal isn't good. I'll try to call you later."

"Sure, later."

"Remember I love you, Rosalind."

"I love you, too."

Before he could say more, the phone went dead.

———

Rosalind sat at the table in amazement. Hearing Allan say 'I love you' sent unusual sensations down her spine and made the hairs on her arms stand. When she and Tom had shared those words, it hadn't been the same. She welcomed what it meant to truly love someone. Those three little words of declaration held a different meaning now.

A knock sounded through the house. Rosalind left the piles of papers and pictures on the table, hurrying to the front door.

"Evening, Max. You're done early."

"Evening. Walt helped finish. Do you still want to go over the applicants?"

"I do. Come on in," she motioned with a sweep of her hand. "Would you like coffee?"

"That would warm these old bones of mine."

Max had discarded his outerwear when Helen's voice came from the kitchen. "I'll bring out a fresh pot of coffee in a minute."

They looked at each other and chuckled.

"She has ears like a cat. Come into the dining room. I have everything laid out on the table. I spoke with Allan, and he suggested a third barn."

"Would we have enough help?"

"Manpower might be part of the problem, Max. I punched in the figures and the money isn't there. I've followed a tight budget all year to make the money last."

Rosalind moved around the table and retook the seat she'd vacated. Should she use Allan's money? He'd said it was okay. Where else could she get some from?

She wondered if he knew she'd used the line of credit against his name.

Tapping the pen on the table, she brooded. The decision came easy. She wouldn't and couldn't bring herself to use what was his.

"Let's take a look at what you have so far." Max joined her at the table and took a stack of papers.

"I've separated the emails and pictures into batches by degrees of need. The ones you are looking at are horses in non-friendly animal shelters." She paused to give him a minute to look them over. "They don't have the financial means for long-term care of large animals. That means horses. I've contemplated they should be the first we take."

Rosalind collected the stack to her right and handed it to

Max. He dropped the one he'd been looking through and took the new pile.

"These here are the worst. I'm not sure I'll be able to save or help them."

As he read each applicant, she studied his reaction. He shook his head and swore a couple of times. Same thing she'd done.

"Oh, my Lord, definitely the worst. The owners should go to jail for mistreating animals," Max stated angrily. "Let's have a vet examine each one first. Then, based on their condition or their chances of recovery, we can supply meds to ease their suffering or agree for them to be your guests."

"Yes, yes, awesome. Giving them the medicine they need would leave us with space. Let's make that happen."

"Okay, I'll handle the calls to the local vets in the morning," Max said.

"Here you two go. I warmed up some sticky buns too." Helen bustled in with a tray. She unloaded a pot of coffee with two cups, along with a plate of delicious looking caramel rolls on the table.

"Mrs. Knutson, they look very tasty. If you have any leftovers, can I take them to the ranch-hands?"

Helen grinned. Rosalind studied the exchange with interest.

"I'll do better than leftovers. I'll make a fresh batch for you to take." Helen hurried back to the kitchen.

"I'm going to ignore that, but if you steal my cook you're fired."

"I won't. Wrong person." Max shifted in the chair. "You might want to ask Joe. He's the reason we've been having so much extra food lately."

"Joe? Good Lord. Never would've guessed. I've been distracted."

He handed her a file. "What do you think of these racehorses?"

"It's hard to believe that when a racehorse begins to lose competitions, the breeder-owners sell them at auction or send them to the slaughterhouses in Canada or Mexico." Rosalind shivered. "It's inhumane. I've seen it happen too many times."

"I know you're partial to them, but the law says they can do what they want with them." Max rubbed his chin. "What if we sent hired hands to the auctions to obtain those horses before the meat buyers get their mitts on them?"

"Love it. Let's go a step further. I want the racehorses tracked. When we spot horses who aren't finishing well anymore, we can approach the owners before they send them to the auction houses."

"What a great suggestion. Maybe you can use the Dunne name to spread the word you're buying horses."

"Good point." She nodded and made some notes.

For the next hour Max and Rosalind decided which candidates would be her future boarders. Together they read each email and printed out info on the racehorses and the ones being mistreated. They put them into an invite pile to *Heavens Kiss Sanctuary.*

The second largest pile came from horse owners whose family members had outgrown the want of a horse or hadn't expected the huge expense. But most were forgotten horses or ones mistreated by owners.

In her book, no animal deserved such a total lack of concern. As Max read the emails in the last pile, Rosalind opened a new email from someone called 'Help for the Forgotten.'

To whom it may concern,
I love all animals and heard about your new horse sanctuary. I

too own a ranch. I'm unable financially to do what you're doing. I try to help my neighbors in their time of need the best I can, however, I'm strapped financially. There is one horse I'd like you to consider.

A few weeks ago on my way home, I spotted a stallion standing next to the fence with no shelter from the falling snow or the dropping temperature. I slowed down. I could see he didn't have any blankets or food.

I cried all the way home, telling myself not to get involved. However, in the middle of the night I grabbed several old blankets and a bale of hay. I drove back to the horse. I secured him for the night, the best I could.

The next morning, I called the owner. He said the horse was his son's, who'd stopped wanting the horse. The man hadn't received any money in over a year for the animal's care. As far as I could tell the old man is on a fixed income and was doing the best he could.

I called my town's hardware store and asked for lumber. They gave it to me, and I built a lean-to. I drop off food when I can.

Would you allow this beautiful stallion to live out his life at Heavens Kiss Sanctuary? Thank you for your consideration. I look forward to hearing from you,

Sincerely, Lori.

"Max, you have to read this email. I wish the barns were ready right now." She handed him her iPad and counted the invite pile. Twenty-two plus this new one would make twenty-three. Three more than she'd planned.

"We should definitely accept this one." Max tapped the screen. "I wonder if we can use this person as an in-between shelter house. Kind of like a halfway home. We can supply her with funds to take on horses till we're ready to accept them."

"Good thought. I'll email her right away."

Rosalind tapped her email account and hit reply.

Dear Lori,

Thank you so much for caring. You are not alone. Please do as much as you can.

I'm happy to inform you the stallion will be accepted. We are planning on completion of the barns by mid-summer.

If you have a PayPal or Venmo account, send me your account name. I would like to forward you money to help pay for the stallion's veterinarian bills.

Heavens Kiss Sanctuary, Rosalind Smith

She hit 'send' and as if on cue, Helen carried in a covered pan of sticky buns.

Max stood. "Thank you, the guys will devour these in seconds."

Helen lowered her eyes and smiled. "Oh, it was nothing. Can you tell Joe hello from me?"

"Sure thing, ma'am." Max blushed and took the pan. "Well, I better head out. It's gettin' late."

Rosalind grinned at the exchange. "After practice, do you want to meet? I need to run the numbers again and talk to my lawyers."

"Yes, I can help send out the emails. And thank you, Mrs. Knutson."

Max waved and was gone.

"Breakfast will be at seven-thirty," Helen announced. "I shut everything off in the kitchen."

"Thanks, have a nice night."

"You need some sleep too, young lady."

Rosalind pushed the chair from the table. She paused. The quietness was strange without Allan. In the short time he'd been here, his presence had become a familiar fixture. She checked the doors and headed to her room.

She opened the top drawer of her dresser and reached for a

heart shaped memory box, flipping the lid open. The silver wedding band twinkled at her. It was cold as she slid the band down her ring finger, but it warmed up quickly. How plain it looked but held so much meaning.

She stared at the foreign metal against her hand. It felt odd, but if they were to stay married, she should wear it.

Rosalind lay on the bed, not bothering to get undressed, and snuggled the pillow Allan had used. A musky scent drifted to her nose. She fell into a light sleep as dreams of him at the rodeo, the bar, and in the hotel room, played in her mind.

"Rosalind!"

"Rosalind, we need help!"

"Rosalind!"

She rose on her elbows. Disoriented, she scanned her room in the darkness.

"Rosalind!"

At the faint sound of her name being called, she shoved the blankets off and ran to the window. Joe and the others were screaming for her to come outside. In the moonlight, she saw water gushing from a pipe on the side of the barn.

"Rosalind, wake up!"

Max's voice carried upstairs.

"Coming!" She tore open her bedroom door and down the stairs. Thank heaven she hadn't undressed.

"It's about time. It's a madhouse out there." Max held the front door open.

She slipped on a pair of boots, grabbed a coat from a hook, and bolted out into the cold.

"What's going on?"

"Not sure. It looks like a water pipe burst." Max handed her a flashlight.

"How could this happen?"

"I have no idea. We have to move the horses," Max urged.

"The temperature is dropping, and the water is gonna freeze on the ground."

"The horses have to be moved. Did something happen inside?" She tied the scarf as they ran.

"The water has short-circuited all the electricity, which means..."

"No heat."

Without another word, Rosalind raced back to the house, grabbed blankets, and towels. When she entered the barn, the cold, wet air was penetrating. They finished moving and settling the horses into the second smaller barn around midnight.

"Excuse me, Rosalind."

She whirled and found Joe holding some sort of wrench. "Where did you find that?"

Max joined her and took the tool from Joe.

"I found it in the bushes by the water pipes," he replied.

"This was no accident. I'm calling Sheriff Hoffman right now," Max stated.

"I knew something bad would happen today." Rosalind pounded her fist into her hand. "Why would someone want to sabotage the barn?"

The two men shook their heads.

Madder than a yellow jacket on a summer day, she slammed her fists on her hips. "When I find the bastard or bastards who endangered the lives of my horses, they'll pay. No one threatens my animals."

CHAPTER THIRTY-ONE

"Thank you, Sheriff Hoffman." Rosalind gripped the man's outstretched hand.

"The Cities might help. I'll send the wrench to them for DNA testing. Officers will be arriving in the morning."

"Thank you, sir. The morning will give us better light to comb the area," Joe replied.

"Sounds like a plan. Please, if you see something suspicious call it in right away. I have a man posted at the front gate."

"You know we will," she said.

The sheriff and her ranch-hands left. Once again, the house was quiet, with a lingering odor of coffee in the air. She stared at the Christmas tree. Why had she even bothered? It wasn't bringing her joy like it should.

"It's a beautiful tree," Helen offered, pressing her hands together.

Unable to share Helen's excitement, Rosalind blew out a breath. "Did all the commotion keep you awake?"

"Like anyone would be able to sleep. Do you want a fresh pot of coffee?"

"No, I do need some sleep. The tree is special." Rosalind grinned, remembering how Allan had struggled to cut it, and his heated kisses afterward. Not wanting to disclose that personal scene to Helen, she added quickly, "It was one my dad planted years ago."

"Why cut it down, then?"

"There are plenty more. I planted whole fields of them, plus I have another field Grandpa Rodney and I planted."

"What a wonderful tradition. Oh, by the way, Max said to tell you not to practice in the morning, which, by the way, is only a few hours away. You're to sleep in."

"I *am* tired." Rosalind yawned and glanced at the mantle clock. It was two in the morning.

Helen unplugged the coffee machine and wiped down the counter. "I'll delay breakfast till nine. Max also said he'd be coming to the house around ten-thirty."

"Thank you. He's going to help select which horses to accept."

"Go on now, you resemble a walking zombie. I'll turn everything off."

Grinning at the thought of the older woman watching urban fantasy shows, Rosalind figured it was time to get to know Helen better. Smiling, she gave her a hug.

"Sweet dreams." Helen returned the hug.

"Goodnight," she murmured and headed upstairs to her room. This time she put on her pajamas and snuggled beneath the covers.

———

The mouthwatering aroma of frying bacon woke Rosalind. Her stomach growled. Time to rise. The sun was shining through her curtains, which meant she'd slept past her normal time. For once her natural internal clock failed. She took a quick shower, dressed, and unplugged her phone from the charger. No missed calls. Hesitating, her finger poised over Allan's number.

Should she call?

No, he said he'd call when he had time. She slipped the phone into her back pocket and went downstairs for some much-needed breakfast.

"Morning, Helen. I hope you fried plenty of bacon." She poured herself a cup of coffee.

"You know I did. Scrambled or sunny side up this morning?"

"Sunny side up. Maybe they'll bring me some cheer."

Helen cracked two eggs into the frying pan. "Have you heard from your handsome husband?"

Rosalind felt her cheeks warm. "Nope. He said he had meetings. I'm hoping he'll call this evening."

"He's a man of his word." Helen dropped two pieces of bread in the toaster. "If he says he'll call, he will. Would you like to eat in the dining room instead of the kitchen this morning?"

"The dining room is a good choice. I can work and eat at the same time." She took a sip of her coffee.

"Okay, should be ready in five minutes."

Rosalind topped off her coffee and stepped into the dining room. She clicked on the television to one of the local morning shows, vaguely hearing their jokes about the snow and ice fishing. She moved some papers and took a seat at the table just as an excited voice announced, "I have breaking news. Wealthy New York stockbroker, Allan Smith has been arrested."

She rocked backward in the chair, gaping at a film clip of

her husband, surrounded by police officers, being led from a courthouse in handcuffs.

"Oh, my goodness. It simply can't be."

Catching the plate of food Helen almost toppled, Rosalind set it down, then grabbed the remote and cranked the volume. The fragment of happiness she'd been holding on to faded to infuriation.

"Mr. Smith, owner of Smith and Associates Brokerage Firm, has been arrested for insider trading. His company and several of his employees have been implicated. They are being investigated at this time. The insider trading allegations have been linked to Amazon, an account the Smith and Associates Brokerage Firm had been trading for companies and clients. Mr. Smith is being arrested for insider trading."

A second video of Allan being driven away in a police car flashed. Soon it was replaced by a mug shot of her husband plastered on the screen.

Shit. Who was she married to? Is that why he was so rich?

Could he have been using her home as a hideout?

Helen collapsed on the couch, crying, and shaking her head. Rosalind went to her and cupped a supporting hand over her shoulder as the reporter continued.

"Mr. Smith has posted bond. Sources say he used newly acquired property in Minnesota where he'd been staying under the radar of the FBI. If you're unfamiliar with who Allan Smith is, he recently married a local celebrity, Rosalind Dunne, the darling Queen of the rodeo..."

Newly acquired property? Are they talking about her ranch?

Rosalind clicked the television off. Had Allan tricked all of them? Her eyes teared, but she refused to let them fall, knowing it wasn't worth it. You didn't cry over stepping in cow pies. She knew the difference between cow shit and wild honey.

She should've seen through his good looks, smooth talk, and sexy body.

Suddenly the landline rang.

"Hello?"

"Is this Mrs. Smith?"

"Yes, who is this?"

"I'm Kyle Wilcox from the Wall Street Journal..."

"I have no comment," Rosalind yelled and hung up. It rang again.

"Hello?"

"Mrs. Smith, I'm from the Daily..."

"Don't call here again."

Rosalind slammed the phone down on the table.

Before she could say anything, it rang again. She ignored it, but Helen reached for the phone.

"No. Don't answer it. It's damn reporters."

Helen snatched back her hand. "Oh, my goodness. What are you gonna do? You should go to him. You need to support your husband."

"I can't. He tricked us. Used me. Us. He made me think he was helping. Made me believe he cared about the horses!"

Her voice rose to a shriek as she said the hateful accusations aloud.

He had said he loved her. She had slept with him.

"You don't know that, honey." Helen heaved a breath and wiped at a tear as she walked away. "I've seen and heard the two of you. I know you love him, and he loves you. Don't question your feelings."

"News flash. I did love him."

Her rage had reached a new level. She headed upstairs, leaving Helen to stare after her. Her uneaten breakfast sat on the table. Everything was so confusing. What if someone had blackmailed him? It would be worse than rustlers stealing cows or horses.

Entering Allan's room, she frantically searched through his dresser drawers and papers. She stopped when she found a file labeled 'Portfolio Management.' She sat cross-legged on the floor and opened it.

Oh, God.

He owned the land she'd wanted to purchase which had started all this madness. No, *they* owned the land.

She tilted her head and stared at the ceiling. He had stolen it. Why? If he did it to get back at her for the whole marriage farce, what a wrong move. She didn't want the land for personal gain. She'd wanted to save horses from suffering.

Rosalind set the file aside and opened the next one labeled 'Marriage.' Inside she found instructions to his lawyer to add her name to all his assets. The land in Minnesota was to be sold back to her for one dollar, giving her sole rights to the property, if they were to ever get divorced.

Her tears splattered the papers. She'd believed the worst, but the fact was he'd already given the land to her the day before Sam died.

———

"Honey, you've been in here all morning and most of the afternoon. You need to eat. I'll be leaving soon, being Friday and all. Do you want me to do anything before I go?"

Rosalind stared at Helen for a moment, dazed, she realized she was still in Allan's room.

"No, I'll be fine."

"Max came by earlier and I told him you were unavailable," Helen huffed, her breathing hard. "Sorry, those stairs got the best of me. He said to let him know when you're ready to work on the sanctuary applications."

"Oh right, tell him to come at seven."

"He'll be happy to hear it." Helen's footsteps creaked on the stairs.

The blur of white papers on the floor compelled Rosalind to rub her tired eyes. She'd found out more about her husband in the last few hours than she had in the time he'd been here.

He was a very caring, forgiving, and considerate man. Not only with her, but also in his work. Everything she'd read inspired her to love him even more. Her fears had been for nothing.

Pulling a memo with his office phone number on it, she took out her cell phone and tapped in the numbers. The line rang and rang. An afterhours recording came on and she pressed one to leave a message. She left her name and number.

Next, she tried Allan's cell phone. It rang once and went directly to voicemail.

Damn, why wasn't he or anyone from his office letting her know what was going on?

Rosalind stood slowly, easing her sore muscles from sitting in the same position too long, and trudged downstairs. She passed the landline phone and saw Helen had left it off the hook. When she entered the kitchen, Helen offered a half-smile.

"Good timing, the chicken potpie is done. Pull it from the oven, please. I fixed a second one for Max. I'll cover it with foil. He said seven was too late and he'd come over in a spell."

"Thanks. Was there anything new about Allan on the news?"

Helen's eyes began to tear. "No, they keep replaying the same video." She sniffled. "If there isn't anything else, I'll be going now. Should you change your mind and fly to New York, give me a call. Take care, sweetie."

Quietly, she left the kitchen. Rosalind picked at the potpie and heard the front door open, then Helen's voice.

"I'm leaving now. I'll return Sunday night."

"Okay, thanks," Rosalind yelled.

Is Helen right? Should I go to him?

CHAPTER THIRTY-TWO

After a restless night, Rosalind dragged her dog-tired butt out of bed to start her day. She and Max had worked until after midnight, determined to have things in place before the competition in Oklahoma. They'd been able to enlist the help of the local veterinarians to give questionable horses their exams. Most were thrilled to do the work at no cost once they found out the horses would be saved.

Eighteen of the twenty-three acceptance letters and emails had been sent. They'd procured the builders and would begin when the weather permitted. By and large, very effective several hours of work.

She checked her phone. Still no missed calls.

When would he call? He only had a day to make it back before she left for the BFA World Championship.

Disgusted, she headed downstairs. Without Helen, the kitchen was dark and void of delicious food smells.

Rosalind toasted two pieces of bread, spread peanut butter on them, and took a bottle of vitamin water from the refrigerator. She finished the toast on her way to the barn.

Max had set up the serpentine course. Settling in for her workout, she pushed Dawn and herself through the drill, harder than she had all week.

"Enough, Rosalind." Max grabbed the reins out of her hands and held Dawn's bridle.

"What? I need to do it again, it wasn't perfect."

"If you don't stop, Dawn won't have anything left for you in Oklahoma."

"Leave me alone. I'm doing what I need to do."

"No, you're riding 'cause you're mad."

She dismounted, took off her hat, and wiped away the sweat that, despite the cold, had collected on her forehead. "Sorry, I didn't realize my emotions were pushing me. What if they keep Allan in jail?"

"Don't worry. Mr. Smith can handle his problems. The press always makes things out worse than they are." Max squeezed Rosalind's shoulder.

"I'll walk Dawn. It'll be nice to have an inside practice area soon."

"Yes, it will, but I'll have Joe take Dawn through her cool down. You should head inside before you get sick."

Rosalind nodded and headed to the house. He was right, she couldn't afford even a simple cold right now.

As she neared the empty house, she decided to drive out to the family cemetery on the north end of the property. She hadn't been there since Sam's funeral weeks ago. Rosalind felt ashamed. She'd let her emotions for Allan dominate all her time and hadn't given Sam the proper respect he deserved.

The area was nice in the summer with several old oak and pine trees, lined with lilac bushes and a metal fence. Today however, the harsh winter snow and semi-cloudy skies added a dismal effect to the tombstones.

Someone had shoveled a path which made it easier to

reach the graves. Before her lay her parents, Grandpa Rodney, and Sam.

She stared at the stones and her breath came out in white puffs when she spoke. "I'm sorry for not coming sooner. I miss all of you so very much. I have a lot to tell you. Grandpa Rodney, you were wise beyond my understanding about finding someone to marry outside the rodeo circuit. I'm not proud of the way I went about it. Now I find myself loving the man, and I might lose him too."

She clasped her hands tight. "You'd have liked him, Grandpa. He has a gentle soul once you get to know him. He's a lot like you were. I imagine Sam realized we were meant to be together. And for that, thank you Sam, for making me accept my wrongdoings."

She didn't expect the stones to answer but hoped for a sign she'd been heard. A gust of wind blew the newly fresh snow in swirls. Rosalind shifted her feet and brushed at the strands of hair on her face.

"Mom, Dad, I wish you were here to see what I've been working on. I'm making your dream come true. I'm opening a horse sanctuary. I named it *Heavens Kiss,* in honor of you, Mom. I can picture you giving kisses to each of the horses."

Rosalind choked back tears threatening to fall. She'd forgotten her gloves on the front seat of the truck and now rubbed her hands together to warm them. The coolness of her wedding ring distracted her, and she studied it. The band seemed impersonal, but suddenly sparkled, as the sun peeked through the clouds.

She did have someone. Or did she? For how long?

The clouds hid the sun again. The wedding band turned into a simple silver ring. She shoved her hands in her pockets, not wanting to see the reminder.

"I promise to come by after the competition. Bye." She bowed her head and started away, more confused than before.

Why has God taken everyone she loved?

Her question went unanswered. The dark, empty house loomed before her as she parked the truck. Grumbling sounds erupted from her stomach, reminding her she hadn't eaten. The house was eerily quiet as she entered. No one called out to her. No clatter came from the kitchen or above.

The sad realization, that for the first time in her entire life she was completely alone, was a hard-hitting truth.

I have no one.

I am really alone.

The walls and floor creaked and moaned in an odd sort of way. As she stood in the front hallway, Rosalind took in the room.

Today the colors seemed less bright, even a little dull in the fading sunlight. The same, yet different.

The old furniture appeared worn. Sam had called it comfy. She'd simply ignored it.

The hallway and living room walls cried out for a fresh coat of paint years ago. No one heard them; nevertheless, she heeded them now for the first time.

What must've Allan have thought, coming into this house? No wonder he accused her of trying to blackmail him.

Her discarded winter gear lay on the floor as she took hesitant steps to the living room. The Christmas tree stuck out like a sore thumb without any gifts under it. It too seemed out of place. Not off center, but as if it didn't belong. Usually by this time colorful presents would've filled the floor beneath the tree branches. Sam and the guys always spoiled her. With Christmas two weeks away, she hadn't purchased a single gift.

Studying the tree, she viewed it as if seeing it for the first time. She scrutinized the whole picture.

Nothing. Zilch. The ornaments held no memories of her father or mother, only of her grandfather and Sam. Simply things they'd done to create a sense of family. A false illusion. It never replaced or fulfilled the love she never knew she'd craved, until meeting Allan.

Why hadn't she seen this before?

For years, Grandpa Rodney had created a deception of family for her. Everything represented tradition with no real meaning behind it. Sam had followed suit, probably thinking the ornaments and stuff meant something to her. She couldn't, didn't blame him or her grandfather. They'd done the best they could for her.

Allan's face materialized along with the memory of his kisses and his body pressed against hers as she'd decorated the tree. He was her family now.

Would she have him for long? Or had she lost him, too?

The furnace hissed, sputtering out heat. Emptiness once again flushed over her. She didn't like it. She shivered and shook off an ominous feeling. Instead of continuing through the other rooms and their illusions, she went to the kitchen.

Numerous memories of her and Allan in the hallway and kitchen surfaced. A smile came easily to her face as she fingered the butter knife. He'd pushed her that day. Not because of what he did or said, but because he'd made her feel things she hadn't wanted to.

Coffee. She needed caffeine.

Rosalind scooped two tablespoons of grounds into a glass coffeepot and filled it with water. Grandpa Rodney had introduced her to the old-fashioned way of making coffee. It was strong, the way she'd learned to drink it. She beamed as she remembered when Allan had first tasted it.

Once the coffee was brewing, she searched for anything to

show her she wasn't alone. Roaming from room to room, she ended up in Allan's.

All the papers she'd thrown around the night before, she now straightened. She lifted his pillow to her face and breathed in deeply. She tried to hold onto the scent, never wanting to forget it.

She needed to know the truth. And the words had to come from him.

She'd leapt to conclusions, believing the worst of her husband. Helen was right. She should go to him. Show her support and let the media see her at his side.

"Rosalind."

She spun around and the pillow fell to the floor.

"Allan..."

Her breath caught in her throat. No other words came now that he stood before her. He looked like hell, though his unshaven face boasted a sexy ruggedness. Gone was his stuffy business suit, replaced by a down jacket, a flannel shirt, and jeans.

"Rosalind, I'm sorry."

It was all she needed to hear, and she rushed into his arms. Their lips met in a hungry kiss. She cupped his face, enjoying the roughness of his whiskers, and stared at him.

"You aren't a figment of my imagination, are you?"

"I'm real," he replied.

"How did you—they released you?"

"Yes. Let's savor the moment a bit longer."

Allan hugged her and she returned his embrace eagerly.

"I can't believe it. The news made it sound so—I don't know. I was about to book a plane ticket."

Allan removed her hands and held them in his. "Shhh, I'm so sorry for everything. Well, not everything. Number one, I'm not sorry we're married. Second, I'm not apologizing for making love to you."

With his affirmation Allan kissed her again. She didn't need to listen anymore and kissed him hungrily.

When they surfaced for air, he led her to the bed.

"Sit down. I need to explain some things."

Rosalind gripped the side of the mattress, readying herself for the worst.

"You have every right to get mad at me, maybe even hate me, but I'm hoping—no, I'm praying you'll forgive me."

"I know about—"

"No, hear me out. I am the owner of the land you—we're using for the sanctuary. I was so angry when I got here, all I wanted to do was ruin your life, make you miserable. When Sam showed me the horses you were trying to save, I felt like a schmuck. I had to backpedal to make things right. I misled you into thinking I could help you, wanting you to believe I was a hero. Your hero. I'm sorry everything got out of hand. The bigger the lie became, the deeper I dug myself into a hole."

She shook her head slowly. "You made me look like a fool."

"I regret that too. I'm appalled by my actions. Every day I wanted to tell you the truth. I even had Tiffany, issue a buyout plan from the Portfolio Management Company."

"Allan, I began to trust you." Her voice had come out in a soft tone. She eyed him as he paced from one side of the room to the other.

He combed his hand through his hair. "The reason I left abruptly when I did was because the Feds served a subpoena. They arrested me because I refused to grant them access to my company's files, computers, and our list of clients."

"Did you do anything illegal?"

He stopped his pacing. "No, let me start at the beginning. The reason I was in Las Vegas, as you know, was for my friend John's wedding. Remember I told you, he and I went through the foster care system together. We always had each other's back after that. Apparently, last year when he came to visit me at my office, he overheard a discussion about the price of Amazon stock. He used that confidential information to buy and sell the stock."

"And that's wrong because why?"

"There's more, according to the Feds. Allegedly several transactions were made dealing with Amazon from inside my company. It's the law you can't personally gain money when you are involved in corporate legal buyouts. They were asserting John and I benefited from these dealings. Insider trader. Martha Stewart. Does this make sense?"

Rosalind's forehead wrinkled. "Somebody who heard something gave that information to someone else. Then that someone else profited from that information. It's like a who's on first riddle."

"Yes, it's close to what happened. My lawyers have assured me neither I nor my company, Smith, and Associates Firm, could be implicated. I, however, would have to give the Feds access to the computers, clients, and employees to prove John, my firm or I did not profit from the illegal trades based on nonpublic information. Most of my money is frozen by the Feds. To post the five-million-dollar bail, I used your ranch as collateral for part and my lawyers made arrangements for the balance."

Rosalind stayed on the edge of the mattress, stone-faced.

Could she believe him?

"I was released at two-thirty this morning once the bail was paid. I went straight to my plane. I'd put my pilot on a minute's notice."

Allan came and stood at the foot of the bed. She didn't know what to say.

"I didn't waste any time. I came straight back to you." Suddenly he was kneeling in front of her. He clasped her hands as she raised her head and peered into his eyes.

"Rosalind, I love you. I think—no, I now know you were extraordinary when I saw you at the rodeo in Las Vegas. I want to stay married. If you'll have me."

Her eyes widened when he held out a light blue box with a signature white ribbon. This kind of stuff only happens in movies or in books.

Was she daydreaming?

She closed and rubbed her sleep-deprived eyes. A drop-dead gorgeous man on one knee declaring his love to a woman and she was that woman.

When she opened them, Allan was still in front of her holding out the box. Not able to say a word because she couldn't think of anything to say, she took the box with *Tiffany & Co.* printed on the top.

She lifted the lid, and another box greeted her. This one was black velvet. Her hands trembled for the first time in her life, as she flipped the lid open and gasped.

A diamond ring. The gem was the size of Texas. It could've won first place in a bull show. Allan was crazy.

"If it's not big enough we can go shopping for another one once the Feds release my money. I had to have Paul front me the money for this one."

A bit at the disadvantage, being in unknown territory, she swallowed hard.

"Allan, are you positive you want me? Because there aren't any mulligans in marriage where I'm concerned. If we stay married, it's forever," she murmured and stared at him, afraid he'd disappear.

"Yes, I'm sure. Till death do us part. Through the gray hairs, wrinkles, face-lifts, and liposuction."

His sexy charisma brought a smile to her face.

He truly loved her. She *did* have a family.

"Oh Allan," she moaned.

Their lips became one. She moved to the middle of the bed, and he joined her. She'd found a partner. Someone who loved her.

The house wasn't quiet any longer. Rosalind's laughter and Allan's promises filled the air.

CHAPTER THIRTY-THREE

A loud pounding woke Rosalind from her sleep. Through the drowsy fog, she realized the sound came from downstairs.

"Coming!"

It didn't work. The pounding continued. She smothered a groan, unwrapped Allan's arms, and sat up.

"Don't leave," he murmured and reached out to her.

"Someone's at the door." Rosalind shouted louder this time. "I'm coming!"

Allan's eyes flew open instantly. "No, you stay here. I'll go."

"We'll both go."

Even in the darkened room she sensed his displeasure by his silence. Together they dressed quickly and headed downstairs. She reached for the doorknob, but Allan was quicker and got to it first.

Max stood on the step, his lips and jaw tight in the early morning chill.

"Oh, you're back. Good, we can use an extra hand. We have another problem, Rosalind."

"Max, what is it?" She waved for him to come in and Allan moved aside flipping on the lights. "Another?"

"Yes, when I went to check on the trucks and trailers for our early departure tomorrow, I found most of the tires slashed."

"Shit. Oh my God, that's fifteen tires!" Rosalind led the men to the kitchen and got busy making coffee.

"Someone tell me what's going on," Allan demanded.

Max took a seat at the table while Allan stood in the doorway with his hands on his hips. She looked at Max and nodded.

"A water line broke the night you left. We found evidence it wasn't an accident." Max straightened in the chair and combed his fingers through his beard. "The sheriff's ordered a probe and an investigation. That's all we know."

Allan swore under his breath. "I caught sight of a police car at the entrance when I drove in. Why didn't anyone tell me? Or call me."

Rosalind shook her head and exchanged glances with Max. "Allan, I tried calling but they all went to voicemail. I couldn't contact you. Feds and jail."

"Damn, sorry." Allan wandered aimlessly around the kitchen and appeared deep in thought, while Max sat quietly. Rosalind let them contemplate what to do.

Allan broke the silence first. "I'm here now, so fill me in." He joined Max at the table.

The coffee came to a boil and Rosalind set the pot down along with three cups.

"There's nothing more to tell. The deputies have no suspicious activity to report. All the ranch-hands are on alert." Not wanting to let them see her concern, she took a sip of coffee and leaned against the counter.

Max poured himself a cup, adding some sugar. "We have four spare tires on hand. I've already put calls into the Randall and Brainerd tire companies for replacements. I should get them in time for us to leave. Worst case scenario, we'll have to take tires from the unused trailers."

"Okay." Allan nodded. "Let me—us know of your progress."

"I will. Rosalind, no practicing today. Allan, good to know you're back."

Max took one last gulp of coffee and left.

"I'm sorry I wasn't here for you," Allan sighed. "Any thoughts as to who it might be?"

Rosalind took Max's place at the table. She folded her hands in front of her. "Max and Joe have a suspicion it might be Tom Clark."

"Who is he?"

The words didn't want to come. They hadn't discussed past relationships before. "He is an old boyfriend."

She held her breath against an onset of questions, but they didn't come.

"They're always a pain in the butt. Does he live around here?"

His response surprised her, yet in a comforting way. The thought that he really did care for her sent a calming surge through her. "No, he has a place in Tomah, Wisconsin. He's a bull rider and not well-liked on the circuit. He was after my money. He found out how large my inheritance would be if I married him, and he tried to pressure me for a wedding date. When I told him no, he—he got rough."

She caught how Allan's eyes widened and his jaw tightened before she lowered her eyes.

"Did he physically harm you?"

"No, no, he didn't... well, he slapped me. Sam and the others were there right away. I've put the incident behind me."

"Son of a bitch." Allan pounded his fist on the table, rattling the coffee cups.

"Let's talk about something else, okay?"

"I'm not happy about this, Rosalind. The man hurt you."

"It's in the past." She poured more coffee into her cup and her calmness disappeared. She hated to talk about Tom.

"Putting it in your past doesn't mean he's done the same. What makes them think it could've been Tom?"

He reached across the table and took her hand. Rosalind looked at him and saw no judgement in his eyes.

A spark of a memory came to her. "He has a bad temper. I witnessed firsthand his treatment of animals, and it wasn't very nice. Joe says most everyone has blackballed him."

"Blackballed?"

"It's when a rider is banned from competitions for being a troublemaker. As far as I know he doesn't have any friends. He usually arrives by himself. Once he showed me pictures on his phone of bull riders getting hurt. Afterward he laughed and found their injuries humorous."

"This is beginning to make sense." Allan tapped his fingers on the table. "Is there anything else you remember about him?"

Rosalind thought for a minute. She'd been through this with Max, too. "How could the culprit be him? We haven't spoken in two years."

"People can be devious, even cynical to the point of black-mail when they can't have what they want. Tell me anything, everything, no matter how unimportant."

"I don't want to think about him. It was a bad time in my life. Let's have breakfast first. I'm hungry, aren't you?"

Allan slid his chair next to hers and turned her to face him. He enfolded her hands within his. Their warmth touched the sadness that threatened to quench her happiness. She stared into his eyes.

"I'm always hungry for you, but if you mean food, sure. Do you want me to help?"

"No, unless you learned to cook in the last couple of days."

He stood and playfully pointed his finger. "Oh, I know when I'm not wanted. I need to check in with Paul and Tiffany."

Rosalind crossed to the stove. "An omelet or fried eggs?"

"A ham and cheese omelet sounds great," Allan said.

"Easy enough. Give me about twenty minutes."

"Sounds good. We'll continue our discussion." He kissed her cheek before leaving the kitchen.

———

"Paul, I might have found the mole."

"Do you have a name?"

"Tom Clark. Lives in Tomah, Wisconsin. He's a bull rider," Allan added.

"He's not on our list. I'm not sure..."

"I don't care if he's not on our list. Do what you can to procure information on him." He knew Paul would do what he wanted. "Rosalind ran into some unexpected and suspicious mishaps after I left for New York."

"I'll get on it right away. The Feds found two employees responsible for the leak. The company lawyers said John won't be prosecuted since he only made one minor trade and used a different brokerage firm. The ruling held that John's trade was simply a lucky investment. However, our two employees deliberately gave their clients insider information. Those trades and clients are under investigation."

"Do what you need to do. I leave tomorrow for Rosalind's competition in Oklahoma. Call me with any information on Tom Clark once you get it."

"Will do, talk to you later."

Allan ended the call. A delicious aroma filled the air. On

his way to the kitchen, he paused at the dining room table and glanced at the project. For the first time in his life, he could actually say he was about to make a positive difference.

"Mm-mmm, something smells wonderful," he said as he entered and sat at the kitchen table.

"It's just the omelet you requested."

"I know, and I love the chef." He reached out and caressed her butt as she came over to the table.

"Oh, I see how it is." She leaned into him. "You want someone to be your maid with benefits."

"Rosalind, caring about someone besides myself is new to me. You are the first woman to change me from an uncaring, callous man to one who truly cares. I don't know what I'd do if I lost you. When you said Tom hit you, all I wanted to do was pull you into my arms. I wanted to hunt down that mother-fucker and kick the living shit out of him."

"Really?"

He nodded, noticing the catch in her voice.

"Okay. I knew there was something dark about Tom and I wanted to be a rebel. I dated him to infuriate my grandfather. It backfired."

"You can tell me anything. Let's call this our courting stage."

"Aren't we doing this backward?"

Her smirk made him laugh and she joined in. It eased the tension as they finished breakfast. He had her take a shower first, and it was late morning when they entered the barn.

He witnessed firsthand all the water damage. "Where are the horses?"

"We moved them to the second barn, but it's not designed to house that many horses."

Allan eyed the stall where they'd first made love and frowned. The wood frame was covered in ice. The floor had at least two inches of ice on top of thick frozen mud.

"This is horrific. When can we get a crew to fix all this?"

"Max says Wednesday. We have to bring in heaters to melt the ice and blowers to dry everything out."

He followed Rosalind into the other barn. She went directly to Dawn's stall, and he searched for Joe. He found him unstacking straw bales.

"Hi, Joe. Do you have a minute?"

"Sure do."

The old man tugged off his gloves and stuffed them in his coat pocket.

"Max and Rosalind say you suspect Tom Clark for the trouble that has been happening here on the ranch."

"I do. I spotted him in Brainerd."

"How far do you think he will go?" Allan leaned against the wall.

"Don't know. Never liked him," Joe grumbled. "Too cocky. Always ready to fight like a strutting banty rooster."

Joe slipped on his gloves. Allan did the same and they moved a straw bale and cut the wire holding it in place. Together they pitched the straw into a stall.

"Have you talked to the sheriff?"

"Yes, but we have no evidence. Tom is a snake," Joe blurted out in a hard tone.

Allan heard the disgust and wondered how Rosalind had ever gotten involved with someone everyone seemed to dislike.

"Do we have the tires yet?"

He and Joe turned. Rosalind had come up upon them without them knowing. Allan slipped his arm around her.

"Yup." Joe nodded. "Max went into town for them. We won't have to take any from the other trailers. Like I told the sheriff, I found tracks leading away from the trailers to the gate, and all the way to the road."

"Interesting." Allan looked at Rosalind. "If the gate lock

hadn't been damaged was there any signs of it being tampered with?"

"I checked it myself, it was clean," Joe stated. "No footprints, nothing else."

"Okay. Ask Max to come see us when he returns and keep my girl warm," she said.

"Yes, ma'am."

Joe nodded and hauled a straw bale into the next stall. Rosalind moved away from him. Allan had to wonder why she was working so hard to ride in a rodeo. "You never told me what's so important about this competition."

"It's only the most coveted title for a barrel rider. If I win, I'll be part of the first mother and daughter to win the same title."

"Your mother won?"

"Yes, the year before she died." Rosalind returned to stand next to him. "Plus, it has a huge purse."

"Wow, incredible. At least you have those memories. I don't have any happy thoughts about my parents. I remember moving around a lot. My mom and dad worked so much they usually left me home alone."

"That's so sad. We'll make our life full of lasting happy memories."

"I'd like that," he said with a half-smile.

"Let's head to the house. The guys have everything under control." She hugged his arm as they walked to the barn doors. A blast of frigid air hit them. He withdrew his arm and wrapped it around her.

"So, tell me why the purse part of this competition is important. You have money."

She paused in midstride and faced him.

"Yes, I have money, but taking care of horses and running a ranch takes a lot. If I stop competing, my income is gone. I've been trying to build up my cash reserves and this competition will give me a modest cushion."

"If you need money, I can help..."

"No, I'm sure you can, but I want to do this on my own. People and animals will be counting on me for a long time. Did you know a horse can live to be twenty-five to thirty-five years old?"

"Thirty-five years. Wow, I would never have guessed."

"You're such a city boy."

They pivoted around in unison at the sound of a car coming down the driveway.

"It's Helen," Rosalind exclaimed with excitement.

They waited for her to park. When Helen got out of the car, she went straight to Allan and hugged him. "I knew they were wrong about you. Glad you've returned."

Allan kissed her cheek. "And I'm so pleased you're here. Now I don't have to eat Rosalind's so-so cooking. Last night she tried to starve me till we found your frozen home cooked dinners."

"If I were younger, I'd steal you away from Rosalind."

Laughing, Allan helped Helen carry in groceries.

CHAPTER THIRTY-FOUR

"Breakfast!"

Rosalind and Allan grinned at each other. Having been up since the crack of dawn, they were starved. They raced from the bedroom and down the stairs. She beat him by a split-second even with his interference.

"No need to rush, there's plenty." Helen placed a platter of French toast on the table.

"Holy moly, it looks like you're feeding an army," Rosalind blurted out. She rubbed her hands together with anticipation.

Allan took his usual spot and she hers while Helen once again took Sam's old place. They heaped their plates with scrambled eggs, sausages, and thick slices of French toast.

When their plates were cleaned Helen asked, "Allan, is there anything else I can get for you? I can't let the two of you go hungry on your long drive."

He patted his stomach. "No, this is perfect. Way too much food for me."

Rosalind's eyebrows rose at his words. It was plain to see Helen was so sweet on him. She found it funny but couldn't resist giving him grief. Allan avoided her penetrating gaze. So, she kicked him under the table. His eyes flicked toward the ceiling in mock innocence.

"You let me know if you think of anything. I'm gonna have sandwiches, coffee, and fresh cinnamon rolls ready to take with you."

Again, Rosalind glanced at Allan and then to Helen. The whole mother hen scene made her smile.

Her husband did have a way with women.

She pushed away from the table. "We better move our asses. Time is ticking away. Max texted me. The trailer is almost ready."

"Okay boss," he said.

"Remember to come back for your goodies."

At Helen's reminder, he turned toward her. "Like you could keep me away."

Helen's cheeks took on a pinkish glow before she turned away and busied herself in the refrigerator.

"Oh boy, now I've seen it all." Rosalind muttered under her breath and strolled into the hallway.

"What?" Allan came up next to her.

"As if you don't know."

"Do I detect a little bit of jealousy?"

She zipped her coat and opened the door, wishing she was still in the comfort of Allan's arms and their warm bed. "If we had more time, I'd hog-tie you and show you how upset I am."

Outside in the frigid morning air, the clarity of the whole situation didn't make sense. During the last twenty-four hours, so much had changed that it was hard to take in. Allan's surprise return had given her hope for a happy ending.

"Hey wait," Allan shouted. "Hog-tie me? I haven't tried making love that way before. Sounds interesting."

"Come on, City Boy, we have work to do." She gave him a slight shove, wishing they did have time for a lesson.

"I'm so stuffed I'm sure to fall asleep in the truck."

She pointed toward the loaded vehicle. "No, you're driving first."

"I...see."

A chuckle escaped her. "Do you think I'd trust you to drive while Dawn's trailer is attached?" She shook her head while he shrugged.

"When you put it like that, yeah. I don't have the expertise. But I'm a quick learner. Ask John, my best friend."

"Not this trip." The thought of allowing another person into her domain had a nice feel to it, but scary. She'd have to trust him sooner or later.

A flurry of activity met them. Her Silverado HD 3500, with the trailer already attached, sat waiting next to the Suburban at the barn. Walt loaded supplies into the trailer and Joe finished packing the trucks.

"Morning, Joe. Morning, Walt," she called out.

"Morning Rosalind, Mr. Smith. Will we have an on-time departure?" Walt asked.

"Yup, heading to get Dawn now. Joe, Helen's prepared special food packages for us. When you're done, can you swing by the house and pick them up along with our luggage?"

Joe's eyes widened and he smiled. "Sure can. I'll go now."

Rosalind put her arm through Allan's and pulled him into the barn. She didn't miss his confused look.

"Did I miss something?"

"He's sweet on Helen."

"I thought I was her only man." Allan chuckled.

Rosalind punched his arm. "Get real, lover boy. Stop flirting, we have work to do."

She walked to the fourth stall, Dawn's temporary home,

and stroked her velvety nose. The mare snuffled against her fingers. "Do you feel it too, my beautiful girl? A storm is brewing."

She withdrew a sugar lump from her coat pocket and held it out. Dawn snatched the treat, tossing her head, her light brown mane flying from side to side.

"Come on girl, time to get going." Opening the stall, she placed both arms around Dawn's neck. "You know Grandpa taught us to always be on time."

About to move away, the tang of the horses and sounds of the truck engines took hold of her senses. Unwanted scenes flashed before her, a slide show of unpleasant snapshots of the awful night of her parents' death. The ugly ambiance played in her mind. She squeezed her eyes to block them.

Relax. Don't fight it. Breathe.

As quickly as they'd started, the memories stopped.

"Rosalind? Are you ill?"

She lifted her head when she heard Allan's worried tone. He came to her and placed a hand on her shoulder.

"No, sometimes a sound or odor makes me think of my parents. I'll be fine in a minute."

He engulfed her in a loving embrace. "You're not alone anymore. I'm here for you."

The depth of his vow struck a chord at her heart. She marveled at his strength, knowing he'd lost parents too. "Thank you. It's been hard over the years. Even with Sam. I know now I needed more, but never wanted to go for it."

As the intense sadness vanished, she put on her business-like face. He loosened his arms, dropped a kiss on her forehead, and stepped away. His act of kindness seemed unreal to her. She paused for a moment, tilting her head to stare at him. When he leaned in, his next kiss was heated but tender.

"I love you."

She blinked. They were an odd pair. "I love you, too. Now, time to hustle."

"Okay, Miss Business."

"We have to meet and join some friends in Iowa. We always travel together for safety." She steered Dawn outside to the trailer. "When you're pulling horses it's nice to know the vehicle behind or in front of you will respect your space."

Her red and silver conversion trailer sported four new tires, and her Silverado also had six. The cost of them, along with the repairs to the barn, dug into funds she hadn't wanted to touch quite yet. She brought Dawn to a halt next to Max. The rear ramp was down and ready.

He took the reins from her. "Ho, Ho, come on girl," Max cooed. "It's your lucky weekend."

"Wow. This is Dawn's trailer?"

Rosalind smiled at Allan. "Yes, what did you expect? One of those things you see in the movies, rickety and ready to fall apart?"

He walked around the horse trailer, shrugging. "Don't know what I thought. As you so like to call me, I am a city boy, through and through. I can't believe the hard work and time that goes into preparing for a competition. It's a lot like the night before a company debut on the New York Stock Exchange for the first time."

"You hire cowboys to walk horses around your office?"

"No..." His chin lifted higher.

She'd gotten the response she'd wanted. "Just seeing if you were paying attention."

"I am. Why do you keep staring at me?"

"I like the view."

He smiled. "Don't I look like a city boy anymore?"

Her heart pounded faster. No, he didn't. She wished they had more time. A lesson in hog-tying would be fun.

"All secure," Max yelled.

She turned away first and went to Max, giving him a hug. "Wish us luck."

"You don't need luck. Your skill will take you to the finish line." Max nodded to Allan. "Take care of our winner."

"You're not coming?"

"No, I get to stay here and take care of the ranch," Max replied. "Remember, the repairs are scheduled for Wednesday."

Allan's expression was priceless, all arched brows and gaping mouth. "Am I expected to help Rosalind by myself?"

Rosalind bowed her head to hide her grin.

"No, Joe and Walt will be in the Suburban following you. They've done this before," Max said.

"Thank God," Allan paused and then added. "You can count on me to take care of our winner."

Max latched the back gate and took hold of Allan's arm. "Keep an eye out for Tom. I let a friend, David Billy, know about our troubles. He'll be meeting you along the way."

"You know I will."

Rosalind could hear the anger laced in Allan's voice. If Max told David Billy, the whole circuit would know, which meant if Tom tried anything, he wouldn't stand a chance.

She shifted her feet restlessly. "Ready to go? Time is wasting away."

"Whenever you are. I'm the navigator."

His enthusiasm seemed genuine, and she didn't want to burst his bubble, but did it anyways. "Hate to tell you, but I don't need one, the truck has its own."

"Right, GPS."

"Call if we have any more incidents," Rosalind told Max. "I doubt you will, here on the ranch, if your suspicions are true and it's Tom."

"Don't worry, Boss Lady. Keep focused on the run. Let Dawn take the lead out of the gate. Stay on pace..."

"Yes, yes. I know. Bye, Max."

They all laughed, and she waved. Rosalind walked to the driver's side, receiving a kiss from Allan before she hopped into the truck.

CHAPTER THIRTY-FIVE

At the first checkpoint in Iowa, their convoy of two became six pick-up trucks towing horse trailers. The sky threatened to let loose another round of snow.

Rosalind glanced over at Allan who was rubbing his eyes. "So, Mr. New Yorker, ever ride in a truck for hours on end?"

The CB crackled with talk, and she lowered the volume.

"Never. Road trips aren't on my bucket list and weren't as a kid either."

"Not much to see," she volunteered and turned on the wipers as the predicted snow fell. "It's a lot of farmland from here to Missouri. We stop there next."

"Sorry I fell asleep. I haven't recovered from all the traveling. Guess I have jet-lag." Allan yawned and placed his hand on her thigh.

"Nothing to be sorry about. Can you get me a water?"

He reached behind the backseat and took a bottle of water from the cooler, untwisting the cap for her.

"Thanks." She took a couple of swigs. "Do you want to talk?"

"I'm fine just staring at my beautiful wife."

She felt a rush of heat on her cheeks and knew she must be blushing. "Stop. I'm not."

"Yes, you are. You certainly don't realize it."

"Can we talk about something else?" She fidgeted with the heat control.

"Have you ever considered building a new house?"

"That was sure a change of subjects. No, why would I have to?" Rosalind took another sip of her bottled water.

"Okay, then. What about expansion? I don't want to be disrespectful, but can we add on? The house is a little small. Maybe about a few thousand square feet would be perfect."

Change the only home she knew? Rosalind thought for a moment. "Don't you like the homey feeling?"

"Yeah, well—sure—maybe another room for an office?"

She twisted the cap back on the water bottle, placing it in the cup holder. She had him in the hot seat, and he was squirming. "Why not tear down the house and build a three-story mansion?"

"Rosalind, no. I have Tiffany surfing the net for office space in town..."

She laughed. "Gotcha."

"That was cruel. I guess I deserved it. I will be discussing stepping down and promoting Paul to President. I have the paperwork ready."

Taking her eyes off the road for a moment, Rosalind stared at Allan. He seemed serious. Had she'd done it? Turned a city boy into a country—no, a real-life cowboy? Funny how fate had a way of pulling you in a direction which brought you full circle. She'd gone from not wanting to marry a non-rodeo man, to loving one. "You want to stay? Live full time in Minnesota?"

"If you'll have me. I thought we could take long vacations in the winter to the sunshine states or warmer countries."

"I don't know what to say. You have more than one house? Just how many do you own?"

"It doesn't matter. Some are for investments. One is right on the Gulf of Mexico. I—we might want to find something else. Florida zoning laws might not allow horses. Maybe we can look inland so Dawn can come with us?"

Tears welled up. He actually thought to include Dawn. "If I wasn't driving, I'd show you, my answer."

The CB noise increased, and Rosalind turned the volume up a notch. She caught Walt's voice.

"Break, ten-nine."

"Ten-seventy-three at one-thirty-six."

"Ten-four," Rosalind said into the mic. She tapped the brakes, undoing the cruise control, and the speed dropped to the limit.

"Were you speeding?"

"Not really, I..."

"It's a yes or no question," Allan coaxed.

"Fine. Yes. We set our cruise controls at six miles over the limit. Most highway patrol officers won't pull you over for that."

"I'm riding with a law breaker. Maybe I should drive," he replied.

"Oh, be quiet. I have a fugitive from the law as a passenger."

They laughed together and the hours ticked by quickly. They talked about the sanctuary, opening a LLC or a nonprofit business to be able to taken in donations and adding onto the house. Allan fell asleep again, leaving her to contemplate having him at the house full-time.

When the six-pack of her convoy reached the Missouri state line, they merged off Interstate 35 into the rest area. She shifted the truck into park. The other vehicles followed suit. Not seeing David, the newest participant to add to their convoy waiting, she decided to go to the restroom.

Rosalind glanced at her sleeping husband. It was odd to think of Allan as that, even funny in a weird way. He looked so comfortable, she opted not to wake him yet.

She pulled the door handle, slipped outside closing the door, and stretched. A gloved hand covered her mouth, and another grabbed her arm harshly. Rosalind's muscles tightened as she used her free arm to slam it into the gut of the attacker behind her.

The attacker uncovered her mouth and with surprising strength, she was whirled around and body-slammed against the side of the truck. With the wind knocked out of her, she gulped for air. Even though both of her hands were free, she couldn't make herself use them.

Panic had taken ahold of her.

Then, once again a gloved hand was covering her mouth cutting off her ability to scream and she found herself eye to eye with Tom Clark.

Her panic changed to anger.

He pressed his body against her, immobilizing her. Rosalind tried to relax and allow herself to fall to the ground as her self-defense instructors had taught her. But the truck and his weight against her were obstacles she couldn't overcome. She kept trying to raise her arms so she could use them.

His face twisted into an ugly sneer. "Rosalind honey, it's good to see you. Hold still."

Tom pressed his hand harder over her mouth. She stopped her struggles.

"See, now that's my girl. I've missed you. I thought we'd have time for a quickie before we're on the road again."

Horror washed through her. The sweetness of his voice soured Helen's chicken she'd eaten, and she gagged at the thought of him kissing her. Renewing her efforts, she was able to raise her leg up just enough to kick at him.

Winning a victory, his body opened a gap between them, but he kept his hand on her mouth.

Shit. She couldn't see anyone coming to help her.

"That wasn't very smart."

Tom breathed the words into her face, and she smelled alcohol. Inching her arms out to her sides, memories of his long ago slap flashed in her mind.

A hatred like none that she'd ever felt before set in over her. Just as she was about to grab his arm, he shoved her jarring back against the truck and wedged his booted foot between hers, forcing her legs apart, and pressed his body against her again.

Rosalind fought harder this time, twisting her body and head, determined not to be the victim of his temper.

"Tom Clark, get your hands off my wife!"

Allan's knife-cutting demand was electrifying. She ceased her struggles.

"Ah, the husband has balls after all. I'm showing *my* sweet Rosalind I've never stopped wanting her. You must know how satisfying she is."

His hand lifted off her mouth. She gasped as air filled her lungs as she sagged forward. Tom locked his arm around her neck, dragging her alongside him.

"Let me go!"

"Shut up, slut," Tom hissed into her ear.

He tightened his hold around her neck cutting off her air. She couldn't think clearly.

Rosalind watched as Allan advanced toward them. "I said, let go of my wife."

Surprisingly Tom's grip loosened, and she wriggled free, coughing, and stumbling into the safety of Allan's arms.

"Rosalind, are you okay?"

"I-I am," she stuttered as Allan hugged her.

"Go. I want to have a little chat with our friend here."

She hurried to the restroom, never looking back at the two men and somehow, she managed to drum up a semblance of calm.

———

Allan didn't watch Rosalind leave, he heard the click of her boots grow softer, and that was enough.

"This is your final and only warning, Clark. Stay away from my wife. She is mine." He narrowed the space between the two of them. "If you ever, and I mean ever touch Rosalind again, you'll find yourself in jail."

Tom raised his hands high into the air, but his grin held malice and Allan fisted his hands.

"You can't be by her side twenty-four-seven." Tom widened his stance.

He knew Tom was primed for a fight, but tonight was not the time or place to take him up on his offer. "Try me, bastard. If I even hear you're in town, I'll have you permanently banned from the bull riding circuit."

His anger had reached the point of no return. He took a step, grabbed Tom's shoulders, and slammed him into the side of the truck, one fist raised.

"Right, like you even have any clout with the circuit. You don't. Empty threats."

"Oh, I will have you banned. My word is as good as gold. And I mean you'll be banned everywhere." Allan slowly loosened his hold and stepped back, fists ready in case Tom tried something. "You have no idea who I know. I have influential contacts all over the globe."

"I don't like sloppy seconds anyway. Enjoy the fact I was her first. When you're done with her and go home to the Big Apple, she'll come begging for me."

Seething anger took over. Allan drew back his right hand which met Tom's stomach, then his left hand followed. Tom gagged and staggered forward. Allan grabbed Tom's chin, yanking him up. "Stay away from her or you'll regret it."

He shoved Tom away who began to wheeze.

Tom rolled his shoulders and shook his head. "You're the one who needs to stay away from me. Don't get in my way."

"Walk away now, Clark, if you want to be able to do it on your own."

"She was mine first! She shouldn't have married you. The release of the photos and the videos should have been proof. I'm a free man. I can do what I want. We've got unfinished business." Tom straightened and sauntered away.

Allan held himself back from pursuing him. The man was crazy. He waited for his fury to cool before looking for Rosalind. He'd dealt with sickos like Clark all throughout his childhood. Even sported black eyes, a broken nose, and cracked ribs before being sent to the next foster care family.

Tom had picked on the wrong man. He was no fool.

Joe came running up to him. "You, okay? I see you met Tom Clark. I can call the police. Did he try something?"

"Nothing I couldn't take care of. I'll call Sheriff Hoffman myself. We'll need to be on high alert from now on," Allan said.

"By all means. I'll let Walt know too. Tell Rosalind, David wasn't able to meet us here. He'll join us *en* route."

"Sure." Allan's breathing slowed as his adrenaline level lowered.

Joe nodded and returned to the other truck. Rosalind reappeared, and Allan gave her a hug and a kiss.

He held her face in his hands. "Are you injured or hurt?"

"I'm fine. I'm sorry. I should've woken you up, but I thought you needed your sleep."

Allan tried to rein in his anger and irritation at witnessing Tom's hands on his wife. "It's okay. Max and Joe warned me about Tom. I don't think we've seen the last of him. Was he in Las Vegas when we were there?"

"Tom did ride the bulls, but I never saw him."

"Was he at the bar too?"

She shook her head and pressed her lips together. "No. Sam had banned Tom from the ranch, and everyone made sure he never came near me. He didn't dare show his face. Sam relented and we went to the bar the night I found you. He didn't leave until David assured him, he would look out for me."

Allan nodded. "He might be the leak."

"What makes you say that?"

"After you left, he commented that the pictures are proof I can't protect you all the time." Allan cursed under his breath. "He's a sick man. I'd bet my last dollar he'll cause more trouble."

"I need to check on Dawn before we leave."

"Joe said David can't join us till later." Allan took hold of her hand.

"Thanks, I was worried when I didn't see his truck."

He kept pace with her as they walked to the side of the trailer. She opened a small window. Dawn stuck her nose out and in return, Rosalind handed her a sugar lump.

"That's my girl. Only a few more hours," Rosalind cooed and closed the window.

He followed her to the driver's side door. Once she was safely inside, he climbed in the other side. They rode in silence for miles. He played the scene with Tom over and over in his mind, searching for something he or Paul missed. Tom's voice wasn't familiar. Nor was his face, but nothing from Vegas was clear. Allan tapped his phone, wanting to call Tiffany and Paul.

"How much further?"

"About six hours. We'll have one more fuel stop. Do you need something?"

"Cell service."

"A man without the use of his phone. My heart bleeds for you. We could sing a few rounds of 'Ninety-Nine Bottles of Beer.'"

"No, thank you. Never liked that song." He held up the phone. "I need to call Paul and Tiffany and let them know Tom might be the person responsible for releasing the photos and video."

"Thanks for being there for me. You don't know how relieved I was to hear your voice."

Allan placed his hand on her thigh. Her admission tore at him. "I'll always be here for you. I love you."

CHAPTER THIRTY-SIX

The convoy exited for a final rest stop before they reached their destination, the Fairgrounds at State Fair Park. Twelve pickup trucks pulled into the rest area one by one, filling the empty parking spaces.

A moment of panic gnawed at Rosalind as she looked out the windshield. "What if Tom's here?"

"He wouldn't dare show his face." Allan winked and nodded toward the backseat.

His bold statement bolstered her courage, and she met his seductive eyes. "Not enough time, lover boy."

"Are you sure?"

Excitement sparked at the prospect of a quickie. Her pulse quickened as he drew her face to his. Their lips touched lightly at first, then the kiss surged to the next level. She slid her hand between his thighs, feeling him come to life.

"Mmmm. I see what you mean. Maybe we..."

A tap on the window broke them apart. Rosalind looked over her shoulder, and he moved to see who was outside. Walt stood there grinning and mouthed, "Time to go."

Rosalind lowered her head and rubbed at her lips before she opened the door and stepped out.

"Got any extra of Helen's fried chicken? We ate all of ours," Walt said.

"Ask Allan. He's been munching the whole trip."

"I have *not* been munching. I'd call it snacking."

Rosalind rolled her eyes and Walt snickered.

"What?" Allan threw up his hands. "We do have a piece or two left. You can have them when we get back from the restrooms."

Walt slapped Allan on his back. "You're not alone. Helen's chicken is the best. I'll check on Dawn when I swing back this way."

"Thanks, Walt," Rosalind said.

Allan took her hand and they walked to the building. Other members of the convoy called out greetings to Rosalind, but not to him.

"Don't worry. They'll get used to you in time." She smiled as she added, "We're a tight group, and they don't take to newcomers."

"I was beginning to think I stank, the way they avoided me."

"Stank?" She questioned. "For real? Smells are not an issue. Be right back."

"Take your time. I'll wait here for you," he said. She touched his hand for a brief moment.

———

Allan relaxed against the wall and drank a fresh can of Coke as he waited for Rosalind. Scanning the area several times, trying to spot Tom, a touch on his shoulder had him stumbling backward, ready to fight.

He faced a tall man in a cowboy hat.

"Howdy. David Billy. I hope you stay sober this time."

Reaching out, he shook David's hand. An image flashed in his mind, of David at Gilley's Bar. "Allan Smith, nice to meet you. Not one of my best first impressions in Vegas, I mean. No need to worry about a repeat."

"David!"

They both turned. Rosalind ran toward them. David opened his arms, and she rushed into them. "I'm glad you were able to make it. How's the baby?"

"We had a girl, Corinne Julie Billy," David replied proudly. "A whopping eight pounds, two ounces."

She moved out of his hug. "I love the name."

"Suzy's doing fine too. She and Corinne stayed home." David shoved his hands into his front pockets and cleared his throat. "Sorry to hear about Sam."

Allan moved closer to Rosalind. The subject still held a lot of emotion for her when it was brought up.

"Thanks, it all happened so fast." She choked on the words and dabbed at her eyes.

Ready to console her, Allan put his arm around her. She leaned her head on his shoulder.

"Heard you got married," David commented.

"Yes, it was a spur of the moment kind of thing. I am married."

Allan analyzed the exchange with interest, tightening his hold on her.

"It's about damn time someone tamed you." David roared with laughter at his own comment, finally calming and changing the subject. "I heard what Tom did back a ways. We told him to leave our group. If trouble occurs, the boys and I will be ready to help out." David nodded to Allan. "Nice meetin' you again."

Without further ado David strutted away.

"And here I thought I was your only knight in shining armor."

His attempt at a joke sounded dull to his ears, but he was secretly pleased to know others were willing to help. Rosalind flung her arms around him. Allan held her close as their lips met hungrily. They kissed deep and long. Hollering and whistling interrupted their private embrace.

Allan held up his hand in a salute, gathering Rosalind to his side. Laughing, they meandered to their truck and discovered Walt there waiting for the coveted chicken.

"What do you have to bargain with . . ." Allan began, but his cell phone interrupted. He checked the call. "Excuse me, I have to take this." He moved several steps away. "Yes, Tiffany."

"The private-eye we hired came through. We have enough incriminating evidence to sue the asshole, Tom Clark. Paul's contacted the police in Oklahoma. They're waiting to arrest Tom when he arrives at the competition."

Allan once again searched the area and glanced at Rosalind. She smiled. He held up two fingers. "Anything I should be doing on this end?"

"No. I talked to the lawyers. They're ready and will be on call," Tiffany said.

"I'll keep you informed." Allan forced the words out through a rush of anger. Recovering, he added in a more candid tone, "Great job, Tiffany."

"Thank you. There are a lot of sick people out there, be safe."

"Will do, bye." He disconnected. Searching the area for the hundredth time, he saw no sign of Tom.

"Everything okay?"

Allan turned, wiping away his concern as he faced

Rosalind. "They found evidence linking Tom Clark to the release of the videos, website, and pictures."

"That no-good son of a—"

"Don't say it, Rosalind. He isn't worth it."

"I'm so infuriated. How dare he!"

Allan put his fingers to her lips. "Shhh. It looks like everyone is ready to head back on the road."

This had the desired effect because her temper visibly cooled. They climbed into the truck. A horn sounded and the convoy began to pull onto the interstate.

"Tell me what's going on," Rosalind demanded.

Shifting in the seat, Allan picked his words carefully. "The New York Police department has been working with Sheriff Hoffman and the Oklahoma Police. They will be arresting Tom on charges of blackmail and extortion. I've been receiving letters asking for huge amounts of money since I returned from Las Vegas. Whenever the deadlines would pass, since I wasn't about to send money, new information was released about our wedding."

"Shit! No wonder you thought I was blackmailing you. I'm sorry."

He reached across the console and took her hand. "You had your own agenda. That's what was confusing me at first and why I did some of the crappy things I did."

"We both did things we aren't proud of. Fate had its own chart for us."

"That's an interesting view on things." He paused as a passing truck merged into their lane. "I haven't been able to figure out how Tom got videos of us."

"Have you seen more of them? It's creepy, being stalked."

He touched her cheek in a caress. "I have. Tiffany and Paul have taken them down. With Tom's admittance it's beginning to make sense."

"I'm sorry, if I hadn't..."

"We would never be here right now."

CHAPTER THIRTY-SEVEN

"What's wrong?"

"Nothing." Rosalind wiped tears from her face. Pressing her lips together, she glanced at Allan, then at the road. He'd been so quiet for the last hour she'd thought he'd fallen asleep. "It was the song that just played. It reminded me of my parents' deaths."

"I have those moments too, but unlike you, I didn't see my parents die."

In the darkness she felt his pain even if his words didn't reveal anything. Their lives were so much alike but yet so different. "That night haunts me to this day. The screeching tires and my mom's scream."

"I'm sure it does. For me, it's seeing a police car." He cleared his throat. "We've never talked much about our past. A few bits and pieces, but I'll always be here for you."

Allan's reassurance brought on a new bout of caring that went deeper than she thought possible. She struggled with a reply, but he broke the silence.

"I love you. Some higher power has put us together and I can only thank them. Paul and Tiffany are thankful too."

She laughed. "Why would they care we're together?" Yet she savored the feelings of serenity his words gave her, chasing the sadness away.

"They have been doing a happy dance privately since we got married."

"How come? They don't know me." She checked the mirrors and changed lanes. The road sign displayed thirty miles to exit 121-C.

"Tiffany is a romantic at heart. She says if I hadn't wanted to get married in the first place, I wouldn't have. She believes it was love at first sight."

Rosalind laughed so hard she was afraid she'd pee in her pants. "I want to meet her."

"You won't for a while. I owe her an extended honeymoon. She's waited for me to succumb to Cupid's arrow."

"I can't get over how we ended up loving each other." She tapped the steering wheel and grabbed a fast glance at him. "Now's not the time to talk about this, but how often will you be flying to New York?"

Her question went unheard as an exit sign came into view.

"Oh my God, a Starbucks. At the next exit, May Avenue. Can we stop?"

Allan stomped his feet and wiggled around in the passenger seat like a little kid. Rosalind smirked. It was the least she could do for him.

"Sure. I'll have to radio the others we're stopping. The Fairgrounds exit is fairly close. Everyone doesn't have to pull into Starbucks." She took hold of the CB mic.

"Great, I can taste the latte already."

"Break, one-nine."

The line crackled and hissed. "Go ahead, one-nine."

"Stopping for brown gargle for the Gotham dude, over," she said.

"Ten-four. Catch you at the drinking well."

"Ten-four-over."

Before she could replace the CB mic, Allan asked, "What is brown gargle?"

"Coffee."

"And Gotham dude?"

The question made her snicker. "You. A man from New York."

"Clever. I learned something new today. I love this CB stuff. It's like having the walkie-talkies I wish I'd owned as a kid."

She smiled at his usage of northern slang instead of his fancy New Yorker words.

Who would've ever guessed a non-rodeo man would be her undoing and husband? They were so different.

Rosalind considered the one guy who'd been able to make her feel true love. A gentle fire grew, turning to an ache of need, her pulse racing. He was so sexy in his cowboy hat and flannel shirt opened at the top. All she had to do was look at him and she wanted him. He was demonstrating possibilities of turning into a cowboy. No one would guess this was his first time around. With some work, she'd be able to turn him into a full-fledged cowboy if he wanted.

The next exit came, and the other trucks honked their horns. She merged with the traffic.

"Would you like to try some real coffee?"

Rosalind grimaced. "Starbucks doesn't serve gut-strong coffee like I drink."

"It'll be my treat. Come inside."

Shaking her head, she opened her door and followed him. The smell of brewed coffee was strong and tickled her taste buds. Rosalind stared at the menu board. Cappuccino, Macchiato, Frappuccino, or Latte.

Was she in a different country? What language was on the board?

"I usually order a vanilla latte or a cappuccino. Try a Clover brewed coffee," Allan suggested.

"A what? Never mind, I'll trust your judgment."

The girl at the register smiled. "May I take your order?"

She watched as Allan took out his phone and opened a Starbucks app.

"Yes, a—"

"Hey, aren't you the guy that's been on the news?" The girl gasped and looked around the store. "The one who married..."

"Yes, I am, and this is my wife," he replied without missing a beat. "I'll take a Grande Vanilla Latte, and she'll take a Tall Clover brewed with the Peru special blend."

The other Starbucks employees began to stare at them. The girl taking their order stood straighter. "Sorry, it's not every day we get a celebrity in here."

Rosalind was mortified. Allan grabbed her hand. The barista scanned his phone and they moved to a waiting area. "Don't be nervous."

Scenes from how the town had handled the news had her looking for an escape route. "How can I not be? That girl recognized us."

"And?" He casually leaned against the counter.

"Oh, I don't know. What if she asks more questions?"

"I'll give them something else to talk about."

Suddenly she was in his arms and Allan was kissing her. She stiffened at first, and then surrendered, allowing his hands to stroke her butt and back. And she did the same to him.

"Excuse me. Vanilla Latte and a Clover special blend. You might want to get a room," the barista snickered while she set the drinks down.

They ended their make-out session and chuckled.

"Right. Have a nice day," Allan smiled and raised his cup to the onlookers.

They took their drinks and left a very quiet Starbucks. Laughing, they glanced back and everyone inside was staring at them.

"Ingenious. Now they do have something to talk about," Rosalind said.

"Yes, they do."

"I bet all the girls wished it was them you were kissing."

"No, all the men wanted to do what I did to you," Allan said.

She sipped her drink. The taste wasn't as good as her homemade coffee, but damn if he hadn't been right. It was close. "This is good, but I wouldn't pay five dollars for it."

In the truck they chatted about the stunt. By the time they arrived at the Super Barn, Walt and Joe had them signed in and had readied Dawn's stall. Together they unhitched the trailer. Rosalind inspected Dawn. Satisfied she was unscathed from the trip, she led the mare to her temporary home.

"No worries, Rosalind. I'll be here with her," Walt promised.

She halted her fourth scan of the stall. "Thank you. Be on alert for Tom Clark. Phone me if he comes around."

"For sure. You get some rest." Walt gently ushered her out. "Your first qualifying run is at nine."

"You read my mind. See ya in the morning."

Walt nodded and she went in search of Allan. It didn't take long. She found him talking to Joe. Rosalind sauntered over to him, and he put his arm around her. Joe excused himself.

"Ready to hit the sack?" Allan lowered his hand to rest it on her hip.

"I am, but I'm worried about Tom."

"No need, he hasn't checked in yet." He held out his hand. "And I'm driving to the hotel. Give me the keys."

Rosalind handed them over to her adoring, caring husband.

CHAPTER THIRTY-EIGHT

Lying awake waiting for time to fly, Rosalind eyed the clock for the hundredth time.

Only four, I still have an hour.

For the first time in ages, she'd developed pre-competition jitters. The anticipation of today's run brought about a rush of emotion. She loved the crowds, the noise, the smells, and the adrenaline rush of each ride. She'd miss all of it, but her mind was made up. Win or lose, this was to be her last professional ride.

In order for the riding camps and sanctuary to be successful, she needed to stay at home, not on the road. If a student needed her at a competition, she'd attend as an instructor, not to ride.

Grandpa and Sam had been right. Life was too short not to take chances on things.

Allan rolled onto his side, draping an arm across her. Inching slowly away from the comfort of his warmth, she managed not to wake him. Rosalind took a bottle of water and drank from it as she paced the room.

Yesterday's qualifying run time of fifteen-point-eighty-eight seconds had placed her in the lead, not even touching her best time. Most of the other riders were a full second behind. She knew from experience, riders rode slow on purpose in order to hide how they might give the leader a run for the money.

She set down the water bottle, put her hand to her mouth, and rushed into the bathroom. Barely making it to the toilet, she lost her cookies. When the heaves stopped, she sat on the floor with her head in her hands.

She'd never had nerves before. Why now?

She got to her feet, peeled off her panties and bra, turned on the shower, and moved into the stream of cold water. It quickly switched to hot, easing away some of the tension and calmed her nausea.

"Honey, would you like breakfast or me?"

She whipped open the shower curtain. Allan leaned against the doorframe, naked.

"I would love to take advantage of what you're showing off, but I can't have hanky-panky the day of competition. I broke the tradition yesterday for you. It saps your strength. Guess it's just breakfast."

She rinsed her hair, reached for the bar of soap, and did her best to ignore him.

Laughing, Allan shoved the curtain to the wall. "Then get out. My turn."

"Aren't we pushy this morning?"

She stumbled and fell into his warm, wet body. He caught and imprisoned her. She felt his hard erection pressing against her. Their mouths met. For a moment she allowed the sexual hunger to take over.

Rosalind held his hands to stop them from further exciting her. "Allan, please I can't," she pleaded.

"If you say so." He moved away. She tumbled out of the shower in an unladylike manner and grabbed a white towel.

"Close the door. Thanks, honey."

She did as he asked, but then leaned against it, breathing hard. What would be the harm in a little morning delight?

Flinging off the towel, she reopened the bathroom door. One step inside and another wave of nausea hit her. Dropping down to the toilet, she vomited.

The curtain swished back, and a spray of water fell on her.

"Rosalind. What's wrong?"

She raised her eyes to his and shook her head. "Maybe nerves."

He knelt next to her, brushing the hair from her face and helped her to her feet. "Should you ride today?"

"Have to. I need to win. This will be my last professional race," Rosalind replied.

"What can I do for you?"

"Not sure, this has never happened before."

"It's still early, lie down for a while," Allan said.

"Yeah, maybe I should."

Naked, he escorted her to the bed. She sank down and brought her knees to her chest, lying in a fetal position. She felt the blanket cover her and his gentle kiss on her cheek.

"I'll get dressed and get you some crackers and Sprite."

"Thank you." Rosalind closed her eyes and willed her stomach to calm down.

———

Allan hurried into the hallway and almost ran into Joe who was leaving his room. "Morning."

"Morning, Mr. Smith. Everything okay?"

"No, Rosalind's not feeling well. What time should we be at the arena?"

"That's not like her. The run is scheduled at ten o'clock.

She needs to be there one hour before her start time. Me and Walt will take care of Dawn till you guys get there."

"Thanks, any word yet if Tom's shown up?"

"No one's seen him," Walt said. "He has till noon to sign in."

"Call if you hear anything." Allan patted Joe's shoulder.

"Will do. I hope our champion is good to go."

"She should be. See ya." Joe nodded, and they went in different directions. Before he reached the front desk, his phone vibrated in his pocket. The screen lit, *blocked ID.*

"Hello?"

"Mr. Smith, Sheriff Hoffman. We've received notice from the Oklahoma Police. Tom Clark's truck has been found abandoned near the fairgrounds. I've given them your number. You should be receiving a call from them."

Allan paced the length of the small area. "Thank you, Sheriff. Will there be extra protection at the rodeo?"

"Yes. No need to worry."

"I want the man found before Rosalind's ten o'clock run."

"Everyone is working to achieve that goal, Mr. Smith. I'll let the local police know the time frame. I'll keep you abreast of any new developments. Talk to you later."

"Thanks again." Allan scanned the lobby. All he saw were families and men dressed like cowboys. None seemed to notice him. With the crackers and soda in hand he headed back to the room.

Should he tell Rosalind she couldn't compete today and take her home?

He smiled.

Home. Not New York, but home in Minnesota. Crazy how things could change in a month's time. He stopped in front of their room. At a sudden thought, his eyebrows rose. He pursed his lips, bracing his hand on the door.

Could she be pregnant? Holy crap.

His second rule for dating women was to use protection when having sex, but he hadn't with Rosalind. Not once. They had never discussed it, maybe she was on the pill.

The odds just changed. Grinning from ear to ear, he slid the key card into the lock.

CHAPTER THIRTY-NINE

Once the door shut behind Allan, Rosalind ran to the bathroom. Groaning, another round of nausea hit her. When it subsided, she brushed her teeth and washed her face.

What was wrong with her? She couldn't be throwing up before or after her run. Should she withdraw?

No, when pigs' fly.

Not when she was this close to gaining respect as a trainer and the title of a champ.

Gingerly she walked from the bathroom and eyed her show outfit. The blue western shirt with a paisley design on the sleeves and pearl snaps along with her Wranglers lay on the bed. She pushed them aside. Sat and waited. After several deep breaths she stood and put on her sports bra and shirt.

Dry heaves attacked her. She bent forward to ease the queasiness. It left without a visit to the bathroom. She finished dressing by tugging on her Justin two-toned boots. Rosalind stood and held her hands on her stomach. The sick mawkishness had subsided, but would it last?

Was it time for her period? It'd never given her this much trouble.

She counted days. Sixteen, seventeen . . . nineteen, twenty... thirty, thirty-one.

Today was the fourth. It should've come last week.

Her eyes widened. The door opened and Allan came in. Rosalind dropped her hands.

"You're awake? Are you sure you should be?" He set the crackers and soda on the table.

She couldn't look at him when this much concern was evident in his voice. As a distraction so he wouldn't see her suspicions, she bent down and fussed with her boots. "Yeah, I'm fine. Must've been something I ate."

He came up behind her, put his hand on her shoulder. "Perhaps—"

"If you're ready, we should get going. I want to see Dawn." She moved away and snagged her hat.

"I ran into Joe. He and Walt left already. They'll take care of Dawn till we get there."

"Good, saves time. I'll bring these in case I need them." She took the crackers and Sprite.

Allan held the door and they walked to the truck. He chatted about the rodeo. She nodded and smiled, only half listening.

Should she tell him her suspicions? They'd never discussed children.

"You can drive." She knew she wouldn't be able to concentrate on the road as her thoughts kept returning to the possibility, she might be pregnant and if she would throw up again.

"Great! I'm beginning to like driving a truck."

"Don't get used to it, City Boy. This one is mine."

"I see how it's going to be. What's yours is yours." Allan opened the passenger's door for her.

"That's right and don't forget it."

He kissed her. Rosalind gave him a sassy smile and buckled

her seatbelt. She was tempted to fold her arm around her abdomen, but instead slid her hand down her thighs. She had to find a way to get a pregnancy test without Allan knowing.

They arrived at the Super Barn and found it in chaos. Trucks, trailers, and people everywhere. He parked and they went to find Walt. Several people called out greetings. She did the same and to her horror the earthy smells caused her to gag. She puckered her lips together to stop from retching and coughed to conceal her actions.

"Mornin', Rosalind."

She and Allan turned. Walt had found them.

"How's our girl this morning?" She discreetly looked for the closest restroom feeling her stomach was about to explode.

"Dawn is ready. She's been walked and brushed. I put on the shin guards too."

"Thanks, sorry for being late," she said as they continued on their way to the stall.

"We got you covered. Heard you weren't feeling well."

"Something I ate, I think." Hating, she was lying to everyone. Dawn came into view. "I'm well enough to ride. Any word on the competition?"

She held a sugar cube to Dawn. Allan had taken on a serious look and had become quiet.

"Alisa Highland. She arrived after you left yesterday." Walt unlocked the stall. "She did hers in fifteen-ninety."

Rosalind's hands fisted. There was no way, she was going to let her take first. "Point taken."

Then a thought came to her. Maybe Alisa could help get a pregnancy test. She'd know what to do.

"Is there a class I can take?" Allan leaned against the door. "Because I can't understand what you guys say most of the time. Did I miss something? Who's Alisa?" He placed his hands on his hips and waited for an answer.

"She's a rival and is sending Rosalind a message," Walt answered. "The hundredth of a second difference means she's here to win."

"You were riding faster at the ranch," Allan pointed out. "She doesn't have a chance."

Rosalind and Walt exchanged looks. Her lips curved upward.

God, how she loved him.

"She and I go way back. Sometimes I win. Sometimes she does," Rosalind said and put a hand on Allan's arm. "She's running a new colt, but he's been unpredictable. I'll have to shave off time to take the prize."

"Allan, we could use your help unloading," Joe interrupted.

"Sure." He turned to follow Joe.

"I'll stay here," Rosalind chimed in. "If anyone wants to know."

"Okay, sorry." Allan stepped to her and planted a sensual kiss on her lips. "I'll be back."

She appraised the masterful movement of his sexy ass and smiled. The Wranglers she'd bought for him fit like a choke strap did on a Saturday night. She blinked to clear her mind; his ass was what got her into trouble in the first place.

It wasn't until he disappeared from sight that she grabbed the feedbag and placed it on Dawn.

"Hey, girl," she cooed. "Did you have a good night? I did, but my morning wasn't nice."

Dawn nudged Rosalind with her nose, then snorted.

"That's my girl." Rosalind smiled, but it soon faded.

One person was missing. Sam. He would've been telling her what each of the riders had done and given her advice on how to outride Alisa. Now she had to figure it out on her own. Brushing aside a tear, she began her checks.

She was a basket case.

Next, she laid the saddle blanket on Dawn's back, took off the feedbag, and reached for her saddle from the bench outside of the stall.

"If it isn't the love of my loins."

She instantly stiffened. That voice belonged to only one person. Replacing the saddle, she pivoted to face Tom. He stood a foot from her.

Shit.

She looked past him for Allan, Walt, or Joe. They weren't coming. She shifted her eyes to the adjacent stall. It was vacant.

No help there, either.

Rosalind sidestepped in that direction to avert and size-up Tom. He wore his bull spurs and held a short whip. Both dangerous weapons when it came to fighting.

"What do you want, Tom?" She kept moving to find freedom.

Stay calm. Keep him talking.

"It should be obvious, my little filly. We're goin' have us some fun before our day begins. You know, like old times."

He moved closer. She dropped back, hitting the gate. He mirrored her movements, blocking her path. With nowhere to go, she backed into the empty stall. Tom positioned himself in front of the entrance, fingering the leather whip.

She was running out of options. She'd have to stand and fight.

"Not a good idea, Tom. We never celebrated until after the competitions, remember, *Tom*?" She put loud emphasis on his name. The wall met her back. Rosalind slipped off her gloves, letting them fall, and scanned the area to her right.

Thank the Lord, she saw movement.

He licked his lips and took another step closer. "As I recall, we did some pretty heavy tongue twisted kissing in the day."

"That was a long time ago, Tom." She slowly inched to the corner.

He turned toward her, releasing a low, horrible laugh. "My palms are itching to hold a very pretty rose that you have covered." He cupped his groin and gyrated his hips obscenely. "Come on, Rosalind, I know what you like."

Ignoring his words, she forced herself to breathe, in, out and to keep him talking. "I'm married, Tom. Those areas belong to my husband! You need to leave."

Damn. Where is everyone, anyone?

He laughed and took a step toward her. Without any hesitation she took matters into her own hands and rushed at him. He dropped the whip but reached out and got a hold of one of her arms. Screaming, she pounded on him with her free hand and used her booted foot to do as much damage as she could. Dawn snorted and kicked the adjacent wall.

"You whore! You're mine." Tom pulled her against him. "You're gonna suffer for not marrying me."

She struggled and won a small victory when he groaned. It lasted only a second. He shoved her against the metal beams. She cried out at the piercing pain as they dug into her shoulder blades. He came at her. She flinched, but then her self-defense lessons kicked in. She raised her knee, missing his groin, but hit his leg.

Tom raised his hand in the air, and she lifted her forearm for protection from the blow.

———

Allan strode inside the trailer and lifted a bag of feed. "Do you guys always accompany Rosalind?"

"No, Sam was her right-hand man. I've gone a couple of times," Walt stated.

Allan hoisted another sack on his shoulder and Walt locked the trailer. He turned. "What do you . . ."

"Tom's here," Joe yelled from a distance. "The police are combing the area. Have you seen him?"

"Rosalind."

All three of them said her name. Allan dropped his load and sprinted for the stalls.

A woman's scream vibrated through the Super Barn. Horses nickered and whinnied. He ran faster and spotted Tom with his arm raised whip in hand. Allan leapt on him. They fell to the ground. He groaned as his knee hit the hard floor first. Waves of pain exploded throughout his body. Before he could recover, Tom landed on top of him. He shoved him off and they exchanged punches.

"You piece of shit. No one touches my wife!" With his left hand fisted, Allan swung.

Flesh smashed flesh, and he heard the sickening thud of bones cracking. He bucked Tom off. Now they stood face to face, circling each other. Blood ran from Tom's nose.

"She's good, isn't she? She should be mine. She can't love you. She loves me," Tom boasted and wiped his mouth.

Allan lunged forward, fists clenched, but he moved too slow, and Tom's punch connected with his ribs. Allan's feet slipped out from under him. Thrown backward, he landed on the ground again. This time he rolled and braced for Tom's next attack.

"Stop where you are, Tom Clark."

Five police officers with guns drawn crowded into the stall. Two of them grabbed and held Tom.

Scrambling to his feet, Allan found Rosalind with her head lowered, squatting in the corner, and covering her stomach with her arms.

"Honey, it's done." Allan tried to keep his worry from his voice. "It's all over, I'm here."

He knelt in front of Rosalind. She raised her head. He inhaled at the sight of her swollen right cheek, blood smeared from a split lip.

Son of a bitch.

"I tried...tried to get away," she babbled. "I fell and cut my lip with my teeth."

With his thumb, he wiped the blood from her mouth. "I'm so sorry I wasn't here."

He took her hands and pulled her to him. Her body shook. Without hesitation Allan lifted her securely into his arms. The police moved aside as he carried Rosalind out of the stall, through throngs of people.

"Where else..." Allan's voice faltered. "How many times did he hit you?"

"He didn't. I slipped and fell when you came in. My head had a date with a metal bar."

When they reached the sunlight, relief flooded through him, and he let her stand. He brushed her hair behind her ears. "I love you..."

"Excuse us. Do either of you require medical attention?"

Two paramedics stood with a gurney and Allan moved aside. "Yes, she does."

"We'll take her to the medical tent to check her out. Do you need help getting on?"

Allan was about to set her on the gurney, but Rosalind stopped him.

"No, I'm walking," she firmly replied.

"Madam, you shouldn't be walking."

"I'll walk or I won't go." She put her hands on her hips.

"You should use the gurney. But if you insist on walking, please come with us."

She nodded and they ushered her into the tent. The flap closed behind her.

"Sir, I think you should get checked out too."

Allan looked at a police officer, who'd come to stand next to him.

"I'm fine."

"Judging by the beating you gave that man, it's best you should."

Now that the adrenaline rush had faded, he did feel some pain in his side not to mention his knee. "Thank you for your concern. As soon as my wife is cleared, I'll go."

"Very well, sir, but we will need your statement too," the officer said.

"I'm not going anywhere. My name is Allan Smith. Just call that name in."

The officer nodded and walked away. Cheers erupted and he turned. Since he'd passed through the barns, a crowd had gathered. The police shoved Tom into the rear of a squad car. More loud applause exploded when the door closed.

CHAPTER FORTY

Allan paced, talked to the police, and paced more as he waited for Rosalind to leave the tent. He'd been cleared with bruised ribs and knee. The paramedics wrapped his ribs and gave him some pain medicine, which he had no intention of taking. Soon Joe joined him, followed by David.

"Any word yet?"

"No. It's driving me insane," Allan stated.

"Don't worry. She's a tough filly."

David's reassuring comment wasn't helping. "If that son of a bitch hurt her, I'll make sure he never gets out of jail."

He moved away from them, took out his phone, and pressed Paul's number.

"Hello."

"Paul, the police have arrested Tom Clark. They said he's confessed to posting the pics and vandalizing Rosalind's barn and the vehicles."

"Do you need the lawyers to fly to Minnesota?"

"No. Cease all inquiries about the website and pictures. Give me news on the markets."

"The Euro climbed. The US dollar is sluggish," Paul said.

"I received the alert on the decline. We need to start moving the clients' hedge funds." Allan inhaled deeply and regretted doing it. His ribs hurt.

"Don't worry about us. I've already taken the necessary steps."

Still holding the phone to his ear, he took in the scene before him. Trailers, trucks, horses, and smells had him wrinkling his nose. So different from his stuffy closed-in office.

It's time to step away. Live life differently.

"Great, thanks," Allan paused, debating the decision he was about to make for only a moment. "Please contact our corporate lawyers and have them draw up the proper papers to make you the new president of Smith and Associates Brokerage Firm."

"Sir. You don't need to... I couldn't...the company can wait for you to return. You can't step down."

"I've lost my interest in the fast lane." Allan's admission was a self-awareness he'd been feeling for a long time. "See about starting an investment-consulting firm. We can have branches in rural areas to help the farmers and ranchers insure their long-term financial dreams."

"Does this mean you won't be returning to New York?"

Hearing Paul say the words solidified his decision. John wouldn't be too happy, but their friendship had taken new avenues in the last months.

"New York will always be my home. I just won't be returning to my role as president. Everything will be fine, I expect..."

A cheer blasted. He turned as Rosalind exited the medic tent. His group of friends had grown. Several rodeo cowboys and cowgirls stood waiting too.

"Gotta go, Paul. Send the documents so I can sign them."

"Allan, you can't..."

"Bye, Paul."

He ended the call and met Rosalind's searching gaze. She was a welcome sight. Radiant in the sunlight, her green eyes sparkled. He moved toward the crowd.

"You're one lucky guy. She loves you."

Allan grinned at David's comment. "Yes, she does. Excuse me."

Rosalind ran to him. He hugged her and gave her a kiss that said so much. "I love you."

"I love you too."

They were words he'd never thought could bring him so much joy, but they did. And then they were kissing again, and he forgot about his own pain. "I should've stayed by your side. It won't happen again."

"I'm fine. I don't have any broken bones. I might have some bruising."

"Did they say anything else?" He studied her from her head to her boots. When he returned his gaze to her face, he saw her mouth was curved into a smile.

"They asked if I might be pregnant. I had to say there is a chance."

He stared at her. "What did—did you say—pregnant? A baby?"

She took his face in her hands. "Yes, there is a possibility I, we are going to have a baby."

"Oh, boy. What do I do?" Allan caught her hands and held them. "Do you need to go to the hospital?"

"They suggested I should see my doctor when I get home. And take one of those home-pregnancy tests."

"Let's go right now."

She laughed. "No, I'm fine and the baby will be too. I know several barrel riders who have ridden when with child."

"No, I think we should go to the emergency room."

Giggling, she kissed him. "We can go after the competition, I promise. But you could get a pregnancy test if you want to know before then."

"I love you, Rosalind. We'll wait." He hugged her.

"Now that we have that settled, what time is my go-around?"

"Ten, and it's only eight-thirty. We would have time," he coaxed, wanting to see the confirmation, and not just a verbal affirmation.

"No, we won't have time for a run to the hospital. Is Dawn okay?"

He saw the group had given them some privacy. "Walt stayed with her. Oh my God, I can't believe it."

"Shhh, slow down, cowboy." Rosalind put her hand on his arm.

He reached out and placed his palm on her belly. "Do you need to change or something?"

"My shirt has a tear." Rosalind pointed at it. "I have another in the trailer, a red one."

"I'll get it and meet you at Dawn's stall."

"Thanks."

She walked toward the barn, joined by her friends. Allan studied the sway of her hips, amused his earlier suspicions had been confirmed.

Then the realization he was going to be a father settled in.

———

Rosalind forced her arms to stay at her sides instead of cradling her stomach. She suspected Allan watched her every move. She answered questions from David and Joe, but when she was alone in the safety of the shadows of the barn, she touched her belly and debated if she should go to the hospital.

The question the medics had asked about being pregnant had left her speechless. The morning sickness, being tired, and the soreness of her breasts all made sense. They'd phoned in to the doctor on call. He'd confirmed she needed to be seen and couldn't tell her anything without a test.

Holy mud pies. I'm going to be a mom.

In a daze she neared Dawn's temporary home. She blinked. Several rodeo people clustered around Walt.

"Was she hurt?"

"Her husband kicked Tom's ass?"

"Who'd have thought he'd do something so evil?"

She spotted Alisa's signature white hat and black hair. As she approached the stall, the group backed away and dispersed, except Alisa. Even though they were rivals, it had never been a hostile competition. Their friendship came first in an odd sort of way.

"Hi, did you come to check out the next World Champion?" Rosalind halted next to Alisa whose surprised expression gave her the advantage in their word game.

"As a matter of fact, no," Alisa chortled, and they hugged. "I came to see you. Craziness, Tom Clark being such a douche bag. I told you he was no good."

"That's why Sam despised him," Rosalind replied.

Alisa touched her arm. "Are you okay?"

"A handful of bruises, nothing to worry about. I've gotten worse from falling."

"I hear ya." Alisa leaned in. "Wanted to check out the hunk you married. Word is he's a looker."

Rosalind nodded. "He should be here soon. Keep your hands off."

"As if I would do anything." Alisa grinned and raised her palms in a teasing jest. "My, my. Does he have a brother?"

Rosalind didn't bother turning. She could tell by her friend's reaction who was coming.

"Here you go." Allan handed her the shirt. "Anything else I can do?"

Alisa's eyes widened at the sight of Allan. Rosalind coughed in an effort to hide her laughter.

"Hi, I'm Alisa."

"You're the rider who thinks she can beat my wife," Allan replied and held out his hand.

"He's a keeper, Rosalind." Alisa shook his hand. "You'll be chasing my tail this go around. See ya later."

She nodded and watched Alisa squeeze Allan's butt when she passed him. He wobbled.

"Very interesting, your so-called friend." Allan rubbed his ass. "Are all cowgirls this friendly?"

"Only to the ones they like. Come on City Boy, time to see me in action."

Rosalind stepped into the stall, away from prying eyes, and took off her shirt. She held out a hand for the new one.

"Rosalind, people—um, men can see you."

"They know I'm off limits. Hurry up, I don't have time for modesty." She chuckled. "I have to lead Dawn to the practice pen for a warm-up."

He tossed the shirt to her. Aware of his eyes on her, she turned and fastened the snaps. It fit snug against her breasts.

I hope it stays closed.

She led Dawn to the practice pen. Two other riders were there running the courses. They motioned for her to go ahead. Hitching her foot into the stirrup, she lifted herself onto Dawn, ran the clover course twice, and stopped next to Walt. "The dirt is too sandy. It's not like yesterday."

"Be careful. You don't have to have the best time this go around. Save it for tomorrow." Walt took hold of the bridle.

Irritated by his suggestion, she bit down on her lower lip. "I never hold back."

"Go to the alley." Walt shook his head. "Dawn is loose enough."

Seeing the effect her harsh words had on him, she lowered her guard. Walt was only instructing, not judging her. "Sorry, I don't know why I snapped at you."

"No need to apologize. Go show them how it's done."

"Thanks." She rode Dawn to the center entrance.

Alisa was already in position waiting for her turn. "Your man is something else, Rosalind. How did you find him?"

"Don't have enough time, maybe later." Rosalind winked and added, "It's you and me."

"Yes, it is. May the best flirt win." Alisa nudged her dark bay colt to the alley.

The announcer introduced Alisa and she took off. Rosalind moved Dawn to the right to get a better look at her run. Her friend maneuvered the horse with expertise. The colt faltered, slicing barrel one. They recovered and hit the pocket on the other two.

She was in trouble. Alisa was in top form for this go around. Rosalind held her breath and peered at the clock.

"Sixteen-point-twenty, for our very own Alisa Highland."

The crowd went wild and spooked Dawn.

"Whoa, girl." Walt gripped Dawn's bridle and petted her neck.

Rosalind looked down at him. "Alisa had a great ride. I need to buy hundredths of seconds to take the win away from her. Where are Allan and Joe?"

"They went to the stands to watch. Don't push Dawn too hard. Save it for tomorrow," Walt advised her.

The announcer broke in. "Our next racer is Rosalind

Smith. She stands in first after one go around. Let's welcome her to the gate."

Applause rang through the area.

"Go!"

Rosalind pressed her legs into Dawn's sides and instead of going forward, she sidestepped.

"Easy, easy, girl," she yelled. Dawn straightened.

"Go! Come on girl, go!"

They went from zero to fast in one second, passing the electric eye starting the clock. The first barrel came, and they pocketed it. The second one, Dawn rated, and Rosalind misjudged the turn, leaning too far. Her boot slipped from the stirrup.

Crap.

Heart in her throat, pulse pounding, they headed to the final barrel. She replaced her boot and cleared it. Using a firm grip on the reins, she urged Dawn to the line.

"Sixteen-point-thirty-one, for Rosalind Smith."

"Whoa!" She jumped off of Dawn when the mare stopped. Walt, Joe, and Allan rushed to her.

"Shit, I messed up. Besides the bad start, I leaned too far, and my boot came out."

Rosalind kicked at the dirt, took off her hat, and threw it to the ground. Alisa was now ahead of her.

"It's okay." Allan placed his hand on her shoulder.

She shrugged it off. "No, it's not. I have to win this. If I do, people will know I can train a winner. It's a critical part of my plan."

Walt reached for the reins. "I'll brush Dawn and do her cool down. You could use one too, missy."

She hesitated for a split second, gave up, then turned and walked right into Alisa. "Sorry."

"No problem. I wish it had been your hubby."

"You have a one-track mind, girl," Rosalind remarked with a smile.

"I do, don't I? Hey, too bad on the second barrel." Alisa's gaze followed Dawn being led away by Walt. "She's a beautiful horse."

"Thanks. I guess my mind wasn't fully focused on the ride."

"Can't blame you." Alisa nodded. "Guess we'll have to wait until tomorrow to see who's the best."

"You're funny, Alisa. I let you take first place today. Wanted to give everyone a show."

They stood facing each other, the verbal confrontation only a smoke screen. Rosalind knew Alisa wanted this win as much as she did. "Wanna get a beer at Toby Keith's?"

Alisa's request threw her for a loop. The girl could go to the extreme in a single breath. "Toby's sounds interesting, but I have to decline."

"Oh, what a shame, I wanted to dance with your hubby."

Rosalind let Alisa's banter cool her down. She'd been the number one reason Sam hadn't let her go out after an event. They'd gotten in too much trouble partying after their competitions. "Your run was good. Your colt has matured since Vegas."

"Thanks. I'm hoping to use him as a stud. That's why I'm goin' to beat you." Alisa smirked.

"Keep hoping. This is my year."

They chuckled together. Alisa moved away but not before giving Allan a wink, who'd remained quiet during the exchange.

He cleared his throat and gave her an innocent look. "What do we do now?"

Rosalind went to him and kissed his sexy mouth. "Sorry for my temper. I've worked hard for this and with everything that happened, I guess it got to me."

"It's expected. What you need is a quiet afternoon. I'm certain I can find a five-star restaurant to take you to. Once we've confirmed—"

"Allan, stop. Let's keep it a secret for now. Besides, you don't have to impress me."

"Okay, our first stop will be the hospital."

"Yes, I know." She collected her hat, brushed it against her jeans, and they walked out of the arena. She felt his hand pressed in the small of her back and smiled at the sign of ownership.

Time to find out what fate had in store for them.

CHAPTER FORTY-ONE

Not again.

Rosalind clasped her hands over her abdomen and rolled from the comfort of Allan's arms. She moaned and ran to the bathroom as the alarm clock rang.

Six-thirty.

Kneeling, she rested her hands on the toilet seat. "You and I are becoming best friends."

"Rosalind? Should I take you to the hospital?"

She sat back against the wall, shaking her head. "No, this is what's called morning sickness."

Allan knelt in front of her. She met his gaze.

"I suspect you'll be wanting crackers and soda for breakfast?"

She laughed, nodded, and breathed more easily.

He brushed her hair from her face. "I love you. I never thought I'd want children, but knowing we created this child out of love is amazing. Anything I can do for you?"

She shifted her position on the floor. "Sit with me. My insides will start churning again if I stand."

He sat next to her. She laid her head on his shoulder. The

morning sickness lasted about a half hour. Allan carried her to bed and caressed her cheek. "I'll be back with your very special breakfast."

She gently squeezed his hand. "Thanks."

After the door shut, she lay there pondering the idea of having a baby. It had been hard to tell him in the middle of the road with people all around. She'd wanted to wait until after the competition.

Sam would've said, what's done was done. No going back.

They were one unit now. She repositioned her arm from under her breast and unhooked her bra. They felt full and tender. She marveled at how her body had changed so fast.

Her cell phone rang, and she twisted to grab it. The screen showed a text message from Walt.

You dropped to second. Alisa is in first.

Rosalind typed, *Thanks.*

The door opened and Allan came in carrying her breakfast. "Maybe some fresh air will do you good."

"Not yet. I'll take some of those crackers though." She straightened, forgetting she'd loosened her bra.

"Mmmm, I like the view. Are you sure we can't make love?"

"Not yet, stud. But tonight, for sure. Come lie next to me."

He took off his shirt and lay facing her. His hand traced the rose and caressed her nipple. She inhaled and held her breath. "Allan."

"I know, but it doesn't mean I can't touch you, does it?"

"No..." Smiling, she placed one hand on his wide chest, stroking its firmness. Her other hand reached the waistband of his jeans, slid down the zipper, and unbuttoned them.

"Rosalind?"

She kissed him. Their tongues danced.

"Commando?"

"I...left in a hurry this morning."

Wrapping her fingers around his thick, long hardness, she slowly ran her hand up and down the length. He groaned against her lips. With her thumb and fingers, she stroked the tip and gently tightened her hold.

———

Oh my God.

Allan constricted her hand at his breaking point. Her palm stilled and in a feather-light touch, moved to caress his chest again. He fought to control his heavy short breaths. "Are we feeling better?"

Her reply was a smile and a kiss. They held each other and he rested his palm on her non-existent belly bump and fell asleep.

A knock on the door awoke them.

"Hello? Maid service."

"Give me a minute."

He jumped off the bed, adjusting his jeans before zipping them. Rosalind gathered her clothes and headed to the bathroom.

Allan opened the door part ways. "Hello. Can you give us ten minutes?"

The housekeeper nodded and moved her cart down the hall. He glanced at the clock. They'd slept for almost an hour. He ran his hand through his hair and then over his chin.

"Hey handsome, I like the shadow look. Time to hustle."

He glanced at his wife. Today she wore a pink and white shirt with fringe along the back of the sleeves, and a silver belt buckle as big as his fist.

"Wow."

"Thank you," she said.

"Let me take a quick shower, give me a minute."

"One-thousand-one, one-thousand-two..."
Laughing, he closed the door.

———

The Oklahoma Fairgrounds were packed. Food venders, pony rides, and rodeo people walking everywhere. Allan maneuvered the truck to the far end of the arena, reserved for participants. Rosalind took it all in, not wanting to forget the thrill of the day. Or the way her big-city husband looked dressed in Wranglers, a plaid shirt, and new Frye boots.

"How can you leave your life in New York City for this?" She waved her arms in front of her.

"Being raised in many foster homes has given me the strength to let go of comfort for the next step in life. I'm promoting Paul to president and I'm planning on opening some rural offices to help ranchers and farmers live their lives without financial worries."

"What?"

"I told you, I won't be going back. Well, maybe we could spend the holidays in New York."

"Allan, you don't have to give up your businesses or your company. I can manage on my own, if you need to be gone for a month or two."

He took her hand and wiped tears she hadn't known had fallen. "I could never leave you or our baby. You've changed me."

"No, you've changed *me*."

They shared a smile.

"Remember our vows, until death do us part? You've got me till then."

Rosalind hugged and kissed him. "I can hardly wait for the competition to end, so I can show you how much I love you."

"You don't have to wait."

She closed her eyes and shook her head. "You're a devil. Let's get going, cowboy."

As they approached Dawn's stall, they noticed another group of people hanging around, mostly reporters.

"There she is." The group edged closer, shouting questions.

"Was Tom Clark blackmailing you, too?"

"When will Heavens Kiss Sanctuary open?"

"Mr. Smith, why have you stepped down as President of Smith and Associates? Is it because the FBI might arrest you again?"

Allan moved in front of her. "We will answer only questions about the Heavens Kiss Sanctuary and horses. It's slated to open in late summer. As you know, with the cold weather in Minnesota it's hard to construct a building and the training facilities. We have fifteen horses approved to be our guests so far. Our website will be live the first of the year . . ."

Rosalind slipped past him and the curious group into Dawn's stall. Allan superbly manipulated the reporters away from the stalls and down the barn as he talked.

"He's good," Joe commented. "Dawn was agitated by the noise."

"Look at them, devouring everything he says," Walt noted as he handed her Dawn's reins.

"Yup, that's my husband." Rosalind felt pride in saying he was her husband. Seeing both men giving her a questioning look. She shrugged. "Well, he is. Can't a girl be happy about it?"

She pushed open the stall and led Dawn to the practice pen. Yesterday she'd let the day's activities intrude into her mind and concentration. Today was do or die. All the riders were looking to pick up clients, buyers, or breeding agreements. Most in the competition were established, but she wasn't.

She needed the ride of her life now to pass Alisa. She had the second to last run for the final go around. Alisa's time had earned her that coveted last slot.

Time ticked away as Rosalind ran Dawn through the practice course.

Clearing her mind as she waited in the alley, she made her last-minute checks. She touched each snap on her shirt, tugged on her gloves, patted her hat, and positioned the reins.

"Dawn, this is it," she murmured. "Win or lose, we are heroes."

The crowd went wild as her name was announced. She raised her arm to signal she was ready. For half a second, she doubted herself but gazed at Allan standing off to the right. He smiled. It gave her the strength she needed.

"Go," Rosalind yelled.

Dawn didn't need any more encouragement and took off in a split second. She counted and leaned for the first turn. Dawn's weight shifted to her hindquarters. The dirt flew and they cleared the first barrel and raced toward the second.

Rosalind counted again and found herself ahead of her timing. Leaning into the turn, Dawn took this barrel so close she felt it and the dirt at the same time. They straightened and headed for the last barrel.

She and Dawn were in sync. Her friend hadn't let her down. The mare moved with grace and ease. Both knew what the other wanted and demanded.

She didn't bother counting anymore because it didn't matter. They were both so committed to winning. This time around the third barrel her stirrup and boot touched the dirt. Dawn turned so sharp it was amazing. As always on the way to the finish line, Rosalind loosened her grip on the reins, giving Dawn her head. They cleared the timeline.

Walt waved his hands in the air. The crowd erupted in such a crazy frenzy, she barely heard her time.

"Fifteen-point-seventy-five."

Alisa urged her colt forward.

With adrenaline rushing, Rosalind couldn't help herself and moved to watch her opponent and leader, Alisa.

They pocketed the first barrel. The colt went wide on the second and knocked the third one. The crowd aahh'd as it pitched to stay upright. Alisa passed the electric eye at the same time the barrel stopped wobbling.

"Fifteen-point-eighty-five for Alisa Highland. Our new Barrel Futurity of America World Champion is Rosalind Smith and Dawn. We have a first. Mother and daughter have both taken this title. Let's give them a round of applause."

Allan was by her side, and she fell into his arms.

"It was fantastic. No, it was incredible. I'm so proud of you." He swung her around and around.

Cameras went off. Microphones were stuck in her face.

"Tell us, Mrs. Smith, what's a millionaire heiress doing parading around as a lowly cowgirl?"

Security guards arrived and ushered the reporters away. Allan and Rosalind looked at each other and laughed. No one could ruin their day, their love, or their life together. The past didn't matter, only their future.

EPILOGUE

A dust cloud rose into the air, announcing the arrival of the first trailer. Rosalind anxiously waited for it to make its way down the newly graveled driveway. She wanted to run out the front door to meet her first boarder, but she walked.

No, she waddled as calmly as she could. The baby kicked, and she paused. "Hush little one. You'll get your chance soon enough."

She patted her protruding stomach and continued on her mission, needing this moment before she had to alert Allan it was time. She'd been having tiny contractions all morning.

Outside on the new front porch, a cramp came hard and fast. She gripped the handrail.

Breathe. One, two, and three. Exhale. One, two, and three.

Once it passed, she slowly straightened, putting her hands on her lower back. Rosalind stepped off the porch and strolled out to greet the trailer.

"Should you be outside?"

She turned and gave Walt a stern look. "I'm not sick. I'm pregnant."

"Yes, we all know. Should you be—"

"Don't start with me. You men are driving me crazy. Now move aside so I can see Morning Dew."

Walt offered her his arm and she took it.

Rosalind's first glimpse of the neglected mare brought tears to her eyes. Morning Dew had been taken away from an owner who'd starved her and kept her prisoner in a stall for over three years. The vet's report indicated the horse's hooves were severely unkempt, she'd had worms, and needed dental work.

The mare had been quarantined for a couple of months. Dr. Rangle, from Faribault, had given her a clean bill of health this morning. His papers pronounced Morning Dew healthy enough to be exposed to other animals.

Max led the mare off the trailer. "Wait, wait girl. Walk. Easy, girl." Her malnutrition was still very evident.

"She's in good hands. We'll get her back to the weight she should be in no time," Walt stated.

"Yeah, it's so..." Rosalind clutched his arm as another contraction came on.

"You're in labor. I'm radioing Allan."

"No. They aren't very close. I have to wait."

He put his arm around her. "Your parents, Grandpa Rodney, and Sam would've been very proud of you."

Walt's words gave her strength, knowing the choices she'd made had been well worth all the trouble. She'd be able to protect and nurture any horse that was brought to her. The LLC and their non-for profit status enabled them to ask for donations, which was working out. With all of Allan's contacts the Heaven's Kiss Sanctuary had well over one million in its coffers.

An old-fashioned ringtone interrupted their conversation. She reached into her back jeans pocket for her cell phone, swiping the display. *City Boy.*

"Allan, you should see Morning Dew. She's tired and scared. I have you on speaker. Walt is here with me."

"I'm sure you'll have her well rested in no time. How are you doing? Helen said you were having back pains."

"It's nothing," she lied. "Gas, I'm fine."

Walt sighed, shook his head, and gave her a disapproving frown.

"Rosalind, take it easy. I know you won't listen if I tell you to go lie down and let Max and Walt take care of the horses."

"You're right, nothing can keep me away." She prayed he wasn't suspicious.

"I've arranged for the local newspapers to stop by to take pictures."

"Okay. Okay, I have to go." She pressed end, gasping, barely getting the words out as yet another contraction seized her. Tightening her grip on Walt's arm as the pain intensified, she doubled over.

"Rosalind, he needs to know."

Another dust cloud erupted on the driveway in the distance. The second horse was arriving. This boarder had become very dear to her heart these past months.

"Give me time to meet Sammy," she gasped and held her breath.

Walt put his arm around her to support her as the trailer stopped next to the first one. Joe hurried to the ramp and unhitched the lock. The sand-colored stud, Sammy, a past barrel racehorse, emerged.

The previous owner had sold the horse to a dog food factory. She'd tried to sequester him before being sold, but the paperwork needed to transfer the horse across the Canadian border had been delayed.

Thankfully Allan, with Tiffany's help, had stepped in. They'd pulled some strings and sent the local police to stop the transport. The cops successfully interrupted the truck by citing the driver with several violations. Sammy was impounded, which gave her the extra time to produce the necessary papers to rescue him.

"Look at him. He's beautiful." Rosalind's voice quivered. "Joe, remember, he's almost blind."

"I'm being careful," Joe replied. "He's frightened. Dr. Rangle will be here tomorrow to assess the condition of his ringbone."

"I can't believe the owner sold him for simply going blind," Max fumed disgustedly.

"We won't allow him to die this soon. He can live out his life in fields of green grass."

Rosalind choked back a sob as she watched him. Her emotions had been on a never-ending roller coaster since becoming pregnant. After winning first place and taking the title of World Championship Barrel Rider, they'd established a website, a Facebook page, and a YouTube account for *Heavens Kiss Sanctuary*. She'd posted daily blogs on both sites about the horses that would soon be arriving and answered questions on YouTube with videos.

Since going live, they'd been hammered with a thousand hits a day.

That brought about new and wonderful problems. Upon returning from her well-deserved extended honeymoon, Tiffany was appointed administrator for *Heavens Kiss Sanctuary*. Her position entailed taking over all directorial functions necessary to run the non-profit operation as donations came in fast and furious. This eased Rosalind's burden of all the correspondence and requests for assistance.

After Tom's arrest made national news, Allan's lawyers assured them that all charges of insider trading were being dropped and his name would be cleared of any wrongdoing in a few months.

Allan's newly appointed President, Paul Harrington, proved skillful in the management and guidance of *Smith and Associates Brokerage Firm, Inc.* The corporation continued to flourish, holding its top place as a Fortune Five Hundred company despite investigation by the Federal Government and the viral attack on the Internet and by the paparazzi.

Life was good.

The new investment-consulting business Allan founded was a huge success with the local farmers and Rosalind's rodeo friends, ensuring their long-term financial needs were met to enable their lives to be secure for many years to come.

"Breaker, breaker. Trailer three coming. Plus, boss man."

"Ten-four," Max barked into the walkie-talkie, offering Rosalind a smile.

Instead of returning it, Rosalind held her protruding belly. Pain ripped through her lower abdomen. She breathed in and out until the contraction passed.

"It's time to call Allan," Walt said and led her back to the porch.

She turned and took a deep breath as a second set of dust clouds arose behind the first set. "Here he comes in his new truck. I must not have sounded too convincing on the phone. He's been such a worrywart since the beginning of the pregnancy."

"You sit. I'll wait here with you." Walt pointed to a chair on the porch.

Rosalind debated whether to sit or stand. Both seemed to be uncomfortable, so she chose to lean against the railing.

Still, she fretted. "Make sure our new boarders are taken care of. The training camps can be scheduled four to six weeks out. Check with the contractors."

"Rosalind, everything will be fine. Don't worry about us. It's time to concentrate on you and the baby," Max stressed.

"You're right," she gulped and breathed. "I can't help it. This is my dream come true."

The third trailer halted as Allan exited his new black Suburban and strolled casually over to the porch. "Honey, what do you think of my new truck?"

Rosalind rubbed her tummy in a circular motion, willing the contraction not to be a strong one. "It looks...like a city boy pretending to be a redneck."

"That hurt." Allan paused at the stairs and glanced back at the truck. "You mean I'm not getting the hang of being a cowboy?"

Walt and Max waited to the side with their hands on their hips. She stepped down. He kissed her and put his hand on her bulging belly.

"Does it have a full tank of gas?"

He shifted his gaze to her. "Sure, why?"

"We need to leave for the hospital. We can call the doctor to let him know we're on our way."

Allan looked to Walt and Max, and then back to Rosalind. "It's time?"

"Yes, our little girl is ready to make her entrance."

"Can you walk? Should I carry you?" Allan took a couple of steps in one direction, and then turned. "What am I supposed to do?"

Rosalind laughed along with Max and Walt. She silently thanked Grandpa Rodney and Sam for their insight. Her new life would never be dull with her City Boy Cowboy in the picture. "We've got this."

THE END

THANK YOU FOR READING

———

Did you enjoy this book?

We invite you to leave a review at your favorite book site, such as Goodreads, Amazon, Barnes & Noble, etc.

DID YOU KNOW THAT LEAVING A REVIEW...

- Helps other readers find books they may enjoy.
- Gives you a chance to let your voice be heard.
- Gives authors recognition for their hard work.
- Doesn't have to be long. A sentence or two about why you liked the book will do.

———

Don't miss out on your next favorite book!

Join the Satin Romance mailing list
www.satinromance.com/mail.html

ABOUT THE AUTHOR

 I was born and raised in the cold and beautiful Minnesota, but I escaped to Illinois for seventeen years to raise my two boys, and now I call Florida home. My husband Andy, who's always been my hero, has put up with my late night computer typing and endless stacks of papers with my stories on them. We have two furry friends as family; Cookie, an Assui-Po dog and Chip, a ragdoll cat, that their sons compare to Eeyore. They are both getting up there in years now.

Life has been full of ups and downs, but I've made it through the hard times. I love to travel and go to Disney World to trade pins. I've been a bowler for many years, and you can catch me writing my next novel at the lanes.

I encourage you to check out my website for more info and don't be surprised if I let my Norwegian heritage come through in my stories.

Go Vikings! You betcha!

www.sonjagunter.com

www.ingramcontent.com/pod-product-compliance
Lightning Source LLC
Chambersburg PA
CBHW031152050726
47495CB00019B/1602